Crave

AND

Torn

Crave
AND
Torn

A BILLIONAIRE BACHELORS CLUB ROMANCE

MONICA MURPHY

AVON

An Imprint of HarperCollins*Publishers*

CRAVE. Copyright © 2013 by Monica Murphy.

TORN. Copyright © 2013 by Monica Murphy.

All rights reserved. Printed in the United States of America. No part of this book may be used or reproduced in any manner whatsoever without written permission except in the case of brief quotations embodied in critical articles and reviews. For information, address HarperCollins Publishers, 195 Broadway, New York, NY 10007.

HarperCollins books may be purchased for educational, business, or sales promotional use. For information, please email the Special Markets Department at SPsales@harpercollins.com.

Originally published separately as *Crave* and *Torn* in the United States by Avon Impulse in 2013.

Designed by Diahann Sturge

Part title image © tomertu/Shutterstock

Library of Congress Cataloging-in-Publication Data has been applied for.

ISBN 978-0-06-338301-2

23 24 25 26 27 LBC 5 4 3 2 1

Table of Contents

Acknowledgments

As always, I'm thanking my husband and children for putting up with me while I work extra hard at my desk, giving myself eyestrain while I stare at the computer all day and night. You are all so awesome and supportive and rarely complain (ha ha). What would I do without you?

To the readers—I would be nothing without your continued enthusiasm and love. Thank you, you all mean the world to me. This book (and this entire series) is a little different and I hope you love reading it as much as I've enjoyed writing it. Hopefully we can't go wrong with sexy billionaire bachelors . . .

A big thank you to my editor, Chelsey Emmelhainz, for slapping my words around and making this book so much better. To the entire team at Avon for their enthusiastic support of this series—y'all rock. To KP Simmon and Kati Rodriguez for keeping me straight. And to Katy Evans for loving Archer from the very, very beginning.

Crave

Chapter 1

Archer

There are few things I can resist in life. This is probably why I got into so much trouble during my younger years. Control is everything—and that is the one thing I've learned from my bastard of a father. You gain nothing by letting yourself go, by revealing your emotions, by becoming vulnerable.

If you're unable to resist the things that draw you in, it's a surefire way to ask for unwanted chaos. I've had enough of that in my personal life growing up. Hell, in my professional life too, though I've finally turned that corner these last few years.

But the few things I can't resist? A challenge. A bet.

"He's an absolute sucker to get married," Gage says, his disgust-filled voice pulling me from my thoughts. Gage Emerson is my best friend. Matt DeLuca is too. I've known them both since high school. We're standing together at our college buddy Jeff Lewiston's wedding reception, lurking in a dark corner of the crowded ballroom and muttering over the so-called sanctity of marriage.

Marriage represents a noose around my neck that tightens with every miserable day. My parents are a shining example of the worst marriage in the history of marriages. They hate each other. They cheat on each other. They fight. Yet they're still together.

Makes no damn sense.

"He seems happy," Matt, the more optimistic of us three, starts, and both Gage and I shoot him a look that shuts him up.

"His wife is attractive, I'll give her that," Gage concedes, sipping from his glass of champagne. "But the moment they come back from the Tahitian honeymoon, she'll turn into the biggest bitch on the planet, I guarantee it."

"You don't even know her," Matt mutters, shaking his head.

"Don't have to. They all do it. Sexy and beautiful and sweet when you first meet them, you don't know what to think. The sex is amazing and you're having it constantly. They'll drop to their knees whenever you ask and give you a grade-A blowjob. Next thing you know, you're buying them a ring." Gage pauses, takes another swig of his champagne, draining the glass.

We've talked about this before. We've watched our friends go down one by one like fallen soldiers to marriage, especially this last year.

"You get that ring on their finger, go through this whole marriage ceremony bullshit, and then you're left with nothing but a nagging wife and a limp dick in the aftermath. Always giving you shit because you're never home and you work too much."

I grimace because holy hell, that sounds like my worst nightmare.

"They sure as hell never complain when they're spending your money, though." Gage gestures with his empty glass.

"Hear, motherfucking-hear," I say, returning the gesture with my glass before I finish it off.

"You guys are such cynics. Both of you act like you've done this sort of thing before." Matt crosses his arms in front of his chest. "When was the last time either of you had a girlfriend." He doesn't phrase it as a question because he already knows the answer.

"Never," I sneer. Serious girlfriends aren't a consideration. None of them interested me enough to want to keep them around.

With the exception of one woman and I absolutely cannot touch her. She's too young, too sweet, too good, too everything I'm not. She's so fucking tempting and so completely off limits, I'd be a damn fool to attempt anything with her.

But I want to. Desperately.

"All this talk about how a woman is nothing but shackles and chains like some sort of lifetime prison sentence. I can't wait to see you both fall and fall fucking hard." Matt laughed.

Gage and I both glare. "I have no plans of falling any time soon," Gage mutters.

"More like never in this lifetime," I add.

"Please." Matt snorts. "You'll both eventually realize you don't want to do this thing called 'life' without a woman by your side. Then you'll be scrambling at some ungodly age, like forty-five, the eternal bachelors looking for some hot piece to be your bride. None of those young babes in their twenties will look at you unless you flash some cash their way."

"Now who's the cynic," I retort, earning a glare from Matt.

"I speak the truth," he says with a shrug. "And you know it."

"You bag on us for being single, yet you're single too," Gage points out. "Why haven't you settled down yet?"

Gage's question earns another shrug from Matt. "Haven't found the right woman yet."

His answer is so simple and sounds so damn logical I want to smack him.

"There is no right woman," I say, wanting to burst Matt's happily-ever-after bubble. "You'll eventually settle. Trust me."

"And you won't," Gage says, though I know he's not disagreeing with me. "I know I don't plan on settling. I don't plan on tying myself down whatsoever."

"Neither do I," I agree. "Settling is for pussies."

"Absolutely," Gage says grimly.

Matt focuses his attention solely on me. "I'll bet big money you'll be the first to go down."

"Go down how? On a woman?" This earns a laugh from Gage. "Go down in flames? What the hell are you talking about?"

"You'll be the first to fall in love with a woman and beg her to marry you," Matt says.

My mouth goes dry. It feels like an invisible noose just tightened around my neck, making it hard to breathe. "Yeah, right," I finally manage to choke out.

"You two are so damn resistant to being in a relationship, I figure you'll both be slapped upside the head and fall hard. And it's going to happen sooner rather than later," Matt says, his voice full of confidence.

That smug tone irritates the hell out of me.

"There is no way I'll fall in love anytime soon," I say.

"Me either," Gage agrees.

"If you guys want to believe that, then cool. Live in your world of denial, I don't care." Our friend is trying to piss us off. And it's working.

"You wanna make that bet you just mentioned? Because I'm in. I'll prove it to you. I don't need a woman or a relationship."

I cross my arms in front of my chest. Matt's done this before. He enjoys getting a rise out of the both of us. Drives me crazy.

So let's see if he goes for it. Always running that mouth of his. Time to put up or shut up.

Gage snorts. "Don't just bet him. Let's all three get in on this one."

"How much we talking?" Matt scrubs his hand along his jaw. The guy is loaded. We're all loaded; we come from wealthy families and we lived in the same neighborhood during high school. When we all turned twenty-one within a few months of each other, we started going to Vegas and dropping big money like a regular person plays the quarter slots. Once we graduated college and got real lives, we had to stop that shit. I still miss it. Sort of.

"A million bucks to the last single man standing," Gage throws out, a triumphant gleam in his eye. He acts like he's already won the prize.

"A million dollars?" Matt's eyes practically bug out of his head. Asshole acts like he's not good for it despite having to recently bow out of a lucrative pro baseball contract due to a career-ending injury—and he didn't lose a dollar of that contract either. The guy has buckets full of money. He recently invested some of it in a winery not far from where I live just so he could claim a loss for his taxes.

He's definitely not hurting financially. Neither is Gage. He's one of the top real estate investors in all the Bay Area, right behind his father. They both have the magic touch, finding properties and businesses for a song and turning them around for a tremendous profit.

The hotel industry claims I have the magic touch as well, despite my father's irritation at that particular assertion. I can't help that I saw a need and filled it with the loser hotel he gave me. He firmly believed I'd fail.

I proved him wrong. Hell, I'm getting ready to expand. And he hates that.

It's almost as if my own father would relish seeing me fail.

"What, you scared?" I say this because I know there is no way in hell I will lose this bet. No woman can sink her claws into me so deep I can't escape.

No way, no how.

Gage laughs and shakes his head. "Don't be such a pussy, DeLuca. A million bucks is chump change in your bank account."

"Not really," Matt mutters. "Not that I'm worried. I'll win."

Ha. Matt making that confident of a statement pushes me to prove him wrong. "You really think so?"

"I know so." Matt smiles. "I'd even bet an extra fifty grand the next woman you talk to, you'll end up marrying."

"Sucker bet, bro. Take him up on it," Gage chimes in, nudging my shoulder hard. "Give us a break, Matt. I can't think of one woman in this entire room Archer would want to talk to, let alone *marry*."

I remain quiet. There is one woman I wouldn't mind talking to. Spend time with. Not in the serious sense or the potential marriage sense, because hell no, that's not in my future. I'd make some poor woman a terrible husband and I know it. Which is why I leave her alone.

She wants that sort of thing. A husband and kids and a white picket fence around the pretty little house she decorated. I know she does. She's a dreamer, a romantic, a woman who deserves to be treated like a queen. I'd only end up hurting her and I couldn't live with myself if I did. Gage wouldn't let me live either.

He knows her well, considering I'm referring to his baby sister.

Once upon a time, when she was younger, I thought of her like a baby sister too. But then she blossomed into this hot teenager that had me thinking all the wrong thoughts every time I got near her. Seventeen-year-old Ivy made me feel like a pervert. Didn't help that every time I tried to avoid her, she wanted to talk to me. As if she knew she drove me crazy and was determined to get under my skin with her sweet, thoughtful ways, how she laughed at my jokes and looked at me as if she could see right through me.

And when she grew into this beautiful, sexy, confident woman, I knew without a doubt I had to avoid her at all costs. I wanted to be with her in the worst damn way. She's the first woman I ever truly cared for. I don't want to hurt her, because I would. I hurt all the women in my life. Ask my mother. Ask any female who thought she had a fleeting chance at being with me.

"Maybe you could go babysit Ivy for a little while," Gage suggests.

I turn to him, incredulous. Can he reach inside my brain and read my thoughts? Fucking scary how he just did that.

"What do you mean?" I ask warily.

"You want to win an easy fifty grand? Go be with Ivy. Like she'd marry your sorry ass." Gage laughs, though I don't. Why am I a sorry ass? Yeah, I know I'm not worthy of Ivy, but damn, his words still hurt.

When I don't say anything, Gage continues.

"She broke it off with the guy she'd been seeing a few nights ago. Not that he was worthy of her, but she's been down in the dumps ever since," Gage explains. "You could go hang out with her for the rest of the night, use her to fight off any other female who might approach. Ivy's always liked you, though I don't know why since you're such a jackass." He pauses, his eyes narrowed. "I realize you enjoy chasing everything in a skirt, but I know you won't take advantage of my sister. Right?"

The pointed look he gives me rings loud and clear. I want to promise him I won't take advantage of her. But he's talking about Ivy . . . and I always want what I can't have.

Especially her.

"She doesn't count anyway," Matt says with a chuckle. "After all, it's just Ivy."

"Right. Just Ivy." I nod as I look around, hoping to spot her. She's here. I saw her earlier, though she avoided me. Most of the time, I choose to aggravate the shit out of her rather than let on how I really feel. "You mean she doesn't count toward that crazy-ass bet you just made me?'

"Yeah, she totally doesn't count. Besides, Gage would kill you," Matt says matter-of-factly. "There are approximately twenty-five women spying on us at this very moment, all of them sorority sisters or whatever of the bride. They're dying for you to even look their way, Archer. First one that talks to you, I guarantee you'll marry."

"Bullshit," I mumble. My friend has lost his damn mind.

"Whatever." Matt laughs as does Gage, but I ignore them.

Glancing across the room, I see her. Ivy. Sitting at a table alone, watching couples sway together on the dance floor to some sappy love song. Her long, brown hair is wavy when she usually wears it straight, and I'm tempted to run my hands through it, see if it feels as silky soft as it looks. Her dress is a rich, dark blue and strapless, revealing plenty of smooth, creamy flesh that my fingers literally itch to touch.

The wistful longing on her face is obvious and I'm compelled to go to her. Ask her to dance. Pull her in close, feel her curves mold against me as I breathe in her sweet scent.

Damn.

Yeah. She'd probably tell me to go to hell before she'd dance with me.

"I don't want to touch her," I say, which is a lie because I would fucking love to touch her. "You can trust me."

More lies. Gage should kick me in the nuts just for thinking about his sister. Let alone actually doing something to her. With her. Over her, under her, any way I can get her. She's the only one who could tempt me to break the crazy bet I just made. Who could make me want to go against everything I've ever believed in since I was a kid.

But I won't. I refuse to give in. She's not for me.

No matter how badly I want her to be.

Ivy

There's nothing worse than going to a wedding alone, especially when I'd had a date approximately forty-eight hours ago. Before I realized the guy I was seeing was also still seeing the woman he claimed he'd broke up with well over six months ago.

How did I find out this amazingly bad news? The supposed ex called my cell and chewed me out while I was looking over wallpaper samples with a client. Talk about humiliating. Talk about my life turning into a Jerry Springer episode. She made me feel like a cheating whore-bag out to steal her man, the very last thing I am. I am not a man-stealer. I know some women are attracted to men in relationships, but not me. Taken men are too much trouble, thank you very much.

I hung up on the still-ranting, supposed ex-girlfriend and promptly called Marc, letting him know I couldn't see him any longer. He'd hardly protested—no surprise. What a jerk.

So now I sit here alone. At the single and dateless table, because when I called the bride and told her I wasn't bringing my date after all, Cecily flipped out. Claimed I would mess up her carefully orchestrated seating arrangement and *oh my God, couldn't you just bring your date anyway and deal?*

I think my saying an emphatic *no* resulted in me ending up at the desperate and single section as punishment.

Sighing, I prop my elbow on the edge of the table and rest my chin on my fist, watching all the couples dancing, the bride and groom in the center of the floor, grinning up at each other like fools. They look happy. Everyone looks happy.

I'm jealous of all the happiness surrounding me. Weddings remind me I'm alone. For once, I wish I could find someone. I've had a string of bad luck with men my entire dating life. I pick wrong, my mom has told me more than once. She describes me as a fixer. I take the broken guys and try to put them back together again. "Humpty Dumpty syndrome" is what she calls it.

Gee, thanks, Mom.

My brother says I'm too young to want to settle down, but I'm nothing like him. He just wants to screw around and stay single forever. Gage doesn't know what I want. Do I though? I'm not sure. I thought I did. I thought Marc had potential.

Turns out he went splat all over the ground. Definitely couldn't put him back together again.

Maybe I shouldn't take everything so damn seriously.

Maybe I should let loose and do something completely and totally crazy. Like find some random guy and make out with him in a dark corner. I miss having a man cup my face and kiss me slowly. Thoroughly. Unfortunately, Marc wasn't that great of a kisser. Too much thrusting tongue, though I firmly believed I could help him correct that annoying habit.

He didn't give me a chance, which is fine, because really, chemistry is everything. If I don't feel a spark with a kiss, then the guy is clearly not right for me.

If I'm going to consider a relationship with a guy, that's what I want. What I need. A spark. Chemistry. A few stolen kisses, wandering hands, whispered words in a quiet corner where someone might catch us. He'd press me up against a wall, cradle my face in his hands, and kiss me like he means it . . .

I frown. I'm sitting alone contemplating a wild wedding reception hookup with a faceless guy. Since when did I become so desperate?

"What's wrong, chicken?" a familiar voice asks from behind me and I stiffen my shoulders. Great. I'd know that deep, velvety voice anywhere. Archer Bancroft. The absolute last guy I want to deal with tonight.

Talk about a Humpty Dumpty type. Archer knows he's broken and damaged. And he definitely doesn't want to be put back together again. The twisted part? He likes being that way. He revels in his brokenness.

No thanks. Even I know my limits. Despite how freaking gorgeous he is, because oh my God, Archer is beautiful. Dark hair, dark eyes, tall and broad with a body that's hard and muscular without being over the top; he's downright swoonworthy.

And he's my brother's best friend. I've known Archer since

I was twelve and he moved in next door with his cold-as-ice parents. I'd developed an immediate crush, because back then he was the most exotic thing I'd ever seen in my never-changing, no-one-ever-moves neighborhood.

The crush died a swift death when I realized what a player he was. Even at twelve, I could see the ugly truth.

Smart girls don't mess around with Archer.

He trails his finger across my bare shoulder, knocking me from my memories, making me shiver. "You're looking aw-fully down during this happy occasion, chicken."

Glancing over my shoulder, I find him flashing that trade-mark panty-melting smile at me. I absolutely refuse to let my panties dissolve for even a fraction of a second. "I really wish you wouldn't call me that," I say irritably, scowling at him. Calling me chicken twice in as many minutes is a sign he's trying to drive me crazy.

What else is new?

Chuckling, his dark brown eyes flash. It's not fair how pretty he is. He has that strong jaw and lush mouth. The dimple that makes such a rare appearance that whenever I see it, I immediately want to kiss it. Lick it.

My frown deepens. I should *not* be thinking about licking Archer's face. What the hell is wrong with me? Too much champagne or what?

More like too much dreaming about being pulled into a dark cor-ner and kissed until you can't breathe.

"No, 'Hi, Archer, how are you?'" He shakes his head, rest-ing his hand on the back of my chair. His knuckles brush against my bare skin and I try to repress the shiver that over-takes me at his casual touch. "And you're usually so polite."

"Archer, cut the shit." I meet his gaze, watch with satisfac-tion as the smile falls from his face. Have I ever talked to him like this? Probably not, but I can't deal. Not tonight. "I'm not in the mood. I've had a bad week."

"Yeah, I heard," he says quietly, his eyes full of sympathy. "Sorry about the guy."

I'm going to kill my brother for blabbing. Now I feel extra pitiful. Archer probably came over because he felt sorry for me. I saw him talking with Gage and Matthew DeLuca a few minutes ago, though they didn't notice me. Were they laughing at my yet again failed attempt at finding a decent guy? Probably. Those three have mocked me for years. It's become habit now. "It's no big deal. He was a total jerk."

"I'd say, for letting you go so easily."

Did he really just say that? What did he mean? "Is there something you wanted to talk about?" I'm eager to get rid of him. For whatever reason, with only a few words he's confusing me tonight and I don't like it. I'm confused enough, what with my secret wishes for random hookups with hot guys.

Hot like Archer . . .

"Yeah, there is." The smile returns, gentler now, not full of the usual bravado. "Want to dance?"

"With you?" I'm incredulous. And I want to laugh when I see he's obviously offended by my question.

"Yeah, with me. Come on." He holds out his hand. "Be my shield before some crazy woman tries to drag me out onto the dance floor. They're circling, chicken. They're about to jump me if I don't watch it."

He's right. I can see a few women starting to approach us. Suddenly overcome with the need to let them know that he's not available, I let him take my hand, his long fingers clasping around mine as he pulls me to my feet. He blatantly checks me out, his gaze running down the length of my body, lingering on my chest, and I simultaneously want to punch him and ask if he likes what he sees.

Yeah, definitely confusing.

A woman appears before us, her smile so wide I wonder if it hurts her face. "Hey, you're Archer Bancroft, right? From Bancroft Hotels? The Hush Resort and Spa?" she asks, her voice falsely bright.

"I am." He pulls me closer, releasing my hand so he can wrap his arm around my shoulders in a proprietary way, like he's claiming me. His thumb rubs circles against my skin, making my breaths come a little faster, and I drop my gaze to the floor, trying to gather my composure. "Have we met before?"

"Once. Long ago, but I'm sure you don't remember me." I glance up and watch as her smile grows. How is that even possible? "I've always wanted to go there. To Hush."

Hush Resort and Spa. The hotel Archer's father gave him as some sort of punishment after he barely graduated college. He turned it into one of the most exclusive and successful couples-only resorts in all the country, if not the world. He became white-hot in an instant, in demand. Gorgeous and sexy, intelligent and ruthless, women wanted to do him, men wanted to be him. And the arrogant jackass knew it.

"I suggest you make a reservation." His voice is full of irritation. He's trying to steer us around her but she's not budging.

"I can't. I'm not part of a couple." She literally bats her eyelashes. "Maybe you could help with that?"

"I'm sure we could find one of your friends to hook her up with, don't you think, baby?" I smile up at Archer, sending him a meaningful look so he gets what I'm trying to do. He blinks down at me, no doubt startled by being called baby, which is fun. He's sort of hot when he's confused, and it's hard to frazzle Archer. So I decide to do it some more.

Leaning up, I nuzzle his neck, inhaling his unique spicy scent. God, he smells amazing. Why have I never noticed this before? Not that we're ever standing this close together, but I'm tempted to rub against him like a cat.

I wonder if she's bought we're a couple yet. If I have to keep this up I might do something crazy. Like . . . bite him. "I'm sure that could be arranged," he says, his voice rough as his arm tightens around my shoulders.

I slip my arm around his back. He's as solid as a rock. Makes me wonder what he looks like beneath all the finery. I haven't seen him shirtless since I was in high school, and he's filled out since then considerably. "If you'll excuse us," I tell Miss Persistent with a sickeningly sweet smile before I turn it on Archer. "Let's go dance, baby."

He leads me out onto the dance floor wordlessly, pulling me into his arms just as another slow song starts. His hand rests on the small of my back as we begin to move to the music and my entire body tingles at his nearness. Which is odd because 1. I have no desire to be with Archer like that and 2. I've been immune to his charm for years.

Weird.

"You're good, with the 'baby' bit and rubbing your nose against my neck," he murmurs close to my ear. His hot breath makes me shiver and I wonder if he felt it. He had to.

And I don't really care. I'm hyperaware of him, of his size and his warmth and the sheer strength of him. His big hand shifts lower on my back, his fingertips grazing my backside, and I inhale sharply. I bet he knows just how to use those hands, too.

Oh my God, this is Archer you're drooling over. Stop it!

"Think she bought our act?" I ask breathlessly.

"Not sure." He hesitates for the slightest moment, causing me to look up at him. I'm struck dumb by his smoldering gaze, the way he's staring at me like he wants to gobble me up. I wonder if I'm returning the same look, because I have the sudden urge to kiss him. For hours, if possible. "But I know I did."

Chapter 2

Archer

Well, that was totally unexpected.

I'm still reeling, though I'm trying my damnedest to act like she doesn't affect me whatsoever. All that "It's just Ivy" talk flew right out the window when I saw the glint of determination in her gaze as she realized she could help me get rid of the clingy woman. How she'd draped herself all over me and called me baby. Flashing me a sexy, secretive smile as if she knew exactly what I looked like naked and liked it.

Then she went and nuzzled my neck with her nose, making me so hard I'm still aching with the memory just before she moved away.

Talk about torture. No wonder I avoid her. Within a few minutes of being near her, I'm sporting wood and plotting how I can get her out of here so I can strip her naked and have my way with her. All night long.

"You're teasing me," she chastises, her pretty hazel eyes watching me carefully as we dance. There aren't many couples on the floor but the bride and groom are nearby, the lights are dimmed low, and the atmosphere is scarily romantic. "You so didn't buy into that act. Come on."

Fuck, she's the tease. I'm not sure she gets just how much

she affects me. I know she doesn't. I wonder if she ever thinks of me. Her brother's best friend, the jerk wad who does nothing but give her a bunch of crap. Knowing her since I was sixteen seems to transform me into my idiot teenage self every time I'm around her. It's like I can't help it.

I'm a grown-ass man worth billions who runs one of the most successful, exclusive resorts in the country and this is what Ivy Emerson reduces me to.

"I pretty much did buy into it," I offer with a shrug. Going for nonchalant. "I'm surprised you didn't take it to the next level. Grab my dick and claim it as yours."

A dark brow rises, her lips quirked to the side. Damn, she's hot, even when she's irritated. Especially when she's irritated. "You are so crude."

If only she knew the extent of my so-called crudeness. I want her.

Having her in my arms is not helping my plight, but she's soft and she smells so damn good I can't resist her. Her dark hair shines beneath the golden lights and the top of her strapless dress appears fairly easy to tug down if I wanted to do such a thing.

Not that I do. Not really.

Liar.

It's not just her beauty that does me in, though. There's so much more to Ivy. How she listens to me, how proud she seems to be when I tell her what I'm doing in my career. It's like she really cares.

"You've always appreciated my blunt honesty," I assure her, pulling her in just the slightest bit closer as I twirl her around the dance floor. Her breasts brush against my chest, her hand slides over my shoulder, and her touch burns me.

Through my suit jacket and shirt, like she's touching bare flesh, branding me.

And I want to be branded by her. Despite my reluctance of ever becoming involved with a woman, Ivy's the only one who I both want to be with and want to run away from.

Yeah. I make no damn sense.

"Really? According to whom? When was the last time we had a scintillating conversation, hmm?" She smiles. It's faint but there, and the sight of it encourages me.

Plus, she just made the word *scintillating* sound hot. The woman is either some sort of sex goddess or I've turned into a complete pervert. "Maybe we need to renew our friendship. Get to know each other again," I suggest, trying my best to still sound nonchalant.

"Like you care about getting to know me again." She rolls her eyes. "We've known each other for years. It's not like you've ever shown any sort of interest in me before."

"I've always been interested, you just never noticed." I pause, taking in the way her eyes widen the slightest bit. I bet my revelation surprises her. "Every time I see you, Ivy, I remember what you looked like when you were twelve, the first time I met you. All gangly and skinny with braces." Look at her now. She's filled out in all the right places and she's the sexiest woman at this stupid reception.

"Great. So you see me as an eternal twelve-year-old," she mutters, curling her lip.

Shit. I've somehow stepped in it with a few choice words. Could I be more of an idiot?

"I definitely don't see you as a twelve-year-old," I murmur, tightening my hold on her hand. "You have to realize that, right?"

She meets my gaze, her eyes full of wariness, her pouty lips curved in the tiniest frown. "What do you see me as, Archer? Gage's pain-in-the-ass little sister? The girl you made fun of her freshman year when you were a mighty senior? Remember how you did that?"

Well hell, is she going to list all of my faults or what? I'm not proud of the way I acted when I was younger. I'd been a self-centered bastard. Some say I still am. "I was a jackass back then," I mutter.

"From what I've observed, you're still holding on to some of those jackass tendencies." Her hazel eyes flash as she lifts her chin in subtle defiance.

"What's that supposed to mean?" Damn, maybe I avoid her because we tend to argue every time we're around each other. Yet I want her. I've wanted her for what feels like forever. But she acts like she despises me. Like my very presence fills her with disgust. No other woman has reacted to me like this—ever. I don't get it.

I don't get her. And I definitely don't get my attraction to her.

Glutton for punishment maybe?

Yeah. I shove that nagging little voice straight to the back of my brain.

"Forget it." Her gaze cuts away from mine.

"Tell me what you're talking about, Ivy."

"Nothing." She meets my gaze once more. "Drop it, okay?"

I let her drop it and we dance quietly, the sharks still circling. I can spot at least three women who are contemplating me standing on the edge of the dance floor. Ready to jump on me the moment the song is over.

I gotta get out of here.

"Let's go outside," I tell Ivy, my gaze trained on one woman in particular who's vaguely familiar. I swear the groom tried to set me up with her once. We went out to some dinner when Jeff and Cecily were first dating.

"Are you serious? No way will I go outside with you. You'll probably try to maul me."

That sounds like a fantastic idea but I know she won't go for it. "Maybe you need a good mauling to get that stick out of your ass."

"What did you just say?" She stops dancing so abruptly she nearly trips over my feet, what with those fuck-me high heels she's wearing.

Tightening my arm around her waist, I save her from sprawling. "I speak the truth and you know it. You need to loosen up, chicken. No wonder the last guy didn't stick, what with how uptight you are." Her eyes widen and her jaw drops open. She looks ready to tear into me and I immediately regret what I said. "Ivy, I'm sorry," I start, but she cuts me off.

"Fuck you," she whispers harshly, shoving at me so I have no choice but to let go of her and watch as she escapes the dance floor.

A woman swoops in within seconds, the same one Jeff tried to hook me up with long ago. I remember she had stalkerish qualities, what with the way she Googled me prior to going out to dinner. I know it's the norm nowadays, but her admission turned me off. "Archer. It's so good to see you again. Want to dance?"

I glance toward the open doors that lead onto the giant terrace. Ivy's headed straight toward them, her hips swaying, her legs looking incredibly long. She's gorgeous and sexy as fuck and I said she needed to get the stick out of her ass.

What the hell is wrong with me?

"Archer?"

I turn my attention to the woman who's looking at me expectantly. I don't even remember her name. Ivy's right. I still have plenty of assholeish tendencies and I just unleashed them all over her. "Sorry, I'm going to have to pass. I need to go apologize to a woman."

Ivy

The moment I'm outside, I take a deep, gulping breath, the cold air filling my lungs, kissing my skin, and making me shiver. I'm angry, but thankfully the air cools my heated emotions and I lean against the railing that overlooks the golf course, happy no one else is around. Considering I'm in the farthest corner of the terrace from the open doors of the ballroom, that's no surprise.

I still can't believe what Archer said to me. He is the biggest jerk on the planet, I swear to God. He actually said I have a stick up my ass. I mean, what the hell? Could he hurl any more insults at me? Oh wait, I'm sure he can.

No wonder I always avoid him. This is what usually happens between Archer and me whenever we spend any time together. I try to be nice. He's his usual jerky self. I get defensive. He insults me. We argue. We then avoid each other until for whatever reason we're forced to see each other again.

We're like a broken record. No matter what, we can't get along. He is the most frustrating person I've ever met. He drives me crazy. And that I'm in his territory tonight, in Napa Valley where his resort is located—not too far, as a matter of fact—also makes me uneasy. Why, I'm not sure.

I wish I were back home in San Francisco, in my comfort zone. At my little apartment, where I'd watch a movie while contemplating going to bed early on another exciting Saturday night.

Frowning, I sigh heavily and hang my head. I've turned into this pitiful, dateless creature all in a matter of hours. What confuses me more? That despite our arguing and the constant animosity that brews between Archer and me, I felt something else between us earlier? Something I would never dare contemplate before?

Sexual attraction.

Tilting my head back, I drink in the night sky. Away from the city lights, I can actually see the stars and there are a bazillion of them stretched across the night's velvety blackness. They twinkle at me, full of mystery and hope and opportunity.

My life is good. I shouldn't let guys hang it up and make me miserable. Marc is a jerk who happened to be a bad kisser. Archer is an asshole who could probably kiss the pants off of me, but I won't go there.

Damn it, I should be happy. I'm working my dream job as an interior designer under one of the best designers in all of San Francisco. I have my own apartment—no more living with my parents, and thankfully no more college roommates. I have great friends and a supportive family. I shouldn't let this sort of thing bother me.

But what Archer said . . . it bothers me. I don't have a stick up my ass, do I? I'm not uptight. I swear I'm not uptight.

Maybe I can be a little controlling, but never stick-in-the-ass uptight . . .

Whipping out my phone, I send my friend Wendy a quick text and wait anxiously for her reply.

She responds in seconds, which impresses me since I know she's out on a date tonight.

> No, you're NOT uptight. Who told you that? Let me guess ... Marc. What an asshole.

Laughing, I shake my head. I appreciate her immediate defense of me. That's what friends are for, right?

Not Marc, I respond. Someone else. Someone I've known since high school.

Since I'd met Wendy in college, I don't think I've mentioned Archer to her, have I? God, I don't know. We talk about all sorts of stuff. She's my closest friend.

So of course I've mentioned Archer to her.

One of your brother's friends? she texts back.

> Yeah.

> Which one? Let me guess ... Archer Bancroft. He's hot. But he also must be a complete asshole for calling you uptight.

Laughing, I type her a quick reply. "Isn't that the truth," I mutter.

"Isn't what the truth?"

Gasping, I whirl around to see Archer standing there, his hands shoved in his pockets, looking absolutely miserable.

Good.

Oh, and also absolutely gorgeous, which sucks. Why, oh why, did this man have to be so handsome?

"That you're an asshole?" I smile as serenely as possible, ignoring the buzz of my phone indicating I have another text. I shove it in the pocket of my dress, thankful it came with one. A girl and her phone can never part.

"Listen, I came out here to tell you I'm sorry." He runs a hand through his hair, messing it up completely. Which of course makes him even sexier, and that's so unfair it's ridiculous. "It's just . . . every time we're together, we somehow end up arguing."

"I can't help it if you're rude," I say with a sniff. I sound like a complete snot but I don't care.

"You push all my buttons," he admits, his voice quiet and edged with a mysterious darkness that sends a thrill shooting down my spine. He keeps his eyes trained on me as he slowly draws closer.

"Right back at you." Why do I sound so breathless? It doesn't help that he's stopped directly in front of me, his big, broad body obliterating everything else until he's all I can see.

"I'm hoping you'll find it in your heart to forgive me." He reaches out his hand toward me and I stare at it, not sure what he wants me to do. "Please?"

Did Archer Bancroft just say *please*? I'm sure this is a rare moment in history. "Why do you care about having my forgiveness?" I keep my gaze trained on his hand for fear he'll see the confusion and emotion in my eyes.

Shit. What is wrong with me?

"Fuck, Ivy, why do you always have to be so difficult?" His hand drops.

I chance looking up at him, see the irritation and frustration written all over his face and I'm so overcome with the need to comfort him I take a step forward, ready to grab hold of his hand and . . .

And what?

"Archer?" a woman's voice calls from nearby, causing the

both of us to look at each other. The slightly panicked look on his face indicates he knows exactly who this woman is.

"Who's looking for you?" I ask.

"No one."

I raise an eyebrow. "Clearly someone is, since I can hear her call your name."

"She's not important. I went on one dinner date with her, Jeff, and Cecily a long time ago. She had us married and planning for babies by the end of it," he says irritably, glancing over his shoulder.

"What's her name?"

He turns to me. "What?"

"Her name? The no one who's looking for you?"

"I, uh . . . don't remember." He runs a hand through that sexy hair again, strands falling over his forehead, and I'm filled with the sudden urge to push his hair out of his eyes. Comb my fingers through it.

Stop!

I need to remember he's a complete jackass. I should run. Right now. In fact, I'm fully preparing to let him know exactly how much of an ass I think he is when the woman's voice sounds again, closer this time as she continues to call Archer's name like some worried owner looking for her pet dog.

"We should—*oh*."

He practically shoves me against the railing, the rough concrete scratching my back through the thin fabric of my dress and he immediately slips his arm around my waist, protecting me. Holding me. His chest is against mine, my breasts pressed flush to him, and I release a skittering breath, my mind hung up on having him too close.

"What are you doing?" I whisper, incredulous.

"Shh." He rests his hand over my mouth, silencing me. His palm is big and warm, his fingers long, and I swear his skin tastes the slightest bit salty—not that I'm licking him or anything.

Oh God, I think . . . no, I *know* I want to lick him. Desperately. Slip one of those long fingers in between my lips and suck. And that is just so, so wrong . . .

"Maybe she won't find us," he whispers, dipping his head so his gaze meets mine. "Stay still."

I slowly nod, his hand still over my mouth, his eyes locked with mine. His touch gentles as he takes another step closer and I want to melt at his nearness.

"Archer, are you back here?"

I flick my eyes to the left and see the woman. She's standing about fifty feet away, her head whipping this way and that, almost frantically searching, and I press farther against the ledge at the same time Archer steps into me. His arm is still around my waist, protecting me from the rough concrete, and he's standing so close I can hardly breathe.

There's a giant pine tree giving us cover, throwing shadows over the corner we're standing in, and I don't think the woman can really see us. She's oblivious to the fact we're not that far from her.

Which I'm thankful for. I shouldn't be. I should be kicking Archer in the shins and letting the woman know he's right here and then throwing him to the she-wolf. Let him deal with the poor soul he rejected God knows how long ago who still harbors a thing for him.

He's a complete womanizer. I'd be wise to stay away from him.

My head tells me this. But my body is singing a completely different tune.

Our gazes lock, his thumb sweeps back and forth across my cheek so slowly I want to die. It feels so good. This . . . is not right. His nearness confuses me. The way he looks at me, touches me, it makes me want him.

Desperately.

My earlier thoughts come rushing back, when I was being all "woe-is-me" wishing for a random stranger to make out with in a dark corner. Being with Archer like this is the next best thing. He's looking at me like he's thinking the same thing I am. Which is scary.

Exhilarating. Exciting.

As I stare up at him, I see how absolutely perfect his lips are. How come I never noticed this before? And when his tongue darts out to lick them, why are my knees suddenly shaking?

Oh, this is bad. So, so bad.

The woman finally gives up and leaves and I slump against the railing, ready for him to move away from me. Ready for him to grab me by the hips and lift me up onto the concrete ledge so I can wrap my legs around him and beg him to do me.

Wait, what? I so can't do that. Clearly, I've had too much to drink, if two glasses of champagne could be considered excessive drinking. Which it must be, because I am making absolutely no sense.

"Ivy . . ." His hand slips from my mouth to cup my cheek, his thumb drifting across the corner of my lips. "I'm sorry."

His touch distracts me as I try to frown. He's doing everything I longed for not even an hour ago. Touching my face, nestled against me in a dark corner where anyone could find us. "What are you apologizing for?"

He cradles my face with his big, warm hands and dips his head, his gaze locked on my mouth for a long, breathless moment before he lifts his lids, his dark eyes meeting mine. "This," he whispers just before he kisses me.

Chapter 3

Archer

I take it slow for fear Ivy will push me away, and at this very moment that's the last thing I want to happen. Her lips part easily when I persist and within seconds she's completely open to me, her tongue sliding against mine. She winds her arms around my neck, her fingers buried in my hair, and I groan at her touch.

Slow goes straight out the window when I smooth my hand down her side, over her hip, curling my fingers into the fabric of her dress. I hitch it up the slightest bit, my mouth never straying from hers, and I feel her tremble beneath my palm as I slip my hand beneath her skirt.

She tastes amazing, feels even better, and when I touch the bare flesh of her thigh I feel her shudder, a soft gust of breath brushing against my lips as she shakily exhales. Her eyes open and meet mine as I smooth my other hand over her hair, fingers tangling in the loose waves.

"You're beautiful," I whisper, because she is. So damn beautiful, I ache with wanting her.

She presses her swollen lips together, her eyes closing as I continue to stroke my fingers through her hair. My other hand is completely still, resting on the outside of her thigh beneath her skirt, and I don't move for fear she'll tell me to let her go.

I don't know if I can.

"Archer," she whispers, and I kiss her to cut off whatever else she wanted to say. If it was a denial, an argument, a declaration, I don't care. I don't want to hear it.

I just want to feel Ivy in my arms, her mouth meshed with mine, our tongues dancing, her entire body trembling as she melts into me. I've waited for this moment for what feels like forever.

Finally, I'm holding her. Finally, she's responding to me like she wants me rather than wanting to kick my ass. While the opportunity presents itself, I'm going to jump all over it. And if that means I get to jump all over Ivy, then I'm going for it.

I let my hand on her thigh inch upward, slowly. Closer to her hip until my fingers skim the lacy scrap of her panties and my dick twitches behind my zipper. The fabric is thin and doesn't amount to much and I wish I could push her against the ledge, yank her skirt up to her waist, and drink her in.

But we only have a few minutes. I'm desperate to touch her. To make her gasp with wanting me, so I have to be quick.

My mouth never straying from hers, I slip my fingers beneath the thin strip that stretches across her hip and touch bare, soft flesh. Her chest heaves against mine, her breasts pushing into my chest, and adrenaline rushes through me at the way she reacts to my touch.

That reaction emboldens me and I trail my fingers forward, across her hipbone, the soft flesh of her stomach. I can feel the tremors beneath the surface of her skin as I skim my fingers down farther . . . farther . . . until the heat of her engulfs me and I slowly slip my hand between her legs.

"Archer," she chokes out against my lips when I touch her,

test her. She's drenched, so wet my fingers glide easily over her folds.

"Damn, you're wet." She grips my shoulders as if she needs to. Like I'm some sort of lifeline and she's afraid to let go. "Tell me what you want," I whisper close to her ear, my fingers between her legs, searching her hot, wet depths. She moves with me, her hips thrusting against my hand, and I close my eyes, fighting for control. Scared out of my mind I'm going to come in my pants and make a fool of myself.

She says nothing in reply, just a little whimper when I still my hand, my thumb resting on her clit. "Tell me, Ivy."

"Touch me." She tightens her arms around my neck, her hands clenching my hair. "Don't stop. Please."

Satisfaction rolls through me as I try my damnedest to make her come and quick. We're on the terrace of my friend's wedding reception, for Christ's sake. Her brother—my best friend—is inside. Gage could come out at any time in search of us.

If he caught me with my hand in his sister's panties and her body draped all over me, I'd be a dead man.

Increasing my tempo, I stroke her clit, watch her face as she reaches for her orgasm. She's so responsive, already close to coming, I can tell, what with the way her entire body tenses, her hands squeezing my shoulders, her hips moving against my touch. I tilt my head back to watch her, filled with the all-consuming need to see her as she comes all over my hand. Knowing that I'm the one who did that to her. Made her feel like that. Made her want like that.

Me.

A ragged little cry escapes her and she stills, her eyes going wide as they lock with mine. Then she's coming apart, sagging against me as the orgasm takes over her completely. My name falls from her lips and triumph surges through me. I fucking love it. At least she knows I'm the one who did this to her, who made her feel this way.

Shudders still wrack her body as I lock my mouth with hers, my tongue tangling languidly with hers. Her breaths slow, her grip on my shoulders gradually loosens, and I know she's coming down off her high.

I don't want her to lose it. I want to keep her there. That I could make her come like that so fast blows my mind. I know I've wanted her for what feels like forever. Has she ever wanted me before this moment?

Breaking the kiss first, I press my forehead to hers, trying to calm my accelerated breaths, my racing heart. I need to gain some control before I lose it. She opens her eyes, staring up at me, all sorts of questions in their hazel depths I can't begin to answer.

"Come home with me." The words fall from my lips before I can even stop them.

Her brows furrow. "What?"

"I want you to come home with me." I press my mouth to hers gently, inhaling her breath. I want more from her. I suddenly want it all from her.

And I have no right to ask for it.

"I don't know . . ." Her voice trails off when I press kisses to her jaw along her soft neck.

"Stay the night with me," I whisper against her throat. "Say yes, Ivy."

"Yes." The word falling so easily from her lips sends pleasure rippling through me. Lifting my head, I kiss her, drown in her like a starving man, telling myself I need to stop now before I lose all control and take her right here on the goddamn terrace.

"Jesus, Archer, you can't even keep your dick in your pants at a fucking wedding reception? What the hell is wrong with you?"

I let go of Ivy so fast at the sound of Gage's voice, I hear the click of her heels as she stumbles, though thank God she doesn't fall. Turning quickly, I face him, doing my best to compose myself. The way I'm standing hides Ivy completely and I wish like hell Gage hadn't found us.

"What are you doing out here?" I ask with a snarl, feeling like an asshole. I shouldn't have let Ivy go like that. Like I'm ashamed to be seen with her.

More like she should be ashamed to be seen with me.

"Looking for you. And I was looking for Ivy. I see that you're preoccupied, though . . ." Gage's voice trails off when he glances around my shoulder to see Ivy standing directly behind me. "What the fuck? Ivy, what are you doing out here with *him*?"

"Nothing," I say for the both of us. "She, uh . . . she was having a bad night. I was trying to comfort her." Holy hell, what a choice of words.

Gage's frown is so fierce he looks like he wants to tear me apart. But his expression is also a mixture of doubt and disbelief. As if he can't believe the two of us are out here together. "Archer, I swear to God if you laid one finger on her . . ."

"I didn't," I assure him, lying through my teeth. "I didn't touch her. Did I touch you, Ivy?"

She steps up so she's standing beside me, her body tense. Damn, I hope I didn't make her angry with my remark. "What did you ask?"

Shit. I did make her angry. She sounds furious.

"You better not have fallen for this dick's charms," Gage says, pointing his finger in Ivy's face. "You know how he is."

Lifting her chin, she glances at me out of the corner of her eye. "I know exactly how he is."

I now feel like a bug Ivy's ready to squash with her pointy heel. "Like I would mess with your sister, Gage. Come on. I'm not that stupid. I know you'd kick my ass if I so much as looked at Ivy the wrong way."

Gage stares at the both of us for long, quiet seconds. Seconds that feel like they stretch into hours, they're so uncomfortable. Doesn't help that Ivy is fuming mad. She practically has steam coming out of her ears, not that I can blame her.

I fucked up with her. Again.

What else is new?

Ivy

For a grown man who runs a multibillion-dollar business, Archer Bancroft is a complete idiot when it comes to women.

My body was still shaking from the most amazing orgasm I'd ever experienced in my life when Gage stumbled upon us, giving Archer crap for fooling around with a woman on the terrace. Not that I blame my brother. It's such an Archer thing to do and here he is, doing it with me.

Shocking.

I hate to admit it, but Archer completely rocked my world. As in, no other man has ever made me come like that. Or come, period. I was ready to say yes to his asking me to come home with him. Passing up an opportunity to have sex with him after five amazing minutes with his fingers between my legs? I'm not stupid. I know sex with Archer would've been amazing. I came so fast, it's almost embarrassing.

Then Gage had to appear. And Archer had to open his mouth and completely ruin the entire moment.

I'm an idiot to think there could ever be anything real between us. Whatever just happened surely meant nothing to him. An opportunity to get with me—get with any woman really—and mess around for a few minutes. He's a known player.

And I just got played.

"I'm leaving soon," Gage finally says, his gaze falling on me. Since I came with him to this stupid wedding, I know what he's going to say next. "Are you ready to go, Ivy?"

"Yes." I nod and start toward my brother, barely withholding the gasp that wants to escape when Archer reaches for my hand, his fingers tangling with mine for the briefest second before they fall out of his grasp.

I glance over my shoulder and glare at him. He looks pitiful. Worried. Sorry.

Good. He should. Not that I care. I can't believe anything that just happened between us was sincere. I should be incredibly embarrassed. I fooled around with Archer. We almost got caught. Talk about a disaster waiting to happen.

"Call me Monday," Gage tells Archer as he rests his hand at my back, ready to guide me back toward the ballroom. "Let's do lunch this week. You're still coming to the city, right?"

"That's my plan." Archer's deep voice resonates within me, and I repress the shudder that wants to take over. I refuse to react in front of Archer. He doesn't need any more evidence that he affects me.

"Great. Let's definitely get together. See ya."

"Hey," Archer says softly, and my brother and I both still, though I refuse to turn around like Gage does. I don't even want to look at Archer, let alone talk to him. "Are you both headed back home tonight?"

"Well, yeah," Gage says with a shrug.

"You should stay the night at my place. It's not that far," Archer suggests, sounding innocent as all get out.

Gage glances at me and I glare back. Oh hell, no. I'm not staying the night at Archer's house. "I want to get home," I whisper.

"It's almost midnight," Gage whispers back. "We won't get back till past two, knowing traffic. I'm beat, Ive."

"I'll drive," I insist. "I'm wide awake. I can make it."

He raises a brow. "Like I'd let you drive my car. Give me a break. You're a hazard behind the wheel."

I roll my eyes. One minor fender bender when I was seventeen and he never, ever lets me live it down. "I won't wreck, I swear."

"It's my Maserati. No way am I letting you drive it." Gage slowly shakes his head.

He wants to stay. I can tell by the look in his eyes. "Gage, no."

"I have plenty of bedrooms," Archer says, his voice hopeful.

I don't want to acknowledge him. Really, I don't. The more I think about what he did, the angrier I get. He said he would never touch me, all incredulous-like. As if he couldn't fathom me as anything but silly, gangly, awkward Ivy the teenage loser. What a jerk. After he just had his hand in my panties and begged me to stay the night with him . . .

Finally I chance a look at him. God, he's gorgeous. His suit is rumpled, his tie askew, his hair a mess. From my fingers. His lips are a little swollen and I remember how he kissed me, his taste, the sounds he made, the way he growled in my ear. Just like that I'm lightheaded and the feeling alone makes me want to slap myself back into reality.

Or maybe slap him for being so damn good at . . . everything. Ugh.

"Come on," Gage says, nudging my side with his elbow. "We'll stay the night, grab brunch at that fancy hotel of his in the morning, and then be on our way."

Hmm, I've never been to Hush. The chance to see it intrigues me, but it shouldn't. Not after everything that's happened between us. "I have to get home. I have to . . . work."

"On a Sunday?" Gage sounds skeptical. Damn him. "Someone wants to have an emergency wallpaper meeting or what?"

Oh my God, I want to punch my brother so hard. I'd relish seeing him fall on his ass.

"Gage, shut the hell up. She probably does have to work," Archer says in my defense, which surprises me.

This is the guy who wanted me to come back to his place so he could get me naked in his bed. Maybe he has ulterior motives. Maybe he'll sneak into my room after Gage falls asleep and strip me and press me into the mattress and . . .

I frown, my hands tightening into fists. I shouldn't want this. I shouldn't want him, especially after the way he spoke about me as if I don't matter to him.

But my body is singing a different song. As in, my skin is still humming after that amazing orgasm and my legs are a little shaky. Not from the stupid shoes with the four-inch heels either.

No, more like from the stupid man.

"Fine. We'll stay." I cross my arms in front of my chest. I probably look like a pouty baby, but I don't really care. I can't believe I'm agreeing to this. "But we wake up, we grab brunch, and we get out of here. I really need to get back."

"Thanks, sis." Gage grabs my hand and brings it to his mouth, kissing the back of it quickly. "You just saved me from an exhausting drive home."

"Such a hardship since you're driving that precious car of yours." Cars are Gage's weakness. He owns too many of them. His addiction is so ridiculous his garage looks like an exclusive, high-end dealership.

"Glad you two are staying. I have guest rooms that are always prepared," Archer says.

I turn to glare at him once more, both uncomfortable and aroused at all the potential that comes with staying at his house. I'm sick in the head. I have to be to even consider . . . no, I can't go there. I blame the champagne. And the amazing orgasm. "You better be on your best behavior."

He throws up his hands in defense. "No funny business, I swear. I'll keep my hands to myself."

"You better, Bancroft, or I'll kick your ass," Gage mutters, his words backed with steel. "Ivy is hands-off when it comes to you."

"I get it," Archer says, slowly dropping his arms to his sides. The slight smirk falls from his face and his eyes meet mine, his gaze imploring. I'm not sure what he's trying to communicate, but I do know one thing.

When it comes to Archer and whatever's happening between us, I'm beyond confused.

Chapter 4

Ivy

His house is amazing, of course. I've been in plenty of beautiful homes in my life. My parents still reside in the palatial house Gage and I grew up in. It's older but large, and has all the warm, lived-in touches that our mom has added through the years. It's nothing compared to the modern, spacious, perfectly designed house Archer lives in in the heart of the Napa Valley.

Not that I can see much of it, considering the late hour. The interior is shrouded mostly in darkness, with only the occasional lamp turned on, but from what I can see, it's beautiful. Sleek and simple, yet warm.

Archer leads Gage and me through the wide hallway toward the guest wing, as he calls it. One wall is made entirely of glass and I can make out a giant pool in the backyard, surrounded by lush, perfectly manicured landscaping that looks like something out of a park.

The man certainly knows how to live, I'll give him that.

"Nice, right?" Gage murmurs in my ear as we follow Archer. "I spend all my money on cars. Archer spends it all on his house."

"Not that I'm ever here," Archer says, revealing he eavesdropped on our conversation. No surprise. Since our encounter out on the terrace, I feel like he's hyperaware of me. And I'm hyperaware of him. "I spend most of my time at Hush."

"Do you have a room there?" The resort is treated as some sort of secret amongst my brother and his friends. At least, they keep it a secret from me. Always made me wonder if there are kinky secrets going down at that place.

Wouldn't put it past Archer, at least.

"I keep a suite there, yes." Archer slows so he can be closer to us. His scent reaches me, filling my head, reminding me of what it feels like to be wrapped in his arms, his broad shoulders beneath my palms. His hair is still a mess and he's shed the jacket and tie, the first couple of buttons on his shirt are undone and revealing a sliver of bare chest that I have the sudden urge to lick.

I really need to get a grip.

"So you stay at the resort most of the time?"

"Not as much as I used to. When it was being renovated I never left. I didn't even own a home then. Hush was my home. Now that the resort has been up and running for the last few years, I finally feel confident enough to leave it on occasion and actually have a life." Archer flashes me a smile, making my heart flutter.

Stupid heart.

"Hush is his baby," Gage adds like I don't know this, though it's fairly obvious. Considering Archer and I don't see each other much, let alone talk, it makes sense Gage would make that assumption. "He created it out of nothing but his own sick and twisted mind."

"Shut the hell up. I met a need that wasn't being filled.

Pure and simple." Archer presses his lips together and his eyes narrow. He looks a little angry.

He also looks a lot sexy.

Stop!

"I'm intrigued. I'd love to see it," I say, pleased when his expression eases. "Maybe you'll take me on a quick tour of it tomorrow?"

"I thought you had to get right home tomorrow," Gage starts just before I jab him in the ribs with my elbow.

Yeah, Gage is right. But I'm curious to see this side of Archer's life that I know absolutely nothing about. I mean, come on. Not even an hour ago this man had his tongue down my throat and his fingers working me straight into oblivion. Any woman would want to know more about a guy after that sort of experience, right?

That's what I'm telling myself.

"I'd love to give you a tour of the resort," Archer says, his voice warm, his gaze hot as he rakes it over me. My skin ripples with awareness. It's as if he just physically touched me. "We'll have brunch and then I'll show you around."

"Sounds great." I smile, he returns it, and for some strange reason it feels like we're all alone, grinning at each other like idiots.

But then Gage clears his throat, bringing us both into reality, and I jolt at the sound, clasping my hands together to keep from reaching out and grabbing Archer.

I can't grab Archer, especially in front of my brother. No matter how badly I want to. Gage knows all of Archer's secrets, all of his faults. He loves his best friend, but Gage would never really want us together. At least, I don't think he would.

Better to pretend there's nothing between us rather than

risk Gage's disapproval. And there's nothing going on with us. Between Archer and me. Really. A hot kiss and an orgasm. That's it.

That's sorta major.

I ignore the rotten little voice in my head and try to focus.

Regaining his composure, he shows us the guest rooms, which are directly across from each other, and I can't believe how beautiful my room is. The colors are soothing blues and grays, the bedding lush, the furniture dark and sleek. The entire room reeks of sophistication. I take it all in, fixating on the bed covered in plush fabrics since I'm so tired and I can't wait to collapse in it.

Or maybe the idea of Archer coming to this room later and making me come again and again is what really gets me going . . .

Overcome with a coughing attack at the thought, I wave Gage away when he shoots me a strange look. "I'm fine," I say as they both head toward the open doorway. "Show him his room, Archer. Good night."

Not giving either of them a chance to reply, I shut the door behind them and slump against it, thumping my head against the solid wood once, twice. Trying to knock sense into my brain, because clearly, I've lost it.

Sighing, I push away from the door and glance about the room, noting the open door that leads to a small connecting bathroom, and I go inside to check it out. All the amenities are here, with the exception of what I might wear to bed. Not that I want to change into something left over from one of Archer's sexual conquests, but still. I'm surprised there's not a fresh, clean nightgown waiting for me to change into for the night, considering he seems to have everything else. I guess I could wear my bra and panties . . .

Or wear nothing at all.

A little smile curling my lips, I find a plush terry cloth robe hanging from a hook on the back of the door. Running my hand over it, I contemplate taking a shower and start to shed my clothes, kicking off my shoes and letting the dress, my panties, and my bra fall into a pile on the floor.

I'll look like I'm doing the total night-after walk of shame tomorrow morning at Hush, wearing the semiformal dress I wore to the wedding. Something I never considered until now. I chew on my lower lip, staring at the gigantic glass-enclosed shower calling my name.

Maybe I should ask Archer if he has something for me to wear. Though how do I approach him? Sure can't do it at the moment, since I'm standing here naked. He might not mind finding me this way, though.

Stop thinking like this. You don't want him to find you naked . . . do you?

Oh my God, maybe I do.

A knock sounds at the door and I jump, grabbing the robe off the hook with lightning speed. Throwing it on, I approach, figuring it's Gage ready to tell me something lame before he goes to bed. He's always been a little overprotective, so he's probably just checking up on me.

"I'm fine, Gage. Really," I say as I open the door, stunned silent when I see who's standing before me.

"Really?" Archer raises a brow, one hand in his pants' pocket, the other clutching an article of clothing. "Why wouldn't you be anything *but* fine?"

Oh. Shit. He should so not be standing in front of me right now. "What are you doing here?" I whisper, glancing over his shoulder to thankfully see Gage's door is closed.

"Making sure you're comfortable." He thrusts his hand out toward me. "I brought you something."

I'm ultra-aware of the fact that beneath the terry cloth, I'm wearing absolutely nothing. The impulse to untie the sash and let the robe drop to my feet just to see Archer's reaction is near overwhelming.

But I keep it under control. For now.

"What is this?" I take the wadded-up fabric from his hand, our fingers accidentally brushing, and heat rushes through me at first contact.

"One of my T-shirts." He shrugs those broad shoulders, which are still encased in fine white cotton. "I know you didn't have anything to wear to . . . bed. Thought I could offer you this."

His eyes darkened at the word *bed* and my knees wobble. Good lord, what this man is doing to me is so completely foreign, I'm not quite sure how to react.

"Um, thanks. I appreciate it." The T-shirt is soft, the fabric thin, as if it's been worn plenty of times, and I have the sudden urge to hold it to my nose and inhale. See if I can somehow smell his scent lingering in the fabric.

The man is clearly turning me into a freak of epic proportions.

"You're welcome." He leans his tall body against the doorframe, looking sleepy and rumpled and way too sexy for words. I want to grab his hand and yank him into my room.

Wait, no I don't. That's a bad—terrible—idea.

Liar.

"Is that all then?" I ask, because we don't need to be standing here having this conversation. First, my brother could find us and start in again on what a mistake we are. Second,

I'm growing increasingly uncomfortable with the fact that I'm completely naked beneath the robe. Third, I'm still contemplating shedding the robe and showing Archer just how naked I am.

"Yeah. Guess so." His voice is rough and he pushes away from the doorframe. "Well. Good night."

"Good night," I whisper, but I don't shut the door. I don't move.

Neither does he.

"Ivy . . ." His voice trails off and he clears his throat, looking uncomfortable. Which is hot. Oh my God, everything he does is hot and I decide to give in to my impulses because screw it.

I want him.

Archer

Like an idiot, I can't come up with anything to say. It's like my throat is clogged, and I can hardly force a sound out, what with Ivy standing before me, her long, wavy, dark hair tumbling past her shoulders, her slender body engulfed in the thick white robe I keep for guests. The very same type of robe we provide at Hush.

But then she does something so surprising—so amazingly awesome—I'm momentarily dumbfounded by the sight.

Her slender hands go for the belt of the robe and she undoes it quickly, the fabric parting, revealing bare skin. Completely bare skin.

Holy shit. She's naked. And she just dumped the robe onto

the ground so she's standing in front of me. Again, I must stress, naked.

My mouth drops open, a rough sound coming from low in my throat. Damn, she's gorgeous. All long legs and curvy waist and hips and full breasts topped with pretty pink nipples. I'm completely entranced for a long, agonizing moment. All I can do is gape at her.

"Well, are you just going to stand there and wait for my brother to come back out and find us like this or are you going to come inside my room?"

More like I'm going to come inside her, if I'm lucky. Which I'm thinking I'm gonna be.

Moving fast, I crowd her, my hands going to her waist as I push her inside. I kick the door shut, snaking out a hand behind me to turn the lock before I settle it back on her waist.

The mention of Gage finding us like this got me moving. He'd tear my balls off with his bare hands if he knew I was touching his sister at this very moment. And then there's that whole stupid bet I just made with him and Matt. Here I went on and on about not letting any chick tie me down and the one woman I secretly consider worth having a relationship with is finally showing a glimmer of interest.

Well, more than a freaking glimmer considering she's naked and nestling that bangin' body all snug up against me. I stare into her eyes, see them clouded with lust, and I lean in ready to kiss her. To take her deep and hard and make her moan with the pleasure of it all. Just like I did earlier, when I touched her out on the terrace. How easily responsive she'd been. Before I ruined it all and blew off what happened between us. Last thing I wanted was to make her angry, but I still managed, all because I didn't want to piss off Gage.

I'm in a total no-win situation with Ivy and I know it. Yet here I am, her naked body in my arms, her lips leaning in close to mine, her breasts coming into contact with my chest . . .

"Hey." I squeeze her hips, my fingers pressing into her flesh, and she glances up at me, her eyes wide, her lips damp. As if she'd just licked them. Fuck, everything she does unravels me. But I need to know where we stand—where she stands. I can't risk making this a bigger mess than it already is. "What are we doing here?"

A perfectly arched brow lifts. "Do I need to explain it to you?"

"You know what I mean." I'm not taking this any further until I'm assured we're both on the same page. "What do you want out of this?"

Ivy reaches out and starts unbuttoning my shirt, her fingertips brushing against my chest with every button she slides out of its hole. "One night of mind-blowing sex?"

I ignore the "one night" comment for a moment, absorbing her words. I shouldn't want more. I never want more.

With Ivy, I think I could.

Well, isn't that fucking terrifying?

"And that's it." My voice is flat, though I suck in a harsh breath when her fingers brush my stomach with that final button she undoes before tugging my tucked-in shirt from the waistband of my pants. "That's all you want from me."

"Isn't that all you want from anyone?" Her gaze locks on my chest and she exhales loudly. "I knew you were bigger than the last time I saw you, Archer, but oh my God."

I smile, loving the way she's looking at me. Like she wants to eat me up. "And when was the last time you saw me without a shirt on?"

"I don't know." She shrugs, her gaze lifting to meet mine. Her eyes are full of hunger, full of want, and I reach out, settle my hand on her cheek, and caress her soft skin. It's like I can't resist touching her. "When we were teenagers?"

"Well, I've changed a lot since then." Leaning down, my mouth is at her ear when I murmur, "So have you."

She slides her hands up my chest, her touch causing sparks to ignite along my skin as she pushes my shirt from my shoulders. I shrug out of it, settling my hands back at her waist, pulling away a bit so I can drink her in.

Jesus, she's gorgeous. I'm hard as a rock just looking at her and I start to back her toward the bed, pushing gently at her shoulders so she falls onto the mattress with a little huff of annoyance. Her long hair falls around her shoulders in tousled waves, the ends barely covering her breasts, tempting me to rake my fingers through the silky strands. Without warning she hooks her finger through the belt loop of my pants, pulling me forward and tipping me off balance so I fall onto the bed.

Fall onto her.

"Now I have you where I want you," she murmurs just before she lifts her head and kisses me deep, her tongue immediately sliding against mine. She skims her hands down my back so lightly I shiver.

Damn, her touch feels good. She feels good beneath me, her hands on me, her legs winding around my hips. I still have my pants on, but I can feel her. My erection nudges against her heated sex and she tilts her hips, grinding against me as she devours my mouth.

She's turned into a wildcat, rubbing against me, her mouth on mine like she wants to consume me, and I willingly fall under her spell. Let her take completely over, as

I'm lost to her delicious taste, the way her tiny hands are all over me, at the front of my pants. Undoing the snap, sliding the zipper down until she's reaching inside and stroking my cotton-covered cock.

"Wow, Archer, you're packing," she murmurs after breaking our kiss, her fingers curling around my erection and giving me an agonizing squeeze.

I burst out laughing at her comment. "Is that supposed to be a compliment?"

"Oh yeah." She slides her hands around my hips, pushing my pants down until they bunch up about mid-thigh. "Take these off. Take everything off."

"Bossy little thing, aren't you?" I whisper against her mouth just before I swipe at her plump lower lip with my tongue.

"I never act like this," she says when I climb off her to shed the rest of my clothes. Her greedy gaze never leaves me. "I think it's all your fault."

"My fault?" Her admission shocks me. How can she blame me for her crazy behavior? "How so?"

"It's you or the champagne I drank earlier." Her gaze drops to crotch level and she's checking me out, her eyes widening the slightest bit once I shed my boxer briefs. "Um, wow."

"Scared?" I rejoin her on the bed, grabbing her by the waist and hauling her over until she's lying beneath me. "You should be," I whisper before I kiss her. Devour her. It grows wild in an instant, my hands roaming her skin, mapping her curves, her hands just as busy as mine, diving straight for my cock. I'll blow if she keeps touching me like that, and I'm not about to go that route, so I grasp hold of her wrists and pull her arms up above her head. Holding her captive as she wiggles against me, making little noises full of frustration.

Driving me fucking insane.

She breaks the kiss first, glaring at me as she jerks her hands against my grip. "I want to touch you."

"You keep on touching me and I'm going to explode all over your fingers," I growl.

Ivy laughs, arching against me so her breasts brush my chest. I can literally feel the hard points of her nipples press into my skin.

This woman is going to kill me. I just know it.

Chapter 5

Ivy

Archer Bancroft has a body like no other man I've been with before, let alone seen live and in person, up close and in my face. All solid mass and smooth skin, defined muscles and broad chest and shoulders. He's all I can see and hear and smell and taste while he lies on top of me, his long fingers curled around my wrists, holding my arms captive above my head.

What we're doing is so completely unexpected, so unbelievably exciting, my entire body is shaking in anticipation. He's kissing me like he's a starving man and I'm the only thing he craves. I can feel his erection nudging between my legs, and I'm so wet for him it's almost embarrassing.

But I don't care. I'm drunk on the sensation of his body pressing into mine, his hungry mouth, his insistent tongue, those big, rough hands pinning me to the bed.

I had no idea being held down would arouse me so much, but oh my God, I'm so hot for him I feel like I'm going to burst.

"Promise not to go straight for my dick?" he whispers in my ear after breaking our kiss.

I want to laugh. I also want to moan. His blunt words turn me on too. "Maybe I really want to go straight for your dick."

His eyes lock with mine. They're dark and full of smoldering heat. "I already told you what might happen if you did that."

Oh yes, he sure did. I might want to witness that too. In fact, the idea is amazingly hot. Me stroking him, Archer losing all control and coming all over my fingers . . .

Restlessly I rub my legs against his, and he chuckles as if he can read my mind. "Promise me you won't make a grab."

"I can't promise you that," I whisper.

"Then let me touch you." His voice lowers as his fingers loosen gently around my wrists. Until they're slipping away and he's nuzzling my neck with his face, his hands skimming along my sides. "I want to explore you."

I'm not going to protest. That's exactly what I want him to do. So instead of making a grab for his dick—as he so kindly says—I sling my arms around his neck, my hands in his hair, gently guiding him down as he rains kisses across my collarbone, my chest, the tops of my breasts, the valley between my breasts . . .

He's teasing me. My nipples ache for his mouth to wrap around them and his lips are everywhere but my nipples. I don't know if I can stand this exquisite torture, his hands gripping my hips, his mouth all over my sensitive skin. I tighten my hold on his hair, tugging hard until he mutters a curse word against my flesh before he licks one nipple.

Then he licks the other.

The ragged moan that escapes me is nothing like the usual sounds I make in bed, and I clamp my lips shut, momentarily embarrassed. But then he does it again, his velvety damp tongue flicking back and forth over my nipple, driving me absolutely wild. Another shuddery moan leaves me, and I tangle my fingers in his hair, holding him to me as he licks and sucks and edges his teeth on my flesh, gently nipping. Testing me.

It feels so good I want more. Oh God, I'm crazed with wanting his teeth on me, his hands all over me. "Harder," I whisper, my request shocking myself, and he bites my nipple, hard.

Between my legs I go loose and damp and when he glides his fingers through my soaked folds, his thumb sweeping over my clit, I shake my head frantically. "No, not like this. Please."

"Want me inside you?" He whispers the heated words against my breasts, and I crack open my eyes to find him watching me. His gaze is dark, full of forbidden promise, and I nod, a whimper falling from my lips. His answering smile is deliciously wicked. "Good. Because I can't fucking wait to be inside you."

No man has ever talked to me like this. I love it. I want more. So much more . . .

Moving up, he leans over me, his chest in my face as he reaches for the bedside table and pulls open the tiny drawer. He withdraws a condom from inside, and I'm momentarily stunned.

Though I shouldn't be. Everyone knows how Archer operates.

Pushing the worry from my head, I lean up on my elbows and press my mouth to the center of his chest. His scent surrounds me, the warmth of his skin, his salty taste. I'm licking a path down to his abs and he pulls away from me, hissing as if I've burned him.

"You're dangerous," he murmurs, tearing open the wrapper and rolling on the condom. The sight of him entrances me and my heart rate accelerates, my mouth going dry when he catches me staring. He shakes his head with a slight smile curving his perfect, swollen lips. "I want to take my time but I doubt I'll make it, Ivy. I want you too damn much."

Again, he stuns me, this time with his words. If I think about it too hard, the entire situation is mind-blowing. I'm naked with Archer Bancroft. We're about to have sex. If someone told me a month ago—heck, a few hours ago—that I would end this night having sex with Archer, I would've laughed in their face.

I'm not laughing now, though. More like I'm grabbing for Archer, bringing him down on top of me, his big body pushing me into the mattress. I wrap my legs around his hips, curl my arms around him so I can stroke down his smooth, damp-with-sweat back as our mouths find each other, lazily kissing, nipping at each other's lips, tangling our tongues.

He tastes amazing. I love the sounds he makes, the way he holds me. And when he slowly slides inside my body, inch by excruciating inch, a shudder sweeps over me, my eyes shutting against the intensity of emotions swirling within. He doesn't move, doesn't so much as breathe, and I'm breathless too. I've never felt so connected to another person before.

It's frightening. Exhilarating.

"Christ, you feel so good," he whispers close to my ear as he slowly begins to move. I shift with him, lifting my hips, tightening my legs around him. He's thrusting faster, almost as if he can't help himself, and I'm fine with it. More than fine with it. I rock against him, sending his cock deeper inside my body, and he's groaning, straining above me, already close. I can see it in the tension in his face, across his shoulders.

He warned me it would be fast, but I don't care. I'm close

too. I've been on edge since he made me come on the terrace. There'd been no relief with that orgasm. More like it ratcheted me up, helping me realize what I was missing, not being with him like this.

"Say you're going to come," he whispers, his ragged voice sending a shiver over my skin. "Say it." He reaches between us, his fingers slipping over my clit, rubbing circles around it, driving me straight out of my mind.

"Yes," I moan. "So close."

Archer rears up on his knees and grasps hold of my waist, pulling me closer as he pounds into me. I watch, breathless at the brutal way he's handling me, truly fucking me, and I wonder if any man I've ever been with has done this. Fucked me like Archer is at this very moment.

That would be a firm no.

The men of my past always handled me gently, as if I were made of glass and might shatter at any moment. Not Archer. He's all macho, primal fierceness, his hands gripping me, his cock pounding inside of me, his mouth brutalizing mine. It's as if he's completely overcome.

I love it.

Closing my eyes, the familiar sensations threaten to wash over me, and I try to hold them off. Whimpering, I shake my head, pant his name, and then I can't hold back any longer.

I'm coming. Lost in the deliciously warm pulsating sensation as the second orgasm of the night takes me completely over the edge.

He collapses on top of me seconds later, his warm weight comforting, yet making it all feel far too real. His mouth presses to my neck, wet and hot as he whispers unintelligible words. I smooth my fingers down his back, feel the shivers still trembling through him, and I kiss his cheek, murmuring, "You should probably go soon." I wince the moment the words leave my mouth. I really don't want him to leave.

But he needs to. If he lingers . . . I might want him to stick around. Then I might do something stupid. Like admit how much I care for him, how much I wish he were a permanent part of my life.

Yeah. He'd flip out and run like a scared little boy if I ever said something like that.

Lifting up so he can meet my gaze, he studies me, his brows furrowed, his mouth curved in a frown. "What?"

Uh-oh. Did I say the wrong thing? Come on, Archer isn't one who lingers in a woman's bed, is he? "You, um, you should probably go, don't you think? I don't want my brother to see you sneak out of my room."

"He's probably asleep. That guy sleeps like the dead." Archer's studying me like I've lost my mind.

"Yeah, but . . ." He's right I'm sure. I don't want to risk the chance. Besides, I need time alone. I need to process what just happened between us.

"So you're kicking me out." He sounds incredulous, looks angry.

"No . . ."

"Yes," he cuts me off, his voice tight. "I get it, though. Don't want Gage to find out. I agree with you, actually. He'll hang me by my balls from a tree, and I happen to like my balls, thank you very much."

He climbs out of bed, snatching his clothes off the floor impatiently, giving me an unintended eyeful of those very balls he happens to like so much.

Crap, I've made him mad. I didn't mean to, but I can't have him lingering. It's bad enough what we just did. I don't do one-night stands, especially with guys I know and run the risk of seeing again. Worse, I don't want to get attached. Or put expectations on us that this sort of thing might happen again.

Because no way should it happen again. That would be a big mistake. Huge. No more fooling around for Archer and me.

Even though I want to. I hate that I'm pushing him away. His reaction is confusing. He acts like he's hurt by my denial.

I'm hurt too. More than I would ever dare admit. Deep down inside, I think . . . I want more. For once, I'm ready to take that risk and go for it. Do something so completely out of character just to see what would happen.

"You still want to see Hush later today?" he asks, his voice quiet, his back to me. He has on his underwear, nothing else, and I let my gaze wander over him, drinking in all that pure masculine beauty.

He *is* beautiful. I wish we had more time. I'd explore every inch of his skin with my mouth, given the chance.

Your chances with Archer just expired.

"Yes," I answer after I clear my throat. "I would love to see Hush." We can handle a mistaken sexual encounter between friends, right? Of course we can . . .

"Great. Well, it's been real," he says after he slips on his pants, still sounding sort of huffy, and I watch him go without saying another word. He quietly shuts the door behind him.

I flop against the pillows and rest my arm over my eyes, groaning out loud. What the heck is wrong with me? I had amazing sex with a man I've known almost half my life, and then I push him out like he's some sort of stranger I secretly banged.

I can't help it. I start laughing.

My life has turned completely surreal.

Archer

Damn, could I feel any cheaper?

I'm skulking down the hall of my very own home, shirtless and shoeless, my clothes and shoes clutched in my hand, my pants unbuttoned, for the love of God, and ready to fall from my hips. My footsteps are light as I'm literally sprinting across my house. If Gage came out at this very moment, he would take one look at me and know exactly what I'd just done.

His baby sister.

Grimacing, I shake my head and head toward my bedroom suite, which is on the other side of the house. I'm breathing a little easier now that I'm out of the guest wing, but I could still get caught. That I'm even thinking like this makes me feel like an absolute jackass.

This is my house. I'm twenty-fucking-eight years old. I shouldn't have to sneak around like some sort of teenager out screwing around with my secret girlfriend.

But here I am. Sneaking.

I'm still shocked over how Ivy kicked me out of bed before the come dried on her skin; she was that ruthless about the entire encounter. Crude, I know, but true. I'd been ready to wax poetic and go on and on over how amazing that entire experience had been. Because as quick as I'd come—embarrassingly quick, I'll admit, but damn I was overwhelmed with the fact that I was actually inside her—sex with Ivy had been mind-blowing.

I wanted to tell her how much I wanted to do it again. Clutch her close and cuddle, for Christ's sake. I don't fucking cuddle. I'm the one who kicks them out of my bed. I'm the one who says, *Hey, it's been real, but you need to get your pretty little ass out of here.*

Always, I sleep alone. For once, I wanted to sleep with someone else. Really and truly sleep. Hold her close, feel her skin on mine, smell her. I can still smell her. Feel her. Taste her.

She gave me the boot instead.

Yeah. Bizarre. I feel like the tables have been turned on me completely. I don't like it. Not one freaking bit.

But ever since I saw her earlier this evening at the wedding reception, she's flipped me on my head. What's up is down and all that other bullshit. I haven't felt right since. It fucking sucks. I have a business to run, employees to take care of, the potential to open another Hush location on the horizon, and a volatile father to handle.

The last thing I need is some woman twisting up my insides.

I stride inside my bedroom, slamming the door behind me, and head toward the bathroom. I need a shower. Maybe if I wash away the memory, the feel of her skin on mine, her scent, her taste, then I can forget her. Ivy.

Doesn't help. As I stand under the scalding hot water battering my body and scrub at my skin, I can still smell her. Hear her panting, frantic breaths, the way she said my name just before she came. Smell her flowery, delicious skin, taste her greedy lips and tongue . . .

Fuck. I glance down, the water beating a rapid tattoo on the top of my head, and see my erection. Fucking stupid thing. No wonder women loved to go on and on about how men only think with their dicks.

They're pretty dead on in that observation.

Restraining myself, I refuse to jerk off. I just came not fifteen minutes ago, you'd think I'd be over this. Over her.

Apparently not. Having her once wasn't enough. I want Ivy again.

I furiously wrench the faucet off and grab a towel, rubbing it haphazardly across my skin, not really drying it. The soft terry cloth slides across my erection and I grimace. Pissed that I'm teasing myself. What the hell is wrong with me?

Ivy Emerson is what's wrong with you, jackass. She's played you at your game and actually came out on top. Where does that leave you?

Miserable. Pissed. Eager to go back to her room and have my way with her again . . . slower this time. So I can linger over her body, see what she likes, where she prefers to be touched, taste her between her legs and see how long it takes to make her come with just my tongue . . .

Rubbing the heels of my hands against my eyes, I blink them open, stare at my reflection in the steam-covered mirror in front of me. I'm a wreck. Eyes wild, skin still wet from the shower, mouth and jaw so tight I look like I might shatter. Rigid and tense.

All over a woman.

I let loose a loud, growling "Fuck!" and hit the lights off, stride back into my room. Climb into bed naked and still damp, yanking the covers over my head in the hopes I can shut off my whirling brain.

Doesn't work. I want her with me. Snug against me. I need to come clean with myself. I've lusted over her for years. Since her high school graduation, like some sort of pervert, considering I have a solid four years on her and the last thing I should've been doing was wondering if she could possibly be naked beneath her ceremony gown.

Of course, she wasn't. She'd been eighteen and pure and beautiful. She'd given me a hug and thanked me for coming and all I could think about was how much I wish I *was* coming. Inside of her . . .

Yeah. I had it bad for her then. I still do. And I shouldn't. I'm not the relationship type. My parents warped me for good. Ruined me for any woman. I might be able to hold my shit together for a while, but she'd wear me down eventually and discover the real me.

I'm not worth it, not worth making it last. I'm selfish. A complete prick. She'd find out quickly, if she doesn't know already, and she'd bail. Wonder why she wasted her time on me, if she'd even consider me, that is.

And then there's that stupid, fucked-up bet I made only a few hours ago. A million dollars rides on the idea that I won't let any woman trap me.

The crazy thing? I know Ivy Emerson is worth a million dollars.

But am I?

Chapter 6

Ivy

Somehow, Archer arranged for a fresh set of clothes to be waiting for me when I opened my bedroom door earlier. They sat in a neat, folded pile, tucked in a bag that was set in front of my door. A pair of black cotton cropped pants, a bright pink T-shirt, and a pair of my favorite brand of flip-flops. All in the proper sizes, all of it cute and something I would probably pick out on my own if given the chance.

How the hell did he know my sizes? Sorta scary.

I never heard anyone pass by the door either. And I would've. I'd tossed and turned, hardly getting any sleep, what with my thoughts consumed by what happened between Archer and me.

Images had flashed all night. The way he looked at me. How he touched me. The things he said to me.

I can't fucking wait to be inside you.

God, I melt just remembering how dark his voice had sounded, the way he whispered those words close to my ear, his hands all over my body.

A shudder moves through me and I let loose a frustrated huff, then proceed to take a long shower in the hopes the hot water will wash away all of my useless and overwhelming feelings for a man I have no business feeling anything over.

Unfortunately, it didn't work. Considering I'm in Archer's house after being in his arms the night before, he permeates everything.

I both secretly love it and openly hate it.

I get dressed quickly, pulling my wet hair into a low ponytail with a band I found in the bottom of my purse. Slicked on some lip gloss because that's all the makeup I brought with me.

No one's called me, no Gage, no Archer. No one has even knocked on my door, and finally curiosity gets the better of me. I open the door and peek my head out, glancing left, then right, but the hall is empty. Gage's door is closed. The house is quiet—it's like I'm staying in a museum or something—and I step fully out of the room, contemplating going to knock on Gage's door.

What if he's still sleeping? It's already past nine and Gage isn't one to sleep in. Deciding I need to know what's up, I approach the door and knock, stumped when he doesn't answer. No way can he still be in bed. And if he is, what a total bum.

"He's outside, waiting for you."

I jump and turn at the sound of Archer's deep voice, surprised to find him standing in the middle of the vast hallway. Like a ghost, he magically appeared. And what a good-looking ghost he is too. He's dressed in jeans and a black polo shirt, his dark hair is still damp, as if he just came out of the shower, and oh wow, he looks amazing. I'm filled with the urge to take him by the hand, drag him back into my bedroom, and strip him. Run my hands all over his delicious body. Ride him into oblivion.

Stop!

"Oh." I can't come up with anything better to say so I don't.

Ridiculous how I thought a little sex between two age-old friends—acquaintances, really—would be no big deal, but it's like the giant elephant filling the entire house, sitting directly between us. I meet his gaze and all I can do is remember how close his face had been to mine a few hours ago as he thrust deep inside my body. How I craned my neck and met his mouth with mine, our tongues sliding against each other's.

Yeah. This is . . . awkward.

"We're leaving for Hush soon. Are you ready?" His velvety smooth voice sends shivers running over my skin, and I press my lips together, searching for composure.

So far, I can't really find it.

"I need to grab my purse." I gesture toward the open door, then let my hand fall helplessly at my side.

"Did you sleep all right?" His question is innocent and courteous considering I'm his guest. But he mentions sleep, which makes me think of a bed, and then I'm remembering how he was in my bed and how fantastic he felt between my legs.

"I slept fine. Great," I lied. "Um, thank you for the clothes."

"You're welcome. You like them?"

"They're . . . perfect." I frown and he does as well. "How did you know my sizes?"

"I took a wild guess." He said this with a shrug, looking a little sheepish. This of course makes me skeptical. Just goes to show how well Archer knows his way around the female body when he can guess my size accurately.

My gut clenches at the realization.

"Oh." I'm at a complete loss of words. His explanation makes perfect sense. Our being together makes absolutely no sense. Clearly, we made a huge mistake. And now we're paying the price with the awkward silences and uncomfortable vibe between us.

"I'll get my purse and then I'll be ready."

"Meet us out front then?" He smiles at me, but it's grim. And it doesn't quite light up his eyes.

"Yes. Give me just a second." I nod once, shooting into the bedroom the second he turns away from me.

Going to the bed, I sit on the edge heavily, chewing on my thumbnail as I give myself a mental pep talk.

You can handle this. So you've seen him naked. So what? And you know what he looks like when he comes. Big deal. Focus on the old days. When he used to be such a jerk to you and treated you so terribly. Remember how you felt last night at the reception, when he first talked to you and called you "chicken." Jerk. Yeah, he irritated the crap out of you. Hold on to that feeling. The Archer-Bancroft-drives-me-out-of-my-mind-he's-such-an-asshole feeling.

Forget all about the Archer-Bancroft-drives-me-out-of-my-mind-when-he's-kissing-me-senseless-and-fucking-me-into-oblivion feeling. That is so the wrong feeling to hold on to.

Picking up my purse, which I left on the bed, I stand, tug at the hem of my new, cute T-shirt, smooth a hand over my hair, and decide to go face my reality.

I can handle this. Because really, I don't have a choice.

Archer

"What the hell is taking her so long? I'm starved."

"Grumpy bastard," I mutter, irritated with Gage's incessant miserable chatter. He hasn't quit griping about his empty stomach since the moment I ran into him in the kitchen. I offered him an apple but he wouldn't take it. Heaven forbid he eats something healthy. And besides, it's not my fault his sister is taking so long to get ready.

Why, I'm not sure. I saw her no more than five minutes ago, looking absolutely gorgeous in the simple outfit I left for her to change into. I'd been half tempted to grab her by the waist, walk her backward into the bedroom, lock the door, and have my way with her for the rest of the day. Talk about an ideal lazy Sunday.

But I knew Gage was waiting and besides, the panicked expression on her face when she first saw me deflated my ego completely. She looked ready to jump and run.

Did she regret what happened between us last night? I don't, but I gotta admit, the vibe between us just now was uncomfortable yet hyperaware.

Were we going to pretend it never happened? That was probably best: act like what we shared last night was some sort of weird—and fucking amazing—dream. Acknowledging it the morning after only asked for trouble, especially since Gage was present.

A grumbling, moody Gage. He's acting like a bear you'd regret poking too hard.

"You need coffee or what? I told you there's a freshly made pot in the kitchen," I say, unable to stand his moodiness one second longer.

"Bah." Gage waves a hand. "I've had your coffee before. It's complete shit."

I don't bother reminding him that I had the housekeeper make a fresh pot of coffee every morning. Just one of the many perks of having a lot of money. Gage is still stuck on us being college roommates when I used to make coffee that tasted like black oil sludge.

"Whatever. You're missing out." I glance toward the door, standing up straight when it opens, revealing Ivy, who stops on the top step. She's looking fresh as a damn daisy, her hair still wet from the shower and pulled into a ponytail, showcasing that pretty face of hers. Her eyes sparkle, her cheeks are flushed, and when she catches sight of the both of us standing in front of my Mercedes, a smile curls those sensuous lips. Lips I tasted again and again last night.

Lips I'd like to see curled around my . . .

I frown. Damn it, I really need to stop thinking about her like that.

Her smile fades just as quick as it appeared. Like she caught herself doing it and realized her mistake. Or she noticed my frown.

Hell.

"Finally," Gage calls out. "Let's get going before they stop serving brunch."

"They serve it until two," I mutter, wishing like crazy Gage wasn't with us. Of course, if he wasn't, we wouldn't be going to Hush either, and I'm excited to show off my baby to Ivy.

"I forgot what a grump you are in the morning until you get some food in your stomach." She approaches us, her eyes soft when they light on me. "Sorry to keep you waiting."

"You're right on time," I assure her, because at this very moment she really can do no wrong.

"I call shotgun," Gage says as he reaches for the passenger-side door handle.

I slap my hand against the door, stopping him from opening it. "Are you so freaking hungry that you lost your mind? Let your sister sit in the front."

"Why?" Gage sounds boggled. And clueless.

I should be thankful for clueless. If he was feeling a little sharper this morning, he might catch on to the weirdness going on between Ivy and me.

"Stop being such an infant and just sit in the back seat." I jerk my thumb toward the back of the car.

"I can sit in the back . . ." Ivy starts, but I shake my head, cutting her off.

"Sit in the front." I say it like a command, which gets those perfectly arched eyebrows of hers rising, and I round the front of the car without another word, sliding behind the steering wheel and starting the car.

I don't mean to be such a bossy ass but Gage is getting on my last damn nerve.

She slides into the passenger seat, sitting right beside me, her usual floral scent not as strong. I can only assume that's because she didn't use her own products. Shampoo, body wash, perfume . . . I wish I knew exactly what made her smell so good. Perhaps it's a mixture of everything, plus her own unique scent.

"It's a beautiful morning," Ivy says, her head turned away from me, nose practically pressed against the glass of the window. "I wouldn't be able to get any work done if I had this sort of view distracting me every day."

I pull out of the driveway, taking in my surroundings, ignoring the snort that emanates from the back seat. I thought I turned into an adolescent when I got near Ivy. Gage was ten times worse, switching to jerk big brother mode within seconds of Ivy making an appearance.

"After living here for so many years, I don't even notice it," I say, turning left and heading toward Hush. The resort is not far from my house, so the drive is easy. Beautiful.

Definitely beautiful, not that I've noticed it much. Too distracted with work, too distracted with the business opportunity that suddenly came up. Thankfully, it's an opportunity that will keep me in Napa Valley, but I know my father worries it might be a mistake, working on a new venture so close to the already successful Hush resort. Why mess with a good thing, is basically what he told me.

Not for the first time in our lives, I completely disagree with him. I know what I'm doing. So I screwed around in college and didn't get the best grades—so what? I might've spent more time chasing women and going to parties versus studying and actually attending classes, but guess what? I got my education in the real world. Growing up in the Bancroft Hotels gave me the hands-on experience and vision needed to take the company to the next level.

Too bad my father didn't realize it.

"Do you miss the city?" Ivy asks, knocking me from my thoughts.

I glance over to find her studying me. "Sometimes. Not that it's far, but I haven't had much time lately to make it over. Not as if I want to visit my parents . . . I like the pace here, though. It's a little slower. More reflective."

"Are you trying to say you're reflective?" Gage pipes up from the back seat. "Give me a break."

I press my lips together to keep from calling Gage an insensitive prick.

"Ignore him," Ivy whispers, reaching over to pat my thigh. "He's just jealous."

"Yeah, right," Gage laughs, but I don't reply.

I'm too caught up in the fact that she touched my thigh, and just like that I'm sporting a hard-on. A full-blown one too, all from a light touch of her fingers on my leg.

This is . . . bad. If I can barely handle her touching me on the leg for a brief second, then I need to get her out of my life pronto.

Or pull her so deeply into my life there's no way she'd ever want to leave my side again.

Keep dreaming, asshole.

Funny how the nagging voice inside my head sounds just like Gage.

Chapter 7

Ivy

The resort is gorgeous. Unlike anything I've ever seen, and I've been to more than a few exclusive spas and resorts in my life. My mom loves to indulge in spas and she's taken me on many a "girls only" trip the last few years. She's all about the detox.

But the Hush Resort is more than just a simple spa. And it's definitely more than a hotel too. From what I can see since Archer's taken us on a tour of the lush grounds, it's all about promoting a lifestyle.

Indulgence. Decadence. Sex. That's the message Hush is sending me, albeit in a sophisticated, understated package. I noticed from the moment we were seated in the small on-premise restaurant that we're surrounded by couples. Young, old, middle-aged, every one of them is so in tune with each other, so focused and seemingly happy, I can't help but admire each and every one of them.

And also feel a little jealous.

I sat with two men, the lone oddity in the entire restaurant. One is my jerk of a brother who can't quite stop giving Archer grief while stuffing his face. I have no idea what's gotten into Gage, but it isn't a pleasant sight.

Then there's Archer, who's been quiet since we arrived. He seems almost . . . nervous, and I've never seen Archer nervous. Of course, I'd never seen Archer naked either, but I sure remedied that last night now, didn't I?

I feel like I'm seeing all the bits and pieces that make him up. It's rather fascinating, though I tell myself I most definitely should not be fascinated. What happened between us was a mistake. Why I can't seem to remember that, I'm not exactly sure.

Hormonal issues maybe? Yes, that must be it.

After breakfast, he takes us for a tour, showing us the gorgeously landscaped grounds with what seems like miles of lush green grass spread around the facility. The rolling hills that surround the hotel location are dotted with the vineyards' neat rows and my eyes are constantly drawn to their simple, efficient beauty. The day is crisp and clear, the sky a startling blue, the sun warm on my skin, and I glance around in utter amazement, overwhelmed with all the natural beauty that's surrounding me.

"You like it?" Archer asks, sounding eager.

"I do." I smile up at him, unable to contain it. I don't want to give him any wrong ideas, but wow, I'm blown away with his resort. "The location is unreal."

"My father bought the property years ago, before I was even born," Archer explains, his gaze going to the vineyards, just like mine does. "The old Bancroft Hotel in Napa that's not too far slowly turned into a complete loser, a financial drain. Couldn't turn a profit, was considered in a less-than-ideal location."

"I'm surprised," I say, interrupting him. He turns to look at me, his eyebrows raised, and I shrug. "Just the beauty of the location alone is breathtaking. And you haven't taken us inside any of the buildings yet besides the restaurant. I'm sure I'll become even more impressed."

Gage wanders off, seemingly bored with the conversation, but I'm sure he's heard it all before. Funny, how Archer and I have never spent any sort of time alone together like this. Until now.

"Well, I had the original hotel building razed when my father sent me out here. I started over completely from scratch. And when I say it wasn't an ideal location, it's because so many other hotels were built in another, much more populated area. This one was considered out of the way." He slips his hands into the front pockets of his jeans, looking so gorgeous as the breeze ruffles his dark hair I want to lunge at him. Grab hold and never let go.

I keep myself in check instead.

"You've done an amazing job," I say softly. "You must be proud."

"Yeah, I am." He smiles, his eyes warm. "It wasn't easy. My father sent me out here to fail."

I frown. "He did?"

"Of course he did. He had no faith in me. I was a world-class screwup, I'll admit it. I didn't want to work, not directly for him, at least. So he said since I thought I knew what the hell I was doing, he'd give me this." Archer's smile turned rueful. "I showed him, didn't I?"

"How long ago was that?" I knew his relationship with his father wasn't the best, but to send his son out to purposely fail with a bad location? Awful.

"Over three years ago. Construction took a solid ten months to a year and we opened when only a few buildings were completed, expanding as each one was finished. Hush made Bancroft a lot of money in the first six months it was open." He studies the vineyards in the near distance, his expression serious, not the usual smiling, charming Archer.

My heart aches for him, no matter how much I tell it to stop.

I'm impressed with his success story. I remember how it was when we were younger. His dad constantly disappointed in him. His mother never around, or always drunk and crying over the way her husband treated her. No wonder Archer spent all of his time at our house when he and Gage became such good friends. My parents weren't perfect, but at least they get along for the most part and they have a relatively normal relationship.

No drunken yelling or icy-cold neglect.

"Such a great story," I say, wincing the moment the words fall from my lips. More like such a lame comment for a truly amazing accomplishment.

"Yeah, well, tell that to my father." His voice is tight, as is his jaw.

I hate that he feels this way. He should be proud of what he's done in such a short amount of time, versus fixated on his father's shoddy treatment of him over the years.

"Is this hotel part of the Bancroft chain or is it separate?" I'm not quite sure why I'm asking him this, but I have to know.

"It's all mine. He signed it over to me." He turns to look at me. "I told you he thought I would fail. He had no problem giving it to me figuring I would lose my ass over it."

The pain in his voice is undeniable. "You certainly proved him wrong," I say softly.

"Sure as hell did." His gaze meets mine, dark and mysterious, his mouth grim. My heart flutters and I step toward him. Somehow wanting to offer him comfort, solace, something. Anything. He's hurting and it makes me hurt for him.

"What made you decide to create a resort like Hush in the first place?" I'm desperate to change the subject. The last thing he ever wants to talk about is his dad or his mom.

"I knew it would turn a profit." He waves a hand. "You know how many people I've heard complain that their sex life was dead after being in a relationship for too long? That they didn't spend enough time with their significant others and they were desperate to connect? I realized it was an untapped market so I created Hush and fed the need. The new location takes the concept a step further."

"It's all a business decision, then. Not because you wanted to help people." Disappointment crashes through me, and I try to push it away. Of course. It's always a business decision. My brother thinks the same way. So does my father.

I sorta hoped Archer was different. Clearly, he's not.

"I'm not looking to help anyone. I'm no one's savior." He tips his head toward me. "You of all people should know that."

I most definitely know that. "I find it funny that the man who is the epitome of anti-commitment creates a safe haven for couples looking to spice up their sex life." I shake my head. "You must see the irony."

"Oh, I do. Trust me." He smiles and the sight of that dimple I adore momentarily takes me aback.

"You should show Ivy some of the rooms," Gage suggests as he approaches us, breaking the quiet spell that had settled over Archer and me. I step away from him, smiling faintly at my brother, though really I'm irritated. I should be glad he spoke up before I did something foolish. Like touch Archer. Give away that I might . . . feel something for him.

I definitely feel nothing for him beyond a fondness for a man I've known for what feels like forever.

Ha. And a yearning for his body.

"I'd love to see the rooms," I say, trying to push the confusing thoughts from my brain.

"Yeah, Arch. Show her everything. Explain the concept behind the resort so she can get a better understanding." Gage smirks.

The look that crosses Archer's face is nothing short of uncomfortable. "Do you want to see them, Ivy?" he asks stiffly, his gaze flicking to Gage before it returns to me.

"Absolutely." I'm surprised he asks. I wonder more at his discomfort. Is this entire scenario misleading? Is he hiding some sort of secret sex den in one of the buildings? Oh, good lord, I know Archer's reputation precedes him, but he was pretty vanilla last night when we had sex. Nothing too outrageous.

But he was certainly the tastiest vanilla I've ever experienced.

We walk down a meandering gravel path, Archer leading us to a row of detached cottages that each individually house a room. They all have quaint front porches with a pair of large, comfortable-looking chairs on either side of the front entrance, and he approaches the largest one, me following right behind him and stopping while he opens the door.

Inhaling as discreetly as possible, I breathe in his scent, closing my eyes for the briefest moment. He smells . . . amazing, fresh and clean and delicious. I sway toward him, afraid I might fall into him, and he turns just as I right myself, his brows furrowed as he studies me.

"Ladies first." He points toward the door and I follow the length of his arm, realizing a little too late that the door is open and he's waiting for me to enter.

I'd been so caught up in my obsessive sniffing, I didn't realize he opened the damn door.

My cheeks hot, I walk inside, glancing about the space, which I instantly love. It's got a contemporary feel with dark wood floors, a giant fireplace dominating the room, and sleek furniture. I do a slow circle, taking everything in. I catch a glimpse of the giant bed within the bedroom, a deck off the back of the cottage with a beautiful view, and—is that a . . .

"Is that a tub?" I point toward it lamely, feeling like a little kid.

"Yes, it is." He sounds amused, and he starts toward the French door that leads onto the deck. I follow him, curious to check it out, and I glance over my shoulder, seeing that Gage isn't following us.

In fact, he isn't in the room at all.

Frowning, I turn back around to see Archer studying me carefully, his hand curled around the door handle. "Your brother took a phone call. He's out front."

"Oh." Swallowing hard, I nod once. Is that all I can seem to say when he makes those types of statements? The ones that worry me and make me realize that I can pretend I don't want him but it's all a lie.

I still want him. More now that I've had him.

"Well, let's check out the view then," I say, hoping he doesn't notice my wavering voice.

Being alone with Archer, even for a few minutes, is going to test my very patience.

Archer

Ivy's looking at me like she wants to eat me up with a spoon and fuck me, I'm returning the feeling a millionfold. But Gage is out front and who knows how long he's going to take with his call.

I can't risk it.

I want to risk it so bad my hands literally itch to touch her.

Being near her flat-out arouses me, there's no denying it. Her scent, her smile, the way she looked at me when I explained Hush's background. I saw the glimmer of sympathy in her eyes. She knows what an asshole my father is.

The last thing I want from her is sympathy. I'm not a charity case.

She walks out onto the private deck and I follow her, admiring the curve of her ass, the little gasp of pleasure she gives when she catches sight of the rolling hills covered with what looks like endless rows of vineyards.

"So beautiful," she murmurs, and I wholeheartedly agree. She's gorgeous.

"You like the view?" Because I sure as hell do. I take a step closer, noting how I tower over her. Her hair is mostly dry, the ends wavy, and I want to grab hold of her ponytail. Yank her head back and kiss her until the both of us are stupid with lust.

"It's stunning." She glances over her shoulder at me, the smile on her face slowly fading. "You're looking at me weird."

The sexy whisper of her voice doesn't quite go along with what she's saying. "How am I looking at you?"

"Like . . . like you want something from me." She turns to face me but backs up a few steps, until she's leaning against the deck railing. Her hazel eyes are wide, her cheeks flushed. A few wisps of hair have escaped her ponytail, brushing against her face. I move toward her, slow and easy, not wanting to startle her. Not wanting to ruin this.

"I want nothing from you that you don't want to give," I murmur, and I note the rapid beat of her pulse at the base of her throat.

"Archer." Her voice is a warning, with the slightest bit of waver. That waver gives me hope. "My brother is right out that front door. What if he finds us?"

"We're not doing anything that we need to hide." I'm directly in front of her, crowding her, and I rest my hands on the railing on either side of her body, effectively trapping her.

"Yet," she whispers, and that one single word gives me so much damn hope, I do what I've been dying to do since I saw her in the hallway of my house.

Dipping my head, I nuzzle her hair with my cheek, breathing in her scent, closing my eyes. My entire body tingles at having her close, hearing the catch of her breath, feeling the slight tremor that moves through her. She doesn't touch me, doesn't so much as move, and I settle my mouth close to her ear. "All I can think about is last night."

"Archer." She sounds like I'm torturing her.

Good. Feeling's mutual.

"Do you think about it? I swear to God, Ivy, all I want to do is drag you into that bedroom right now and fuck you until you can't see straight." My control is about to snap. And I never let it snap. But this woman pushes all my buttons, does everything she can to tear me apart with just a look. A smile. It blows my mind how much power she wields over me.

She has no clue about her power either.

"You shouldn't talk to me like that. Last night was a . . . mistake." She settles her hand on my chest as if she's going to push me away, but her fingers curl ever so slightly into my shirt. Pulling me just a fraction closer to her.

Triumph surges through me. She can't resist this pull between us either. "You really think so?"

"I know so." She pushes at my chest so I have no choice but to look at her. She's not strong enough to get me to step back, though. No way am I moving from her yet. "We can't continue this."

"You want to." It's a statement, not a question.

"No, I don't." But she's nodding as I lean into her, and when I brush my mouth with hers, the shuddering exhale she breathes against my lips twists up my insides. "Archer . . ."

I love hearing her say my name, even if it's in protest. Because really she's not protesting. She wants this just as bad as I do.

"Just one kiss," I murmur against her lips, darting out my tongue to lick. The soft moan that escapes her is my answer, and I settle my mouth fully on hers, our tongues meeting, circling, tasting. I rest my hand on her hip, stepping into her, wanting to feel her.

The breeze sweeps over us, a shiver moves through her, and I slip my arms completely around her waist, tugging her lower body close to mine. Fuck Gage. Fuck anything else. I want to pull her into that bedroom, slam the door, and keep her in the bed pinned beneath me for the next twenty-four hours.

It wouldn't be enough. But when it comes to Ivy, I'll take what I can get.

A buzzing sound rings through my head as I continue to

kiss her, lose myself in her. I slide my hands over her ass, groaning when she grinds subtly against me. The buzz gets louder, more insistent, and I break the kiss first, staring down at her, my breath coming in pants. "What is that?"

She blinks up at me, looking as wrecked as I feel. "I think it's your phone."

Shit. She's right. I can feel it vibrating in my jeans pocket. Yanking it out, I see it's a text message from Gage.

> I gotta get back home. Meet me at the car.

"It's your brother." Damn it, I'm not ready to send her back to the city with Gage. I want to keep her here with me.

Like she'd ever go for it. She has a life. A relatively new career, friends—she probably has little time to spare, especially for me.

I'm delusional if I think I can make something between us work. Not that I want something real or lasting. A fling. That's all I want. And then there's the bet to consider.

You're really going to let a bet guide your decision?

I ignore the shitty little voice in my head.

"What did he say?" She licks her lips as if she's trying to get one last taste of me, and my cock twitches as I reluctantly step away from her.

"He's ready to leave."

"That's probably best." She pushes away from the railing, glancing to her left, looking at the tub that sits outside near the deck. "You never did explain the reason for the tub being outside."

"It's built for two. The decks are all private; none of the guests can see each other." I smile, imagining the two of us in that tub, our naked skin slick and soapy, Ivy sitting in my lap, her long legs wound around my waist. "It's, uh, one of our most popular features."

"I'm sure." The sarcasm is thick and I take another step away from her, surprised. "Archer, what happened between us last night . . ."

"Was a mistake. I totally agree," I finish for her, needing to be the first one who said it.

Weird thing, though, is the look on her face when I do. Like I slapped her when she least expected it.

"A mistake," she says slowly as she nods. "That's what you think?"

"Absolutely. I mean, come on. We could never work. I don't do relationships. You know this." I sound far more confident than I feel. Maybe it's because I always say this sort of thing to women, or really more to myself. I've never been in a relationship. I know I would fail at one. I would most definitely disappoint her. Ivy.

But secretly? I wish she would give me—give us—a chance.

"And I do."

"You most definitely do," I agree a little too quickly.

"And you're yet another Humpty Dumpty." She sighs.

"What?" Okay, that made no damn sense. Why is she calling me Humpty Dumpty?

"The kind of guy who's all broken up and can't be put back together again." She smiles at me, but it's sad and the sight of it makes me feel like a complete jerk. "I have a type. And I think you top my type list."

"I'm on your type list?" I never believed Ivy had any sort of crush on me. Not beyond the *push-pull-we-hate-each-other-maybe-we-should-tear-each-other's-clothes-off* thing we've been suffering through for years. Though I always figured that was more one-sided on my part.

"I never realized it until now. You're so right. We could never work. I'm too nice. And you're too . . . you." She drops that bomb like it makes all the sense in the world.

"What's that supposed to mean?" I rub my palm against my chest, irritated with myself. I'm acting butt-hurt over a woman. This is crazy.

"Do I really need to explain myself, Archer?" She doesn't let me answer. "Let's go meet Gage. I need to get out of here."

Without a word, I follow her out, trying to ignore the disappointment settling over me like a heavy wet blanket.

But I can't. Her rejection, her words, hurt far more than I care to admit. And I'm the one who rejected her first.

We're quiet as we head back to the car, Gage waiting beside it with his arms crossed in front of him, tapping his foot impatiently. We all get inside, Ivy taking the back seat this time, and the mood is dark as I make the quick drive home.

They both hop out of my car as if they can't wait to get away from me the moment I pull up in front of my house and I climb out, chasing after them.

"Sorry to be so abrupt, bro," Gage tosses out apologetically as he yanks his keys from his pocket and hits the remote, unlocking his car. "I have a client wanting to meet for dinner. He owns a piece of property I've been after for months and I think he's finally going to cave."

"I understand. You'll have to call me when you make the deal."

"Prepare for a call late tonight then." Gage grins at me and I chuckle.

I get it. I'm a businessman. When an opportunity presents itself, you have to go for it, and that's exactly what Gage is doing.

Sort of what I did with Ivy.

Sprinting ahead of her, I approach Gage's Maserati and open the passenger door for her, watching as she slides into the seat. She glances up, her eyes fathomless as she studies me. "Thank you, Archer," she murmurs. Then adds meaningfully, "For everything."

"You're welcome," I automatically say, though I'm not quite sure what we're referring to.

Rolling her eyes, she huffs out a breath and yanks the door closed, effectively shutting me off.

Shutting me out.

And as I watch the car speed away, I feel like I'm watching my heart leave with it, forever in Ivy's possession.

Fucking crazy, but true.

Chapter 8

Ivy

One week later

And so you had sex with him."

I nod miserably, trying to ignore the glee in my friend Wendy's voice. She's really enjoying my story—a little too much. "I did."

"And it was awful. Terrible. He was selfish and didn't bother getting you off."

"Wendy," I whisper harshly, glancing about the restaurant, at the people sitting nearby. Nobody's paying us any mind. "What if someone heard you?"

"No one heard me. And quit trying to change the subject. Give me all the dirty details." Wendy sips from her water glass, her brows raised expectantly.

I sigh, completely put out and embarrassed that she wants to hear everything, yet also perfectly willing to reveal all. I've had no one to talk to about my encounter with Archer and I've been holding this inside me for an entire week.

Then I see Wendy waiting for me at our usual restaurant for our Saturday lunch date, and I immediately tear up like a baby when she asked what's new.

I reached my breaking point.

She took one look at my tear-streaked face, my watery eyes, and demanded I tell her what the heck was wrong with me. After purging the entire story of my encounter with Archer in twenty minutes, she's contemplating me with a gleam in her eye, as if she sees me in a new light. She's probably impressed—or in shock. I don't normally do this sort of thing. Wendy's the adventurous one with men. I'm the boring one who tends to choose wrong and stay too long.

I definitely don't do one-night stands with sexy-as-hell men who know just how to touch me to make me go off like a rocket. No man has ever been able to make me go off like a rocket. Ever.

Until now. Until Archer.

"He wasn't selfish," I say primly, pressing my lips together to keep from saying what I really want to.

He's amazing. Hot as hell. The best kisser ever. Oh, and his hands . . .

A slow smile curves Wendy's mouth. "Meaning he was all right."

Better than all right. "He knew what he was doing."

"Quit being so vague." Wendy sounds irritated. Not that I can blame her. I'm being vague on purpose.

"I'm not about to give you any more detail than that. Sorry," I say chirpily, sipping from my water glass. "I don't kiss and tell."

"Since when? We've dished about plenty of men. Now I want details about the one who was actually decent in bed and you're not talking." Wendy's eyes narrow as she contemplates me. "What gives?"

I squirm in my seat. I don't want to admit that my night

with Archer is . . . special. She'll probably make fun of me. She *should* make fun of me. I deserve it. I'm thinking like an idiot. "I really don't want to relive what happened between Archer and me. It's too weird. We've known each other for too long."

I'd have hoped he would call but he hasn't. We agreed it was a mistake, what happened. I walked away from him. The subject was closed, in both my mind and his.

But I lied to myself. Since I came home from Napa, he constantly invades my thoughts. I'm trying my best to focus. I throw myself into my work, which is easy considering how busy we are. Sharon Paxton is one of the most coveted interior designers in the city and her clientele keep her—and me—busy. Learning from her, working with her, is a privilege, one I take very seriously.

I've lost concentration more than once, though, since the Archer incident. I missed an appointment with a very important client. I brought the wrong fabric samples to another one. I was acting so out of character, Sharon sat me down yesterday afternoon and asked what was wrong. I made up some sort of excuse, promised I would do better, and escaped her hawk-like gaze before she asked any more questions.

This is what Archer's done to me. Turned me into a terrible employee. I can't sleep. I sit around on the couch at night and watch really bad reality TV. All the while I stare at my cell phone, willing him to call me, text me, something.

Yes. I've turned into one of those girls. God help me.

Our waiter magically appears with our lunch, setting our salad orders in front of us before he takes off, leaving me alone once again with my too nosy, too perceptive friend.

"You like him," she says, stabbing her fork into her salad with relish. Like she's killing the lettuce.

"No way," I reply too quickly. I'm such a liar. "He drives me crazy. He always has."

"Because you like him. You just didn't realize it yet. Now you do. The two of you have sex and it's like roses and romance and you want more," Wendy says, full of logic.

The sex between us was definitely not roses and romance. I can't begin to describe what it was like, but not soft and sweet like I was used to. It was hard and fast and immensely satisfying. "No, it wasn't quite like that."

"But it was good."

"It was amazing," I admit softly, earning a giant smile from Wendy.

"Knew it." She munches happily on her salad while I sit and watch her, my appetite having fled a while ago. "Call him. Tell him you want to do it again."

"No way." I shake my head, jealous of Wendy's hearty appetite. I've hardly eaten since my night with Archer. He's all I can think about and it's so stupid, I don't know why I'm acting this way. "I don't want to do it again."

"Liar."

"Okay, your smug, short answers are starting to bug me," I say, grabbing my fork and stabbing the lettuce, much like I saw Wendy do a moment ago. Damn it, I'm going to eat even if it kills me. "And they're totally not helping my situation."

"Well, what are you going to do then? You and Archer Bancroft have a past. A history. There's tension there and it finally resulted in the two of you having hot, amazing, outrageous sex."

I don't answer. I'm not going to give her the satisfaction of an acknowledgment.

"Now you're all mopey and sad. Wishing you could see him. Well, go see him then. Call him up. Greet him with, 'Hey sexy, let's do *that* again.' See what he says." Wendy smiles. "I bet he'd take you up on your offer."

But what if he didn't. "I would never call him and say something like that."

"Maybe that's half your problem."

I glare at her and she bursts out laughing. "It's not funny," I insist.

"I think you like him more than you want to admit, and you don't know how to deal with it. I'm trying to tell you how to deal." Wendy offers me a sympathetic smile. "Maybe you need to fess up to your feelings. Why are you acting this way? Is it because you're disappointed in yourself for doing something so crazy?"

"Partly." I shrug. "I don't know why I'm acting like this. Why he has me all twisted up in knots."

"I've already told you why," Wendy says gently. "There's nothing wrong with you contacting him. I'm sure you're waiting for him to call because that's your usual MO. Well, guess what? Having a one-night stand with Archer broke your pattern. Calling him will continue to break that pattern. And there's nothing wrong with doing things a little different."

Sighing, I stare at my still full plate. My appetite has completely evaporated. "I was about to tell him that maybe I wanted to see him again, and he called our one night together a mistake. He doesn't want me, not like that." I should confess I called it a mistake too, but I can't. I hate to admit how much it hurt, him saying that. It's one thing for me to think it, another thing entirely to know he feels the same way.

But do I really feel that way?

No.

"Ah, honey . . ."

I interrupt her. I really don't want any sympathy. There's no one to blame for this but me. "Yeah, I might've changed up my pattern, but look where it got me? Miserable. Angry at myself for making such a stupid, *stupid* decision. He's not the one for me. Not that I ever really thought he was." I shake my head. "I need to focus on my anger over this."

"Yeah, you do," Wendy agrees.

"Not sit around wishing he would call." Whoops, wish I hadn't admitted that part.

"Forget him. Screw this guy," Wendy said vehemently.

"I already did." I scrunch my lips together.

We stare at each other across the table for a few seconds before we both burst into laughter.

"You sure did," Wendy says after she gets herself under control, slowly shaking her head as the occasional giggle escapes her.

Yeah. I sure did. What a mistake.

The realization hits me like a swift kick in the ribs. Yet again, I did it. I went after a man who has no intentions to do right by me. Heck, I have no intention of doing right by him. To do so would be utter foolishness. The man is a mess. He's a complete and utter mess and I have no one to blame but myself for getting involved with him.

I almost want to laugh at my mental choice of words. Involved. As if what we shared contains any sort of involvement beyond the quick and dirty sexual kind.

Archer Bancroft is my ultimate failure. That Humpty Dumpty of a man can never, ever be put back together again. I won't even bother trying.

Archer

H ey, what's up? Haven't heard from you in a while."

"I've been busy." So damn busy I can hardly breathe. Not so busy that I haven't been thinking of a certain someone constantly. Hence my reason for calling her brother—I'm digging for information. "You make that deal you told me about?"

"I sure did. Purchased the property for an absolute song. Already have a buyer lined up, and my end of the deal isn't even closed yet." Gage chuckles, sounding pleased with himself. "It all came together way too easy."

"That sort of thing usually makes me nervous." Struggles and roadblocks actually make me feel better when it comes to business. And life. When it's too easy, there's always a catch.

Always.

"I've been working this guy for over a year. This was definitely not an easy deal. I finally got him to cave. I'm a persistent motherfucker when I need to be." Gage full blown laughs.

Wasn't that the truth? One of the many traits Gage and I share. "Congrats, man."

"Thanks." He pauses. "There must be another reason you called. You're not one for chitchat."

I blow out a harsh breath, working up my nerve. "Listen, I need Ivy's work number," I say as nonchalantly as I can, leaning back in my chair so I can stare out the window.

"Why? Call her cell." Gage sounds distracted. "Or are you afraid she won't answer you."

Damn Gage for being too perceptive. "I need to talk to her

about a business proposition." Not a lie. The new location is going into fast-forward mode and the interior designer I hired to transform Hush is unavailable. I need someone quick.

I need Ivy.

"Are you serious? She's just a junior associate, you know. I have no idea if she's up to snuff with what you might need." Gage mutters something under his breath, and I hear a female's soft laugh.

"Way to bag on your sister." I shake my head, irritated with him. "And where the hell are you anyway?"

"Work. Where the hell are you?"

Doesn't sound like he's at work. And he's awfully quick on the defense. "Come on, just give me her number."

"Hold on, I need to scroll through my contacts. Give me a minute."

Tapping my fingers impatiently against the edge of my desk, I wait. I can hear Gage say something, hear the light tones of a woman answering him, and I wonder who he's with on a Monday afternoon. Can't help but feel a little jealous too.

Jealousy is an emotion I'm not used to and definitely not comfortable with. There's no need to get jealous if I'm never with a woman beyond a night or two, right? I move through life with no entanglements, no relationships beyond my friendships, and even then I don't let many into my inner circle. Hell, I don't even stay in regular contact with my mom, not that she cares. She's too busy hitting the bottle or fighting with my father. And I deal with him only because I have to.

More than one woman has described me as a loner. Fairly accurate. I surround myself with plenty of people but it's meaningless. A good time for a few hours before I go home alone. Socially I've withdrawn as I become more consumed with work. This latest project has kept me constantly going these last few weeks.

I miss Ivy. I regret calling what happened between us a mistake. It wasn't. Screw the bet, forget my friends, forget everything. I want to see her. It's been over three weeks. Three long weeks without seeing her pretty face, that gorgeous smile. Hell, I miss hearing her all exasperated with me, insulting me, telling me to leave her alone.

I miss the way her body felt beneath mine. How she tugged on my hair tight, the hot little words she panted against my lips just before I made her come.

"All right, here you go," Gage says, interrupting my thoughts as he rattles off a number. I scribble it across a notepad, my mind still foggy with images of Ivy, and I blink hard, banishing her as best I can. She is the last thing I need to think of while I'm talking to her brother.

"Thanks," I mutter, dropping the pen on my desk and scrubbing my hand over my face. I need to get a grip.

"You're serious about wanting to hire her?"

"I am. The new Hush location's completion is ahead of schedule and I'm pushing it forward. Our previous designer is heavily involved with another project, so she's unable to get on board. I thought I'd ask Ivy if she's available." I say this as casually as possible, not wanting him to figure out my other motive for contacting her.

"I know her boss would probably like a chance at it," Gage says.

Sharon Paxton probably would. But I know for a fact she's beyond busy with her own clients. She has a waiting list, for the love of God. This probably doesn't bode well with getting

Ivy's help, but I'm willing to pay whatever it takes to have her work with me on this project.

I want to see her that badly. This is the perfect excuse. That I have to use my business as a way to get her back into my life is probably underhanded, but I don't care. I'm at the point where I'll do anything to see her again.

Prove to her that maybe I am worth being put back together again.

"I'm sure she would," I say. "I'd rather have Ivy."

Gage is quiet for a moment before he finally asks, "Do you have a thing for my sister?"

"Not at all," I say easily. "Hell, we argue most of the time when we see each other."

"Then why would you want to work with her if all you do is argue?"

Valid question. Shit. "I trust her. I've known her for years. She's your sister. She'll do a good job and not try and screw me over."

"Huh." Gage doesn't sound like he believes me, so I push forward.

"This project, this location, it has to be handled delicately. Discreetly. I can't hire any designer off the street. I need someone I can trust to keep their mouth closed and not leak what I have planned."

"You haven't even told me what you have planned," Gage points out.

"Exactly, and I'm not going to either. That's why I think Ivy is the perfect fit." This part is true. I do want her to work for me. I trust that she won't blab what I have planned for the remote location. An even sexier, more intimate resort than Hush, it will cater to wealthy couples that want an indulgent getaway with their significant other.

Private gourmet meals, couples massages, the small hotel will be exclusive to only eight couples at any given time. The location will be the ultimate in intimate, quiet luxury.

"Well, good luck. Give her a call. I'm betting she'll say no."

"Why does everything circle back to a bet?" I ask irritably, not needing the reminder. "And how do you know she'll say no?"

But she doesn't count toward the bet, right? Didn't Gage and Matt count her out? After all, she's just Ivy.

"She doesn't particularly like you, Archer. You know this." Gage makes it sound like common knowledge. "And besides, I'm going to guess her boss won't let her take on the project. Sounds like it'll be over Ivy's head."

"I want her. Only her." I clear my throat, realizing how that sounds. "For the project," I add weakly.

"Good luck. I doubt you'll get her, but more power to you."

Gage's words are just the challenge I need to hear.

Chapter 9

Ivy

Chicken, I need your help."

Icy shock moves through my veins at the first sound of Archer's familiar, deep, and sexy-as-hell voice. The very last person I expected to call me at my office on an early Wednesday afternoon—and just how did he get my work number anyway?

Duh, your brother.

Freaking Gage.

"No, 'Hello, Ivy, how's it going?' And I really, *really* wish you wouldn't call me chicken." I'm trying to joke. Or more like trying to figure out if he really does need my help. I mean, come on. Like hearing from him out of nowhere nearly a month later, after what happened between us, is no big deal.

It's *such* a big deal.

"So nice to hear from you, Archer. What's it been, a couple days?" Almost twenty-five days, not that I'm keeping count.

"Very fucking funny, Ivy. I'm not kidding," he growls irritably. "I need your help, and I needed it yesterday."

"And you're calling me? Why? How exactly can I help you?" Wow, I sound remarkably cool and calm, but deep within my insides are trembling. And for whatever crazy reason, my nipples are hard. All from his gruff, commanding tone. So ridiculous, but it's like the second I hear his voice, my body reacts. I haven't been able to get that night out of my mind. Images of a naked Archer above me, kissing me, buried deep inside me are burned on my brain.

"You're still single, right?" he asks, knocking me from my thoughts.

"How is that any of your business?" My heart lodges in my throat. As if he would care. "And who told you that?" Fine. I so am. I haven't talked to Marc, the jerk, since I broke it off with him. And I haven't talked to any other guy either, let alone gone out on a date since my night with Archer.

Has he somehow ruined me forever? God, I hope not. I'm only twenty-four. I don't want to die a shriveled up old lady pining for a man who had sex with me once and then walked away.

"Gage told me."

I'm going to kill my brother. "Why do you care if I'm single or not?"

"I have a proposition for you." He pauses and my heart falls into my stomach with hope. "A business proposition."

Of course. Not that I expected a sexual one. Hello, been down that road once before and look where it got me? A lot of lonely, achy nights waking up after sweaty, too-graphic dreams involving me and him naked. "What sort of business proposition could you possibly have for me?"

"We're getting ready to open a new set of suites at Hush. There's only a handful, but they're bigger, much more exclusive—and expensive—and I need someone to design the interior." He pauses and my heart squeezes. "I want you."

Hearing his familiar, deep voice say he wants me in that commanding way of his sets my legs shaking. And I'm sitting down. Ridiculous. "Maybe I'm busy," I say haughtily, which is true.

"Come on, Ivy. You're not too busy for me, are you?" He's teasing me, but there's a sexual edge to his voice. One I want to ignore.

"Actually, I am. I have a lot of projects I'm working on currently for clients." I sound like a prim schoolteacher, but damn it, I know I have an appointment I need to get to soon. I really don't have time to listen to him go on and on about how much he *needs* me. Getting my hopes up only for them to come crashing down when he never contacts me again.

He's real good at that.

"I'll make it worth your while." His voice lowers, deceptively soft yet edged with smoky, sensual heat.

Tingles sweep over my skin. "I'm sure you will," I say sarcastically. I refuse to let him know how much he still affects me, especially after he so callously ignored me this past month.

We got naked together. We had sex. And he acts like it never happened. I do too, because how else should I handle it? Confront him?

Hey, what the hell was that night all about anyway? I felt the earth move and thought maybe . . . you felt the same?

Can't go there. No matter how badly I want to. And wasn't he the one who called it a mistake?

Yeah, so not going to bring any of that up to him. He'd rather forget. Just like I would.

Liar.

I wish he hadn't called. Just hearing his voice works me up. Archer Bancroft is dangerous for my well-being and I know it. Delicious. Wicked. Appealing. Wrong. At least, he's wrong for me.

"I have to go, Archer." I keep my tone brusque as my gaze

lands on my computer screen. My to-do list mocks me, it's so long. And my calendar app dings, reminding me I have an appointment with a client in thirty minutes.

Which means I need to leave now if I want to make it on time.

"Listen, I'm in town and I want to see you," he says, shocking me. I didn't expect him to say that. "Let me take you to dinner tonight and I'll explain everything. How about we go to Spruce?" He refers to an ultrapopular restaurant not too far from my office. I've been there before and it's amazing. Amazingly intimate too—the perfect restaurant for a date. Not that we're going on a date.

Yeah, right.

"I'll pick you up at your office, we can have a few drinks first, then dinner," he continues.

"No," I say vehemently, rendering him completely silent. I'd bet a million dollars not many women utter that word in his presence, but the very last thing I want is Archer invading my private workspace, spreading his devastating charm all over it.

I really don't need that reminder lingering around long after he's gone. Some things should remain sacred from the Archer effect. "How about I meet you at the restaurant?"

He's silent for a moment. Like he doesn't approve of my suggestion. As if I care. "That should work," he finally says, his words clipped.

"Is seven too late?" I glance at my calendar, see that I have one last meeting with a new client at five-thirty to go over wallpaper samples, but the restaurant he suggested isn't too far. I could probably make it on time.

"I'm staying the night in the city so seven's perfect." He

pauses, the silence heavy with unrecognizable . . . tension. "It'll be good to see you again, Ivy."

Clutching the phone tight, I close my eyes for the briefest moment, all those unwanted memories bombarding me. The way he kissed me, the taste of his lips. How he'd touched me, his big hands everywhere, settling between my legs, teasing me while he murmured the hottest, sexiest words I'd ever heard.

And that was only the moment out on the terrace. Never mind later, when we ended up naked in a bed. I can't even go there. Not now, with his velvety deep voice in my ear.

"Seven o'clock at Spruce," I confirm, opening my eyes to glare unseeingly at the computer. "See you then."

I hang up before he can say another word, proud of myself. Women don't hang up on Archer either. Hell, no one really hangs up on him. He's a force to be reckoned with.

And now he calls me out of nowhere declaring he needs me—please. He's stringing me along, I'm sure. Why, I haven't a clue.

But when do my past experiences with Archer ever make sense?

Deciding my client can wait a few minutes, I bring up Google and type in Archer's name, waiting breathlessly as a list of recent articles pop up. Talk of Hush and how he made it such a huge success. One article written a week ago catches my interest, about the expansion of the Hush brand and how he's refurbishing a location in Calistoga.

Frowning, I click on the link, reading the few details they have about the new Calistoga spot. He never mentioned it during the phone call. Or when we were last together and we were actually at Hush. He'd been so proud showing me everything. You think he would've at least mentioned a new location.

So why didn't he tell us about it?

Weird.

I close out Google and gather my things, my mind awhirl with what I read. Was this the job he referred to, the one he so desperately needs me for? All logical thought flowing through my brain is telling me not to bother meeting him. Cancel via text with no explanation. He would totally deserve it.

Curiosity rules me, though, it always has. There's no way I can pass this dinner up. Despite how difficult it will be, sitting across from him for hours in a dark, intimate restaurant, gazing adoringly at his beautiful face. Wondering yet again how stupid could I be, having sex with him. Nursing this renewed crush of old that can go absolutely, positively nowhere.

I'm pitiful.

Archer

glance at my watch for what feels like the millionth time, wondering where the hell Ivy is. She's close to twenty minutes late, and I know for a fact she's ridiculously punctual.

With the exception of tonight when she's meeting me. Shit.

Drumming my fingers atop the white tablecloth in a steady rhythm, I glare at the entrance to the restaurant. I hate it when people make me wait. In business, I flat out don't tolerate it. That this woman I've known since she was a gangly teenager with a mouthful of metal leaves me waiting almost desperately for her arrival blows my mind.

And rarely is my mind blown. Funny, how the one person who keeps doing it on a regular basis is Ivy.

She's angry with me. I could hear it in her voice when I spoke to her on the phone. It had taken me two days to work up the courage to call her. Like a complete wuss, I rehearsed that conversation in my mind a thousand times.

The reality had turned out worse than my imagination. At least I got her to agree to see me. But what if she decides not to show and leaves me hanging?

I push the thought from my mind, refusing to acknowledge it for even a minute.

"Another drink, sir?" The waitress appears, her gaze full of sympathy. She probably thinks I've been stood up.

Hell, I've never been stood up in my life. "I'm fine," I mutter.

"Perhaps you'd like to order dinner? An appetizer, maybe?" She sounds hopeful and I'm beyond ready to crush her dreams.

Shaking my head, I glare at her. "I'll wait a few more minutes."

She takes off after flashing me a wan smile, leaving me to brood. If Ivy doesn't show, I can hire someone else to do this job. It wouldn't be a problem, there's a goddamn list of designers who would give up their firstborn to work with Bancroft.

But damn it, I trust her. I want her. And not just for her amazing design skills.

She isn't *just* Ivy. Could I really fall for her? Why else would I act like such an anxious asshole? This woman has me so twisted up in knots I'm ready to do anything to have her back in my life.

Anything.

Scowling, I glare at the door, as if that'll make her magically appear. I'm thinking like a chick but I can't deny it. I want her with me all the damn time. It's scary how bad I need her. Trying to ignore her didn't work. I went almost an entire month without contacting her, but she's all I could think about. The moment I get into the city, I'm reaching for the phone, demanding that she meet me.

I remember how put out she sounded on the phone, her voice full of irritation. The first indication I'm most likely going to screw this up.

Hell. I cannot screw it up.

And then there's the stupid bet. Matt sends me the occasional email asking about my dating situation. Hell, he haunts my Facebook page, probably just waiting for me to change my status from "single" to "in a relationship."

As if I ever would do that. I know his ass is watching. I won't give him the satisfaction.

The front door opens, letting in a gust of cold air that chills my skin, sending a rush of awareness through me that nearly steals my breath. *She* enters the dimly lit restaurant, windblown and gorgeous, her curvy body covered by a black coat. I greedily drink her in as Ivy pushes wild strands of long dark brown hair away from her face, her gaze searching the room before those pretty hazel eyes light upon me.

I work to keep my expression neutral, my mouth curving into a subtle closed-lip smile, but inside I burn.

For her.

She smiles in return, though it's faint, and the sight of it is like a punch to the solar plexus. I wait impatiently as the hostess takes Ivy's coat before leading her to my table.

The way Ivy moves captivates me. Sinful and sexy yet with an innocent air, her hips sway as she heads toward me, the skirt of her black dress swishing about her legs. The dress covers her completely, but I know exactly what it's hiding beneath the clingy fabric. All I can think about is slipping my hands beneath her skirt so I can touch her thighs. I remember the first time I touched them, how they trembled. How smooth her skin was . . .

"Sorry I'm late," she says as she sits quickly, not giving me time to stand and greet her like I want to, with a hug. I wanted another chance to get my hands on her again, however briefly.

Ivy smiles up at the hostess as she pushes the chair in for her before hurrying away. "My meeting took much longer than I anticipated," she explains apologetically. Always polite, though I see the strain around her mouth, in her entire expression. She's uncomfortable being with me. I get it.

I don't like it, but I get it.

"Trying to keep me on my toes?" I raise my brows and she frowns.

"I didn't do it on purpose, Archer." She exhales shakily. "I'm not interested in playing games with you."

"I don't want to play games with you either, Ivy," I say. God, I wish I could reach out and touch her. Rest my hand on hers. Tell her how much I miss her.

She sounds breathless, which makes my body twitch. Reminding me how breathless she'd been the last time I saw her—naked. How she begged for more when I had her pinned beneath me, her body shaking as I made her come with my name falling from her lips.

Having her sitting in front of me after not seeing her for a month is like a shock to my system, leaving me tongue-tied. Frozen. She picks up the menu, oblivious to my dazed stupor, and smiles when the waitress approaches, ordering a glass of wine.

"Want another beer, sir?" The server's cheerfulness grates.

"Yeah," I bite out, scowling at the waitress just before she hurries away. I catch Ivy sending me a secret smile as she shakes her head. Makes me wonder if she thinks I'm some sort of joke or something. The way she looks at me, like I amuse her.

Better than sending me the cold glare of death, which I suppose I deserve after how I've treated her since we were together.

"You look good," I say, my rough voice startling her from her quiet perusal of the menu.

She flicks her gaze up, those pretty eyes meeting mine. "It's . . . nice to see you too, Archer." Her voice is the stuff of my wet dreams, low and melodic. "Have you already ordered?"

"I was waiting for you." Damn, does she think I'm a total rude bastard or what?

Most likely—you are, after all.

"Oh. Well, isn't that sweet of you." She checks out the menu again, biting her lip as she looks over her options. The restaurant's packed, the buzz of conversation a low hum that falls away the longer I watch her.

What would it take to get back into her good graces? What do I have to prove?

Everything.

The waitress reappears, snapping me from my thoughts, and I order the steak while Ivy orders seared scallops. The server takes our menus, promises our drinks will be ready in minutes, and then leaves us alone.

Finally.

Ivy watches me expectantly as she takes a sip of water, the

delicate gold bracelets on her arm jingling with the movement. "So tell me about this job and why you need me so badly," she says, getting right to the point.

I toy with my empty beer bottle, unsure how to start what will surely be an awkward conversation. It's going to take everything I have not to blurt out why I really want her to work for me. "I'm opening a new location."

A little smile teases the corners of her lips. "I saw."

"Where? Ah, let me guess. Online." Her gaze meets mine and I stare at her, probably looking like a lovesick fool. She nods in answer, her gaze cutting away from mine, and I feel oddly defeated. "It's in Calistoga. I've been in negotiations on the property for a while and at one point it almost fell through. But I finally put the deal together and we've been doing a quick renovation on it the last few months. "

"So you knew about this when you—when you showed Hush to Gage and me?" Her smile disappears when I nod. "Why didn't you tell us about it?" She sounds shocked.

"I've been keeping it a secret. I didn't want anyone to know. Most details about the location are pretty limited and I made sure of that. I don't want anyone to know what we're offering to our guests until we open." I shrug.

"So now the new resort is almost ready?" She's studying me like I'm crazy, which I probably am.

"Two months, give or take."

"So why are you here when you should be back in Calistoga supervising the remodel?"

Here comes the tough part. The stuff I don't want to admit for fear she'll laugh in my face. "I wanted to meet with you," I say, my voice stiff.

"You came here for the sole purpose of seeing me?" She

sounds incredulous, visibly swallowing as she reaches for her water glass, her shaking hand making the ice rattle against the glass when she sets it down. She looks nervous.

Welcome to the club. I'm nervous. And women don't make me nervous.

With the exception of Ivy.

"This project is important. I want you by my side, Ivy, working with me."

"I—I don't understand where this is coming from. You've never come to Paxton before. You haven't even seen my portfolio."

"I saw samples of your work online." Everything's online, both a wonderful and scary thing. "Your portfolio is on the Paxton website."

"Oh," she says weakly, settling back in her chair, her shoulders sagging, her lips parted as if she wants to say something but can't come up with the words. She looks like she's in a state of shock. "Wha—what did you think?"

"Of your work? It's amazing." Giving in to impulse, I reach across the table and grasp hold of her hand, giving it a gentle squeeze. "I know we'll be the perfect fit, that you'll be the perfect fit for Crave. Your sophisticated touch is just what the suites need."

"I—I don't know, Archer. What you're proposing is coming so out of left field, I don't know how to answer. I don't know if I can answer." She presses her lips together and shakes her head. "I have to talk to Sharon and see what she says, but I can already guess."

"What do you think she'll say?" It won't matter. I want Ivy on this project and I will pay and do whatever it takes to make that happen.

"She won't let me work on the project. She'll want it." Exactly what Gage pointed out, not that I'm surprised. In fact, I'm fully prepared, having already called Sharon and proposed my suggestion.

I'm not quite ready to admit the outcome of that conversation.

The waitress magically appears, interrupting what I might've said next by setting our drinks in front of us and I release my grip on Ivy's hand. We both thank her, our smiles polite and false. I see the way Ivy sneaks glances at me. Like she thinks I might've lost my mind.

I probably have.

The tension that has been brewing between us returns tenfold the moment the server makes her escape.

If I wasn't so damn agitated I might find it amusing, how Ivy took such a big gulp of wine, nearly draining her glass before she leans across the table. "You just can't come out of nowhere and demand I work for you, Archer," she whispers. "I answer to someone else. I just can't up and do what you want me to at the snap of your fingers."

"I already have approval from your boss."

Her eyes widen in shock. "What?"

I nod slowly. "I spoke with Sharon earlier. Explained my situation, how much I appreciate and am inspired by your talent, and knowing how busy she is, I would love to hire Paxton Design to work on this project for me. With the sole purpose of having you lead it."

She sucks in a harsh breath. "So I'm working for you."

"She cleared your schedule for the next two weeks. It'll be an intense, rushed job, but I know you can do it." I do. She's smart. Her employer had nothing but wonderful things to say about her, not that I'm surprised. Ivy is amazing.

So amazing, I can't stop thinking about her.

"What if I don't want to be a part of this project? What if I don't want to work directly with you?"

Damn, not the answer I expected from her. "Does it bother you?" Pausing, I study her, drinking in all that dark hair waving past her shoulders, her beautiful but shrewd gaze, her lips pressed together as if she's afraid she's going to say something she'll probably regret. "We've already done this, Ivy, and we were pretty damn compatible. Would it be such a hardship, having to spend time with me?"

Her jaw drops open, and she glances around as if she wants to make sure no one's listening before she leans across the table. "If you're implying that I'm going to have *sex* with you, you couldn't be further from the truth. Been there, done that, don't want to go through with it again."

"Ouch." I rub my chest, surprised by her words. Why, I'm not sure. I asked for them by saying all that. "Harsh."

"It's the truth," she retorts, draining the last of the wine in her glass. "God, I need a refill."

"I've made some mistakes. A lot of mistakes," I correct myself when she narrows her eyes, looking ready to blast me. "The biggest one is how I've treated you. I'm sorry I haven't called or contacted you since we were last together. I've been—busy." And too chickenshit to make the first move.

She rolls her eyes. "Like I was sitting beside the phone waiting for your call. Please, Archer. Don't flatter yourself."

She's extra feisty tonight, which I assume means she's extra mad at me. I need to tread lightly. "It's not that I was purposely ignoring you, you know. I've been swamped trying to put this new resort together." It's the best excuse I have—and the truth, for the most part. Hopefully she believes me.

Thankfully she doesn't acknowledge what I said. "Explain the new location. I'd love to hear more about your little secret," she says, settling back into her chair as if she's going to stay awhile.

Excitement rises within me. Her wanting to hear about it means she's interested. And once I get her fully hooked, she'll be on board to happily work with me. I know it. "It's the ultimate in luxurious comfort. Every need will be taken care of at the Calistoga location. It's a more intimate resort that caters exclusively to only a handful of couples at any given time. Couples that are looking to put intimacy back into their relationship. Even sexual intimacy." I stress the last two words.

"A swingers club," she states flatly.

I shake my head, chuckling. "Hell, no. What sort of pervert do you think I am?"

Ivy doesn't say a word, just arches a delicate brow in challenge.

I sigh and shake my head. "Fine, I'm a pervert. But I don't run a swingers resort, Ivy. There's no swapping with others or wild orgies going on at either location. It's all about a one-on-one level." Ironic, considering I have no clue what that's like.

"Then what exactly is this new place supposed to be?"

"It's whatever your heart desires," I say softly. "Whatever your lover wants. Hence the name Crave, considering it fits so perfectly. A discreet, comfortable, safe place where you can discover your secret fantasies, indulge in your secret wants. The new location will provide whatever you might need, no questions asked."

Her cheeks are pink, her eyes wide. She looks almost . . . aroused. "It sounds—interesting."

I smile. Damn, she's beautiful. "It is. Very interesting."

She remains silent, tracing the stem of her wineglass with

the tip of her index finger. I fixate on that finger, how delicately she touches the glass, the short, darkly painted nail. My
skin suddenly feels too tight, I'm getting hard from watching
her finger, for the love of God. Taking a deep breath, I try to
regain some control.

But hell, I'm dying to feel those fingers all over my body
again . . .

Leaning across the table, I lower my voice, ready to cut to
the chase. "I need you, Ivy. I want you to bring a sexy, sophisticated touch to my resort."

A little sigh escapes her. "You've already arranged it with
Sharon. Why feel the need to ask me?" She sips from her
wine, her gaze steady on me over the rim of her glass.

"Because I want you to willingly work with me. I know I
should've told you first before I spoke to Sharon, but I was
getting desperate. I'm running out of time and I need to get
this project finished. And I trust you." It's the truth. I hardly
trust anyone. I definitely don't trust any women. They're all
the same.

Except for Ivy.

Reaching for her hand again, I press my palm against hers
and entwine our fingers. Hers are slender, delicate, and I
swear they tremble in my grip. A jolt moves through me at
the connection, as if my body missed being touched by hers.
"Say yes, you want to work with me."

"It's not that easy . . ."

"Say yes," I repeat, refusing to take no for an answer.

"I shouldn't. I should be mad that you went above my head
and made it happen anyway, with or without my approval."

I smile, feeling cocky. "Come on, you've never been able
to resist me."

She tries to extract her fingers from mine but I squeeze tight, not about to let her go. "You're such an ass."

"You think I wouldn't use that to my advantage?" I lower my voice. She's going to kill me for saying this, but I'm overcome. Having her hand in mine, our fingers laced together. I'm gripping her so tight, I feel like a desperate man. I haven't forgotten her no matter how hard I try. "I absolutely cannot get the last time we were together out of my mind."

"Please. We haven't spoken since. Until today." She glares at me with narrowed eyes, tugging against my hold, but I refuse to release her. "You know, I really can't stand you. Seeing you tonight only reiterates my feelings."

I don't doubt it for a minute. Most women hate me once they get to know me.

Not Ivy. She knows all my faults yet she still wants to be with me. Or at least she used to. I want that again. The closeness, that connection I share with no one else. She somehow understands me, she always has.

I know for a fact that not many people do.

"Fine, hate me all you want. Just say you'll do this."

"It's not that easy for me to walk away from my life, you know. I have responsibilities. And what if Sharon's mad that you did this?" I smooth my thumb across the top of her hand, and she releases a shuddering breath. "I'm asking for trouble, working with you."

"Ivy, please."

Her eyes widen at my choice of words. I rarely say please. I just take what I want. But please is not working with Ivy at this very moment. She looks ready to run.

"Archer . . ."

"Please, Ivy," I say again. "I need you."

Chapter 10

Ivy

I t's hard for me to believe you're serious." He's driving me
crazy with how he's touching me. I can't think. And the way
he's looking at me isn't much better.

At this very moment his sole focus is on me. That penetrating dark gaze of his locked on my face. As if nothing and no one else matters. All that intensity is tough to deal with.

Of course, he wants something from me. Not like he can be a complete ass and expect me to be agreeable.

Despite my instinct to scream *No!* and flee the restaurant, I take this moment to study him, my gaze roving over him greedily. He's wearing a black sweater that stretches across his chest, emphasizing his broad shoulders. His dark hair gleams beneath the soft glow of the lights shining from above.

More than one woman has glanced in his direction since I sat down. Power, wealth, authority, it radiates from Archer in palpable waves. Funny how I can forget that when I'm not around him. How potent he is to my well-being.

Couple all that potency with a devastatingly handsome face and outrageously sexy body, no woman is immune.

Including myself, as much as I'm loath to admit it.

"What's so difficult for you to believe? I've already gotten your boss's approval. We're ready to move forward." He smiles, drags his thumb across my knuckles yet again. A bolt of heat rushes through me at the seemingly innocent touch. He knows what he's doing to me, how he affects me. This is an act to make me agreeable.

Stupid idiot that I am, I'm falling for it despite the warning bells screaming inside my head. "For how long again?"

"Two weeks tops."

How simple he makes it sound. He snaps his fingers and makes it all happen, just like that. Could I really stand to be around him for any extended length of time? I have no willpower when it comes to Archer. He's a weakness of mine. Like indulging in too much chocolate and bad movies on a Sunday afternoon.

Only a million times worse.

"And Sharon readily agreed to this without protest?" I found it hard to believe. She needs me around, she's so busy. I don't know how she can afford to let me go, even if it's only for two weeks.

"The prestige of her design company working with Hush and Bancroft is more than enough incentive for her to have you come work for me." He pauses, the confident expression on his face downright breathtaking. "You really think she'd refuse me?"

Could anyone refuse him? He's a Bancroft, after all. And so arrogant with it, I wish I could tell him no. Just once. Right now would be the perfect time—but the opportunity he's offering me is just too tempting and Sharon would kill me if she's already agreed. He knows it too. "What you're suggesting . . . it's crazy. You really think we can get this project off the ground and ready in two weeks?"

"We can do whatever we set our minds to. Just say yes, Ivy." His gaze drops, landing on my mouth, where it lingers a fraction too long. My lips literally tingle, as if he physically touched them.

Extracting my hand from his grasp, relief floods me as I finally break the physical connection between us. When he touches me, I can't think. I have a problem thinking when he's looking at me too, so I drop my gaze. Study the table-cloth in front of me, which is a stark, pure white, made of fine, thick linen.

That I'd rather contemplate a tablecloth shows how powerful Archer's influence is on me. God, I'm weak when it comes to this man.

His sinfully deep voice breaks through my thoughts. "Stop playing this game, Ivy. It's going to happen."

Sighing, I reluctantly lift my gaze. "Fine. When do we leave?"

"Tonight?" He flashes that dazzling smile, the one that dissolves my panties. *Sexy, no-good jerk.*

Grabbing my wineglass, I drain it, my skin instantly warming from the alcohol. I'll definitely need more wine to get through the rest of this evening. "No way. Tomorrow."

"All right. Tomorrow works," he drawls. "But it'll have to be first thing. I have a few stipulations too."

"I'm sure you do."

"I'll need you to consult with me on everything. Every choice, every decision you need to make. It's not that I don't trust you, but there's a certain aesthetic I want at both locations and I need to ensure your choices meet that aesthetic."

I nod once. Nothing unusual there. "I don't have a problem with that."

"And if I don't like what you suggest, you won't try to convince me otherwise. I have final word." He wraps his fingers around his beer bottle and brings it to his mouth, taking a drink, gorgeously sexy when he swallows, which is insane.

He makes me insane. His scent, the way he watches me with that calculated, hot gaze. His mere presence warms my skin, sets fire to my blood. Floods me with memories of our one amazing night together. I both cherish and hate those memories.

And he's drawing out the suspense on purpose. I'm literally sitting on the edge of my seat, waiting to hear what he might say next. "I also want you to move in with me," he finishes once he sets the bottle down.

My mouth drops open, shock rushing through my veins. "Move in with you?" I squeak, clearing my throat.

"I'll need you on site every single day. I'm rushing this project. All decisions we need to make must be quick. I can't have you coming back and forth from San Francisco. I need you with me. Every day. Every night, until the project is finished. At the very least you can stay at Hush."

"Oh, I get exactly what you want from me." A slow-burning rage sweeps over me, making me shake. I push back my chair and stand, glaring down at him. "I'm not going to be another one of your sexual conquests."

Tilting his head back, he watches me, calm as ever. "Don't be angry, Ivy. I'm not asking you to have sex with me in order for you to have this project. I'm not that much of an asshole."

God, his words sting. What sort of woman does he think I am? "Yeah, right. Next thing I know I'm flat on my back in your bed. No thank you. You're not going to bribe me with career recognition either." Bending, I grab my purse from the floor and sling it over my shoulder.

"I know the idea of staying with me doesn't make you comfortable, but it's best for the project considering the timeline. Besides, I'm not asking you to wait for me naked in my bed every night, though the idea is appealing." The arrogance dripping from his voice makes me want to hit something. Preferably him. "Come on, I know you haven't forgotten how easy it was between us that night, Ivy," he murmurs, his voice low. Sexy.

Ugh.

His words enflame me, filling me with both lust and anger. I really hate that I still want him. "You're a bastard," I say through clenched teeth before I turn and head toward the door, desperate to escape the suddenly too warm, too confining restaurant.

I hear him call my name. Hear his chair scrape across the floor as he stands and starts to come after me. But I refuse to look back. Choose to ignore the hostess who's calling after me that she still has my coat.

Pushing open the door, I step out into the dark night, deeply breathing the cool air. A flash goes off in my face, I swear I hear them call Archer's name, and I head in the opposite direction, avoiding the paparazzi at all costs. How could I forget they follow Archer everywhere?

God. My head is spinning, and not just from the wine. The stupid photographer is just the tip of my overwhelming iceberg—that Archer demands I work for him, went above my head to ensure I have no choice but to work for him is infuriating. Never mind that we had sex and he has to bring it up. Like he's trying to use that night against me. I could blame it on the champagne I drank too much of, I suppose.

So freaking embarrassing.

Worse? I know I would've done it without the champagne.

I can't blame too much alcohol on my one night with Archer. I was completely sober.

But he's an asshole. A controlling, arrogant jerk who thinks I'm some sort of spineless, stupid girl. I wish I could refuse him but he's effectively trapped me. And why didn't Sharon talk to me about this? I can't quite wrap my head around how he made all of this happen and so quickly.

He's just that powerful, that influential to gain the things—or people—he wants with a simple phone call or snap of his fingers.

Not knowing which way to go, I turn right, heading blindly into the night. Cars pass by, I hear the loud rumble of a city bus as it speeds down the street, and I blink hard, my strides quick, my heart pumping like crazy. A shiver moves through me and I rub my arms with my hands, wishing I had my coat. It's a total favorite; I love that jacket and I'm pissed I left it in the restaurant like an idiot.

God, he's so distracting, it's unfair. Why did he have to be so gorgeous? So freaking irresistible?

I increase my pace, furious at my thoughts. I can hear him right now, following behind me, his determined steps hitting the sidewalk, his huffs of aggravation.

Good. I'm irritating him. Glad to know the feeling is mutual. I need to get away from him.

Far, far away.

"Ivy." The man is as tall as a god with legs as long as my entire body, meaning he easily catches up with me. His strong fingers clamp around my upper arm and he turns me so I face him. "Don't run away from me."

His words are spoken as a demand. "Let me go." I struggle against his hold and he tightens his fingers, making it impossible to escape.

Archer pulls me in close, his body heat wrapping around me, his potent scent filling my head, making me weak. "Stop fighting this."

I need my willpower to kick in. It has to or I'll never survive him. "There's no 'this' to fight. I'm not helping you."

Archer looks downright offended at my words. "You don't have a choice. I need you."

"You don't need me. I'm just an easy target." The urge to punch him comes over me, stronger than ever. He has the advantage, knowing how easily I react to him. He's not above using it against me fully either. "I hate that you've done this," I murmur.

"Why?" His voice is deceptively soft. As persuasive as his fingers stroking my lower back, he's trying to lull me into a false sense of security. Like I'm some sort of cat he can pet and stroke and ease under his spell. I was strong enough before to send him away, to walk away on my own. But am I strong enough now? Can I resist him again? I don't know.

"You've already fooled me once." Not really, but it sounds good. We fooled each other. "I shouldn't let it happen again."

Reaching out, I rest my hand on his chest, desperate to push him away. It's as if my fingers have a mind of their own, though. I curl them into the soft, smooth fabric of his sweater, feeling the steely strength of him just beneath. A trembling sigh leaves me, and I keep my gaze locked on my hand, afraid to look at him. Afraid he'll see everything I feel for him reflected in my eyes.

"I was fooling myself," he finally says as he touches my cheek, slipping his fingers beneath my chin to tilt my head up. "I didn't mean to hurt you."

I frown. Did I hear him right? Did Archer just admit he'd done something wrong? "Well, you did."

Our gazes hold for long, quiet moments heavy with tension. I want to run. Break free of him for good and pretend this night never happened. Yet another part of me wants to stay. Wants to agree to what he's asking me. Maybe then I can get one of two things.

Either I can convince Archer we're truly meant to be. Or finally get him out of my system once and for all.

Archer

Ivy's fingers still grip my sweater, her innocent touch driving me fucking wild with wanting her. Holding her close, she fits against me perfectly, as if she were made for me. It was like this between us last time. The moment I pulled her into my arms, it was like we were two pieces of a puzzle that finally clicked together.

Half the reason I'd been scared shitless before. Still. No other woman feels this . . . right in my arms. And I haven't even kissed her yet. It feels damn good just to hold her, which is ridiculous because I don't need to just hold a woman.

I should have her sprawled naked and needy beneath me, screwing her brains out at this very moment. Forget emotion, forget everything but that driving need to consume. That's how I usually operate.

Yet here I am. Acting like I'm in junior high and holding hands with a girl for the first time. Terrified and out of my mind with it.

"Is this just an excuse to get in my pants?" she finally asks, her voice wary. She's so damn smart. "You wanting me to work for you in such close circumstances? Seems pretty desperate if you ask me."

Slowly shaking my head, I let my thumb drift across her plump lower lip. Only a month since I last kissed her and I can vividly remember her taste. The sounds she makes. The way she wound her arms around my neck, her slender fingers threading through my hair. Her touch had felt so damn good. Too good.

Fuck. That's exactly it. She's too damn good for me. I need to remember this.

"You're the only woman I can trust, Ivy," I murmur, my heart lodging in my throat, making it hard to speak. "The only woman who understands me and my life and my career and what's required. I know you won't leak any information about the new location. And I know I can trust you to help me make the right decisions when it comes to designing the interiors."

A trembling breath escapes her, the gust of air brushing against my thumb. My heart rate kicks up into a steady gallop and I inhale deeply. Trying my damnedest to act like she doesn't affect me.

But holy shit, does she ever affect me.

"How can I understand you when I don't even really know you, Archer? We've never been close." Her gaze drops to my lips, lingering there. "Despite what . . . happened between us last time, there's nothing between us."

I feel like there's too much between us, but I won't go there now. "You've been a part of my life for a long time. You've known me since I was a teenager. Before I became . . . this." The consummate playboy who can have any woman I want at any time. The workaholic hotelier who throws himself into his business until all he can do is live and breathe Hush. And now there's Crave . . .

"Yeah, well my feelings still haven't changed about you. I think you're crazy." She gasps when I lean in and brush my lips against the right corner of her mouth. That quick sample of her soft skin makes me ache for more. "Wh—why are you kissing me?"

"Because I need to." I kiss the left corner, moving to capture her upper lip between both of mine, nibbling a little bit before I release her. "I need your help, Ivy. I can't get the resort ready without you."

"Stop it." She's pushing at my chest, but I'm not going anywhere. "Don't say things you don't mean."

"You really think I don't mean it when I say I need you?" I'm incredulous. I sure as hell need her. More than I care to admit.

I have to convince her to come back into my bed. At least one more time—possibly a few dozen times before I let her go back to her world and I go back to mine. She was there the night of Jeff and Cecily's wedding reception. All that pent-up chemistry swirling between us, exploding the moment my lips first touched hers. She knows how combustible it can be between us.

So why is she full of so much doubt?

"You don't need me. You just want me to bail you out of trouble. I've never mattered to you. Not really." She tilts her head away from mine when I lean in for another kiss.

"Damn it, Ivy," I start, but she cuts me off.

"You abandoned me, Archer." Ivy's voice is so soft, I can hardly hear her. "I know we agreed our having sex was a mistake, but the way you touched me in the suite at Hush right before Gage texted you, I was so confused. I thought you wanted . . . oh my God, I don't know what you want. Not really. I don't get you. Since I left you that afternoon, you haven't called. I haven't heard one peep out of you—not that I expected to." She takes a step back, withdrawing from me completely, and my arms feel empty without her in them. "This back and forth between us is . . . difficult. I can't risk getting close to you again only for us to end it before we really gave ourselves a chance. Not that there's an 'us' . . ." Her voice trails off and her cheeks turn pink. She probably didn't mean to admit such a thing.

Her small admission gives me hope.

"I won't touch you. Unless you want me to." I smile, but she doesn't return the gesture. Heaving a big sigh, I cup her cheek, briefly sliding my fingers across her soft skin before I let my hand drop away from her. I can't help but touch her, but if she doesn't want me to, I won't. "I promise."

Pressing her lips together, her hazel eyes go wide as she trembles. I draw her back into my arms, protecting her from the cold. She has to be freezing since she left her coat in the restaurant. "Let's get out of here and you can come back to the hotel with me downtown. I have the penthouse suite and the view of the city is amazing. It's too damn cold out here to talk."

Ivy stiffens in my arms just before she withdraws from me yet again. "Come with you back to your hotel room? I don't think so. Next thing I know, I'm flat on my back and you're all over me."

I smile. Damn, that sounds amazing. "And that's a bad thing, why?"

"Stop, Archer. I already told you I refuse to let that happen again." She crosses her arms in front of her, contemplating me with her shrewd gaze. "Besides, if we ever did have sex again, you'd run like you always do."

When shit gets serious, I definitely run. But not anymore.

For once, I don't want to bail. "I can't run any longer, Ivy. This is it. I need the new resort to open with a roaring success. I need those suites to look amazing. Together, I know we can do it."

"Fine." She sighs. "We need to come up with a budget. A timeline." She taps her finger against her pursed lips, driving me wild with wanting her. Damn, she's beautiful. Even shivering in the cold, angry with me and most likely thinking I've lost my damn mind, she's gorgeous. Fucking amazing, really.

I don't deserve her help. I don't deserve Ivy Emerson whatsoever.

But I still want her. Desperately.

"We can plot and plan back at the hotel, Ivy," I tell her. "Come on. I won't try any funny business."

A perfectly manicured brow lifts at that remark. "Promise?"

Nodding, I make an X on my chest with my index finger. "Cross my heart."

"You swear? I can't think when you push yourself on me, Archer. And if you want my help in figuring out how we're going to do this, then you need me to be able to think."

Is it wrong that I'm pleased with her remark? That she can't think when I'm around? I love that, especially because I feel the same way.

"Come back to the suite with me, Ivy. We'll figure this out."

"Fine." She offers a jerky nod. "Let's do this."

Sweeter words were never spoken.

Chapter 11

Ivy

The penthouse suite is amazing, not that I expect anything less. It encompasses nearly the entire top floor of the hotel, is larger than my apartment, and has three bedrooms, which reassures me. There will be no sleeping in Archer's bed tonight.

No matter how much I'm tempted.

I've stayed in more than a few Bancroft Hotels over the years, considering the Bancroft family comped my family all our rooms when we traveled, and I've never been disappointed. But I've never had any reason to stay at the Bancroft in downtown San Francisco. It's my hometown, after all.

"You like it?" Archer shuts the door and strides toward me, his voice full of pride. Despite the burden the family business has put on him his entire life, and specifically today, I know he's still proud of Bancroft, as he should be.

"The view is amazing." I approach the windows, staring out at the glittering view of the city before me. The moon breaks over the fog, shining its silvery light on the bay, and I withhold the sigh of longing that's desperate to escape me.

The beautiful suite, this gorgeous night . . . is made for lovers. I yearn for that to be true, no matter how bad I know Archer is for me.

But Archer knows he needs to keep his distance. It's the only way I can stay sane.

God, how stupid could I be, pushing him away when I want him more than anything?

"I stay here whenever I come to the city. Better than staying at my parents', that's for sure." The bitterness in his voice is no surprise. He doesn't get along with his parents; he never has. Not that I blame him. His father treats him terribly. Their fractured relationship has always broken my heart.

He comes up behind me. I catch his reflection in the window and I hold my breath, marveling at how we look together. He towers over me, his dark hair mussed, his expression strained. As if he's as tense as I feel.

I can imagine his big hand sliding down my back, pushing gently so I have no choice but to bend forward. Hearing his dark, sexy voice commanding me to brace my hands on the shockingly cool glass. His skilled fingers would settle on my hips, slowly gathering the fabric of my dress so he could touch my bare skin beneath. Those assured fingers would slip beneath my thin panties to find me already soaking wet for him . . .

Lust surges through me and I stiffen my shoulders. God, I'm a wreck. He stands too close and I'm imagining how he'll take me right here, in front of a window for everyone to see.

"There is no 'us' in this room tonight, Archer," I say, my voice firm. No matter how much I want it to be true, I have to hold strong. The man is dangerous to my well-being. I want to smack myself for even contemplating going along with his stupid plan. I am so weak when it comes to him, it's pitiful.

"Well, that's unfortunate," he drawls, and I want to punch him.

God, I'm starving, and that's what's making me extra irritable. We left the restaurant before our dinners arrived, though Archer said he'd paid for them when he came out of Spruce. He called in room service from the car moments before we arrived at the hotel, ordering an enormous amount of food I would normally never eat. An assortment of appetizers, fried this and that, and I swear he even mentioned a pizza.

My stomach growls at the thought of pizza.

"Hungry?" He raises an eyebrow and I look away from him, embarrassed. Not that I'd ever admit to him I'm actually starved. Women don't eat, not in front of perfect men like Archer. We might nibble on a leaf of lettuce and drink copious amounts of water to purge any sort of bloating, but that's it.

"The food is on its way and it shouldn't take long," he reassures when I don't answer him. "Don't worry."

I offer a jerky nod, thankful to change the subject. "Great. I'm starving." I'm also a liar. I can't eat around him. My stomach is tied up in knots just having him so close.

"Do you want to back out?" he suddenly asks, shocking me.

What brought that on?

No, I want to scream. What I want is to throw myself into his arms and beg him to kiss me. Feel those warm, soft lips settle on mine, the delicious, velvety hot glide of his tongue as he searches my mouth. I want to hear him whisper wicked words in my ear while his hands are sliding all over my body.

More than anything, I desperately want him to take off my clothes, push me to the bed, and have his way with me all night long.

But my wants are pointless. And ridiculous.

"Of course n—" I'm ready to tell him no, but he cuts me off.

"I know I'm being incredibly selfish, but I can't have you

back out, Ivy. Still, I would never force you to do something you're not comfortable with."

His soft, beguiling tone warms me from within. When he looks at me like that, his dark gaze full of heat, his expression so sincere, I can almost believe him.

A knock sounds at the door, startling me. Irritation flashes in Archer's eyes at the interruption and I watch his long-legged stride eat up the floor as he heads toward the door. He throws it open, growls his greeting, and takes the cart from the hotel employee before the guy can push it inside.

I almost want to giggle, watching Archer pushing the cart laden with plates covered by silver domes into the room, as if he were the lowly employee and it isn't his family name on the outside of the building. "I hope you at least tipped him," I say.

His gaze darkens when he looks up at me. "Of course I did. I'm not totally heartless."

I wish I had the balls to say, *Prove it.*

But I hold the words back.

Archer

"You're staying here with me tonight."

I don't bother asking after I've downed my third slice of pizza prepared by the hotel's gourmet chef. She's staying with me whether she likes it or not.

We're sitting in the dining area of the suite. The table is small, giving me the perfect excuse to sit close to her. Her scent lingers in the air, the warmth of her presence easing my earlier tension despite her obvious reluctance to come here.

And her obvious reluctance to agree to my plan. I know she still feels this way without her having to say a word. I can read her. I've always been able to.

Ivy picks at her food. "You're kidding, right?"

Christ. The woman throws up roadblocks every chance she can get. "Hell no, I'm not kidding. It's late. I don't want to make the trek across town this time of night. You can stay in one of the other bedrooms. I swear I won't make a move." I scrub a hand across my cheek, my frustration mounting.

Clearly, Ivy has no plans on making this easy.

"Did you plan this too? Bringing me here tonight? Forcing me to stay?" Lifting her head, her gaze meets mine, her expression almost pained.

God, she exasperates me. "Of course I didn't."

"Seems like you did."

"Are we really going to go round and round about this?" I wipe my hands with a napkin, wad it up, and throw it on my plate. "You hardly ate."

She shrugs. "I wasn't that hungry."

"So your growling stomach lied? I ordered all of your favorite foods." She used to gorge herself on junk when she was a teen. We all did. Hell, I still do. I also work out like crazy, so I can afford the occasional indulgence.

A sigh escapes her. "I haven't eaten this type of food in years."

"You used to."

"Back when I was a teenager and didn't need to watch everything I eat," she retorts, irritation flaring in her eyes.

I let my gaze slide over her. Damn, she's hot. With a killer bod and curves in all the right places. Places I wish I could explore again with my hands. Or even better, explore with my mouth. "One night isn't going to kill you, Ivy." I'm trying to tempt her, since all she has to do is sit there. I'm beyond tempted to jump her and show her how much I need her.

But not yet. I have to be patient, even if it kills me.

"I'll have to run extra hard if I bother eating one of those mozzarella sticks." She eyes the plate I specifically ordered for her, her tongue darting out to lick her upper lip. They'd been a weakness in her past.

"You run?"

"On a treadmill. At the gym." She shrugs.

"Come on, live a little." I push the plate toward her.

"Are you going to taunt me like this the entire two weeks we're together?" She arches a brow and I smile at her in answer.

I don't want her scared of me. Or worse, angry.

She plucks the mozzarella stick from her plate, dunks it in ranch dressing, and takes a huge bite. Watching her eat pleases me for some weird reason. Pleases me even more that she spoke about our being together in a positive light.

"You deserve to cut loose and have a little fun every once in a while, you know. All work and no play makes Ivy a dull girl."

Ivy glares at me. Damn, she's pretty when she's angry. "Life isn't all fun and games." She takes another bite of the cheese stick, a little moan escaping her as she chews.

The sound sends a swift bolt of lust straight to my groin. "Isn't that the damn truth," I mutter.

"You certainly make it look that way, though. Always out with two or three women hanging off your arm, drinking and having fun at clubs all over town," she points out.

Hell, she thinks I'm a complete jackass. Especially with the way I've ignored her since we were last together. If she only knew the truth. How difficult that had been, how much she scared me. How much she *still* scares me. "You really think all I've done is fuck around and spend my family's money these last few years?"

"Of course not." She pops the last of the mozzarella stick into her mouth, chews and then swallows. "Gage has told me how hard you work."

"And maybe you need to learn how to let loose more and have a good time," I return. Here we go, returning to our standard argumentative selves. I swear it's like foreplay between us. It masks all that sexual tension that's constantly brewing whenever we're together.

"I know how to let loose." Her voice is defensive.

"Then prove it." I am practically daring her. She's always worried over what everyone thought of her, ever since I've known her. Cultivating a certain image, not allowing anyone too close for fear they might see the real Ivy.

Not that there's anything wrong with the real Ivy. In my eyes, she's damn near the perfect woman.

"How can I prove it to you?"

I can't answer her for fear I'll say something so incredibly stupid, I'll fuck it all up.

I can't chance it. Too risky.

"Can I be honest?" she asks suddenly, shocking me from my thoughts.

"Please. By all means."

She watches me, her gaze direct, her expression serious, and I want to squirm. "You scare me."

Great. The feeling's mutual. "I won't do anything you don't want me to."

"That's not what I'm scared of." She exhales loudly. "Just being in your presence is like going on an exhilarating roller coaster ride, and I'm constantly terrified I might fall off and plunge to my death at any moment."

"Well. That sounds . . ."

"Pretty scary, right?" She smiles, though it doesn't quite reach her eyes. "I want to help you, Archer. I really do."

"Then quit waffling," I say vehemently. Fuck, I swear I'm losing her. She's slipping right out of my grasp like tiny granules of sand, and I can't do anything to stop it from happening.

"I've already agreed to help you. I don't have a choice but to agree, what with the way you handled this." She pauses, her tongue sneaking out to wet her lips. My heart lurches at the sight of her pretty pink tongue. "I'll help you, if you help me."

Relief floods me, leaving me weak. "Anything. I'll do anything you want. Name it and it's yours."

Ivy jerks her gaze from mine and bends her head, studying the table. "When we were . . . together last time. The night of Jeff and Cecily's wedding. It was good between us. Right?"

Uneasiness slips over me, sending a chill racing down my spine. Where is she going with this? "Yeah."

"So, what if we worked together and spent time together as if we were a real couple?" She keeps her head bent, sketching invisible doodles on the tabletop with her index finger.

"What do you mean?" Lusty hope rises within me. She couldn't be asking for what I think she is . . .

No way. This is Ivy. She wouldn't be so bold as to ask me to have a fling with her, would she?

I'd say yes. I'd get her any way I could, just to be with her.

"I want to spend more time with you, Archer. I want to get to know you. The adult you, not the rude teenager from our past." She shrugs those slim shoulders of hers, her voice sounding downright hopeless. "Over the years, we've grown apart, moved on with our lives. Having you back in my life makes me realize I've missed you."

Disbelief fills me. That she could be so honest, so incredibly forthright in what she wants from me is shocking. Normally I'm the brutally honest one. But Ivy changes everything. I would've hemmed and hawed and wondered how the hell I might approach her.

Hell, I'm doing that very thing right now. Yet she comes right out and asks for what she wants from me. I can't help but admire her for that.

"I've missed you too," I admit because she deserves those words. She jerks her head up, her wide-eyed gaze meeting mine, and I smile at her. "I thought you hated me."

"I do." She returns the smile. "But there's more between us than fights and hate and constant irritation. Don't you think?"

Oh, I know. But I'm not sure if I'm brave enough to tell her yet. Scrubbing a hand over my face, I'm half tempted to ask her why she's here. With me. I flat out don't deserve her.

"Yeah," I murmur, not sure what else I can say. I'm shocked she's willing to give me—us—another chance.

"But it'll be temporary. Once Crave's design is complete, we're finished. I'm sure you'll be ready to move on by then anyway." Her smile turns unnaturally bright. "From everything."

Not true. I'm ready to deny it, but she cuts me off.

"We walked away from each other before and you never called. I guess I could've called you, but I don't operate like that." Her smile becomes more brittle and I'm tempted to lunge for her. Tell her exactly how much I want her and watch the wariness leave her gaze. And become replaced with pleasure.

And of course she doesn't operate like that. She's a traditional sort of woman who deserves a man who will chase after her without fear and make her his forever.

I suddenly want to be that sort of man. Only for Ivy, though. Not for anyone else.

"This is so embarrassing." She sighs and drops her head, keeps her gaze focused on the table in front of her. "The guys I've been with, they were all hopeless, you know? I wanted to fix them and they definitely didn't want to be fixed. And I get you don't want to be either. You're perfectly happy in your broken, messed-up state. But you, Archer, you were the first one I truly felt comfortable with. Like I could finally let go and . . ."

"And what?" I prod.

"Have an . . ." Her voice trails off again and her cheeks are pink. "You know."

Pride fills me even though I know it's a jackass move. But what man doesn't want to hear those words slip from the lips of a woman he's attracted to? "Have an orgasm?"

"Yeah." She gives a jerky nod. "They don't usually happen easily for me."

Well, hell. I have to help her. Prove to her she's a beautiful, desirable woman who deserves to have as many orgasms as she damn well pleases. Let her know just how much she undoes me with only a look. A smile. A glimpse of skin, a brief hug. Everything about her screams "take me," and my body is more than willing to do just that.

Clearing my throat, I decide to get down to business. After all, I'm a world-class negotiator. "So you want me to help you."

"Yes." She bites her lower lip, her expression full of worry.

"Have plenty of orgasms." This turn of events is downright surreal.

I'm not complaining.

Her cheeks color a pretty pink. "Yes."

"And in return, you'll help me."

She nods, not saying a word. "I still can't believe you want me for the project."

I roll my eyes in answer. "I can't believe you doubt your abilities."

"It's not that. It's just . . ."

"What?"

"I don't understand why you want me around," she whispers. "What's happening between us, Archer? It's confusing."

My heart lurches. I feel the same exact way. "I'm confused too, Ivy."

"You don't act like it. You're the usual smug, arrogant Archer."

"Deep inside, I'm petrified you'll tell me to fuck off." Couldn't she see that? I hardly uttered a word for the last five minutes. I just let her do all the talking.

She laughs, the tension easing from her expression at my confession. "I would never say that to you."

"Never say never."

"So we're in agreement then," she says, releasing a shuddering breath.

"Design skills for orgasms? I think so." I grin and she glares at me.

"You make it sound sleazy. You're paying me for my design skills." Worry flits through her gaze. "Right?"

I chuckle. "Of course. You know this." Pausing, I contemplate her. "But you don't have to pay me for the orgasms, you know. I'll handle that task for free. Gladly."

"Oh my God, this is the most embarrassing thing ever. I should've never told you." She buries her face in her hands.

I stand and slowly start to approach her. "Don't be embarrassed." My voice is soft and I stop directly in front of where she's sitting. "I'm glad you were honest with me."

She tilts her head back, her gaze meeting mine. "Will you be honest with me?"

I think of the bet. I think of Matt laughing his ass off at me. Of me owing him that extra fifty grand because damn it, he was right. I think of Gage wanting to murder me for defiling his sister.

"I'll try my best," I say because it's all I can offer.

"That works," she murmurs, a smile teasing the corners of her mouth. "I'm excited to see the new resort."

"I'm excited to show you."

"Calistoga is gorgeous."

"I agree. Wait till you see it. Hopefully you'll think the hotel is gorgeous too."

She nibbles on her lower lip, looking unsure and incredibly sexy. "I want to thank you for the opportunity. Letting me work with you," she says softly.

"I'm grateful you're willing to help." Reaching out, I skim my hand over the top of her head, my fingers tangling in the silky soft strands of her hair.

"Like I said, you really didn't give me any choice." She shakes her head, but I don't remove my hand. I never want to stop touching her. "I hope I don't disappoint you."

"You could never, ever disappointment me," I tell her, knowing I'm one hundred percent right. Though I'm starting to wonder if she's talking about disappointing me in a non-work-related way.

Again, she could never, ever disappointment there either.

"I don't know about that," she says, her voice full of doubt as she watches me approach.

"Let me prove it to you." I take her hand so I can pull her to her feet.

"How?" Her voice is trembling, her gaze meeting mine expectantly.

"Like this."

Chapter 12

Ivy

Archer's mouth settles on mine before I can utter a single word, and I'm completely lost. In the taste of him, the scent of him, the way he moves into me as if it's his every right to be there. Touching me, holding me, drawing me close, his arms circling my waist.

This is what I really want. Working with him will be a great boost to my career; the Bancroft Corporation a stellar client to put into my portfolio and an opportunity that I would be a fool to pass up.

But this is what I not-so-secretly crave. Being in Archer's arms again, his persuasive lips caressing mine, gently encouraging me to open to him. I do so easily, letting the soft sigh escape when his tongue touches mine. After all my arguments and protests, I still can't believe I confessed to him what I really wanted.

A chance to be with him, to lose myself with him. Freely.

He's the only one who's able to coax an orgasm out of me. Men have tried numerous times before with a variety of methods. And when it wouldn't work, when *I* didn't work, they made me feel like a freak. A few had even declared me frigid. Unresponsive. Unfeeling.

Jerks. They'd tried to tear down my self-esteem and for a

while, I let them. Until I realized I didn't need any of them to give me an orgasm. I was fully in charge of that task. Quite happily, I might add.

Until Archer. And then *bam*. Instant orgasm. I'd like to experience that again.

And again and again and again.

"I've missed you," he whispers against my lips, his husky voice sending a scattering of gooseflesh across my skin. "So damn much, Ivy."

I'm about to tell him I missed him too, but he's kissing me again, more forcefully this time. His tongue strokes mine, his hands clutch at my waist, and I step into him, run my hands up his chest, my fingers molding to the wall of hot, firm muscle beneath my palms. He shivers from my touch, and I realize he enjoys my touch as much as I enjoy his.

Such a powerful, overwhelming discovery.

As our hands move, our lips search, the kiss becoming deep. Hot. I slide my tongue into his mouth and I rest my hands at his sides, my fingers slipping beneath his sweater so I can touch the smooth, bare skin of his back. He grips my waist, guiding me backward, until I'm bumping against the wall and he's got me trapped. Deliciously, wonderfully trapped.

He toys with the tie at the waist of my dress, his fingers playing with the ends, and then he's tugging. Pulling the tie undone until my dress loosens and he's pushing either side of it wide, exposing me to his perusal.

Breaking the kiss, he studies me, his smoldering gaze raking over my body, making me aware of how on display I am for him. I thrust my chest out and let him look his fill. Remind him of what he's missed out on for the last month.

Me.

"You're killing me." He slips his fingers beneath the strap of my black bra, moving to trace the scalloped lacy edge across one breast, then the other. "So fucking beautiful."

Pleasure swarms me, making me dizzy, and I lock my knees for fear I'll collapse. I almost cry out when he leans in, one hand braced on the wall beside my head, his mouth at my throat, then my collarbone. Dropping sweet little kisses on my chest, the tops of my breasts, sampling me. I grip his hips, holding on to him for dear life as he licks and kisses my skin.

Everything he's doing feels so good I'm afraid I might pass out from the pleasure of it all. My belly clenches, between my legs I grow hot and damp, and I bite my lip when he trails his fingers down my stomach until they're toying with the waistband of my matching black panties.

"I can see through them," he whispers, and I crack my eyes open to find his dark head bent, no doubt staring intently at the tiny scrap of material that's barely covering me. "I really think you are trying to kill me."

A soft burst of laughter escapes me and he glances up, a sexy smile curving his delicious lips. Tilting my head back, I brush my mouth with his, licking his lips, a soft moan escaping me when his tongue touches mine. I could get drunk off his kisses. His fingers are teasing me, sliding across my stomach, dipping just beneath the waistband of my flimsy panties, not quite reaching where I really want him to be.

"I think I'm going to enjoy this orgasm task," he mutters against my mouth, making me laugh again. I love how blunt he is. How honest. Spending time with him is never, ever boring.

Especially now.

"Let's take this off," he murmurs, pushing my dress off my shoulders so it falls to the crook of my arms. I straighten them as he steps away and the dress flutters to the ground in a heap around my feet. I kick the fabric away, standing before him in just my panties and bra and my black heels.

His gaze drops, running up the length of my body, frank appreciation in his eyes. "Holy hell, woman."

I feel hot from his words, the way he's looking at me. Thrusting my chest out farther, I contemplate him, heat blooming between my legs when he studies my breasts, no doubt seeing my nipples poke against the thin fabric of my bra.

Without warning he's on me, his mouth fused with mine, his hands cupping my breasts, thumbs circling my nipples. I arch into his touch, a long agonized groan escaping me when he tugs on my nipples. The pleasurable pain shoots through me, landing between my legs, and I rub against his thigh, sparks of heat blistering through me.

"I want to fuck you right here. Against the wall." His hand sinks into the front of my panties, finally touching me exactly where I want him. "So wet, Ivy. *God.*"

He sounds tortured. I *feel* tortured. Without thought, I grab him, mold my hand around the length of his erection, stroking him over his jeans. I wish I could touch his bare skin. I wish I could go down on my knees and draw him into my mouth . . .

Deciding that's the perfect idea, I frantically undo the snap and zipper on his jeans, shoving them down with impatient, shaky hands. They fall to his feet and he kicks them off, his mouth locked with mine once again, his hand between my legs. I ride that hand unashamedly, whimpering as his fingers work a sort of magic over me, and I lose myself in the sensation. My breaths leave me in shuddery exhales and I throw my head back, my eyelids fluttering as his fingers circle and stroke my clit again and again.

"Come for me, baby," he whispers against my lips just before he kisses me. "Reach for it."

A ragged little cry escapes me and I close my eyes, moaning when I feel his lips on the side of my neck. He drags his hot tongue over my skin as I grind against his palm and I'm close. So, so close, I'm almost afraid it's not going to happen.

"I can feel you. Hot and clenching so tight around my finger. You want more, don't you, Ivy?"

His hot words send me straight into oblivion. My body is racked with tremors as my orgasm pulses through me, taking me completely over the edge until all I can do is ride the wave. I grip his shoulders for fear I might collapse as he continues to stroke me, his fingers featherlight and so gentle I almost want to weep at how amazing his touch feels.

God. He makes me fall apart with a few hot kisses and delicious touches like some sort of sexual miracle.

As I slowly come back down to earth, I realize he's still touching me, licking my collarbone, pressing up against me. I can feel his erection brush against my stomach, still covered by his boxer briefs, and I reach for him. Brush my fingers down the light trail of dark hair that lines a path from his navel downward. Sliding my hands beneath the waistband of his underwear, I touch bare, hard skin, my fingers curling around his length.

"Jesus, Ivy," he chokes out.

Smiling, I slide my back down the wall until I'm level with his cock. Slowly I tug his underwear down, revealing him to my gaze, and his erection springs out toward me almost eagerly.

I feel just as eager. Exhilarated. Reaching for him, I curl my fingers around the base of him and lean in, dropping a kiss on the tip. His agonized groan fuels me and I lick him, wrap my lips around just the head as I suck and work him deeper.

"Not like this," he gasps, tugging on me so hard I have no choice but to stand and face him again, my feet wobbly since I'm still wearing the damn heels. I'm about to kick them off when he rests his hand on my cheek, making me look up at him. "Keep the shoes on."

Archer

This is my every fantasy come to life. Ivy in my arms, spent from the orgasm I just gave her. Ivy kneeling in front of me, drawing me into her mouth, her enthusiastic tongue whipping me into such a frenzy I knew I wouldn't last long.

No way was I going to come too fast again. This time around, I want to make it last as long as possible. So I yank her to her feet and push impatiently at her tiny panties, wanting them off. Then I'm unsnapping her bra, watching her toss it to the floor before I'm on her again, nestled close, our mouths locked, our tongues dancing, my hands wandering.

We're both naked save for her heels and I pick her up, her legs automatically going around my waist, her pointy heels poking into my ass, but I ignore the sharp pain. I press my cock against her, dying to plunge inside her.

Fuck. I need a condom first.

"I'm on the pill," she whispers as if she can read my mind, and I lean back to study her. Her lips are puffy from our frantic kisses and her hair is in wild disarray about her head. Red marks dot her neck from my mouth and her chest is flushed; her nipples so hard I'm tempted to suck one into my mouth right now and pull and tug with my lips until she's whimpering from the pleasure.

"Yeah, uh . . . despite what you've heard, I'm clean. I swear." I swallow hard, overwhelmed with the idea of taking Ivy with no barriers. Just skin on skin. All that wet, silky heat sucking me deep . . .

"I want you, Archer." She tightens her legs around my hips and I can feel her. Hot. Slick. Tempting me like no one else ever has. "I trust you."

Her simple statement threatens to unravel me.

Reaching between us, I guide myself in, teasing her with the head of my cock before I finally sink into her depths. She throws her head back against the wall with a loud groan when I fill her completely and then we're moving. Grinding. We're in absolute perfect sync as she slowly rides the length of my cock.

Closing my eyes, I press my forehead to hers, breathing hard, trying to keep my shit together. She feels fucking amazing, surrounding me, all over me until she's the only thing I can see, hear, smell, taste. I turn my head and bite along her neck, soothing the nips with little flicks of my tongue, and she releases a shuddering sigh, my name falling from her lips.

That little sigh spurs me on, and I increase my pace. Her arms and legs clutch me close and I nuzzle her damp hair, breathe in her heady scent. I've never felt closer to a woman than I do at this very moment with Ivy. She's all I want. All I'll ever want.

The realization is so staggering I fumble for a moment, my hands gripping her ass tight. I pause, trying to keep my control, desperate to make this good for her, but she's circling her hips and sending me deeper. So much deeper I'm afraid I'll never find my way out of her.

"Harder, Archer," she breathes against my ear, making me shiver. "I want to come with you inside me."

Ah hell, she's as good of a tease as I am. Increasing my pace once more, I fuck her hard against that wall, her body thumping loud with my every thrust, our sweaty skin clinging to each other, my hand tangled in her hair as I grip the back of her neck and bring her in for a kiss. Our lips meet, our tongues stroke, and then I'm groaning against her, coming so fucking hard I swear I see stars.

She's coming too. I can feel her clench all around me, milking my orgasm further until I'm absolutely spent. We stand together for long, quiet moments, the only sounds our stuttering breaths, our frantic heartbeats. I'm not ready to let go of her yet, not ready to slip out of her hot depths, and I stay there. Wrapped tight in her embrace, never ever wanting to move again.

"I . . . uh. Wow," she murmurs minutes later, and I chuckle as I lift my head away from her to meet her gaze. "That was . . . I didn't mean for that to happen."

"Really?" I kiss her, not insulted in the least. I don't doubt for a second she didn't mean for that to happen. I really didn't either.

But when she was sitting there talking about her lack of orgasms, it was like she threw down a challenge. I had to prove to her that she was wrong.

Did I ever.

"I just . . ." She laughs and shakes her head. "You make it hard for me to form words, after all that."

"Mmm." I kiss her again, her swollen lips parting for me easily as I search her mouth with my tongue. "We're amazing together."

"We are, aren't we?"

"I'm going to enjoy showing you just how amazing again and again over these next two weeks." I say it like a promise. A vow. Because it is.

She presses against my chest with her hands so I move away from her, but I still don't let her go. "That sounds promising."

I meet her gaze, schooling my expression, needing her to know the truth. "I was an idiot for pretending what happened between us didn't exist. And I'm sorry about that." Leaning in, I drop a soft kiss on her swollen lips. "I'm sorry I let you down. I can't wait to start working with you. I trust your instincts. I believe in your skills. And I can't wait for us to work together on this project and make my resort the best fucking thing the entire industry has ever seen."

A slow, sexy smile curves her lips and she kisses me again. "I love it when you talk like that."

"What, like an arrogant asshole?"

"Yes." Her lips linger on mine. "I find your arrogance . . . arousing."

"Really?" I'm doubtful, but I'll go with it.

"Yes. Really." She licks my cheek and I flinch. What the hell was that for? "Take me to bed, Archer. Show me what else those magic hands and fingers can do."

"Wait until you see what my magic tongue can do for you." I get hard just thinking about it.

"I can't wait to see."

Chapter 13

Ivy

Eleven days. I've been in Calistoga with Archer for eleven days and I can't believe how wonderful it's been. Busy and tiring and exhausting, but also . . . freaking amazing.

I don't ever want to come down off this high.

We've been working nonstop on Crave. It's small and quaint and gorgeous and sophisticated all at once. I've poured over endless fabric swatches, paint colors for the interiors, and searched through enough furniture catalogs and websites to make my eyes cross until I finally came up with the perfect color scheme for all eight of the suites, plus the lobby and spa accommodations.

All with Archer's approval, of course, and he's loved everything I've come up with. Considering we have similar taste, it's been a relatively easy road. For all our arguing and fighting from the past, it's hard for me to believe just how easily and well we work together. He's brilliant and smart and comes up with the best ideas. I constantly compliment him as if I can't help myself.

And then he thanks me by kissing me stupid, stripping me naked, and having his way with me. Again and again and again.

Every night that we're together it's like this. We come together in a frenzy of heated breaths, delicious kisses, soft sighs, and wandering hands over naked skin. During the day we're on our best behavior, working hard, going over plans, all sorts of plans, or returning to Hush where Archer has to take care of his day-to-day responsibilities, which are tedious and sometimes irritating, but he always handles them with ease.

He's so good at his job, it's a joy to watch him in action. I admire the easy way he has with people. How efficiently he handles a guest complaint, an employee complaint, a call from some reporter inquiring about the Calistoga location. It's nonstop, everything he has to do.

As each day passes, my admiration for him grows. I care for Archer far more than I want to admit. I think he cares for me too. Spending so much one-on-one time with this gorgeous, frustrating, adorable, volatile, sweet, stubborn man, I can't get over how much I didn't know about him until now.

His drive. His passion. His intelligence. He so believes in what he's doing, the service he provides for people, he will do everything he can to ensure that he offers his guests the absolute best service their money can buy. And he's pulling out all the stops for the new resort. It's costing him a fortune. He'll charge his guests a fortune too. But I have a sneaking suspicion they'll love it and come back for more.

And he'll become an absolute success all over again.

Running my fingers through my hair, I scratch the back of my head, squinting at my laptop's screen. I've been searching for the lobby rugs and I can't find them. I have a visual in my head, but so far nothing comes close to my imagination. I'm afraid I'm going to have to settle.

I know if I told Archer that, he would flip. Demand I continue my search until I find rugs I absolutely love. He's definitely not about settling, even for rugs.

Hunched over my laptop, I curl my leg beneath me on the chair and sigh, scrolling through yet another textiles website, looking through a ton of ugly rugs that are all wrong, no matter how much I try to make them right. My vision is blurry and my neck aches. It's past seven, I'm so ready to call it quits, but I'm trying to wait for Archer to return.

Silly, yes, but I can't help myself. I want to see him.

When we're not in Calistoga, we're headquartered in Archer's office at Hush. That's where I'm at now, waiting for him while he handles some sort of urgent issue. There are always urgent issues for Archer to handle. He does everything at Hush. The man has so much on his plate it overwhelms me, and I'm not the one who has to take care of it all; I'm only an observer. Most of the time he's putting out various fires, which must get super old.

But I guess this is what comes with being the owner.

Stretching my arms above my head, I grimace when I hear and feel my neck pop, then settle back into position. I curl my fingers around the mouse when big, warm hands settle on my shoulders, making me yelp in surprise.

"So tense," Archer murmurs, his deep voice sounding directly in my ear.

"You scared the crap out of me." I sink my teeth into my lower lip to keep a moan from escaping when he starts to rub. Oh my God, that feels so good. I think I might melt into a pool of nothing if he keeps it up.

"Sorry. You were too busy scowling at your laptop." He continues to massage my shoulders and I close my eyes, savoring his touch. How good he makes me feel. "Find what you want?"

If we're talking about you, yes, I sure did. "Not really," I admit with a sigh.

He's standing directly behind my chair, rubbing my shoulders, his fingers digging into my flesh. My entire body warms and loosens at having his hands on me and I want to turn around, grab him, and tell him let's go back home.

Scary, how I'm starting to think of his house as home. I'm certainly not spending my nights in the guest room, that's for sure. Or at Hush like we'd originally planned. No, I get to spend them in his amazing, humongous bed in his equally amazing, humongous bedroom.

The man certainly knows how to live with every luxury available. My parents may be wealthy, but they're downright modest compared to Archer.

"You should schedule a massage," he murmurs, dropping a kiss on top of my head.

My insides warm at the sweet gesture. I'm dying to have that mouth of his on mine. "Why would I need to when I have you?" Opening my eyes, I heave a big sigh. Yes. Yes, I've lost it. All over Archer.

All for Archer.

"True." He sounds amused, his voice warm, his touch gentle as he squeezes my shoulders. "I'll give you a more thorough massage when we get home."

"I like the sound of that."

"It'll involve special oils from the spa and you completely naked." His voice drops to a husky whisper, sending shivers down my spine, and I smile at my laptop screen.

"Sounds absolutely amazing."

"It will be, I can promise you that." He crouches beside me, his face level with mine, and I cut my gaze to his, marveling at his handsome features. His dark brown hair falls across his forehead, making me want to reach across and push it away. So I do, my fingers sifting through the silky soft strands. "Still looking for rugs for the lobby, huh?"

"It's been a rather . . . frustrating process." I click out of the website I was perusing and turn more fully to face him.

"I know someone who designs rugs. Has a studio where they're handwoven." He smiles. "Every one of them is like a work of art."

"I'm sure they are. Very expensive works of art," I stress. We're completely over budget, but he flat out doesn't care. He spares no expense. It sort of drives me crazy.

And makes me admire him even more.

He shakes his head. "I've never seen a person so obsessed with rugs before."

"That's because I have an idea in my head I can't shake." I tap my forehead. "And it sucks because I'm forever disappointed in every stupid rug I see."

"That does it. I'm calling her right now and we'll make an appointment to see her tomorrow. She can create whatever you want, she's that good." He whips out his phone and starts scrolling through his contacts. "Actually, I'll text her, see if she's available in the morning."

"Archer, we only have a few days until we're open. No way can she get them done in time." I shake my head, shocked he would go to such lengths to please me.

"Then we'll throw some solid color rugs out for a few days to cover while I insist she rush the process. Trust me, they'll work on the rugs twenty-four-seven if I pay her right."

"They're not worth that much . . ." I start, but he silences me with a look that I find so incredibly sweet and sexy I feel my heart crack a little more every time I see it.

Like right now. It's cracking wide open, all for Archer.

"If it makes you happy, it's worth it. You've already sketched out what you wanted for me, remember?"

I nod, a little embarrassed that we're having this discussion over freaking rugs. "That you're willing to go to such lengths when you don't even know what it will look like says a lot."

"Like I'm crazy?" His smile grows, that dimple of his flashing and I lean in, giving it a kiss.

"I'm the crazy one." *Crazy for you* . . .

Just thinking that freaks me out a little.

"Yeah, you are, baby," he drawls. I love it when he calls me baby. My stomach flutters as he leans in closer, and I can make out every speck of stubble on his cheeks, see the tiredness in his dark brown eyes. He looks as exhausted as I feel and I have the sudden urge to comfort him.

"You're definitely crazy, though," I say, entranced with the gold flecks in his brown eyes, the way they look at me full of so much emotion. Emotion I can't quite figure out, but I don't want to. It's a little scary to contemplate, and I'm not ready to face it yet. "You're drastically over budget."

"You're the one who put the budget on me. The sky's the limit for this place. I already told you that." He kisses me, his lips lingering, and just like that I want him.

He makes me want to lose all control . . . and gladly.

Pulling back, I roll my eyes. The budget I tried to get him to agree to has flown right out the window. No wonder he drives his father crazy. Don Bancroft plans and plots to the finest detail. He has a list and a chart and a spreadsheet for every little thing. He doesn't go a penny over budget unless he's absolutely forced to, at least according to the stories my brother has told me. And when he does go over budget, he's grumbling and griping the entire time.

Whereas Archer tends to fly by the seat of his pants and hope like hell it all comes together. It worked for him before with Hush. I know it's going to work this time around too with Crave. I can feel it. His love and excitement for this opening far outshines anything else.

Well, his excitement for me is pretty shiny too. Love? Yeah, I doubt that, but I'm going to revel in what we share while we have it. Because it's fleeting, I know this.

I think he knows it too.

Our two weeks together are almost up, and I can hardly stand the thought of being away from him.

"We shouldn't have your friend make those rugs. I'm sure I can find something that'll work. I like the solid color idea. It's simple. Won't put me through so much torture while I look for the perfect pattern. Now I just need to find the perfect color." I turn away from him, my finger poised to resume scrolling, and he touches my arm, causing me to look at him again.

"I already texted her. We'll meet with her tomorrow first thing. Your work day is officially over." He smiles, softening his demanding words. "I'll take you to dinner if you'd like."

"Where?" I ask breathlessly, my arm tingling from his touch. His palm is wide, his fingers long, and he's smoothing his hand up and down my arm, making my breath come a little quicker. "I'm kinda tired. It's been a long day."

"We could stay here tonight. There are a couple of suites available. We could order room service, maybe?" He raises his brows, waiting for my answer.

I've wanted to try out those outdoor bathtubs built for two since I first saw one. Working with Archer has turned into a kind of torturous foreplay, one I both delight and agonize in. All the wanting and the yearning throughout the day, the lingering glances and the quick touches.

Archer Bancroft makes me feel like a confident, smart,

and desirable woman. And I'm going to wield my newfound power on the very man who gave it to me.

Archer

"Room service sounds perfect," Ivy says after a too-long pause. Hell, for a minute there I thought she was going to say no.

It has been slow at Hush, which works out in my favor since I spend half of my time in Calistoga lately. Always with Ivy by my side, helping me, offering her suggestions, guiding me when I go off track, me pushing her when she is being too conservative.

First day in, I realized pretty quickly we make a good team. There are enough differences between us that balance our personalities and allow us to work well together. Hard to notice when in the past, all we ever did was argue every time we came together.

But the arguing was a result of all that troublesome sexual attraction getting in the way. Not that it's disappeared. Hell no. But we're taking care of that issue every single night. We're both exhausted after a heavy and long workday, but we always make time for each other. In bed. Wrapped around each other, naked limbs entangled. My ultimate task of the day is making Ivy moan with pleasure.

I'm falling for her. Hard. Fast. I don't want her to leave. She feels like a true partner in every sense of the word.

That scares the shit out of me.

Working side by side with Ivy since she came here has been

exhilarating. Getting to know her, watching her in her element has left me impressed. She may be young and at an early point in her career, but she's smart and instinctive, with excellent taste. Without a doubt, I know my resort is going to look unbelievable when we're finished.

I just hope we can wrap it all up and have it ready in the next few days. That's the only thing making me anxious.

Well, that and the fact that as soon as Crave opens, Ivy's gone. Out of my life.

Fuck, that fills me with so much despair I can barely stand thinking about it. She doesn't think I'll stick. And sometimes I doubt myself too. I don't want to subject her or myself to a relationship that's doomed to fail.

But are we really doomed? I don't know. I'm so used to thinking that way, it's hard to believe anything else.

"So you want to get a room? Or eat here in the office then head on home?" I definitely don't want the formality of my office this evening, eating at my desk, talking business like we've been doing constantly since I've brought her here.

I want to be in a suite tonight, alone with her and shut off from the rest of the world. We can eat, plan our schedule for tomorrow, and then indulge in each other. My favorite part of the day is the nights. Being alone with Ivy.

Being inside Ivy.

How will I feel, though, when it's all over? Normally, with women, it's never an issue. Hell, I don't allow women to become this close to me ever. Their expectations grow to insurmountable proportions, and I'm left fending off their disappointment and sense of abandonment.

I have this feeling that with Ivy, it will become difficult to let her out of my sight, let alone out of my life. I'll be the one with the sense of abandonment when she leaves me.

"How about you call the order in and I'll go get us a suite?" I suggest.

She smiles, her hazel eyes sparkling. When she looks at me like that, I feel ten feet tall and like I can do no wrong. It's too easy, what we share.

I remember complaining to Gage that it made me nervous when things were too easy. I should be feeling that way at this very moment.

But all I can do is think about how pretty she is. How much I want to kiss her. How I enjoy spending every waking moment with her. Every sleeping moment with her too.

"Sounds perfect. I've been wanting to try one of those outdoor bathtubs, you know," she admits coyly. "Do you want me to order for you? I love how the menu is always changing."

That's because I hired a world-class chef who's a pain in my ass and worth every penny I pay him. "Yeah, order me something. You know what I like. I'll come find you in about ten minutes, okay? I have a few things I need to wrap up first."

"All right." Shutting her laptop, she stands and I grab her, pulling her into my arms. She turns more fully into me, her gaze meeting mine, eyes large and unreadable as she grips my tie and pulls me in for a kiss. I bury my hands in her hair, messing it up completely, not giving a shit. I love it when she's messy and looking dazed, her cheeks flushed, her lips swollen from our constant kissing.

Damn it, I have it bad for this woman. And I don't really care if anyone knows it or not. Even Matt.

Even Gage.

Yeah, I need to tell Gage. They both need to know what's going on. Not that I'm coughing up the money, not yet. They said she didn't count, but damn it, she counts to me. But I won't be paying off any sort of bet until I put a ring on her finger.

I can't believe I'm contemplating putting a ring on Ivy's finger.

"I'll see you in a bit then?" she murmurs when I finally break the kiss. Her face is turned up to mine, her lips still slightly pursed, her lids heavy, giving her a sultry, sexy look. Her scent surrounds me, heady and sweet, and I'm tempted to jump her right here. Wouldn't be the first time we fucked around on top of my desk. Last time, I'd pushed her skirt up, tugged her panties aside, and made her come with just my tongue in record time. Had to, since there'd been a meeting I needed to attend and they were all waiting for me.

I'm getting hard just remembering it.

"Yeah, I'll be quick, I promise." I'm already anxious to see her and she hasn't even left yet. She smiles as if she can read my mind, and I lick my lips, staring at her mouth, ready to give in and kiss her again. She sways toward me, a little sigh leaving her as our mouths come closer, closer . . .

My fucking cell phone rings and I spring away from her, running a hand through my hair, sending it into a haphazard mess. We've been rudely interrupted before, and I hate it. "Shit," I mutter as I pull it out of my pocket and see the number, watching as Ivy steps back, smoothing a few loose strands of hair behind her ear, nibbling on her lower lip.

Damn it, I wish I was the one nibbling on her lower lip.

"What the hell is going on with you and my sister?" Gage says. No hello, no what's up. Just launches right in with the diatribe.

"She's working for me, Gage. You already know this." I look at Ivy, who's pointing at the door and mouthing *See you later* before she dashes out of my office without another word.

Lucky her, she doesn't have to deal with her pissed-off brother.

"Yeah, but I saw some cozy picture of the two of you together. It looks like you're about to kiss her." Gage is literally yelling at me. "What the hell, man?"

"What picture are you talking about?" Oh. Shit. Who took a photo of us? And where? Do I have the paparazzi trailing my ass?

Of course I do. How easy I forget.

"I don't know. You guys are outside somewhere. You're standing real close and she's leaning into you. It seriously looks like the two of you are about to kiss or were just kissing." Gage pauses, takes an audible deep breath. "If you're with her, you better not break her heart. I'll fucking kill you, Archer, and you know it."

"I'm not with her," I automatically say, wincing the moment the words fall from my lips. I've turned into a liar.

Easy as that.

"So what's up with the picture? Oh yeah, and did I mention your arm is around her?"

Damn, did Gage withhold that bit of information on purpose?

"I have no idea. I'll admit, we've become closer. We spend a lot of time together working. And we're actually getting along. Can you believe it?" Nothing but silence on Gage's end, which of course makes me want to squirm. "There's nothing to worry about, Gage. I swear," I say as I walk around my office and gather up miscellaneous papers and whatever else is lying around, cleaning it up for the end of the night. I'm full of nervous energy, and I need to keep myself occupied before I bust out a *Fine-you-caught-me-I-think-I'm-falling-in-love-with-your-sister-tell-me-what-to-do* confession.

"Tell me you're not sleeping with her."

Well, hell. Leave it up to Gage to get right to the point.

"I'm not sleeping with her," I automatically say because I'm not—not really. When I get Ivy in my bed, there's rarely any sleeping involved.

"Don't forget the bet," he reminds me, like I ever could. That bet is burned into my brain, making me feel like shit because if she ever finds out, especially now, she'll probably hang me by my balls and let Gage have his way with me. Not that I could blame her. I feel like a liar. Like I'm hiding the bet, hiding our relationship as if I'm ashamed to be seen with her. And that's definitely not the case. "And don't forget she's my goddamn sister."

"I'm not involved with Ivy," I mutter, falling into my desk chair with a thump. Shit. I do not need this sort of lecture tonight. This is going to kill my mood for sure if I let it. And I'm already letting it. "She doesn't count, remember? You and Matt both said that."

I hate even saying it, let alone thinking it. She counts far more than I could ever imagine.

"Yeah, I know what we said, but she's still pretty and sweet and hell, for all I know you've wanted her for years. I have no clue." Damn, Gage's too close to the truth for comfort. He sounds worried and that makes me feel like hell.

Does he really think I'd be a ruthless jerk, going after his sister with no thought and callously hurting her? "She's a friend. She does her job well. You already knew this was going to happen when I called you a few weeks ago, remember?" How easy Gage forgets. I swear he's in his own little world. "Why the panic now?"

"I didn't think you'd actually ask her to work for you." He

pauses. "And I've been . . . distracted. Not around much. I had no idea she wasn't even in town."

"Well, I did hire her and she's staying here with me. At the resort." Lies again, but damn, I don't want him knowing she's staying at my house. In my bed. "And she's doing a fantastic job." I lean back in my chair, glancing up at the ceiling. "Don't worry. Your sister is safe with me."

"She'd better be. Normally I don't trust you as far as I can throw you, but this is Ivy we're talking about. You hurt her, I hurt you."

I know without a doubt, Gage will make good on his promise.

Chapter 14

Archer

Opening night

S o what do you think?"

I turn to find Ivy standing in front of me, wearing a dress that should be outlawed, she looks so damn good in it. Too damn good. "Uh . . ." I can't find my tongue, and I nearly swallow it when she does a little twirl, the skirt flaring out to reveal her pretty knees, her slender thighs.

"I love it, but I don't know," she says when she's facing me once again, a giant smile on her face. Her hair is up, her elegant neck exposed, little tendrils of dark brown hair curling against her cheeks and neck. She's so beautiful it hurts to look at her. "Say something, Archer, before I think you hate it."

The dress is white lace and sleeveless, the neckline dipping into a deep V that exposes all that smooth, kissable skin. A simple gold satin ribbon winds around her, just below her breasts, tied in a pretty bow at her back, and I'm tempted to slowly pull it undone. Unzip the dress, peel it off her, and kiss her everywhere.

But we have an opening party to go to for Crave. That we're already running late to.

"I think you look amazing." I go to her and drop a gentle kiss to her lips. She looks nervous and I grab her hands, giving them a squeeze. "What's wrong, baby?"

"What if they hate it?" she blurts out. "The interiors? All of it? I'll never be able to forgive myself."

"They're not going to hate it. Everything looks fucking amazing." It does. She did a phenomenal job. We did a phenomenal job together. Proving to me yet again that we make a great team.

"Really?" She's looking at me, really looking at me, and I know she needs my reassurance now more than ever.

"Really." I kiss her again, this one a little longer, leaving her breathless when we break apart. "I wouldn't lie to you."

That in itself is a lie. I'm keeping something from her right now. Like that stupid bet. It's the most juvenile thing I've ever participated in, and I don't want her to hear what Matt and Gage had to say. How she didn't count. How none of them think I could possibly be interested in her.

I need to come clean before Gage or Matt ruin it and tell her first. They're both supposed to be attending tonight, but they won't get a chance to talk to her alone. I'll make sure and keep her by my side the entire evening.

"Archer . . ." She breathes deep, as if gathering strength, and I squeeze her closer, not wanting to break this physical or emotional connection we have. "What's going to happen after tonight?"

"What do you mean?" I know exactly what she means. I'm just stalling for time so I can come up with a logical answer.

"Between us. I—I have to go back home. I need to go back to my job." She drops her head, pressing her forehead into my chest, and I wrap my arms around her waist, holding her close. "I don't want to leave you," she whispers.

My heart constricts. This has happened so damn fast. And I let it. Enjoyed it, really. "I don't want you to leave either," I admit.

She sighs, and I feel all the tension leave her body as she melts against me. "You don't know how glad I am that you said that."

Slipping my hand beneath her chin, I tilt her face up, see the tears shimmering in her pretty hazel eyes. They're more green than brown at the moment and I kiss away the tear that drops on her cheek, my heart aching at seeing that physical display of emotion coming from her. "I'm falling in love with you, Ivy." I've already fallen. And there I went, fucking admitting it. What is wrong with me?

I'm in love with Ivy. That's what's wrong with me.

"Oh." She presses her lips together and closes her eyes, but another tear falls onto her cheek. I kiss that one away too. "God, Archer, I—I'm falling for you too."

She didn't say love, not that I'm going to hold it against her. For once, I'm laying it all on the line for a woman. For this woman—the woman I love. The woman I think I've always loved, I just never knew it until this very moment.

"We need to go, baby." I kiss her again, because after making such a confession from the deepest, darkest part of your soul, you have to be reassured your woman is on the same page.

The responsive way she kisses me, clings to me, tells me that yes, indeed, she is more than on the same page. We're writing the same damn book. Together.

"Can we talk later? Tomorrow? About . . . us?" she asks when I finally, reluctantly pull away from her.

"Whatever you want." I cup her cheek, staring into her eyes. Feeling myself fall more and more in love with her.

"I CAN'T BELIEVE how much you transformed this place." Matt glances around the lobby, his eyes wide as he drinks it all in. "It looks incredible, Archer. You should be proud, man."

I am. So damn proud, I feel like I'm going to burst. "Yeah, you saw it in its barest, ugliest, pared-down state, didn't you?"

It had been a dilapidated, falling-down-around-my-ears building that had once housed a premiere spa. Before the recession came along and took down the previous owner's business with a mighty, ugly fall. The building stood empty for about four years, allowing looters and whatever other bums came through to completely trash the place and gut it of anything valuable.

But I'd known from the moment I walked inside, it had potential. I'd purchased the building and land for pennies on the dollar. Best decision I ever made. Not only did I have a new business to be proud of, but creating this resort brought Ivy and me together.

"I sure did and I thought the place looked like something out of a horror movie. Might've tried to discourage you from buying it too, not that you would have listened to me. But you're the one with the vision, not me." Matt shook his head, his gaze still sweeping the interior. "And Ivy helped you with it all, huh?"

"Yeah, more like she chose everything. The furniture, the art that covers the walls, the light fixtures, the accessories, all of it is Ivy's vision, which complements mine, thank God. I just signed off on all the invoices and didn't bother arguing with her. Everything she chose totally works, don't you agree?" I want to hear him praise her. I need someone to join in with me, since I sound like an overeager boyfriend too proud of his woman.

Which I sort of am.

"I do agree. The place is gorgeous. And there was no arguing between you two, huh? That's rather unlike you and Ivy," Matt jokes.

"I know. We uh, work well together." Understatement of the year. Ivy and I do everything well together.

"I'm sure," Matt said wryly. "You got something going with her and hoping to hide it from us? Is that it?"

"Of course not," I retort, nerves eating at my gut. Ivy's close by but out of earshot, and the last thing I want is for her to walk in on this conversation.

"You two looked pretty cozy to me when you first arrived."

We'd run a little late but still arrived before the start time of the party, so we hadn't expected any of our guests to be there yet.

It was just like Matt to screw it all up and actually show early. And witness Ivy and me walking into the lobby with my arm around her waist. Making her blush and giggle when I whisper how fucking sexy she looks.

Though Matt greeted each of us with an easy smile and a friendly hug, I felt the nerves radiating off Ivy. I wonder if she could feel the nerves vibrating off me.

Most likely. We haven't been caught by the outside world yet. Well, not to her knowledge. I never told her about the picture Gage called me about.

"I'm not going to deny we've become closer," I finally say when I realize Matt is waiting for an explanation. "But we're just friends. There's nothing going on between us." Now why the hell did I say that?

"Really." Matt's voice is flat and clear of emotion. Meaning he doesn't believe a word I say.

"Really," I agree with a nod. "She's so damn talented,

though. You should consider hiring her when you redesign the winery's interior."

"Who said I was redesigning it?" Matt asked, looking slightly taken aback.

"Have you taken a look around the place? It could use some sprucing up. Bring in a more modern feel." The winery he recently purchased was dark and dreary, the furnishings in good condition but old. He needs a new look if he wants to make a splash amongst the many wineries in this area.

"Is she expensive? I'm sure that snob Sharon Paxton charges a fortune for use of Ivy's services," Matt mutters.

"She's worth it." I spot Ivy standing not a few feet away from us, talking with one of my Hush clients who I invited to see the new location. The opening party is small and intimate, much like the resort itself, and I invited only a select few to catch that first glimpse of Crave.

We'll open the suites in a week. A few finishing touches need to be made, but for the most part, Ivy's job is done. Though we're talking tomorrow, maybe even later tonight. If I have my say in any of this, she won't leave my side again. I want her to move in with me.

Gage is going to shit a brick. Matt is going to call me out on all the lies I'm telling him. But I don't care. Maybe I should just come clean right now. I want Ivy with me for the rest of my life, forget that stupid-ass bet. She's worth a million bucks. Hell, she's priceless to me.

"I'm sure you think she's worth every penny," Matt says, the amusement in his voice clear.

"I told her she should start her own design consulting business." I slip my hands into my suit pockets, my gaze locked on her as she walks away from the client, only to be stopped by one of the waitstaff who hands her a glass of champagne.

"I'll be her first client. Tell her if she's considering it, she needs to sign me up," Matt says. "She does fabulous work." He's looking at me again and I tear my gaze away from Ivy to find him smiling at me, looking infinitely entertained. "Nothing going on between the two of you, huh? Your eyes were eating her up just now. As if you know exactly what she looks like beneath that dress."

Asshole. Panic flares within me. I don't want to deal with this right now. "Where the hell is Gage anyway?" I ask, trying to change the subject.

"I don't know. He's been a hard fucker to pinpoint lately. I'm not sure what's up with him." Matt steps closer to me, his voice lowering. "Come on, Archer. Tell me the truth. I won't say anything to Gage. Are you and Ivy together?"

Guilt settles heavy on my chest. I can't talk about this here and now. I need to talk to Gage. Get his permission, convince him I won't do wrong by his sister. I love her. But I can't confess everything yet. Not here, not now.

"No," I say emphatically. "She's just Ivy, remember? She doesn't count." Even as I say the words, they don't feel right. She's not just Ivy. She's never been *just* anything.

Just the girl for me, but that's it. And that's enough.

"What did you say?"

Icy dread slithers down my spine as I turn to find her standing before me, her eyes wide, all the color drained from her face. Ah, hell, she heard me. "Hey, baby," I start, but she cuts me off with a look.

"I want to hear you say it, Archer." Her voice is cold, her eyes hard, and my heart sinks.

I'm in big-ass trouble. Damn it, I need her to listen to me.

"Ivy, let me explain." But again she stops me, this time with a shake of her head.

"No. There's no need for an explanation. I heard exactly what you said. I don't count."

"You misunderstood me . . ." I need to make this right, get to her to listen to me. Her expression is tight, her mouth so thin her lips practically disappear, and she's so rigid I fear she might shatter if I so much as touch her.

I don't dare try. She'd probably kick my ass, she looks that pissed. And I can't blame her.

Yet again, I fucked it up royally. I didn't even mean to.

"There's nothing to misunderstand. You said it yourself, Archer. I. Don't. Count." She takes a step toward me, throwing her hands out and shoving my chest so hard I have no choice but to take a staggering step backward. "I can't believe you. After everything I said earlier. After everything *you* said, then you deny what's happened between us to Matt like I don't matter. What an idiot I am to think we could actually have something together."

I'm losing her. Fuck, I can't lose her. Not like this. "Come on, baby, let's talk about this somewhere else." If only I could get her alone, I can make this right. She needs to listen to me. Not in front of Matt and whoever else is nearby, listening in. Matt's watching us like we've both lost our minds and a few guests are lingering, trying to catch bits of our heated conversation, no doubt.

Shit. I'm not just losing the only woman who's ever really mattered to me all in a matter of minutes, I'm also making an ass of myself during Crave's opening night.

Feeling helpless, I try to grab her, but she yanks her arm out of my grip, her eyes wild and full of angry fire. "Please, Ivy. I need to explain everything to you. Privately."

"I don't want to hear your explanations. They're worthless. Absolutely worthless. Just like whatever happened between us the last few weeks is worth nothing. I should've known it was all an illusion. That you would dismiss me so easily to Matt, I just . . . I can't do this, Archer." She walks away, holding her head high, but I can see the wobble in her step. I hurt her so badly, I don't know if I'll ever be able to recover from this.

I wonder if she'll be able to recover from this. That she would jump to the conclusion that I don't care about her hurts too. After everything we've shared, she wouldn't even fucking listen to me.

It makes no sense.

"Well, you sure went and fucked that all up," Matt mutters as soon as she's gone.

"Shut up," I mumble. I can't just leave to go after her and it's killing me. This is my damn party. I have to be here to greet everyone and it's only started.

But I want to chase after her and explain. I need to explain. That she heard me say that . . . breaks my fucking heart for her.

"Why didn't you just tell me the truth? I knew you were lying anyway," Matt says.

"So why did you keep on asking then?"

"Because I wanted to hear you admit it. I have to say, it made me happy for you, man, seeing you when you first walked in with Ivy. Your entire face lit up when you were staring at her, and she looked at you like you hung the damn moon." Matt shook his head. "Leave it to you to say something so stupid, you fuck up a good thing with two simple words."

Yeah. Leave it to me to fuck it all up with two words. Just Ivy.

The woman I'm in love with.

Just Ivy.

The woman I hurt.

The woman I failed.

Chapter 15

Ivy

Two weeks later

W e're still on for lunch, right?"

Sighing, I check my schedule and see that my lunch hour is completely free. How unfortunate. I've become so unsocial it's painful. "I don't know if I'm up to it, Wendy," I start, but she cuts me off with an irritated snort.

"Screw that business, girlfriend. I'm taking you out to lunch whether you like it or not. We're going to that sushi place you love, we're going to order not one but two of our favorite rolls, and then we're going to devour them until we feel like we're going to burst. What do you say?"

Sounds like a nightmare. But I can't say that to Wendy. She's my best friend and she's only trying to cheer me up after that fiasco of a so-called relationship with Archer. "Fine. Want me to meet you there?"

"Yeah, if you don't mind. Say around twelve-thirty?"

"That should work." Luckily enough, Sharon doesn't mind if my lunch hour is flexible, as long as she can get a hold of me whenever she needs me. The more I've worked with her, the more I enjoy it.

She didn't ask questions about the Archer experience either. I forwarded her pictures for my online portfolio, she expressed her pleasure with the interior design I came up with, and that was that. Nothing else was said.

Just the way I prefer it. Talking about Archer—heck, even thinking his name—hurts too much.

"See you then." Wendy pauses, and I clutch the phone tight, scared of what she might say. "Chin up, okay, hon? Don't let this get you down. He's just a man, after all."

"Right, just a man," I say weakly, wondering if she realizes she's mirroring the same hurtful thing he said about me.

Just Ivy . . . she doesn't count.

If he walked into the room right now, I'd probably slug him in that too-pretty face of his. Let's see if he would refer to me as *just Ivy* then.

God, I miss him. I want him back—I'm in love with him. But I can't forgive him for saying what he did to Matt. Doesn't help that I spoke to my brother, and he told me some story Archer had spun to him as well. Denying that we were together, swearing up and down nothing was going on between us. Something about a picture Gage saw online of the two of us together, smiling at each other like we're in love.

Archer didn't bother to tell me about that picture either.

He lied to everyone. He lied to me. My heart still aches.

But would I ever get over him? I really, really hope so.

Someday.

I throw myself into my work because it's the only thing that keeps my mind occupied and off my troubles. I move through my days like some sort of ghost. Functioning, able to complete my tasks, meet with clients, answer the phone, only to go home and crawl into bed. Watch sappy movies and cry into my pillow, wishing I wasn't alone.

I am a pitiful, horrible wreck.

In my sleep, he comes to me. Smiling that beautiful smile of his, the dimple flashing, and then I'm suddenly in his arms. Slowly melting when he whispers how much he loves me. Until I'm falling completely under his spell, ready for him to make love to me.

Then I wake up and realize it was all just a dream and I'm alone. Without him. I tell myself it's better this way. He would've hurt me sooner or later, and it was best that it happened sooner, no? Now it's out of the way, and I can move forward.

But my mind and my body are stuck in the past, still longing for Archer. I can't help it.

Not that it's been that long since the incident, as I refer to it. Less than two weeks, that's it. He's called. He's texted, but I refuse to answer him or talk to him. At least he hasn't called my work, or worse, my parents.

God, that would be mortifying. Bad enough he's phoned Gage repeatedly, who calls him all sorts of vulgar names before he hangs up on him.

Gotta love a big brother who defends you no matter what, even against his best friend.

My desk phone rings, knocking me from my morose thoughts, and I pick it up, surprised to hear Sharon's voice. "Ivy, I have a huge favor to ask of you," she starts.

"Sure." I grab a pen, ready to take notes in case I need to. Sharon talks fast, and I feel like I'm constantly scribbling across a notepad when I talk to her in the hopes I'll remember what to do. "What's up?"

"I have a client coming by in fifteen minutes and there's no way I can be there in time to meet him. Could you do it for me? I hate to ask this of you, but I don't have a choice. I'm stuck in traffic, and I already had a late start back to the office."

"Sure. Who are you meeting with?"

"Matthew DeLuca. Have you heard of him?"

"What? Of course I have. He and my brother are good friends." I'm in shock. Why would Matt want to meet with Sharon? Why wouldn't he meet with me? If this has anything to do with the winery, I'm almost offended. I heard rumors he was going to refurbish it. I totally wanted to check it out and see what exactly needs improving.

Not that I want to be in the same vicinity as Archer . . . do I?

Of course you do, you lovesick idiot.

"Well, perfect. Ought to be easy for you to talk to him and find out what he's looking for since you know him so well." She rattles off a few other facts to me before she hangs up. I settle the phone in its cradle, surprise still coursing through my veins.

Okay, now I'm irritated. Why didn't he reach out to me first? I'm so calling Matt and chewing him out for not wanting to meet with me.

Of course, seeing Matt will also remind me of Archer and that will hurt. It especially hurts because Matt was the one Archer said all of those horrible, hurtful things to about me. He witnessed our entire argument, the reason why we fell apart.

I hate that. But I'll need to face him sometime, so it may as well be sooner rather than later.

Within minutes I hear the front door buzzer. The entrance is kept locked during the day so we don't have any strange people busting in uninvited. I stand, smoothing my hands down my skirt as I exit my office and enter the lobby, only to stop short when I see who's standing on the other side of that door.

It's not Matt.

It's Archer.

Stiffening my spine, I stride toward the door, stopping just in front of it. "Go away," I tell him, knowing he can hear me.

He slowly shakes his head, looking so devastated, so sad, he's breaking my heart.

Stupid, too-soft heart.

"I can't go," he says. "Not until I talk to you, Ivy."

"I don't want to hear what you have to say."

"Too damn bad. If you don't let me inside, then I'll just tell you everything through this stupid glass door."

Stubborn ass. "Where's Matt? I thought the appointment was with him."

"He made the appointment so I could come see you." He pauses and takes a deep breath. There are dark circles beneath his eyes, his cheeks are covered in stubble despite him being impeccably dressed in a gorgeous suit, and his hair is mussed. As if he's run his hands through it repeatedly. "Though he really does need your help, Ivy. That winery of his is a disaster."

I love that he's such an admirer of my talents, but it still doesn't change the fact of what he did to me. And how much it hurt. Maybe I overreacted, but so what? I need to be protective of my heart when it comes to Archer. "So you're lying again. Using Matt to see me."

"You won't take my calls, you won't answer my texts. What do you expect me to do?"

"Leave me alone?" I suggest.

He's still shaking his head. "I can't do that."

"Why not?"

"Because I'm in love with you."

My heart cracks wide open. "I don't believe you."

"It's the fucking truth." He grabs the handle of the front door and yanks on it, making the glass rattle. "Open the damn door, Ivy, so I can tell you this sort of thing face to face."

"We are face to face."

"I feel like I'm in goddamn prison, talking to you through the glass." He glares at me, his mouth thin, and I almost want to laugh.

Almost.

I should not open that door. Everyone I know would urge me to tell him to screw off. I don't need his trouble. And he's full of trouble.

But he's also fun . . . and sweet and lovable and sexy and smart. He claims he's in love with me.

I'm in love with him, too.

So I jumped to the worst conclusion, but would anyone blame me? Archer doesn't have the best track record when it comes to women. I wanted to believe he was in love with me, but I was scared. Afraid he'd bail on me after the two weeks we were together because that was our original deal, right? Two weeks. Next thing I know, I'm ready to turn it into a lifetime, and that's scary.

Maybe I overreacted because I was scared to commit too. Neither of us is perfect.

And then there's that stupid bet Gage told me about. Why didn't Archer mention it from the start? I wouldn't have cared. Those three are always making ridiculous bets with huge payouts. They're ridiculous. The bet is ridiculous.

Yet he kept it from me like some deep, dark secret. Doesn't he know I'm used to their behavior by now? And I still love him for it?

He's watching me, his dark eyes looking so haunted I automatically reach out and hit the keypad, punching in the code that deactivates the alarm and flicking the lock so the door can open. Next thing I know he's rushing in, rushing me, and I'm in his arms, being clutched so tight I can hardly speak as my face is pressed against his chest, breathing in his familiar, delicious scent. He buries his face against my hair, his entire body trembling, and it's like I can't help myself.

I wrap my arms around his solid warmth and close my eyes, savoring being in his arms again.

"I'm sorry," he murmurs against my temple just before he kisses it. "I fucked up and I'm sorry. Will you ever forgive me? I need you to forgive me, Ivy. I need you in my life. I feel lost without you."

Tears threaten. Of course. When do they not threaten lately? "I'm sorry too."

"For what?" He sounds stunned.

"I overreacted. I blamed you and made such a big deal about the bet being a secret, but maybe . . . maybe I was scared too." I pull away slightly so we can face each other. It feels so natural, so right, having him here. Touching me, looking at me with all that love and emotion shining in his eyes. It gives me hope. "If you'd been honest about the stupid bet from the beginning, I wouldn't have cared."

He frowns, his brows drawing down. "Really?"

"Archer. I know how you guys operate. I would've helped you win that million dollars if you'd let me in on the secret." I so would've. Not anymore, though.

Nope. Now I'm ready to throw him to the wolves and make him pay up.

"I'm an idiot," he says with a sigh. "Your brother said so too."

"You talked to Gage about me?" I'm in shock.

"I wanted his blessing." His face turns solemn, his dark brows drawing together. "Considering I'm in love with his sister, I had to clear the air between us and make sure I had his approval."

"And do you?" I hold my breath for fear of my brother's reaction.

"I do." He smiles faintly, though his jaw is still tight. "I think he gets how much I love you. Thank God. Remember, I'm an idiot when it comes to this sort of thing."

I nod in agreement. He so is. "You are. So am I. Maybe that's why we're so good together."

His expression clears at my words. "I also really messed this up."

"You definitely did."

"You've never, ever been just Ivy to me." He cups my cheek, his fingers drifting lightly across my skin. "You've become my everything."

My heart flutters when he touches the corner of my lips with his thumb. "I've missed you."

"I've missed you too." Leaning in, he kisses me, breathing against my lips all the pent-up hope and love I've held deep inside me as well. "I love you, Ivy. So damn much it's killing me not to have you by my side. I need you. I want you to be my partner in every sense of the word."

"What do you mean?" My heart is beating so fast I swear it's going to thump right out of my chest.

"Come live with me. Work with me. Start your own design business in Napa. Do you know how many calls I've taken since the opening, all of them asking about you? I could give you a ready-made client list."

Pride suffuses me. I had no idea. "Including Matt?"

He chuckles. "Yes. He's reluctant, but I'm trying to sway him. Cheap bastard."

I laugh, feeling lighter than I have in weeks. "What about us?"

Archer sobers immediately. "I'm in love with you, Ivy. I want you by my side forever."

"Forever?" I ask breathlessly.

"Yeah." He kisses me again, deeper this time, my lips parting for his persuasive tongue. "Marry me, and we can go into business together. Bancroft and Bancroft," he says after he breaks the kiss.

"Bancroft and Emerson?" I joke, though my head is spinning at his words and what they all mean.

"Baby, if you're going to marry me, you have to take my name. I'm kind of old-fashioned like that." He frowns. "I can't believe I just said that. I sound like a macho ass."

Laughing, I circle my arms around his neck and press my fingers against his nape, forcing him to kiss me again. "I loved that you just said that. I will gladly take your name, Archer. Though I'll be the first Bancroft in Bancroft and Bancroft, I hope you know."

"I don't think so," he murmurs against my smiling lips. "My first name starts with an A. Yours with an I. I'm afraid I'm first."

"Shouldn't you be polite? Ladies first, after all," I tease as he pulls me in closer.

"I think I can do that." He presses his forehead to mine, staring deep into my eyes. "I need to hear you say it, Ivy."

"Say what?" I'm confused. Dazzled. Lost in his dark brown gaze, those golden flecks dancing with so much happiness.

He doesn't say a word, merely continues to stare at me until realization slowly dawns. "Oh." Tipping my head up, I kiss him. Softly. Reverently. "I forgive you, Archer."

"I forgive you too, Ivy." He's smiling, knowing I'm teasing him, drawing it out. "And?"

"And I love you. So much, I thought I might die without you these last two weeks."

"I feel the same way, baby. The same exact way. Don't ever leave my side again."

"I won't. I promise."

"Become just my wife. Nothing else. Just mine." He's teasing again and this time his words don't hurt.

This time, his declaration fills me with so much love I know he's the man for me.

"Only if you become just my mine too," I say with a smile.

"I already am," he admits. "You own me, Ivy. You own my heart. There's no one else I'd rather belong to."

I kiss him, unable to stand it any longer, my heart and soul completely transformed when I hear him whisper two simple words.

"Just you."

Torn

Chapter 1

Marina

"Tell me your name."

A shiver runs down my spine at the commanding, deep voice that sounds in my ear. I keep myself still, trying my best not to react considering we're surrounded by at least a hundred people, but oh, how I want to.

If I could, I'd throw myself into the arms of the man who's standing far too close to me. He's demanding to know my name as if I owe him some sort of favor, which I can't help but find hot.

Irritating, but hot.

"Tell me yours first," I murmur in return, turning my head in the opposite direction, so it appears I'm not even talking to him. He stands behind me, tall and broad, imposing in his immaculate black suit and crisp white shirt—the silvery tie he wears perfectly knotted at his throat.

I might not be looking at this very moment, but I'd memorized everything about him the moment I first saw him not an hour ago. He'd drawn plenty of attention without saying a word, striding into the room as if he owned it, casting that calculating gaze upon everyone in attendance. Looking very much like the mighty king observing his lowly subjects—until his eyes lit upon me.

He watched me for long, agonizing minutes. Butterflies fluttered in my stomach as I felt his hungry eyes rake over my body, and for a terrifying moment I wondered if he could see right through me. I shifted the slightest bit, inwardly cursing myself for coming tonight, but I held firm. I refused to react.

I still refuse to react.

"You don't know who I am?" He sounds amused at the notion, and I'm tempted to walk away without a word. My earlier nerves evaporate, replaced by a steely spine and an even steelier attitude. He's so confident, so arrogant, I'm sure he believes he has me.

He doesn't know who he's dealing with then, does he?

We're at a local wine- and beer-tasting, and I'm here representing the bakery my family owns. The one I was recently allowed to take over and run since I'd graduated college. The business they all believe is going to fail. *So why not give it to Marina? She can't screw it up too badly.*

That's what I overheard my father telling my uncle. The memory of his words still cuts straight to the bone.

Finally I chance a glance at the man behind me, drinking in his thick brown hair tinged with gold, the way it tumbles across his forehead, his twinkling green eyes, the faint smile that curves his full lips. The combination gives him a boyish appearance. It's a complete illusion because there is nothing boyish about this virile man before me.

"Perhaps you can enlighten me." I offer a carefree smile and turn to face him, the nerves returning tenfold when he takes a step toward me, invading my personal space. His scent hits me first: clean and subtle, a mixture of soap and just . . . him. No cologne that I can detect.

Rather unusual. Most of the men I know slather themselves in expensive scents all with the purpose of drawing in us silly women. Instead, they end up choking us.

With the exception of this man. I find the uniqueness refreshing.

A slow smile appears, revealing perfectly straight white teeth. "Gage Emerson." He thrusts his hand toward me. "And you are . . . ?"

He's not very subtle. And he's exactly who I suspected, not that I had any real doubt. The very man who recently bought up what feels like half of the Napa Valley, all in the hopes of turning it around and selling it to God knows who just to earn a hefty profit.

Not caring in the least that he's forever changing the landscape of the very place I've grown up in. And devastating my family in the process.

"Marina Knight," I say. God, I sound breathless, and I want to smack myself. I'm not here tonight because of him. I came for other reasons. To promote the family bakery, to mix and mingle with local business owners, many I consider friends. My life in the Napa Valley is all I know.

And this gorgeous man standing in front of me is trying to take what I know away from me for good.

His smile grows and a slow, burning anger—combined with hunger, which makes me angrier—threads its way through my veins. I inhale sharply, desperate to control the unwanted emotion. I knew he was handsome, charming, well spoken. I'd recently done my research; Googled him for a solid hour, trying to find any sort of weakness—since he certainly knows my family's—but it appears he has none. Like he's some sort of untouchable superhero.

I didn't expect my reaction to him, though. My body is

humming in all the right places at his closeness. My skin literally tingles, and when he clasps my hand in his to shake it, my knees threaten to buckle.

"A pleasure to meet you, Marina Knight." His voice rumbles from somewhere deep in his chest and he draws his thumb across the top of my hand in the quickest caress before releasing it.

He's just a man, I remind myself. A dreamy, sexy man, in that polished, overtly masculine, deliciously commanding way that I don't normally find myself drawn to, but . . . hmm.

A girl is always allowed to change her mind.

"Lovely to meet you too," I say automatically, sounding just like my mother. Wincing, I look away, feeling foolish. I'm twenty-three years old. I've moved amongst the revered social circles in the Napa Valley all my life. My family is one of the most well known in the area. You'd think I'd know how to handle myself around charming, ruthless men.

But I don't know how to handle myself—at least around this one. Gage Emerson is intimidating. Gorgeous. Captivating.

I should run. Right now. Just turn tail and run. I don't know what I was thinking, hoping to talk to him. He's after my family's extensive property holdings throughout the valley. And I want something from him too.

The venue is small, at one of the many local wineries in the area. I'd found out Gage was coming so I planned to attend as well. I'd already talked to the winery owner, giving him my card in the hopes he would discuss the offer I made him earlier tonight, right before the party started.

The artisan breads my aunt bakes every morning would go perfectly with his wines. I've been trying this tactic for a while, approaching local businesses the bakery could pair with for promotional purposes, but so far, no luck. I'm starting to believe the word "failure" is tattooed on my forehead, and the only one who can't see it is me.

"Would you like a drink?" Gage asks. When I look at him once more he inclines his head to the side. "I'm headed to the bar. Care to join me?"

I follow him wordlessly through the crowd, murmuring hellos to the people I know as we pass, which is most of them. I've spent my entire life here. The towns that make up Napa Valley may be large, but the community is small, and everyone seems to know each other.

The gossip will probably be rampant with the fact that I spent time in the company of the calculating, interloping real estate shark Gage Emerson, but I don't mind. Ultimately I'll get what I want.

Though he probably won't.

He settles his hand at the base of my spine, steering me toward the bar, and I feel his touch in the very depths of my soul. My knees weaken as we come to a stop, standing in a short line to order our drinks.

"So what brings you here this evening, Marina Knight?" he asks, making idle conversation. He doesn't sound overly flirtatious, but I can never be too sure. At least he's not touching me any longer. I don't know if I'd be able to form words with his hands on me. My brain seems to go into temporary lockdown just having him close.

"My family," I say, not wishing to give too much information away. If he can't figure out who I am after my introduction, then I really don't want to give him any more hints.

He lifts a dark brow. "Your family?"

"We own a few businesses in Napa Valley," I finally answer vaguely, stepping forward as the line moves.

He keeps pace with me, his gaze roving over my face, as if

he's trying to figure out if we know each other. "Family businesses? Have we met before?"

I slowly shake my head. "Hmm, not that I can recall." I'd rather have him think he's utterly forgettable.

Not that he is. Oh no. It's only been a few minutes, but I'm afraid he's burned himself onto my brain forever.

"Huh." He sounds stumped. Looks it too. Which means he looks adorable.

His squeaky-clean image is the stuff of legend. Well, really his public image is one of all business, no play. Yes, he always has a beautiful woman on his arm at various public events. Yes, he's been linked to a few relationships, always with women who are as successful and powerful as he is.

So what could he see in little ol' me? The bakery manager with the giant family that's slowly losing its fortune, one buyout at a time?

Ugh, I need to push all the ugly thoughts out of the way and focus on the here and now. Like how can I convince him that the next acquisition on his agenda is off limits. The one he's going to be offering on very soon. The deal my family—specifically my father—won't be able to resist much longer.

I need to hold Gage off from making that purchase. He buys up the strip of businesses my family owns in St. Helena, and my career is over. My entire life I've wanted to run one of the family businesses, specifically the bakery. It was expected. The bakery had been a part of my life since I could remember. Now, with everything being sold off, there won't be any businesses left. After all that my family had done over the years, to be left with nothing makes me sick to my stomach.

I'm a part of the Molina family legacy, one of the oldest families in all the Napa Valley, yet I feel like there's nothing I can do. It's slipping out of my grasp right before my eyes and

I'm powerless to stop it. Though maybe I could stall Gage for a little while . . .

But how can I hold him off? What can I do to stop him from changing my life forever?

You're a smart, strong woman. You can come up with something.

Sometimes I swear it feels like the voice inside my head is not my own.

It's our turn to order at the bar, and Gage asks for a beer while I order a glass of sparkling wine, locally produced. I'm ultraconscious of supporting our area businesses. After all, I'd hope for the same in regards to *my* business.

My failing business, thank you very much.

He pays for my drink, and I let him. He's still trying to figure out who I am; I can tell by his scrunched brows, his narrowed eyes. We move away from the bar but remain standing nearby. His back is facing everyone else still in line, and he's turned toward me while I'm leaning against the wall. He's got me effectively trapped, though I don't feel it. I rather like being surrounded by Gage Emerson.

Even though I shouldn't.

Gage

can't place her, but I swear I've heard of her before. Maybe even met her, though I can't recall where. Archer's hotel opening, maybe? I don't know. I met an endless stream of people at that specific event, though they weren't overly friendly. Most everyone in the Napa Valley still treats me like an outsider.

Marina Knight . . . it's her first name that's tripping me

up. I don't know many *Marinas*. Or even one aside from her. Who does? But this one . . . she's beautiful. And not what I expected—though, really? What the hell could I expect? I don't know her.

At least I don't think I do. And damn it, I'm too distracted by her pretty face. I think she's screwing with my brain.

All that calm, contained elegance she wears so eloquently is seductive. Honey-blonde hair that falls in gentle waves to the middle of her back. Cool, assessing blue eyes that seem to see right through me and are amused with what they find. Her mouth is slicked with a deep, ruby red lipstick and she presses her lips together before she flashes a mysterious little smile. Just looking at the gentle curve of them sets my blood on fire.

Not a good sign.

She's of average height, hitting me at about my shoulder, and she's wearing a simple black dress that covers her completely yet clings to every delicious curve. She screams both ice queen and touch me—an alluring combination I'm finding harder to resist the longer I'm in her company.

Lately, I've sworn off women completely. I enjoy spending time with them. I appreciate them like any other man. But they're a total distraction when I don't need one, always wanting more than I can give. Focusing on my business is the ultimate goal at the moment. Starting up a relationship with the potential for it to turn serious?

I don't think so.

Truly, that is the absolute last thing I want. Especially after witnessing my best friend Archer Bancroft fall hopelessly in love—with my little sister, Ivy, for God's sake. I know that's not the path I'm ready to take.

Plus, there's a hell of a lot of money on the line. The asshole friend of ours who came up with the million-dollar bet, Matt DeLuca, is laughing hysterically at me right now. I can feel it; I can always feel it. I think he's here somewhere, probably spying on me as I talk to this woman I don't even know. All the while he's got that new assistant of his following him everywhere, sending him longing glances while he's an oblivious idiot.

She's got the hots for him, the poor thing.

We were at a friend's wedding when the three of us declared we never wanted to get married. We must've been drunk when we did it, but we all bet each other we'd never let ourselves get tied down to a woman. And the last single man wins one million dollars.

Fucking crazy.

If I have my way, Matt definitely won't win. Smug bastard. He thinks this situation we've all found ourselves in is hilarious. He believes he's got winning our stupid bet covered. Mister Lone Wolf has thrown himself completely into the renovation of the winery he recently bought. Women don't interest him, he told me just the other day. Maybe for a quick romp between the sheets, but nothing that could last. Nothing serious.

All the while, his very attractive assistant is sitting not ten feet away from us, her body stiff. I swear to God, her head tilted toward us so she could totally listen in on our conversation.

I'm with him one hundred percent in that regard. Let Archer take the fall—alone. He's thrilled to be playing house with my sister, which still blows my mind. Ivy's just as enamored with him. Funny, considering how not that long ago they argued all the damn time. I figured they hated each other.

Now . . . hell, they're getting married in a couple of months. I'm going to be Archer's best man. Just thinking of wearing the imaginary noose that Archer's willingly walking into has me tugging at my suddenly too-tight shirt collar.

"So what brings *you* here tonight, Gage Emerson?" Marina repeats the question I asked her earlier, that same little mysterious smile curving her lips. There's a natural sultriness to this woman that calls to me. I can't explain it. I want to lean in closer to her and inhale her scent. Touch her soft cheek, take her hand and press my palm to hers. Something, anything to make that instant connection between us I'm suddenly looking for. Her lips drive me to distraction; they're such a lush, seductive red.

I bet she tastes fucking amazing.

Keep your head straight, asshole.

"Business," I answer firmly, sipping from my bottle of beer. It's from a local microbrewery that's become a recent favorite. That's why I came, that and—as always—to make business connections. Archer got me the invite. The more properties I buy in the area, the more inclined I am to stay here.

I like it. The countryside is beautiful, the people seemingly friendly until you want to take over their turf, and it's not too far from San Francisco, my home base.

I keep my eyes trained on Marina the entire time I drink, noticing how she jerks her gaze away from mine, her chest turning the faintest shade of pink, as if I might've made her uncomfortable.

Yep, I'm such a goner. And when I know I shouldn't be. I'm completely entranced. The women I'm normally drawn to are sophisticated, confident. My equals in age, status, and earning capability. I appreciate more of a powerhouse couple ethic. I sound like a complete jackass in my own damn brain, but I can't help it. I'm drawn to intelligent, confident women.

This one is young, pretty, and seemingly shy . . . with that air of innocent yet sensual mystery that has me eager to get to know her better, despite my current aversion to the fairer sex.

"And what sort of business are you involved in?" I swear she just batted her eyelashes at me.

"Real estate." I take another drink, giving her the side eye as she casually averts her gaze, seeming to scan the crowd from over my shoulder. I glance behind me, seeing no one familiar in the room before I turn to face her once more. Of course, I'm the outsider here. And they're all watching me as if they expect me to grow five heads or something. I feel out of place.

Napa is small and everyone notices a new face. At least back home in San Francisco, it's pretty damn easy to get lost in the crowd when you want to. "I've recently made some purchases here in the area."

"Is that so?" Her lips curl into a knowing smile and I frown, trying my best to figure out who the hell she is.

But I don't know. Not for lack of trying.

"It is. There are a few more that I'm interested in too. That's why I'm here. I'm hoping to find out some information."

She lifts an elegant dark blonde brow and my gaze is drawn to it. So she's a natural blonde? There's a rarity. "What sort of information?" she asks carefully.

"Well, I was hoping to run into someone from the Molina family." I've tried to contact many of them already, but they won't return my calls. "I know they still own a substantial amount of property and businesses in and around the area. And that they've slowly sold off a few pieces they felt didn't fit into their real estate portfolio over the years." I clamp my lips shut, afraid I might've revealed too much. What is it about this woman that makes me . . . forget?

Marina remains quiet for long, tension-heavy seconds. Pressing those sexy-as-hell lips together, she blows out a shuddery breath, her gaze narrowing. "So what you're saying is that you're a vulture."

Cocking my head, I frown. "What did you just call me?"

"You heard me. A *vulture.*" Her voice drips with contempt. She scrunches her mouth into a sexy pout, her eyes coldly assessing. "You swoop in when someone is vulnerable and desperate for money. Then you take everything from them."

I never said any such thing, though she's right. The Molina family is vulnerable and looking to sell off their assets, considering they're land rich and cash poor. "I wouldn't call myself a vul—"

"No need to explain yourself." She holds up a hand, stepping away from me. As if she needs the distance. The seductive smile, the sparkling interest in her pretty blue eyes, it's all gone. Doused like a flame under water. "I understand your type. It was nice meeting you."

My type? What the hell is she talking about? "Wait, Marina!" I call her name, but she's already walking away, not once bothering to look back as she exits the building and disappears completely.

Chapter 2

Gage

"Y ou dumbass, Marina Knight is a Molina." Archer smacks the back of my head like he used to do when we were teens, and I let out a wimpy yelp, twisting out of his reach belatedly. Back then, I was usually quick enough to duck and miss that hard-as-hell-smack.

Now I kind of deserved it.

"I only just realized that. And trust me, I feel like a dumbass." I rub the back of my tense neck. Last night while lying in bed, I'd finally connected the dots and figured out who Marina Knight was. The last name Knight should've been my first clue. I did a little Google research, which enlightened me. Talk about feeling like a complete idiot.

I need a vacation. I can't remember the last time I've been able to let go and just relax.

We're at the restaurant inside Archer's hotel, Hush, having lunch while I tell him what happened at last night's event. Archer was the one who'd given me the invite in the first place since he hadn't been able to attend. Too busy making kissy noises at my sister, I guess. I don't remember his excuse.

So I went in his place. Sounds like I really stepped in it too. Something I never, ever do. I'm careful to a fault.

"A little late with that, aren't you? Her mother is Maribella Molina."

"I know," I interrupt, but Archer can't be stopped.

"She married Scott Knight back in the late seventies and it was considered a monumental merger of two of the most influential, wealthy families in the area. The Molinas and Knights are like royalty in the Napa Valley." Archer pauses.

That I let the Knight reference slip by shows how distracted Marina made me. I'm always on my game. I can always appreciate a beautiful woman, but when it comes to work, I don't let them distract me.

So what gives? Why is Marina the exception?

Yeah, Scott Knight might run everything, but all the businesses are still under the Molina name. Still. I'm irritated that I was such a dumbass.

A waitress stops at our table, refilling our water glasses before she flashes a flirtatious smile at Archer. He barely looks at her, offers a cordial thank you before she hurries away.

All the women love him, and he only has eyes for Ivy; thank God. I'd have to kick his ass if I caught him flirting with some random chick.

"Listen, I know who she is. Thanks for the explanation." All information I already knew. Though I can use it to my advantage. For whatever reason, it's been impossible to get to Scott Knight. And my usual tactics haven't been working. I can definitely put Marina into my arsenal.

That is, if she'll ever speak to me again.

"Can't believe you had the nerve to talk about the Molinas in front of their *daughter*. You're a complete dickhead." Archer shakes his head, chuckling. "To be a fly on the wall . . ."

"Shut up." I sound vaguely whiny even to my own ears. I remember how she glared at me when I started talking about her family. *Holy shit.* So much disgust had filled her gaze. How she called me a vulture before fleeing, not once turning back to look at me despite my yelling her name. She'd hurried right out of that room as if the devil himself was chasing her.

Yeah. I really screwed that up.

"She's very close to her family," Archer goes on with a gleam in his eye. Like he's enjoying my misery by torturing me with more information. "I'm sure she's already run off to Daddy and told him everything."

"I don't need to feel any worse than I already do," I say, my voice low, as low as my mood. "And if that's the case, my chance at that strip of businesses in St. Helena is shot, huh."

"Yep, you're fucked," Archer agrees. A little too easily for my taste, but what can I say? I'm sure he's one hundred percent right.

I royally fucked this up.

Glancing around, I notice the restaurant is pretty empty. We're having a late lunch, and I should probably let Archer get back to work, but I'm frustrated with this entire situation.

"I don't get it. I don't know why I can't make this happen. It's like Scott Knight refuses to see me. I've tried to make an appointment with him multiple times. He never returns my calls." Or takes them either. If it was bad before, imagine how much he'll ignore me now after his daughter shreds my name and reputation?

"I'm surprised you didn't put two and two together, considering you've been hounding Scott Knight for weeks," Archer says, all nonchalant conversation-like.

My mind is spinning; I'm hoping like hell I can come up with a solution and smooth over this incredible blunder I've made.

I don't normally do this sort of thing—blunders. I'm efficient, conscientious, and, above all, careful. Archer is the screwup. This is why we've always balanced each other out so well. He pushes me and I rein him in.

"You're always on top of your game," Archer continues. "What happened last night?" He contemplates me; I can feel his eyes staring at me hard. "You got the hots for Marina Knight, don't you?"

"Fuck no," I say way too defensively, glaring at him in return. "She's an ice queen."

"If so, she's a beautiful one." Archer lowers his voice. "Don't tell your sister I said that. She'd chop my balls off."

"Like I'd tell her," I mutter. "She'd probably chop *my* balls off by association. Marina distracted me. I took one look at her and it was like my brain froze."

"Ha." Archer shakes his head. "She has a bit of a reputation for being . . . indifferent. And for whatever reason, every guy who encounters all that cool indifference seems to get caught in that magnetic spell Marina casts. I don't know what it is about her."

Great. So it was nothing special between us. She's some sort of mythical siren. "I screwed up. I wish I could start over, but it's too late now."

"You could go see her and apologize," Archer suggests.

"See her? Where?"

"She runs the organic bakery in St. Helena. You've heard of Autumn Harvest, right?"

Heard of it? That bakery is in the very block of stores I want to purchase. The Molinas had put it up for sale before, a few years ago, when the bottom fell out of the economy. They took it off the market before I could make an offer—not that I'd been in a position to make such an offer then. My money had been tied up in other properties and, just like everyone else in America, I'd been hit by the economic crash. Thank God I'd recuperated and am now doing better than ever. I'm a lucky bastard.

And, damn it, I want that property. The Molinas own four buildings on Main Street in St. Helena. Half of them need renovating, but they don't have the cash to invest in such major work. The lease was coming up on one of them. Another building sat empty. Revamping those locations would allow me to collect more rent money. And that money would make everything worth my while.

Though I can't make the purchase if I can't get Scott Knight to talk to me.

"So it's really an organic bakery?" I ask. Sounds like a contradiction. I associate bakeries with sweet, sugary goodness, not good-for-you food.

"Well, they say that to please the health-conscious masses. And they make some delicious all-natural artisan breads. It's the cakes that kick ass, though." Archer leans back, patting his stomach. "Ivy brought one home for my birthday. Best damn cake I ever ate."

"What kind? And does *she* bake them?" I found that hard to believe. She didn't seem like the sweet, domesticated type. Definitely doesn't look like a woman who likes to knead dough and frost cakes.

"She's not the baker, her aunt is. Marina manages the business."

Huh. Pulling my phone out of my jeans pocket, I bring up Autumn Harvest in St. Helena, clicking the "About Us" link. Impatiently I wait for the photos to load, sighing when I see the small pic of Marina Knight smiling at me.

This is where I recognize her from—the website. I'd looked

at it before when I was gathering information. Ammo. Whatever you want to call it.

"I knew I recognized her from somewhere," I say as I stare at the picture on my phone.

She looks pretty. Accessible. She's wearing a T-shirt that says AUTUMN HARVEST across the front. Her hair is pulled into a ponytail, her smile wide, cheeks a becoming, rosy pink, almost as pink as her sensuous lips.

I can't take my eyes off her.

"I think you've got it bad for freaking Marina Knight," Archer said, sounding infinitely amused, the jackoff. "This is hilarious. Are you sitting there mooning over her picture?"

Clicking my phone off, I shove it back in my pocket. "No," I mutter, glancing about the restaurant. The place is now packed, and it's a Wednesday, for Christ's sake. I need to change the subject and quick. "You must be making it hand over fist here."

"Business is good," he says modestly. "Brisk. This time of year is always better than others." He grins. "The autumn harvest is almost upon us, you know. The tourists come out in droves. Get it? Autumn. Harvest. You can't get away from her if you tried right now, bro."

Asshole. "You're real funny." I roll my eyes, but he's kind of speaking the truth.

I can't get away from Marina Knight. She's invaded my thoughts the last few days. The last few nights. I regret pissing her off. I regret not getting to spend more time with her.

I also regret that she sounds somewhat like a man-eater according to Archer, though she hadn't given me that vibe when I was with her. Alluring, yes. Seductive, most definitely.

Sighing, I run my hand through my hair, glancing out the window at the gorgeous view of the vibrant green and gold vineyards in the distance. I need to make a gesture. Get on Marina's good side.

But how?

Marina

The bouquet arrived out of nowhere, a gorgeous burst of color, a variety of wildflowers in a giant glass vase with a raffia bow tied around the middle. The delivery guy carried it into the store with both hands curled around the vase, his head hidden behind the blooms.

"What the heck is that?" My aunt Gina stops right next to me behind the counter, her gaze wide, jaw hanging open. Her forehead has a streak of flour across it and the apron she wears is smeared with chocolate.

"I don't know," I answer as the flowers are set rather unceremoniously on our counter, directly in front of me. "They're beautiful, though."

"And they're for a Marina Knight," the delivery guy announces, his tone bored as he chews his gum, contemplating me from around the flower arrangement. "Is that you?"

Curiosity fills me. "It is. Who are these from?"

He shrugs, not giving a crap. "I dunno. Check the card. See ya."

I watch him go, the glass door swinging closed behind him, the tinkling bell above the door announcing his departure. Aunt Gina nudges me in the ribs, her elbow extra pointy for some reason, and I grumble out an *ouch*.

"Check the envelope! I want to know who your new admirer is," she encourages eagerly.

"Hah, I have no admirers." And I like it that way. Men complicate everything. I need to focus on saving the family business, not worry if a guy thinks I'm pretty enough to ask out on a date.

Leaning forward, I breathe deep, inhaling the deliciously sweet floral scent. The flowers are so beautiful they almost don't look real. The arrangement appears haphazard, a casual gathering of gorgeous blooms, but as I look closer, I see that it's artfully arranged.

"They're lovely," Gina breathes, sniffing loudly. "And they smell divine. Even better than the chocolate cake baking in the oven."

She's right. I can't even smell the usual bakery scents anymore. All I can inhale is the fragrance of the flowers. Plucking through the arrangement, I run my finger first over a silky white petal, then a velvety purple one. I notice the pick nestled amongst the blooms holding a small, cream-colored envelope.

I tear it open and pull out the thick, square card, frowning at the sight of the unfamiliar, very bold script.

Marina—
I'm sorry. I hope you can forgive my rudeness the other
night. Perhaps we can start over?

Best,
Gage

Blowing out a harsh breath, I roll my eyes at no one. I'm freaking irritated he didn't sign his last name, believing he was that memorable.

And he had been.

A giddy, fizzy sensation washes over me, and I fight it down as best I can, but it's no use. I like that he did this. That he wanted to apologize by sending me flowers.

It meant he was thinking about me.

Taking a deep breath, I shake my head, focusing instead on why he had to make that apology in the first place. Talk about a grand gesture. The flowers had to have cost him an absolute fortune. Glancing at the back of the torn envelope, I see the name of the floral shop printed in tiny script in the upper left corner.

Oh yeah. I know they cost a fortune. Botanical is the premiere florist shop in the valley—and right down the street from the bakery.

"Who are they from?" Gina asks.

I glance up at her, sad I'm about to disappoint her. My mother's family has already written me off as a dried-up old maid, I know it. I'm freaking twenty-three, but every Molina woman, including my mother and my aunt, were married by the age of twenty-one.

The way they act, they may as well set me up on the shelf and forget all about me.

"A man I met a few nights ago," I start, glaring at her when she begins squealing excitedly. She shuts up quick. "It was nothing. We were at that new winery's open house—remember the one I told you about? We started talking, and then he made me angry, so I stormed off. The flowers are his way of apologizing."

"Some apology," Gina says dryly, her gaze still lingering on the bouquet. "Why did you get so mad at him?"

"He insulted our family."

I knew that would get her riled. She stiffens her spine, her expression gone indignant. "What? How? What an insufferable—"

"I overreacted. He didn't know who I was." I shrug, trying to act like he didn't bother me too badly, but he so did. If I think about it too much, I could get angry all over again.

Angry and some other emotion I'd rather not focus on at the moment . . .

"He didn't know who you were? Who is this imbecile?" My aunt is outraged on my behalf. Gotta love her. "Everyone knows the Molinas!"

"First of all, I'm a Knight—" I start.

"And a Molina," she adds.

"Right." I nod. Proud Italians are the worst, as in the most stubborn people of all the land. At least my family is. "And he's not from the area."

My entire family tends to forget there's a whole other world outside of their Napa Valley glass bubble. As a child, I found it very secure. As an adult, I view them as narrow-minded and self-important. Sometimes.

Didn't you act a little self-important with a certain someone a few nights ago?

I frown. Really didn't need that reminder.

"Where's he from?" she huffs.

"I don't know. He didn't tell me. But I knew he was a stranger. I've never seen him before." I'm lying. Yes, he's a stranger, as in not local. But I know where he's from. I can't tell Gina I did a background check on him, though. Then she'd ask why, and I'd have to tell her, and I'm sorry, I don't have time to answer questions right now.

I need to work. It's all I do lately. I definitely don't get out much; the event where I saw Gage had been a social-working thing, so that doesn't count.

Otherwise, I'm so busy I'm either here at the bakery, help-ing out my parents, or having long meetings at the bank trying to straighten out our financial mess with an advisor who's worked for my dad since before I was born.

Then I go home late at night and collapse into bed, only to start all over again the next morning.

Talk about living in a sheltered little bubble. I'm the complete embodiment of it.

"Well. He sounds horrid." Gina sniffs.

I hold back from rolling my eyes. My mother's younger sister loves to rush to judgment. It's one of her finer qualities, my mom always says. Her steadfast loyalty is always appreciated. And we work well together, despite her occasional moodiness and uneven temperament.

Of course, she could probably say the same about me, so . . .

"He wasn't that bad." Major understatement. No, Gage Emerson definitely isn't horrid. Handsome, yes. Sexy, indeed he is. Confident to the point of smug, oh yeah.

I've always found confidence in a man attractive. I blame my father. He embodies all of those traits in a most handsome package.

"Do you forgive him?"

Blinking, I turn to find Gina studying me, her gaze shrewd. "What did you say?" I ask.

"What with the flowers and the card he sent you, do you now forgive this man who insulted our family? And why would he go so far and apologize like this? How long did you two talk?" she asks.

"I don't know. Ten minutes?"

Her lips tighten to the point of almost completely disappearing from her face. How does she do that? "So a man you spoke to for ten minutes and treated you rudely sends you flowers that probably cost hundreds of dollars? I smell a rat."

"You always do," I tease her, trying to lighten the moment, but she won't have it.

Shaking her head, she rounds the counter and stands on the other side, sticking her face into the bouquet and breathing deep. "This is by far the most beautiful arrangement I've ever seen. And I've seen a lot." That was the truth, considering Gina used to create beautiful cakes for wedding receptions. We gave that up when I took over. I'd streamlined the business completely, something my aunt was very grateful for. She'd been working herself to the bone.

Now I guess it's my turn.

"He's just trying to impress me with his money," I joke, making her smile. "Probably hoping I'll fall to my knees and praise him for his lavish gifts."

"Now that sounds like an interesting scenario," a man's voice says from behind her.

Gasping at the sound of the faintly familiar, velvety deep voice, I glance up to find Gage Emerson himself standing in the middle of the bakery, looking disgustingly gorgeous, clad in another one of those perfect suits he owns. The man dresses to perfection. And why didn't I hear the bell ring over the door? "Oh my God," I whisper, absolutely mortified. His suggestive tone said he found my words . . . titillating. Great.

And while we're standing in the presence of my very overprotective and slightly angry aunt.

"I take it this is the rat?" she asks, making me groan inwardly.

"At your service, ma'am." Gage goes to her, his hand outstretched. Gina eyes it warily, as if it was a snake that might strike her at any moment. "Gage Emerson, aka The Rat."

She laughs and takes his hand, charmed. Just like that. It

might not last, knowing my aunt, but come on . . . everyone seems to fall for him.

Why does her positive reaction rub me the wrong way? Why does *Gage* rub me the wrong way?

If I'm being honest with myself, I could get on board with him rubbing me the right way. And I don't normally fall for smug assholes. I'm attracted to confident men, but there's something about Gage I don't like. His arrogance is over the top. He seems like he'd be bad for me. And I've never had a bad-boy fetish.

Not that he's a bad boy, per se. But he's definitely trouble. Trouble I don't want.

Yeah, you do.

I'm arguing with my own self inside my head. Clearly, I've lost my mind. I don't get it. I don't get my reaction to him.

Correction. I don't want to react to him, and I can't seem to help myself.

Chapter 3

Gage

The two women eye me carefully, the older woman—who I assume is Marina's aunt—relaxing somewhat.

At least someone has a sense of humor around here. You could cut the tension in this cute little European-style bakery with a cake knife.

"How are you, Marina?" I walk toward the counter, noting how she grips the edge so tight she's white-knuckling it. Do I make her that angry? Or maybe . . . that nervous?

I know she makes me nervous. She's all I think about, which can't be healthy.

For once, I really don't give a damn.

"Good." She lifts her chin, her expression neutral. Only her eyes give her away, a hint of nervousness fluttering in their depths. This woman standing before me is completely different from the one I first met a few nights ago. This version looks younger, sweeter. More like the woman in the photo on the Autumn Harvest website. Not quite as poised as the elegant siren luring me in with her dangerous smile and sweet voice. "I'm surprised to see you here."

"My conscience wouldn't let me stay away. I had to seek you out and apologize for how I offended you." I gesture toward the flowers that cost me a shit-ton of money. Cost doesn't matter, though, since I believe she's worth it. Getting me an in with her father, her entire family?

Even more worth it. Plus, I can eventually write off the expense.

Christ, you're a jackass.

I can't even admit to myself that I really wanted to buy her those flowers. That the bright, colorful arrangement made me think of her. Hiding behind it in the hopes of getting an in with her father is only part of the reason I'm here.

Marina Knight. She's the true reason I'm standing here worried I'm going to make a complete ass of myself.

"How did you find me?" she asks warily.

Now she probably thinks I'm a stalker. I can't give away my source. Yet. Archer's the guy I want to hook her with eventually. If I can't charm her, I need to find another way to make her see me again. "I figured out who you were and put it all together."

"Hmmm." That's her reply. She sounds like she doesn't believe me.

Great. I wouldn't believe me either.

"Do you like the flowers?" I ask when she still doesn't say anything else.

"They're beautiful," she admits grudgingly, making me smile. She doesn't return it, screws her lush mouth into a little scowl instead. "Thank you," she mumbles.

"So." I offer her my best, most humble smile in return. "Am I forgiven?"

"You think it's that easy, Rat Boy? That you can just waltz in here and have yourself declared forgiven all because you threw your credit card at the most expensive flower shop on this street and bought the biggest arrangement they've got?" Her aunt snorts and shakes her head. "I don't think so, young man."

Raising my brows, my gaze meets Marina's. Guess the aunt has no problem letting her opinion be known. "It was an honest mistake," I say. "And, well, you sort of jumped to conclusions, you have to admit."

Marina's expression hardens in an instant. Jesus, what is with me constantly saying the wrong thing to this woman? I'm usually a smooth-talking motherfucker—direct quote from Archer—and if anyone is an expert at that subject, it's him. I put women at ease, I make them laugh, and if I'm lucky—on certain, especially rare occasions, at least lately—I get them to agree to come home with me.

"You're two seconds from getting kicked out of here," she whispers fiercely, her eyes shooting fire. Aimed right at me.

"Sorry! Shit." I throw my hands up in front of me defensively, her aunt's mutterings of "stupid Rat Boy" coming from somewhere behind not going unnoticed. "I just . . . I'm sorry."

Marina crosses her arms in front of her chest, the movement plumping up her breasts, drawing my attention. I can't help it, I'm a guy and she has nice ones. She's wearing a black T-shirt with AUTUMN HARVEST written across the front in elegant gold script, her long blonde hair pulled into a high ponytail, minimal if any makeup. She looks tired. There are dark smudges under her eyes and her mouth is tight. "Go on," she prompts.

Hell. I have to say more? Breaking out in a light sweat, I forge on. "I was rude. And I didn't mean to offend you. I had no idea who you were—"

The aunt makes a *harrumph* noise, but I ignore her.

"—and my friend had to point out who exactly you were

a few days later." Stuffing my hands in my front pockets, I shuffle my feet, feeling all of about ten years old and having to confess everything I'd done wrong to my dad. Waiting for the inevitable punishment that was sure to come.

"Who's your friend?" she asks, her voice curious.

What? No "you're forgiven," or "thanks for the apology"? I'm boggled. And I may as well reveal my secret source. I have the distinct feeling she's ready to tell me to get the hell out.

"Uh . . . Archer Bancroft."

Her arms drop to her sides, curiosity written all over her pretty face. "I know Archer. Vaguely. He owns the Hush and Crave hotels, right?"

Slowly I nod, wondering at the sudden gleam in her eyes.

"So how do *you* know him?" she asks.

"Where you going with this, girly?" her aunt pipes up.

"Gina. Don't you have a cake to check on?" Marina asks pointedly.

"Crap! I do. Oh my God, I hope it's not burning. I'll be back." Aunt Gina gives me the evil eye as she passes and pushes through the door I can only assume leads to the kitchen, disappearing in an instant.

"Sorry about that," Marina says, taking a deep breath and exhaling loudly. "So do you mind telling me? How you know Archer Bancroft?"

Hmm. Someone wants something. I can see it in the way she's looking at me. Like her question shouldn't matter but it definitely does. I wonder what she wants from Archer? "We go way back," I drawl. This could be fun, making her work for it.

"Really? So are you two close?"

Best friends since high school, but like I'm going to give her that info. Yet. "Close enough," I say, purposefully vague.

"Hmm. You know, I had this idea I wanted to propose to him, and I keep forgetting to give him a call, I've been so busy. Maybe you can help me with that," she says hopefully, her eyes wide, her expression open.

Is she serious? I can't tell. But I haven't even earned her full forgiveness yet. "I can help you with whatever you want."

Her gaze narrows. "You say things like that, and it sounds sexual."

Guess this attraction between us isn't all one-sided. Good news. Just looking at her and I want to touch her. Run my fingers through her hair. Drop a soft kiss to her very kissable mouth. She might punch me if I try, though. Can't push her too hard. "I guess I can't help but think of sex when I'm near you."

Her mouth drops open. "Are you serious?"

Shit. Yep, there I went, pushing too hard like I can't help myself. I need to change the subject quick. Most women who flirt with me have no problem talking about sex. This one acts like I just asked her to commit a crime. "So, what sort of idea were you thinking?"

Her expression instantly goes blank. "Like I'm going to tell you anything. I don't even know you."

Fine. She wants to play that way? I can play right back. "You want my help talking to Archer?"

She nods so subtly I can almost believe she didn't do it. Almost.

"I need your forgiveness."

"You're forgiven," she says automatically.

Meh. That was quick. And it really didn't count since I know she didn't mean it, but I'll let it slide. "You can't make me feel guilty about this anymore. What's done is done."

"Fine. Great. Works for me." She releases another shaky

breath. I think I make her uncomfortable. Perfect, because she makes me incredibly uncomfortable.

As in the *I want her so much I feel like I'm going to lose it if I don't touch her in the next five minutes* kind of uncomfortable.

"I'll need one more thing from you before I can make this happen," I say quietly, trying to amp the anticipation. I'm dying to see her reaction when I tell her.

Marina rolls her eyes, sexy despite her irritation with me. Since when have I ever been excited by a woman's irritation? I'm a sick bastard.

"Oh, come on. What more could you want?" She sounds completely put out. And clueless.

Well. I'm about to rock her world with one single word.

"You."

Marina

Listen, I'm not some whore you can buy and sell," I say, immediately regretting my words. I sound completely over the top.

The look on his face shows he knows it. "That wasn't what I was implying," he says carefully. "I just . . . like you. I was hoping maybe we could see each other sometime."

The man is insane. Gorgeous and confident and with a surprisingly good sense of humor, considering how deftly he handled crazy Gina, but he's also a complete pain in my ass.

He has something I want though and I can't believe I forgot. Connections: one I somehow missed, so shame on me. And that connection is Archer Bancroft: a transplant, not necessarily considered a local, but definitely a man who's moved into the area within the last five years and done positive things to regenerate the economy. His hotel business is thriving; he's provided lots of jobs and plenty of sales revenue. He's solid, and his reputation is relatively golden, helped considerably since he settled down into a serious relationship. This community is small enough that everyone knows each other's business, and Archer's not shy about making a public statement.

He is definitely someone I want to do business with. I've had these new ideas bouncing around inside my brain, and I think he's the perfect candidate for one of them. Well, his hotel is the perfect candidate. If I could get my aunt's desserts into his restaurants, the extra exposure and revenue might help save the bakery.

And I exaggerated. I don't *know* Archer. I know *of* him. I've met him a few times. We always exchange polite hellos when we see each other at social events, but that's not very often considering I'm always working and rarely out. I just don't have time.

That's the extent of my so-called friendship with him. Whereas Gage really knows him. And even though I don't trust him and know he wants to buy up my family's property— including the bakery—I may as well use him while I can, right?

So, yeah. I want him to get me an appointment so I can propose my idea to Archer.

Not with these sort of stipulations put on me, though. Saying he wants me? That has cheap sexual thrill written all over it.

Sighing, I finally shake my head. "Of course. I know. It's just . . . it's been a long day. And then you send me the gorgeous flowers, and my Aunt Gina flipped out."

"She's quite the character," he inserts politely.

"You're too kind." Smiling wryly, I continue on. "Then you show up begging for forgiveness and . . . you distracted me."

"And that's a bad thing?"

"When a girl needs to focus on working, her business, and nothing else—yes. It's a very bad thing." Deciding to hell with it, I move away from behind the counter and head toward the front door, flipping the sign from OPEN to CLOSED.

"Closing up?" he asks. He sounds incredulous.

"There are no customers in here besides you." And it's near enough to our actual closing time that it won't make any difference.

"So are you going to answer me?" he asks, watching me move around the tiny bakery. His big body seems to eat up all the space, filling the air until all I can breathe and see is him. I do my best to avoid him, straightening chairs, picking up miscellaneous straw wrappers and crumpled napkins that still litter the tables. I'm trying to avoid answering him. Too full of nervous, restless energy he can no doubt pick up on.

What more could you want?

You.

I mean, really. Who says that sort of thing? I feel like I'm in some bad, cheesy made-for-TV movie or something.

"What sort of answer are you looking for? You never really asked me a question," I finally say, glancing out the corner of my eye to see him approaching.

"I did so." He stops mere feet away from me. I can feel his body warmth reaching toward me and I'm tempted to lean in. Absorb all of that strength and warmth and gorgeousness. Though he looks utterly untouchable in the finely tailored suit that I can tell cost a fortune. "I asked if you wanted my help in getting you a chance to talk to Archer."

"Of course I do," I say, my voice quiet, my thoughts a confused jumble in my brain. What is going on here? Why am I even talking to him? Why do I want to be close to him? It makes no sense.

I can't stand him.

Really. I can't. I don't care how good he looks in that suit or how his sexy hair probably needs a trim. How bad I want to run my fingers through it. Or maybe grab his tie and yank him closer, see what he might do if I reared up on tiptoe and kissed him . . .

"Then go out to dinner with me," he suggests, his voice bold, his expression arrogant. The glint in his eyes, the curl of his lips . . . he's too damn confident. Like he knows I won't be able to resist him.

Irritating, because I'm this close to giving in and saying yes.

I slump my shoulders. Seconds ago I was imagining violently kissing him, and now I'm considering some other sort of violence toward him—like bodily harm. He infuriates me, yet he interests me. Usually if I'm interested in a guy, it's because I like him. I don't want to smack him upside the head.

"You're going to force me to go out to dinner with you and in return you'll help me arrange an appointment with Archer Bancroft?" I laugh, though I find no humor in his suggestion. I might find it . . . arousing. Which is wrong on so many levels I lose count.

"I'm not forcing you to do anything, Marina," he says softly, his eyes glowing as they drink me in. "Unless . . . you like it that way."

Well, holy shit. The man needs duct tape wound around

his mouth about twenty times. He says the worst things *ever*. "Did you really just say that?" I ask, my voice sounding deadly even to my own ears.

He seems to snap himself out of a trance. Standing straighter, he blinks, runs a hand along his jaw. God, his hands are big. I wonder what they might feel like on me. Sliding over my arms, my legs, between my thighs—

Get over it!

"Did I really just say what?" He looks dazed. The tension crackling between us has suddenly become unbearable and I have no idea why.

Um, maybe because you're attracted to him?

I push the pointless thought out of my head.

"Is it just me you say idiotic, sexist, disgusting things to, or do you talk this way to all the women you encounter?" I cross my arms in front of my chest again, noting—again—that his eyes drop right to my breasts. Men. They're all the same. And this one is so blatant, so cocky, and with such a rude mouth. He's downright offensive.

Yet my skin is buzzing just being in his presence. My blood is warm, my body both loose and anxious all at once. I only ever feel this way right before I'm going to have sex and I'm all amped up. Excited and nervous.

And I am never—*ever*—having sex with Gage Emerson. Oh hell, no.

A little groan escapes him and he closes his eyes for the briefest moment, gripping the back of the chair directly in front of him. Damn, his eyelashes are thick. Of course. Everything about him is the epitome of male beauty.

He cracks his eyes open. "Did I really say that out loud?"

"Yep," I confirm, enjoying his absolute misery.

"I was thinking it," he admits, looking sheepish. Cutely sheepish. "That probably makes me a pig just the same, right?"

"Right." I nod, letting my arms drop by my sides. "I won't whore myself out on a date with you just to get a chance to talk to Archer. I can do that on my own."

A dark brow rises in challenge. "You really think so? Think about it. I'm offering you an easy in. He might throw up roadblocks, you know."

Knowing Gage, he'd probably ask Archer to throw up those roadblocks just so I'd go out with him. Jerk. "Oh my God. Are you implying I can't see Archer without you? Do you really need to be such an arrogant ass?" I toss back, immediately wishing I could clap my hand over my mouth. This man makes me say things I regret every single time.

"You're right." His vivid green eyes dim. "I'm an arrogant ass and I'm sorry. Forgive me again by coming with me on this date? I'll make it up to you."

I'll make it up to you.

There is a hint of sexual promise in his request, in that one specific sentence. I'm drawn to all that heady temptation, despite wanting to also knee him in the balls and tell him to go to hell. God, I hate rich dudes who think everyone owes them something. They are the absolute worst because usually, in the end, they always get what they want.

I've dealt with plenty in my lifetime. My family is both populated with and surrounded by wealthy, powerful men. We move in the same social circles. I went to high school and college with plenty of those who were going on to be successful, wealthy men—and women too, of course.

Except for me. My family is still drowning in a sea of debt, and it's only a matter of time until they decide to close the bakery once and for all. I think they believe it's a fun little project for my Aunt Gina and me. Like we're pretending to be business owners.

None of them understand how much this bakery means to Gina. Or me. I've only been running it for a year, but I've worked here off and on since I was a teen. It became my after-school job, my summer job . . . I met my first boyfriend here. Had my first kiss out in front of it, too.

Autumn Harvest has tremendous sentimental value to me. I also think it has tremendous potential, if only I could find the extra funds to make it really shine. Not that anyone cares.

"What do you say?" Gage's delicious rumble of a voice draws me from my thoughts and I blink up at him, still caught in hazy longing for the past. I make bad decisions when I'm feeling like this. All based on what my heart says versus my head.

My heart is almost always, always wrong.

"Say about what?" I ask, wanting to hear him ask me out on the dinner date again. I need to stall. I need to rationalize with my overexcited thoughts how going out with this guy is a huge mistake. My change of heart in regard to Gage is confusing even to me.

He smiles, the sight of it sending a flurry of butterflies fluttering in my stomach, and I stand up straighter. Determined not to act like a silly, simpering female.

I want to, though. Just looking at him, listening to him talk, sets me on edge. In a deliciously scary way.

For whatever strange reason, I'm fairly positive Gage Emerson has set his sights on me. And I think I kind of like it.

His smile grows. God, he's pretty. "Go out with me. Come

on, Marina. It'll just be a simple dinner, and in return you can have thirty minutes of Archer's time, or however long you need, to tell him all about this mysterious proposition."

"And what do you get out of this arrangement?" I ask warily.

"Why, the pleasure of your company, of course," he says smoothly. Effortlessly.

Men who speak too effortlessly tend to scare the crap out of me. Usually means they're hiding something. My one long-term boyfriend in college was like this. Very charming . . . and eventually, he became toxic to my mental state. He was a liar and a manipulator. I don't need another one like that in my life.

So what is it about this guy that I'm drawn to? Because I am. I can't deny it.

I study Gage for a long moment, letting the anticipation roll through my veins. Saying yes would be tremendously easy. So would saying no. In fact, refusing him would be even easier. Then I'd never have to worry about Archer Bancroft or the good idea I want to bring to him. I wouldn't have to put on a phony show for Gage while going out on this date with him. Being something that I'm not; I do that constantly.

"Take a chance," Gage murmurs, his decadent tone reaching right into me, shaking me up. "Say yes, Marina. You know you want to."

"Hmm. Funny thing is, I don't want to." I try to sound irritated and instead it comes out breathless. What is wrong with me?

His expression goes from confident to crestfallen, like I flipped a switch. "You hate me that much?"

"*Hate* is a pretty strong word, so let's just say I'm not your biggest fan."

"So you won't go to dinner with me."

I slowly shake my head, disappointment filling me, and I push it aside. I'm doing the right thing. I need to remember that. "You'll probably try to pull some funny business, and I'm a little behind on my self-defense classes."

"Funny business?" His lips twitch, despite his sadness just a second ago over my rejection. "You sound like your aunt."

"You're right. I do," I agree. "Going out to dinner with you would be a mistake, Gage. We both know this."

"We do?" He sounds surprised.

"*I* do. And I can't afford to make any more mistakes in my life. I'd rather date no one than fall for some gorgeous guy who's out to manipulate me. Right?" I offer him a tentative smile, but he doesn't return it. I can't blame him. I just called him a mistake. We've insulted each other, lobbing them back and forth like a tennis ball for the last ten or fifteen minutes. Imagine an entire evening just the two of us? Tearing each other apart with our words. Maybe tearing off each other's clothes with anxious, eager hands . . .

Swallowing hard, I usher him out of the bakery with a few choice words and a firm push on his shoulders so he goes through the door. I slam it shut behind him, turning the lock with a forcible jerk. The loud click rings out—I know he heard it—and he glances over his shoulder at me one last lingering moment before he heads off into the sunset. As in for real, he walks toward the sunset, no doubt in search of his car.

Walking back toward the kitchen, my entire body begins to relax. I'm thankful to be out of Gage's presence. It's too overwhelming, just flat-out too much. He makes me think things, say things I don't normally ever think or say. I'm a nice person. I don't reject people or call them names. And I called him a disgusting pig. Talk about harsh.

What the heck is wrong with me?

Gage Emerson is what's wrong with you.

I barely hold back the snort of laughter. God, ain't that the truth?

Chapter 4

Marina

My eyes burn as I flip through the stack of bills yet again, pulling one out in particular that I've been avoiding for a while. I order flowers from a local florist—not the one Gage used because I *so* can't afford that place. Gina and I use them to decorate around the café where we can, knowing they add a nice touch. The customers appreciate them, as do Gina and I.

The flower order has gotten smaller and smaller over the last year. I'd started choosing the cheapest flowers they had, too. And now it's finally time for me to bite the bullet and cancel the order outright. I hate having to do it but we can't afford the expense. I'm trying my best to cut corners where I can.

And this is the next corner being cut.

Deciding I can piece out the bouquet Gage sent me and use the large variety of flowers for decoration over the next week or two if I stretch it right, I slap the bill on my newly made "call tomorrow" pile and sigh wearily.

Sometimes it feels like we're spinning our wheels. I'm doing everything I can to make this bakery work, but competition is stiff. There are popular bakeries and cafés all over the valley. The locals and the tourists love to get their eat and drink on so we're all battling against each other, trying to fulfill that need.

No one—and I mean no one—can make a cake like my aunt, but not enough people are discovering them or discovering our bakery. I got her out of the ruthless catering circle despite the loss of decent revenue. I had to do it. Baking and decorating elaborate wedding cakes every weekend was both exhausting her and killing her creativity. She does her best work when she can let the wild ideas fly.

Lately she's made some true masterpieces. They taste so delicious, and look so beautiful, it's almost a crime to carve into them. I have about a bazillion photos on my phone of her cakes, like I'm a proud mama dying to show them off. I need to create some sort of brochure featuring them all.

Another sigh leaves me, and I'm feeling stuck. We don't have enough money in our current advertising budget to do much beyond the chalk easel I set outside the front door every morning announcing our daily specials. We do a lunch special featuring sandwiches with our artisan breads and homemade soup that Gina also makes, so we get a terrific lunch crowd. Our morning crowd is okay too, but we're no Starbucks.

Grr. Just thinking of giant conglomerates makes me frustrated. Small towns gripe all the time about Walmart coming in and destroying local businesses. I'm starting to believe them one hundred percent. Walmart, Starbucks, they're all soul-sucking destroyers of the local business economy.

Yet I frequent our local Walmart at least once a month. Don't do Starbucks anymore, though. Why would I, considering I have an espresso machine here in the bakery and I know how to use it? Besides, I can't hand them four dollars plus for a coffee when my place is barely making it.

Propping my elbow on the edge of my desk, I rub my forehead, feeling the unmistakable tension there. I always get headaches when I pour over the bills. Who wouldn't, the task is so depressing. I press my fingertips into my skin in a circling motion, trying to ease the stress, but it's no use. The only thing that could cure my stress is a bottle of wine and a soak in my tub.

I remember my earlier encounter with Gage and glance over at the flowers sitting on top of the filing cabinet. I brought them in with me earlier when I knew I'd get stuck back here going over our bank account and the invoices due. If I'm going to do the drudgework then I need to make the spot pretty, right?

Plus, just looking at them makes me think of him. The things he said—both the good and the bad. And he says terrible things. It's like he doesn't even think. He's a successful businessman worth *billions*. Some of that is family money, but the guy is smart. Right? So how can he conduct business when every time he opens his mouth he says something crazy?

I can almost forget about the terrible things he's said when I think about how freaking gorgeous he is. How those beautiful green eyes seem to see right through me. Just one glance in my direction and he sets my skin on fire. Leaving me so hot I feel almost fevered every single time he looks at me.

And that his touch is my only relief . . .

Closing my eyes briefly, I stifle the moan that wants to escape and sit up straight, shuffling the stacks of bills into their own haphazard organized piles that only I understand. I drop them all into my desk drawer and shut it with a satisfying thud, then wipe my hands. Like I'm all efficient and totally handled yet another stressful workday, going over bills and taking care of business.

I so didn't handle it. I barely made a dent in our past-due

situation. Yet another fun night trying to manage everything at the bakery, while it all falls down around me no matter what I try to do.

I push away from my desk and stand, then grab my sweater and purse hanging from the little coatrack I keep in the corner of the room. Hitting the light switch as I exit my office, I walk through the kitchen, smiling when I see everything shiny, bright, and clean. My aunt prides herself on keeping an immaculate kitchen and scrubs until it's spotless every single evening before she leaves.

Walking through the swinging door that opens onto the front of the café, I turn off the switch next to the doorframe, so the only thing left lit is the glass case that houses the cakes, cookies, bars, and all the other delicious stuff Gina bakes, though it stands empty now. Gina will be back at it tomorrow, arriving before the sun rises so she can make all of her delicious goodness ready for the morning crowd.

She can make a chocolate croissant that would have your eyes rolling into the back of your head it's so good. I'd put in a special request for them tomorrow just before she left. She said she'd make a double batch just for me.

Working at the bakery is going to kill my figure and make my butt big if I don't watch it. A girl can hold out for only so long.

I push in the rest of the chairs, the task forgotten after I rejected Gage and basically kicked him out of the café. Everything else in the area is clean. Perfect and ready for tomorrow—so why am I lingering? Shouldn't I want out of this place since I'm going to be right back and at it with gusto by seven o'clock tomorrow morning?

Where else do you have to go? Not like you have anyone to go to besides your parents, and they sure as heck don't count.

That is the most depressing thought ever. I feel like I've been listening to all the women in my family crying over how I'm a spinster at twenty-freaking-three and it's starting to take hold. If I think about it too much, I believe it. I'm a total screwup.

Blowing out a harsh breath, I hang my head back, staring at the ceiling. Since when did I turn into such a world-class failure?

I hear a faint knocking on the front door, causing the bell hanging above it to tinkle and I startle, looking straight through the glass and right at . . .

Gage Emerson? Standing on the doorstep?

I frown at him, wondering if I've become delusional. I'm hallucinating. No way is he really standing there . . . is he?

Shaking my head, I blink my eyes shut, counting to ten before popping them open again. He's still standing there, though now he's clearly impatient with me, if the glower on his face says anything. His hands are resting on his hips, pushing back his unbuttoned, elegantly cut navy jacket and showing off that broad chest of his, his tie loose around his neck, his shirt wrinkled. He's rumpled and looks absolutely delicious.

Oh God. I need to get rid of him, and quick.

Gage

Marina is looking at me in utter disbelief. Like she can't believe I've somehow magically appeared in front of her. She even closed her eyes for a few seconds. Does she think I might be a figment of her imagination or something?

I don't know. There's an entire building separating us and I want in. She didn't conjure me up.

Nope. I'm real. As in I'm the idiot who's drawn to her despite her obvious hate—or at the very least, disinterest in me. I must be a glutton for punishment because here I am, standing in front of her door in the hopes that just maybe she'll still be inside the bakery. Despite the fact it's past nine o'clock and she shut the place down at five.

Then unceremoniously kicked me out.

Luck's on my side tonight, I guess, finding her here.

Honestly, I don't know what possessed me. I left Autumn Harvest and went back to the house, hoping to get in a few phone calls. Hell, I even tried to call her father, but he wasn't in. Not that he's ever in for me.

I think the guy is on to me. I haven't been sneaky about my approach, so I wouldn't be surprised if he knew all about my sniffing around his property.

But the thrill of the hunt couldn't hold its allure today. I got depressed. And I never get depressed. I've been rejected twice within an hour. First by Marina, then by her father. It's a multigenerational-rejection type of day.

Deciding the house was too quiet and I didn't want to be alone, I left. Wandered down the cute little Main Street in St. Helena, purposely avoiding the bakery. I ended up at a bar and grill, where I ate dinner and consoled myself with a few beers. Watched the baseball playoffs on the flat-screen TV over the bar. Giants were in the lead and eventually ended up winning the game.

The Giants are my favorite team. Hell, my friend Matt used to play for them, so of course I love them. But I couldn't work up even a trickle of enthusiasm for their win. All I could think about was . . . her.

She's consuming my thoughts. I never let a woman do that to me, and I can't believe how fast my attraction for her has grown. I like everything about her, even how much she seems to hate me.

How driven she is, how protective she is of her family. I understand that side of her and I'm drawn to it, too. That she acts like she's attracted to me despite herself is intriguing too. Most women practically beg for my attention, drawn by my bank account more than anything else.

Not Marina. She'd rather I never darken her doorway again. And she'd most definitely benefit from my bank account. Yet she views my wealth with contempt.

I admire her for that. Hell, I want her more because of it. I feel like she sees me, the real man behind all the bullshit. Flaws and all, and despite that, the attraction is still there between us. Like a living, breathing thing. Does she see it?

If she does, she's pretending it doesn't exist.

A shiver moves through me as Marina slowly approaches the door, her expression wary, those pretty blue eyes narrowed as she studies me. I'm this close to leaving, but something keeps me there. I think I want to see what she might say to me. See if she's going to let me in.

I'm freaking desperate for her to let me in.

My problem? Too many beers made me think too much, and now here I am, basking in the bakery's autumnal finery. Late September and there are already a few pumpkins decorating the front. Two large planters flank either side of the door, filled to the brim with giant, rusty, orange-colored mums.

AUTUMN HARVEST is written in elegant black script across the door. The front window is large, allowing passersby a glimpse inside. Tiny tables and chairs fill the room. Large wicker baskets full of fresh fruit and wrapped baked goods line the walls. The bakery has a very warm, trendy Napa feel to it.

Yet she's having trouble with the business. I don't understand why.

Yeah. I really don't know what possessed me to come back here. I mulled over the reasons why Marina sent me packing for hours. I freaking still can't believe she told me no when I asked her to dinner. That she literally pushed me out of the bakery like she never wanted to see me again. I dangled the Archer carrot and she didn't give a shit.

She didn't think I was worth it.

No one tells me no. Well, I take that back. I've heard no plenty in my career. No is a part of negotiations. In fact, when I hear a no it makes me work that much harder to turn it into a yes.

But when it comes to women? They don't tell me no. I'm the one who usually turns them away. The one who has to break it off first. I'm not used to rejection.

Maybe that's why I'm drawn to her. She's the complete opposite of any woman I've ever met.

"What are you doing here?" she asks, barely cracking open the door. Like she might be afraid I'll push past her and force my way inside.

She wouldn't be too far off base. The idea does cross my mind.

"I don't know," I answer honestly, stuffing my hands in my pockets.

She studies me for a long, quiet moment and I stare back. She looks . . . weary. A little sad, a lot irritated. "I usually never stay this late," she admits. "Are you stalking me or what?"

"No, I'm not stalking you." I chuckle, shaking my head.

A cool breeze washes over me, making me shiver, and I nod toward her. "Can you let me in?"

"I was just locking up for the night." She moves to close the door, and for a brief, terrifying moment, I'm afraid she's going to slam it completely and shut me out.

For good.

"Just a few minutes. I want . . . to ask you something." I made that up. I have nothing to ask her beyond *why do you hate me so much*, which has been running through my brain for the last five hours or so.

"Can't this wait until tomorrow?"

Jesus. I have never, ever met a woman so disinterested in me before. I hate it.

I'm more determined than ever to turn her no into a yes.

"No, it can't." I try to turn on the charm and flash her a smile, but even I can feel how halfhearted my effort is. "Come on, Marina. Throw me a bone here."

Rolling her eyes, she pulls the door open and I enter the quiet, dark bakery, brushing past her as I walk inside. I hear her sharp intake of breath when my body touches hers.

Just like that, I'm aware of her. Of every little sound she makes, the intoxicating scent of her, how she looks at me like she's ready to run and hide.

I make her nervous. Fuck, she makes me nervous. I shouldn't want this. Want her. She hates me. I don't like her much either. At least I don't like her attitude toward me or the way she treats me.

"What did you want to ask me, Gage?" She locks the door and leans against it, her tone bored, as is her expression. "It's late so make it snappy. I need to go home and collapse into bed."

Make it fucking *snappy*? I can't even acknowledge that or

I'm gonna lose my shit and say something I really regret. And the bed reference sends all sorts of dirty images into my brain.

The fact that she's able to both turn me on and piss me off is quite the feat. She deserves a medal or something.

"Why won't you go to dinner with me?" I blurt, instantly hating myself for letting the question fly out of my mouth. I don't think I want to know her answer. I don't think she appreciates me asking when I sound like a whiny little baby either.

"You want the truth."

I nod furiously. "Hell yeah, I do."

"You're trouble." She says nothing else, just regards me with those cold, assessing blue eyes.

"I think you have me mistaken with Archer." No one has ever called me specifically trouble. Archer, yes, all the damn time. Me, Archer, and Matt together? Oh, hell yeah. We caused all sorts of trouble together, especially in our younger years.

But me, all alone? I'm not trouble. Not really. I'm a pretty responsible guy. My dad instilled it in me to take care of everything that matters. In business and in pleasure. When I see something I want, I go after it until I make it mine.

Is that what you're doing right now?

I push the scary-as-fuck thought right out of my head.

"I already told you I don't know Archer that well. I do know he has a reputation," she starts.

I interrupt her. "Well earned, let me tell you. He's an absolute dog."

"Hmm. Well, from what I've heard, he's settled down now that he has a fiancé."

My sister, but I don't bother telling her that. I have to keep some of my secrets. I might want to use them someday. And I can't keep up this pretense that Archer's a total dog because he's not. Everything Marina says is true. "Listen, I swear I'm not trouble. Trust me."

She laughs. "Any guy who says 'I swear' and 'trust me' is one hundred percent trouble."

I'm starting to get offended. More than anything, I'm fucking tired of dealing with her. Yet here I stand, still dealing with her. *Wanting* to fucking deal with her. And wanting to prove her wrong too. "You don't know me."

"I know your kind. You think you can get what you want and when you don't, you turn it into a challenge," she tosses at me.

Well, hell. She's pretty dead-on with that one.

"And I think for whatever sick and twisted reason, I've become a challenge to you," she continues, her eyes blazing with newfound anger. "I'm not some game to play and eventually win, Gage. I've already told you I'm not interested in you or your offer. What else do you want from me?"

I move toward her, grabbing her hand and pulling her to me. She presses her other hand on my chest. Her eyes have gone wide as she stares up at me in shock. "I want a chance."

"If you're circling back to the dinner date thing, no. I think it's a bad idea." She takes a deep breath. "I think the two of us together is a bad idea. You don't like me. I don't like you. There's no point to this. We should walk away from each other right now."

Now that sounds dramatic. "I never said I didn't like you." I might've thought it because, hell, the woman loves to throw up roadblocks. I thread my fingers through hers, pulling her into me. Her hand is small, soft, and warm. I like the way it feels in my grip.

"We don't even know each other." Her lower lip trembles as she stares up at me. "You make me nervous, I hope you know."

"Guess what? You do the same thing to me."

She stares at me incredulously. "Really?"

I nod and don't say another word. Something about this woman makes me want to be honest with her. Lay it all on the line.

Whether it's good or bad. Whether I want to know her response or not, I need to hear it. For once in my life, I want to leave myself vulnerable when it comes to a woman. But only for this woman. She has me so twisted up in knots I don't know if I'll ever be able to unravel them.

I don't know if I want to either.

Chapter 5

Marina

Wait . . . did Gage just say I made him nervous? Really? I find that hard to believe.

I'm so tired, so ready to go home and collapse into bed, yet here he is, holding my hand and overwhelming me with his mere presence. He's probably lying. Trying to get an in with me so he can get closer to my dad. Well, forget it. He can't trick me.

Glaring at him, I disengage my fingers from his, taking a step backward, but my butt comes into contact with the closed door, making me realize I'm . . .

Trapped. With Gage directly in front of me, looking all broody and handsome and grouchy and sexy.

I am so screwed.

"Stop trying to act like you're a normal guy with normal feelings," I toss out at him, wincing at how I sound like a sullen teenager. "No way do I make you nervous." I mean, really. He's a smooth-talking charmer. How can little ol' me make him nervous?

"You totally put me on edge. I don't get why you're so hell-bent on pushing me away." He stalks toward me, pinning me between the cool glass of the front door and his extremely warm, extremely hard body. "I can't figure you out."

"Maybe I don't want you to figure me out." I want him to leave before I do something really stupid.

Like let him kiss me.

"Ah, I think you do." Bending his head, he sets his mouth against my cheek, his lips whispering across my skin as he speaks. "Don't you feel it, Marina? Feel the chemistry between us, brewing and popping? Don't you want to do something about it?"

"No." Reaching out, I grab hold of his shirt, tugging him a little bit closer. Wait, what? I should be pushing him away. "This is a huge mistake."

"What is?" He settles those big hands of his on my waist. His long fingers span outward, gripping me tight, and I feel like I've become seized by some uncontrollable force, one I can't fight off no matter how hard I try.

That force would be Gage.

"I already told you." God, he's exasperating. It's like he doesn't even listen to a word I say. "Us. Together. There will never be an *us* or a *together*, got it?"

"Got it, boss." He's not really listening, I can tell. He's pulled slightly away so he can stare down at me, too enraptured with his hands on my body. A shock of brown hair tinged with gold tumbles down across his forehead and I resist the urge to reach out and push it away from his face.

Just barely.

He slides his hands around me until they settle at the small of my back, his fingertips barely grazing my backside. I'm wearing jeans, yet it's like I can feel his touch directly on my skin. Heat rushes over me, making my head spin, and I let go of a shaky exhalation.

"We shouldn't do this," I whisper, pressing my lips together when I feel his hands slide over my butt. Oh my God, his touch feels so good.

What the hell am I *thinking*? Letting him touch me like this? It's wrong. Us together is wrong.

So why does it feel so right?

"Do what?" His question sounds innocent enough, but his touch isn't. He pulls me into him so I can feel the unmistakable ridge of his erection pressing against my belly and a gasp escapes me. He's big. Thick. My thighs shake at the thought of him entering me.

I need to put a stop to this, and quick.

"I don't think we sh—"

Gage presses his index finger to my lips, silencing me. I stare up at him, entranced by the glow in his eyes, the way he stares at my mouth. Like he's a starving man dying to devour me.

Anticipation thrums through my veins. I should walk away now. Right now, before we take this any further. We're standing in the doorway of the bakery, for God's sake. Anyone could see us, not that many people are roaming the downtown sidewalks at this time of night. He's got one hand sprawled across my ass and he's tracing my lips with his finger like he wants to memorize the shape of them.

And I'm . . . parting my lips so I can suck on his fingertip.

His eyes darken as he slips his finger deeper into my mouth. I close my lips around him, sucking, tasting his salty skin with a flick of my tongue. A rough, masculine sound rumbles from his chest as his hand falls away from my lips. He drifts his fingers down my chin, my neck, and my breath catches in my throat.

"Gage." I whisper his name, confused. Is it a plea for him

to stop or for him to continue? I don't know. I don't know what I want from him.

"Scared?" he asks, his lids lifting so he can pin me with his gorgeous green eyes. They're glittering in the semidarkness, full of so much hunger, and my body responds, pulsating with need.

I try my best to offer a snide response but the truth comes out instead. "Terrified."

He lowers his head. I can feel his breath feather across my lips, and I part them in response, eager for his kiss. "That makes two of us," he whispers.

Just before he settles his mouth on mine.

The kiss is just the right blend of soft and hard, demanding and giving. I wind my arm around his neck, slide my hand into his hair and pull him closer. Needing him closer as our tongues dance, our sighs mingling together into one perfect, cohesive sound.

He pushes me against the cool glass, one hand still gripping my butt, his other hand drifting down my front. A barely-there touch over the soft cotton of my T-shirt, my entire body tightens in response; my nipples harden beneath the lace of my bra.

I feel like I'm drowning. In his taste, his hands, his scent, his overwhelming presence. It's so confusing, what I'm feeling while in his arms. I don't like him. I don't want to want him.

But I do.

The kiss grows hungrier, more insistent. Our hands are everywhere, his slipping beneath my T-shirt to touch my belly. Mine slide down to curve over his very firm backside, squeezing, pulling him closer. Until we're nothing but a panting, yearning, straining mess.

I break the kiss first, staring up at him in dazed wonder.

His swollen lips are parted, his hair a mess from my fingers, and he watches me, his breathing rough.

He looks too beautiful for words.

"We shouldn't—"

"I'm sorry—"

We start talking at the same time, his apology making me want to shove him away.

Instead I grab hold of his tie and pull him into me, our lips crashing together, our tongues circling, tasting. It's a frenzied, out-of-control mess, and I fall back against the glass door again, startled when I hear the familiar tinkling of the bell above us.

He ends the kiss this time, his gaze lifting, staring just beyond my head and through the door. "We need to—"

"Move this elsewhere?" I ask, earning a startled glance from him. I bet he didn't expect that. "I agree." I push him away, and he steps back, looking just as dazed as I feel. Grabbing hold of his tie again, I take him with me, walking through the café toward the kitchen, the two of us completely silent.

I can hear him breathing, feel his warmth radiating toward me, and I let go of his tie, take hold of his hand instead. He follows behind willingly, his fingers locking around mine, and I hold my breath, afraid he might say something to ruin the moment.

Thank God he keeps his big mouth shut.

Excitement pulses through my veins. I can't believe I'm doing this. It's a mistake. I know it, and I'm sure he knows it too, but there's something about him I can't resist. The way he looks at me, the things he says, the way I feel when I'm in his arms, his mouth on mine, our tongues tangling . . .

He's irresistible. And I'm tired of fighting it. Fighting with him.

We enter the kitchen and the minute the door swings shut behind us, I turn toward him, wrapping my arms around his neck as he bends to kiss me. Our mouths cling perfectly, the taste of him becoming quickly addictive. I'm fast becoming addicted to the way he touches me, too. His hands race over me, too light, not lingering long enough, and I move against him with a whimper. His answering low moan vibrates against my lips, sending an echo through my entire body, and I shift closer. Restless. Wanting more.

I can't even question what's come over me. I don't kiss men I don't really know. I definitely don't grope them either. I'm no prude, but I've never had something like this happen to me. It feels so random, so completely out of character. Scary and exhilarating and exciting and—

"You're thinking too much." He grabs hold of my hips and guides me backward, until I bump against the wall with a startled gasp. Taking my hands, he raises my arms above my head, pinning my wrists with his firm grip. "You need to learn how to just feel."

Before I can offer any sort of argument, he leans in to kiss me, softly at first. A teasing, gentle caress of his lips that makes me want more. His kiss slowly becomes harder, then hungrier, until I feel like I'm about to lose my mind—my very soul—to his greedy, wicked mouth.

God, he's so right. I need to forget everything and just lose myself in the moment. Lose myself in him. Let go of all my troubles, my hang-ups, my wariness over getting involved with Gage. I want to feel his hands. His mouth. His tongue, his fingers, his . . .

He breaks away to blaze a trail with his lips along my jaw, down my neck. My hands are still pinned in his grip, and I struggle against it, wanting to touch him.

Needing to touch him.

"If I let you go, are you going to run?" He breathes the question against my neck, his teeth nibbling the sensitive skin.

I shake my head. No way am I going to run away from this, though a tiny voice deep inside my mind tells me I absolutely should, that I'm about to make the biggest mistake of my life. "No."

His grip gentles on my wrists, his thumbs sweeping across my wildly beating pulse. I shiver at the contact, shocked at how he can illicit my body's response with the lightest of touches.

"I think I like having you trapped." He pushes my hands together and grabs hold of both of my wrists with one big hand, his other hand sliding down my front, between my breasts, one finger trailing down the center of my stomach to stop just at the waistband of my jeans, sending shivers cascading all over my skin.

"I'm sure you do," I say, trying for sarcastic, but yet again, I just sound breathless. Needy.

Damn it.

A smile curves his lips, the sight of it taking my breath away. "I'd like having you this way even more if you were naked."

Oh my God. I should tell him to go to hell right here, right now. We are so not doing this. Not doing it. Not doing it . . .

He slips his hand beneath the hem of my shirt, his fingers grazing my stomach, and I close my eyes, all protests, all thought forgotten. All I can do is lose myself in the sensation of his touch, the way his fingers curl around the waistband of my jeans before they move for the button. He undoes it easily, sliding down the zipper, brushing against the front of my panties, and I open my eyes, press my lips together to keep from crying out.

The jerk knows I'm holding back. His smile turns arrogant as he pushes first one side of my jeans down over my hips, then the other. He's surprisingly agile with one hand, considering he's still holding my wrists against the wall.

Not like I'd move them anyway. I sort of like being so open and vulnerable to his perusal. His touch.

God, why though? Why should I leave myself so open and vulnerable? Being with him makes me feel free. It's exhilarating in the most scary, forbidden way.

He's temptation personified and for once in my life, I want to completely give in to sin and not worry about the consequences.

"What are we doing?" I ask, my voice low. I need an answer. I need to hear that he's just as lost to this as I am. If he says the wrong thing, I should put an end to it right now. Kick him out and hope like crazy I never see him again.

Liar. You'd be devastated if you never saw him again.

He lifts his head, slipping a finger beneath the thin elastic waistband of my panties, touching the bare, sensitive skin of my stomach. I hold my breath, waiting for him to slip that finger lower, wanting it between my legs. "Do you have to ask?"

Smug bastard. "I don't like you," I remind him. Reminding myself, too. I really don't. He's trying to buy up my family's property so he can turn it for profit, and we'll be left with nothing but some cash in the bank, our legacy gone. I need to focus on that. How he wants to end our presence, how he wants to squash my secret dream.

But all I can do is savor his touch and want more. More, more, more.

"Good," he grunts. "I don't really like you either." All the while that finger trails lower, teasing down the front of me until he pulls completely away and out from beneath my underwear.

I feel the loss keenly, the bastard. "Don't—"

"Don't what?" He grins, leaning in to press his mouth to mine as he lets go of my wrists. "Don't touch you? Don't stop? Which is it, Marina?" He whispers the questions across my lips, his own hot and delicious. I'm torn. I don't know what to do. I want him to stop. But then again, I want him to keep going. I want to know what it feels like to be with Gage.

Feel him move inside me. Know what he looks like when he comes.

Closing my eyes, I fight my inner battle. And surrender myself to him.

Gage

She's a gorgeous sight, pressed against the wall, her jeans hanging halfway down her thighs, wearing the most innocent yet sexy panties I think I've ever seen. They're white cotton, trimmed in delicate lace, the fabric so sheer I can see her pubic hair. A tiny white bow dots the center of the waistband, and the same silky ribbon ties around her hips, bows dotting either side of her.

I want to undo those bows and watch her panties fall away from her body. Then I want to get down on my knees and bury my mouth between her legs. I know she'll taste hot and wild. I wonder how many flicks of my tongue will make her come.

Fuck, I'm beyond eager to find out.

"Come here." She grabs hold of my tie—I think she likes doing that—and pulls me to her, my mouth falling onto hers. She opens for me easily, her tongue doing a wicked dance against mine that has me so hard I'm afraid I'll bust through the fabric of my pants, I want her so damn bad.

I guess the kiss is her answer to my earlier question. I know I shouldn't want this either. That if I think about it too much, I'll put a stop to the craziness. Because this is crazy, without a doubt. She's too prickly for me.

But the prickliness has all but evaporated, leaving a passionate, responsive woman in my arms. This woman shoving at my jacket until I shake it off blows my mind. What the fuck are we doing? We're going to have sex in the kitchen of her bakery. I've known her for only a couple of days. I'm trying to buy out her family because they're desperate for money.

And I'm trying to get in her pants because I'm desperate to be inside her.

She seems just as desperate, furiously attacking the buttons of my shirt before she yanks on my tie yet again, loosening it around my neck. I shrug out of it all then reach for her, pushing her shirt up and over her head, my mouth going dry when I see her breasts barely covered in the white, lacy bra.

Rosy pink nipples press against the lace as if they're yearning to be free. I reach for her, flicking open the front clasp. The cups spring away, revealing her full, perfect breasts, and I cup them in my palms, brushing the tips with my thumbs.

"Oh God." She thumps the back of her head against the wall, her eyes sliding closed as I continue to caress her breasts. I don't want to stop touching her, watching her, enjoying her. She's so damn responsive and I want to savor her, but my body—specifically my overeager and greedy-as-hell cock—has other plans.

Unable to resist, I lean in and suck a plump nipple into my mouth, lashing at it with my tongue, sucking hard. She threads her fingers into my hair, holding me to her, and I lift my eyes, watching her. My skin tightens in response at her expression. How lost she seems, how overwhelmed.

Fuck, I can't wait to see her pretty face when she comes.

Within seconds we're a flurry of hands and mouths. Clothes being shed until they form a big pile near our feet, shoes kicked off, condom retrieved from my wallet, until we're both naked and panting, grinding against each other but not necessarily doing anything about it.

Yet.

I pull away from her to tear open the condom wrapper then roll it on my aching cock. I can't wait to be inside her, can't wait to pound my way to orgasm and lose myself in her at least for a little while. Forget the battle and the angry words and the fact that I'm stealing away her heritage, just focus on the two of us together. Connected.

She whispers my name, and I glance up, find her staring at me with wide eyes and parted, swollen red lips. I go to her, kissing her soundly as I grab hold of her by the waist and lift her up. She weighs nothing; my hands grip her perfect ass as she winds her long, smooth legs around my middle, and I press her against the wall, my cock poised perfectly to thrust forward inside her.

"You're big." She breathes the words, my erection pressing against the soft give of her belly, and I smile, reaching toward her so I can brush stray tendrils of wavy damp hair away from her forehead. She closes her eyes and releases a shuddering breath, as if she has to prepare herself for this moment, and I'm suddenly worried.

Is she changing her mind? Ready to back out? Fuck, I'm

about to enter her. If I think about it too long, I could probably come like an overeager teenager if I don't watch it. I want to make this good, I want to make it last, but not if she doesn't want this to happen . . .

"Now you're the one who's thinking too much," she whispers when I don't say anything, amusement filling her voice.

I meet her gaze to see she's smiling at me, the apprehension still lingering in her eyes, but I can't worry about it now. Carefully, so slowly I know I'm trying to kill myself by torture, I enter her body for the first time. I register the quick intake of her breath, the way her body tenses up for the briefest moment as I push inside. The give of her welcoming body as I go deeper, all that silky, hot wet flesh wrapping around me, sends me straight into oblivion.

Closing my eyes, I hold steady, my racing heart roaring in my ears. I press my forehead to hers and swallow hard, trying to keep my shit together, but it's so damn hard when she feels so damn good.

"Ohmigod." Her words run together as she shifts against me, sending me deeper and we both groan. "Move, Gage. Please."

I do as she asks, surprised at her request. Breathing deep, I pull almost all the way out, feeling her inner walls drag against my length before I plunge deep inside and she clings to me, a low moan sounding close to my ear. Her arms are around my neck, her face buried at the spot between my shoulder and throat. I can feel her lips move against my skin as she speaks.

"More," she encourages. "Harder, Gage. Please."

Christ. With that kind of encouragement I can have her bumping against the wall within seconds but I don't . . . want to hurt her.

My brain registers this weird realization and I pause, swamped with confusion. I always ensure the woman I'm with is satisfied, but I chase after my orgasm as quick as I can like any other guy. Guess that makes me a selfish prick. I think Marina might've even called me a selfish prick today, or at least a variation of it.

Somehow, now that I'm inside her, I don't want to be a selfish prick at all. I want to watch her, learn what she likes best. I want to see her eyes, her entire expression grow fevered as I continue to push and push with deliberate, sure strokes inside her body. I want to hear her breath catch, hear her whisper my name just before I make her completely fall apart.

And only then will I chase my orgasm. I want her satisfaction to come first.

I fill her, again and again, the slap of our damp bodies, the sound of our sighs and moans mingling together. Reaching between us, I touch her; she's so drenched and hot. Circling her clit, rubbing it, I feel her tense all around me, squeezing me deep, and I close my eyes, hold my breath. Desperate to make myself last.

Desperate to make this so good for her she'll forget every man she's ever been with.

She's chanting nonsense. My name and *please* and other unintelligible words mixed together, and all I can do is open my eyes and watch helplessly. Captivated by her expression, her breaths, the way she clings to me, her head tipped back as if she's lost in her own little pleasurable world. I move faster, grinding against her, waiting for her to fall completely apart because holy fuck, I'm dying to see it. Dying to feel it. Feel her.

And then she's coming, a filthy word falling from her lips as she shudders and shakes all around me. I remain still, my cock filling her, my thumb pressing against her clit until her tremors slow, and she becomes a warm, languid woman, limp in my arms, silly, sexy little words still coming from her lush lips in a breathy whisper.

Fuck, that is the biggest turn on ever.

Lacking control or finesse, I resume my pace and pound inside of her, intent on the orgasm that's barreling down upon me. I'm almost there, the familiar tingling starts at the base of my spine, and my thrusts become erratic. Pushing deep, deeper still, until I'm buried so far inside her I'm afraid I'll never find my way out.

Only then am I coming, my body trembling, a loudly proclaimed *fuck* coming from deep within my chest as I come inside her. I clutch her close, bury my mouth against the soft, fragrant skin of her shoulder, and I bite her there, earning a whispered gasp from her for my efforts.

"Damn," I breathe as I turn into her, breathing against her neck. She smells amazing. Like sand and the ocean and flowers. Fragrant and so damn intoxicating I'm afraid I could stay like this forever, breathing her in, feeling her surround me.

"Um." She shoves at my chest and I lift my head away from her shoulder to find she's looking fairly awkward.

As in, *oh my God, I totally regret doing this* type of awkward.

Hell. I've gone and done it this time.

Withdrawing from her, she unwinds her legs from my hips. We're both silent as I set her on her feet, my gaze not meeting hers.

The moment went from hot to uncomfortable in a matter of minutes.

I watch out of the corner of my eye as she bends over and snatches her clothes up, and I do the same. We both get dressed, and when I throw away the used condom in the trash can nearby, I earn a snort that sounds suspiciously of disapproval coming from her direction.

Well, what the hell does she want from me? At least I used protection, right?

Fuck.

I turn to find she's completely covered though rather sloppily, her hair a haphazard mess around her head and her swollen lips still tempting me to kiss her.

By the look on her face, though, I don't think she's in the mood for sweet kisses and a whispered, "That was fucking amazing."

"We shouldn't have done that," she blurts, clamping her lips shut the moment the words are out.

Ouch. I rub at my still bare chest since I haven't buttoned up my shirt yet. Well. That hurt like hell. "Too late," I say, because what else can I say? It is too late. We did it.

Best sex of my life and she's full of regret.

"It was a mistake," she continues, her words like daggers straight to my still wildly beating heart.

"Pretty bad for you then, huh?" I quickly do up all the buttons of my shirt, stuffing my tie into my front pocket. No way she didn't enjoy what just happened between us. "I couldn't tell, what with the way you screamed my name and kept begging me 'please.'"

She glares at me. Great. We're right back at it again. "There you go, resuming the piggish qualities I find so endearing."

I shove my shoes on, not bothering with socks. I just want the hell out of here. My post-climatic high is fading fast. Hell, it's pretty much demolished. She's got me on the defensive, and I don't like it. "I think for once, we're in agreement," I tell her as I leave the kitchen.

Marina follows after me, her bare feet taking her pretty fast, since my angry strides have me at the front door in less than five seconds flat. "What do you mean?" she calls after me.

I turn and pin her with a glare, suddenly furious at her. More than anything, furious with myself. I hate how she's making me feel bad, like I did something wrong. Like we should've never had sex. Maybe she's not too far off the mark, but it's like she's rubbing it in. "You're right. It was a mistake. We should never have done that."

Turning away from her, I flick the lock undone and open the door, exiting the bakery without another word.

Chapter 6

Marina

It takes everything I have to get out of bed this morning. I hardly slept, my mind too occupied with last night's events. Every time I moved, trying to force myself to fall asleep, my entire body ached but not in a bad way. More in a *wow, that was amazing and I came so hard I almost blacked out* sort of way.

Not that I'd ever admit that to Gage.

What had been an amazing moment went south real quick. And it was all my fault.

Regret fills me at the way I spoke to him, how I called what happened between us a mistake. I mean, yeah. I sort of do regret that it happened but only because our "relationship"—I have no idea what else to call it—is so bizarre. I don't know him, not really. And what I do know of him, I don't like. Every time we encounter one another, sparks fly, and usually they're angry ones.

Not last night, though. Those angry sparks turned into chemistry-filled sexy sparks, which then morphed into totally orgasmic sparks. God, the way he touched me, his mouth everywhere, his hands everywhere, his drugging kisses, his big cock moving inside me . . .

My body tingles just remembering it.

Forcing myself to get up, I take a quick shower, scrubbing

my still-sensitive body carefully with soap. My palms brush over my nipples and they harden instantaneously. God, what would I do if he was in the shower with me? His big, soapy hands sliding all over my skin, reaching between my legs, his sure fingers touching me in that exact spot where I so desperately want him to touch. Bringing me to orgasm again and again—

"Marina! It's almost seven! You're going to be late!" Mom yells from the other side of my bathroom door, killing my delicious Gage-in-the-shower fantasy in an instant.

I really need to move out on my own, but I come from a traditional family and haven't really found the need to fight it. Until now.

Finally I get my butt to the bakery to find the pumpkins Gina had set out a few days ago gone, damp spots remaining where they'd been and a scattering of pumpkin seeds. I stride into the bakery and look around, waving at Eli, one of the two college students we have working for us part-time, on his perch behind the register.

"Where's Gina?" I ask as I get closer to the counter.

"Back in the kitchen. She's working on that second batch of chocolate croissants for you." Eli grins and shakes his head.

I forgot all about the croissants. I think I'm still in a Gage-induced haze.

Entering the kitchen, I find Gina standing at the oven with her back to me, peering through the glass window to check on her croissants baking within. "Hey. What happened to the pumpkins outside?" I ask.

"Oh! You startled me." She whirls around, her smile rapidly replaced with a frown. "When I arrived this morning, they were destroyed. Smashed all over the sidewalk."

I frown in return. I stayed at least an hour after Gage left, mopping the floor, scrubbing down the wall he pinned me against. I'd been about to leave when I noticed the streaks all over the glass front door, from where he had me pinned there too. I'd had to grab the Windex and scrub 'til it shone.

Having sex in the freaking bakery was not the smartest thing to do. I still can't believe we did it. I mean, really, what the hell was I thinking? He should be my sworn enemy, not the man who gave me the most intense orgasm of my life.

And if he ever knew that, I can only imagine the smug expression on his too-handsome face. The sight of it would probably make me want to punch him.

"I stayed pretty late last night," I finally say. "What time did you get here?"

"Around four. I came early, couldn't sleep." Gina opens the oven door and reaches inside, a baking mitt covering her hand as she slowly withdraws the cooking sheet from inside. Perfectly formed golden brown croissants fill the tray, the fragrant aroma making my mouth water.

And I left just past eleven, so it had to have happened between midnight and four. "I bet it was kids."

"I'm sure. I already cleaned up the mess. It wasn't that bad, but it makes me reluctant to set out any more pumpkins." Gina shakes her head. "Jerks."

"Yeah." Unable to resist, I pluck a piping hot croissant off the tray, tearing off a small piece and dropping it into my mouth. It melts on my tongue, warm and so freaking delicious I moan loudly. "So good, Gina."

She beams with pride. "Thank you. You know, you can check the security cameras. See if you can see anything."

"You're right." I tear off another piece and chew. I always forget about the security cameras. They're relatively new. "I think I'll go check it out."

"Let me know if you see anything," she calls after me as I leave the kitchen and head to my office.

Deciding I better check before I get on with my normal day and forget, I log into the security site we use, bringing up the outdoor camera. I fast forward through the film, not really seeing anything until around two-thirty in the morning, when two people with slender builds and hoodies over their heads and faces come along and smash the pumpkins against the sidewalk, kicking them over and jumping up and down on them like they're bouncing on a trampoline.

Yep, kids. So stupid.

They don't linger long and I stop checking, knowing there's not much I can do since I can't see their faces. Besides, maybe I could get them on vandalism charges, but come on, what cop is going to go after kids destroying pumpkins?

If it happens again, then I'll contact the police. For now, I'm letting it lie.

Huh. I wonder if the cameras caught Gage and me last night? My cheeks heat at the thought of seeing the two of us kissing in the front entrance, me plastered against the door . . .

Deciding to check the other cameras, I click quickly through the feeds, rewinding and fast-forwarding through the last few days, momentarily startled to notice that business is definitely picking up during the early lunch crowd. I usually don't come out and help behind the counter until around twelve thirty, but customers are coming in even earlier, the place looking packed around eleven thirty.

I know by the daily tallies that business is increasing, but seeing the evidence makes it even more real.

Great. Business is picking up, and I'm thrilled. But are Gage and I on the camera feed or what?

Continuing my search, my heart starts racing when I don't find any evidence of the two of us, when really there should be. The camera system cost a bundle when we initially purchased it, but the monthly maintenance fee isn't that bad and worth the expense. Though maybe I should reassess. Who really needs a camera on the kitchen? Really the only people who are in there are me and Gina and our handful of employees.

Right. And me and Gage last night . . .

Sitting up straight, I go to the kitchen camera feed, my head pounding as I scroll back to approximately ten o'clock last night. I start to fast-forward again, slower this time, until a horrified gasp escapes me.

Gage, with his back to the camera and still clad in his suit, his big hands holding my arms above my head as he kisses me senseless.

Arousal drips through me, slow as honey, and I lean my forearm on the edge of my desk. My mouth goes dry as I watch us. I feel like a voyeur even though I know it's me. And Gage. I can almost feel his lips on mine, our tongues touching, my hand buried in his hair—

"You have a phone call." Gina peeks her head around my office door, and I squeal, clicking out of the camera feed so quick I swear I strained my finger.

"Holy crap, you scared me." I rest my hand against my chest, feeling my rapidly beating heart. If she'd come inside, she probably would've seen the footage. How could I explain that?

And how the hell do I get rid of it?

"Didn't mean to." She lingers in the doorway, wiping her hands on her apron.

"Who is it?" I ask, breathing deep, smoothing a shaky hand

over my hair as I try to gain some composure. Watching the video of Gage and me together has me rattled. And I didn't even really get to see anything.

I saw enough, though, to remember just how good he made me feel.

"I don't know. I happened to pick it up when I went out to the front and he didn't leave a name. Just asked for you." Gina leaves without saying anything else, and I reach for the phone.

"Hello, this is Marina." The person on the other end is silent for so long I wonder if they've hung up. "Hello?"

"Hey," the word is breathed out, the voice undeniably familiar.

"Gage?" I tighten my fingers around the receiver, startled he's calling me. I thought he'd hate me, after what I did to him. "Um . . ."

"Yeah, this is awkward. Listen, I talked to Archer about you."

I'm stunned. Why would he still talk to Archer about me? "You did?"

"He's willing to meet with you sometime next week. He said for you to call his direct number at the office and you two can set up a meeting. You want the number?" Gage asks, sounding efficient. Very business as usual.

Nothing at all like the man who held me in his arms last night, murmuring filthy words in my ear while he pushed inside me so deep I thought I might splinter in two.

"Yes, I want it. Let me grab a pen." I find a notepad and pen and jot down the number Gage rattles off, his deep voice sending tingles sweeping over my suddenly too-hot skin.

Just hearing him talk on the phone and I'm a goner. This is so ridiculous.

"Why are you being so nice to me?" I ask, clutching the phone so tight I know my knuckles are white. "I—"

"Treated me like crap last night? Yes, you did." He pauses, as if struggling with whether he should say something or not, and I silently urge him to go ahead and just say it. I don't care what it is. I might get angry but . . . I doubt it.

Or the anger will just be rapidly chased by arousal, so hey, that works too, right?

The man has turned me into a sick, twisted woman.

I want to apologize to him for being such a bitch last night and kicking him out, but I just can't find it in me to say I'm sorry. And that makes me feel like an even bigger bitch. "I panicked," I say instead.

"Because we had sex in the kitchen of your bakery?"

Closing my eyes, I let my head fall to my desk, thumping my forehead on the thick pile of papers. "Yes," I agree weakly. "I know. I did too."

He didn't seem panicked. He'd been really sweet and aggressive and sexy and gentle. I've never had sex against a wall in my life. I've never been touched, kissed, fucked—yes, definitely never fucked—like that ever. Ever, ever, ever.

So it blows my mind that something so crazy, so absolutely, terrifyingly wonderful, happened with a man I don't really like.

You like him when he has his hands all over your body and his tongue in your mouth.

Lifting my head, I open my eyes and scowl, banishing the nasty little voice inside my head and focus instead on the man I'm talking to.

"I know you regret what happened, and I feel bad for pushing myself on you," he explains. "So I thought I'd call up Archer and get this handled for you. It's the least I can do."

I don't regret what happened. Well, maybe I do a little, but who regrets great sex? "You didn't really push yourself on me. And thank you," I whisper, feeling a little choked up because really, the man could've told me to fuck off and die and I wouldn't have blamed him. I would've deserved it.

"You're welcome." He pauses, again as if he's struggling with what to say next, and I get it. I feel the same way. "I'll, uh, see you around."

Panic flares. I can't let him go. Not like this. "Wait a minute! Don't I, um . . . owe you dinner?"

He remains quiet, but I can hear him breathing. "You don't owe me anything, Marina."

I love the way he says my name, his deep voice seeming to caress every letter. Holy crap, do I have it bad for a man I don't like. "It's the least I can do," I murmur, throwing his words back at him. Maybe . . . maybe we can see each other again. One more time. It wouldn't hurt, right? And I need to make it up to him, how awful I was. How I basically forced him to leave.

We had amazing sex, and then we were almost angry over it. Like we resented each other or something. So weird.

I'm tired of feeling resentful. Can't we just . . . enjoy this connection?

"You're serious." He sounds incredulous. I'm not surprised.

"A deal's a deal, right?" Reaching for my mouse, I bring the security site back up, pleased to see I didn't exit completely out of it after all. The screen is right where I left it, me being held captive by Gage against the wall. I speed it up a bit, to the part where I can see we're completely naked. My legs are wound around his waist, my heels digging into his perfect, flexing ass as he pushes deep inside me.

I'm transfixed. Watching us having sex, having him on the phone, it's like Gage overload.

"You don't owe me this. I don't want you throwing this dinner back in my face like you're prone to do," he says grumpily. "Considering how you believe I always have ulterior motives."

I let the insult fly, too enamored with the sound of his voice while watching him hammer inside of me on the computer screen. I squirm in my seat, feeling like a complete pervert at, what, just after eight in the morning? "I won't throw it back in your face," I swear to him, not sure if I can really keep that promise. "I guess it all depends if you say something stupid to me. Like you're prone to do."

Ha. We sound like little kids fighting on the playground.

Thankfully, he ignores my dig as well. "I'm leaving for San Francisco tomorrow, so how about tonight?"

"Tonight?" I hit pause again on the screen and turn it off, turning away from my computer so I won't be distracted. "That's kind of last minute." Like I have any plans.

"I know. It's either that or we wait until early next week, when I get back."

I can't wait that long. I want to see him, which I sort of hate. I absolutely shouldn't want to do this. But my humming body more than wants to see him. "Fine. Tonight," I say curtly, wincing when I hear my tone so I try and soften it. "That sounds . . . fun."

He laughs. The jackass. "Yeah, you sound thrilled. Look I'm going to try and get Archer to accompany us. He can bring his fiancé."

"Wait, what? You want Archer to go to dinner with us?" Okay, I hadn't bargained on that. I'm going to have to be on my A-game if that happens. I might even have to present my proposition to him, and I'm not quite ready to discuss it yet. I still need to handle a few details.

"Yeah, Archer and his fiancé. Trust me, you'll love her. And Archer, too. This isn't some business dinner, Marina. Just pleasure."

Just pleasure. Oh, now those are two words that take on different meaning when used in reference to Gage and me.

"Okay." I swallow hard. "Let's go out to dinner with Archer and his fiancé." I close my eyes and push my desk chair into a circle. This is probably a really bad idea.

But I can't back out of it now, right?

Chapter 7

Gage

"You want to go on a double date with your sister and me?" Archer chuckles, the sound irritating as it rumbles in my ear, and I pull the phone away, wishing I could tell him never mind and hang up.

I can't, though. Promised a certain someone it would happen, and now I have to come through on that promise. Plus, I want to see her again. If I'm lucky, maybe I'll get her naked, in a bed, where I can take my time and map her entire body with my lips.

Yeah. I can't get the thought of her out of my mind. The way she clung to me, the taste of her lips, the sounds she makes when she comes . . .

I tried calling her father first thing this morning. No dice. The man hates my guts or flat-out doesn't give a shit. So I need to get in his daughter's good graces and maybe eventually she'll introduce the two of us. It could be a win-win for everyone.

Because just as much as I'm attracted to Marina, I'm also attracted to the fact that she's a Molina. Scott Knight's freaking daughter. I am so close to getting an in with him, I can almost taste it. Does this make me an asshole, wanting to get closer to her so I can get to her father?

Yes.

Damn it. That's what I thought. And I hate that I feel this way, like I'm using her. Getting to know her, kissing her, having sex with her . . . it's changed everything. The power has shifted between us.

Not that I ever really believed I held the power when it came to Marina and me. She's been tough on me since the first moment we met.

And I like it.

"I definitely want to go out with you and Ivy tonight," I finally agree, keeping it simple, waiting for the inevitable questions.

"Who's the girl making you want a double date?"

There's question one. "Don't laugh at me," I start, but he answers for me, his tone smug.

"Let me guess." He pauses for dramatic effect. He's having way too much fun with this and the conversation has only just begun. "Marina Knight."

I don't bother responding for a few seconds. I don't need to. He knows he's irritating the shit out of me. When his chuckle grows into full-out laughter, I'm ready to end the call.

"How did you make that happen?" he finally asks when he gets his laughter under control.

Question number two. "I convinced her I was a good guy and now she wants to date me." Lies, all lies. Like I can tell him the truth.

I fucked her against a wall in her bakery. Hottest sex of my life. Dying to do it again.

"I call bullshit."

Well hell, now I'm offended. "Why do you find that so hard to believe?"

"You badmouthed her family. The Molinas and the Knights, they're all about the family. You breathe one bad word against them and they're ready to take you down and tear you apart. Every single one of them acts that way," Archer explains.

I remember her Aunt Gina calling me Rat Boy. That sounded rather . . . mobbish. Is that even a word? "You make them sound like the mob," I mutter, glancing about my temporary office. I'm staying at a house I purchased a few months ago in St. Helena. It's cute, small, and very old. Needs major renovations—we're talking a total overhaul—and I've been getting bids on the job over the last few days. Its central location makes it the ideal place to stay while I'm here in Napa.

"Rumor has it they might be, though I doubt it," Archer says, his tone serious.

"Mob ties, give me a break," I mutter, more than ready to change the subject. "Listen, she wants to talk to you." I'd fibbed a little when I called Marina. I'd left a message with Archer when I couldn't get a hold of him and grew too anxious waiting for him so I broke down and called her anyway.

I knew I could get him to see her, but I haven't confirmed anything yet. I just wanted to call her. Listen to her voice. Imagine the way she sounded last night when she whispered my name as I sunk particularly deep inside her tight, wet body—

"Talk to me about what?"

"Yeah, it's about business. She won't tell me what exactly, but Marina says she has a proposition for you and she kept meaning to call you but hasn't yet," I explain.

"Huh, wonder why she hasn't called. I've talked to her a few times. Nothing extensive, though." He makes a noise; I can hear him shift in his chair, the unmistakable creak coming through loud and clear. "When do you want to go on this momentous double date?"

"Tonight? Maybe?" I wince, waiting for his answer.

"You gotta be kidding me. *Tonight?* You expect us to rearrange our schedules for you or what?" Archer sounds a little angry, mostly amused. His favorite thing to do is give me shit.

"I need to get in her good graces so she'll introduce me to her father," I explain. Well, that's part of it. I also just want to see her again. Want to talk to her, argue with her a little, until she gets that angry little shine in her eyes, and I become so tempted I lean over and kiss her.

"Really." Archer sounds doubtful.

"Yeah. Really. The guy has been giving me the complete shut-out for months. I'm dying to talk to him." Negotiate with him. Make Scott Knight a deal he can't refuse.

"Ah, so there's the heart of the matter." Archer makes a tsking noise. "You're not trying to get in her pants. You're hoping to get in her dad's back pocket."

He's making me feel like shit and I refuse to. Besides, I've already gotten into her pants.

Yeah, you are such an asshole.

"You're not going to guilt me over this." I do that well enough on my own.

"Whatever. I understand. It's just business." Archer sighs heavily. "Let me talk to Ivy, but I think we can do this. I've got no major plans going on, and I don't think she does either."

"Thanks, bro," I say. "I appreciate you doing this so last minute." I mean it.

"No problem. I've called you begging to help me out so many times, I've lost count," Archer jokes, though really, he's serious.

He's the one who usually needs to be bailed out, rescued, whatever. Our friendship has always had that balance. Archer's the fuckup; I'm the one who cleans up the aftermath. Or saves his ass.

Whichever is needed first.

Now look at me, running to him for favors. But that's what friends are for.

Ever since Archer started dating my sister, he's straightened out. It started sooner even, when he received the old Bancroft Hotel his father gave him. He immersed himself in his work, took it seriously and turned that crappy old hotel into the thriving, successful Hush—a premier hotel and spa.

Then he and Ivy started seeing each other seriously, and he really got his shit together. I hadn't approved. Hell, they kept their budding relationship from me for fear I wouldn't like it. I love Archer, he's my closest friend besides Matt. And of course, I love my little sister, and would protect her no matter what.

Archer and Ivy together though? The idea still blows my mind, and they've been a couple for a while now. Hell, he's so in love with her, he's going to marry her.

It's pretty amazing, seeing what the love of a good woman will do to a guy.

Not that I'm looking for anything like that—hell no. Not yet. I'm too damn busy to pay a needy woman any mind.

Fuck around with one, specifically one as hot as Marina? Yeah, I'm on board with that.

Here come my asshole tendencies again. Showing themselves front and center.

"Tell Ivy to not ask Marina a lot of questions, okay?" I request.

"What do you mean by that?"

"It's just . . . she'll be curious and want to know more about this woman I'm dating. And it's nothing. It's not really serious, on my part or Marina's part. I'm trying to talk to her dad. She's trying to talk to you. We're using each other," I explain, hoping like hell that's the truth. If Ivy and Marina start talking and become friends, that would be awful. I don't want to hurt Marina's feelings, but this has to be nothing serious for me.

Despite how amazing the sex had been between us, it can't matter. We're just having fun. Gaining something from each other. She has to know or at least assume I'm talking to her because of the connection with her dad. This makes me feel like an asshole because damn it, I like her. Despite her not liking me, I'm drawn to her like I can't help myself.

Because yeah, I'm pretty sure it's not serious for her. One night of sex. Tonight, just a dinner. A chance to speak to Archer and get to know him better. Hell, she can barely tolerate me. Most of the time, she provokes me enough that I end up making an ass of myself and saying something stupid to piss her off. Being with her doesn't bring out my finer qualities . . .

Except when I'm buried inside her and making her come. Then all is good in the world. All is right.

Yeah. We'll go to dinner, we'll both get what we want, and then we're done. Nice and simple.

Just the way I like it.

Marina

arling, what in the world are you doing?"

I poke my head out of my walk-in closet at the sound of my mom's horrified voice. She's standing in the middle of my bedroom, her eyes wide with shock as she takes in the disaster. My clothes are strewn everywhere. All over the floor, the bed, thrown over the chair that sits in the corner closest to the closet.

It's a pre-date war zone, and so far I'm losing the battle.

"Looking for something to wear." I get up off the floor and stand, wiping my hands on my thighs. "I have nothing."

She's still glancing about the room, checking out all the items of clothing lying everywhere, I'm sure. "I beg to differ. I had no idea you were hoarding that many clothes in your tiny closet."

Funny how it's my "tiny" closet. It's your standard-size master bedroom walk-in. Hers puts mine to shame. It's like an entire room, with an island in the center full of drawers where she organizes her bras and underwear. Lit racks line the wall, showing off her beautiful shoe and bag collections. My father had the closet rebuilt for her about twelve years ago. I remember being in total awe. I'd never seen anything like it.

Then I went on to have friends in high school whose mothers had even bigger closets than my mom. Talk about putting us to shame.

"Fine. I have nothing that I *like*," I stress, throwing my hands up in the air. "I need to go shopping."

"What for? Where are you going that you're so worried over how you look? You always dress so nicely, darling, except when you're working, but what can we expect? Not like you can dress up to dole out pastries and coffee." She smiles, oblivious to how she just completely insulted what I do for a living.

She does that all the time and it's irritating. Even a little hurtful, though I try to tell myself to get over it. But my mom has zero respect for my job or my business, and I don't understand why. I'm actually doing something with my life, but she doesn't even see it.

"I'm going out tonight."

"Oh?" Mom sounds casual but everything else about her demeanor perks up. Great. "And who are you going out with? Anyone we know?"

I really don't want to tell her where or with whom. She's going to jump to conclusions when she hears I'm going out with a guy and it's nothing like that.

"No one special. And no, I don't think you know him." I shrug, moving over to my dresser. Kneeling down, I tug open the bottom drawer and flip through my jeans, finally pulling out my absolute favorite. They're a dark rinse, skinny fit without being skintight, and they make my legs look long when they're really not. "No need to make a big deal about it."

"When you say things like that, darling, I'm assuming it's a big deal. You just don't want to get my hopes up." She clasps her hands together, her blue eyes that are just like mine twinkling with delight. "Is he handsome? How long have you been seeing him? What's his name?"

Look at her. She automatically assumes I've found a special someone—her word choice long, long ago, not mine. The twenty-three-year-old spinster is the disappointment of the family. It's ridiculous.

My friends definitely think it's ridiculous I still live at home, but that's the way it's done in a traditional Italian family. Usually. I'm the need-to-be-protected baby girl in my parents' eyes. Their only girl, since it's just my older brother and me. John is married with two babies, doing his own thing clear across the country in Boston, where his wife is from.

They met in college, the perfect sort of romance that made my mom infinitely happy.

So now my parents focus all of their attention—much of it unwanted—on my lacking love life.

Realizing she's still waiting for a reply, I heft out a long sigh, glaring at her. "Mom. He's no one. I swear."

"Tell me his name," she demands.

"Gage Emerson." Just saying his name out loud makes my skin tingle. I love his name. I loved especially when I whispered it in his ear just before he came. Hard.

Taking a deep breath, I tell myself to calm down. Those are *so* not the thoughts I should be having with my mother in the same room.

Mom frowns, a little crease forming between her scrunched brows. "Hmm, I don't recognize the name. I don't know of any Emersons who live in the area, but I must confess, I'm woefully out of touch when it comes to those who are your age. I haven't been to the country club in forever."

She sounds so old fashioned sometimes, and what is she? In her early fifties? Mom acts and sounds much older. But she grew up in a much stricter world than I ever did. My grandparents wouldn't let her do anything.

It drives me crazy, how she loves to go on and on about me needing a man in my life. Her disappointment that I haven't found a boyfriend is her old-fashioned thinking rearing its ugly head.

"He's not from the area," I tell her, tossing my jeans onto the last spot of empty space on my bed.

"Oh? So how did you two meet?"

"At an event a few nights ago. Remember the brewery- and wine-tasting thing I told you about?"

"Ah, yes. So." She smiles. "What does he *do*?"

He's a shark who's sniffing around Molina property and wants to steal it from us for nothing so he can turn around and make a huge profit.

Oh yeah, and he's a sex god who had me screaming his name when he made me come.

"He's in real estate," I finally answer as I head back into my closet.

My stomach roils, and I press my lips together. Why am I going out with him again? Yes, I'm hoping he'll get me an in with Archer Bancroft so I can talk him into carrying Autumn Harvest bakery desserts at his restaurants in his two hotels.

I hope this entire setup works. More than anything, I hope I can enjoy my dinner tonight and not want to stab Gage in the chest with my fork. As long as he keep his mouth shut and looks pretty, we should be good.

You are such a bitch.

Maybe I am. But the man provokes me like none other. Both in a good and bad way.

Mom follows me, hovering at the open door. "Residential or commercial?"

I can practically hear her brain calculating how much he could possibly be worth. "I don't know. I'm guessing commercial."

"Ahh. That's nice. How old is he?"

"Um." I swallow hard. I don't know all the pertinent information about Gage Emerson beyond his name, that he and Archer are friends, and he's a jackass snake in the grass who's really good with his hands. And his mouth. And his . . .

Wow, isn't my opinion of him top-notch?

"I think he's in his early thirties?" I wince, not one hundred percent sure my answer is right. Looks like Google and I need a second date tonight.

"Sounds like you don't know much about your young man."

I barely restrain from rolling my eyes. "He's not mine, Mom."

"Oh, someday he will be. If he's smart and realizes what a fine catch you are." She sounds so confident. I almost hate to disappoint her.

So I don't.

"He's very intelligent. I think he's fairly successful at his job." From the way he dressed and his arrogant attitude, I would say he's definitely doing all right. Plus, there was all that research I did on him. Not that I'm telling my mom anything. "He's handsome too."

Too handsome, is more like it. All that dark hair tinged with gold, the intense hazel eyes, rugged bone structure, and too tempting mouth—he's definitely gorgeous.

Not to mention that amazing body and big ol' . . .

"He sounds delightful. Is he coming here to pick you up?" Mom asks, her expression beyond hopeful.

"I'm meeting him at the restaurant," I answer, ignoring her disappointment. I can't let it bother me. If I had Gage pick me up at the house, he'd get the third degree. My father would probably make him fill out a questionnaire to see if he's good enough to go out with me or not, and we'd end up here for hours. In the end, Gage would run screaming from my house, never to return.

And I wouldn't doubt for an instant that Gage is using me to get close to my father. Considering I'm using him to get an in with Archer, I guess I can't complain.

"I don't know if I like that," Mom murmurs, shaking her head.

I start going through my clothing again, pushing aside one hanger after another. "Let's see if this goes any further before I bring him around here, okay?"

"Of course." Mom nods but she still looks a little heartbroken. "I understand. Well, I'll let you get back to your search. Let me know if you need any help."

I watch her leave, jumping a little when she slams the door behind her.

I've disappointed her. Again. This time it hangs heavy over me. She makes me feel like a little kid. When am I ever going to do anything right in her eyes?

Exiting my closet, I grab my cell from my bedside table, shocked to see I have a text message from Gage. We exchanged phone numbers before we got off the phone earlier, but I didn't expect to hear from him.

> How about I come pick you up tonight? Instead of meeting at the restaurant?

I frown. Did the man bug my room or what? It's like he heard the conversation between my mom and me.

I'd rather just meet you at the restaurant. It's easier, I reply.

He immediately answers.

> It's no trouble. Really.

The guy doesn't quit. From what I can tell—and I barely know him—he's always determined to get what he wants. It's rather annoying. I need to nip this in the bud.

> I'd rather you not meet my family. And I'd rather drive my own car.

There. Brutally honest might shut him up. Though I immediately feel guilty for sending such a bitchy text, I push the unwanted emotion aside. I need to remind myself he's a jerk who only wants one thing from me.

And it's not sex. He wants to make money off my family.

This time he takes a little longer to reply.

> I have met your family. Your aunt . . . remember?

I let out a sigh. He fights just to fight, doesn't he? I think he likes going round and round.

> Then meet me at the bakery at seven. Though I'll probably be alone. Gina leaves early.

I should make Gina stick around as the buffer. The last thing we need is to be at the bakery alone again. He might try and spread me naked across my desk and have his wicked way with me.

Lord help me, that sounds delicious.

> I'll see you at the bakery at seven then.

Nothing else. No more trying to convince me to let him come to my house, no more nothing. I think I might've offended him.

I know I shouldn't care. I know it's pointless, but . . .

I feel bad.

Chapter 8

Marina

"Hope your Boy Toy shows up soon. I'm about ready to take off," Gina mutters as she wipes her hands on a rag at the sink. She's just finished making a new creation, and I told her I'd wanted her to stick around for Gage's arrival so I could use her for protection.

She'd been surprised but hadn't made me explain myself too much, thank God. Just nodded, told me she was in the mood to experiment and since it was my Uncle Joe's poker night, she would stay after work and hang out with me.

So I watched her make a chocolate raspberry cake that smelled divine and had the best frosting I've ever tasted. All the while, we talked. About the bakery, what our individual plans were for the next year, what we thought we could to do take the bakery to a higher level.

It was fun. My aunt is savvy about business, creative, with an endless list of ideas. I briefly explained how I was going to meet Archer. She thought it was a fabulous idea, which pleased me. I wanted her on board. I consider Gina my business partner, and I hope she feels the same way.

Plus, she helped ease my nerves about Gage coming to pick me up and take me to dinner. As the time draws closer to Gage showing up, I'm worrying about potentially bad situations. Like the two of us alone in his car on the way to the restaurant. Yeah, that could be scary.

Scary and exciting, if the two emotions can coexist.

I believe when it comes to Gage and me, they definitely can.

"Where's he at?" Gina asks, interrupting my thoughts. "It's almost quarter after seven."

I push down the threatening irritation, glancing down at my black sparkly top and picking off a piece of lint. I finally decided on a top that shows off a lot of skin without looking sluttish. Because I don't want to tempt Gage or give him the wrong message. I refuse to have sex with him again tonight.

And if he keeps me waiting much longer, we will most definitely not be having sex tonight. Or any other night.

"So he goes from Rat Boy to Boy Toy?" I ask her, wanting to change the focus of our conversation. If we keep going on about how late he is, I'm just going to get madder.

"Oh, yes." She smiles. "Rat Boy is quite handsome, so that's a bit of a stretch for a nickname, you know? He's got that pretty face I'm sure you enjoy staring at."

I feel my cheeks heat but don't say anything. I do enjoy looking at that pretty face. She knows me too well.

"And who wouldn't? I don't mind looking at it either." Her smile blossoms into a full-blown grin. "Has your mama met him yet?"

"God, no," I mutter. "She'd flip out and have us engaged within minutes."

Gina laughs. She knows it's true. "She'd probably be picking out your wedding china patterns and prepping the baby announcements."

I laugh with her. "She knows I'm going out to dinner with him, but I told her it was nothing serious. That it's just business."

"Business, huh? You know, the more I think about it, I find it hard to believe. He's a charmer, that man. I think you might've fallen under his spell." Gina raises a skeptical eyebrow, but I ignore it.

"Really, Gina. This has nothing to do with his charm and everything to do with talking to Archer Bancroft about your desserts in his hotels. Remember?" When she nods reluctantly, I continue. "He's good friends with Archer. We're going out to dinner with him and his fiancé. I hope to present my idea in the next week or two, but tonight will help break the ice."

"Ah, such a wonderful idea. Truly." Gina takes off her dirty apron and tosses it into the laundry hamper, then comes toward me and wraps me into a big hug. "Such a smart girl you are, Marina. I wish your parents could see how much you love the bakery. I'm afraid they're going to sell it."

My heart sinks into my toes, reminding me of the other reason Gage is in my life. He plans on taking everything away from me anyway.

Makes me wonder why I'm trying to get in with Archer's hotels when the bakery might eventually disappear. "I wish they could see how much the bakery means to you, too."

Gina shrugs as she withdraws from my embrace. "Perhaps we should make a presentation to the family as well. Convince everyone that we need to keep the bakery for the both of us."

That sounds like an impossible feat. The bakery is right smack in the middle of the block of buildings that my family owns. I really doubt they'd sell all around it and let us have this space. "We can try, right?" I ask weakly.

She cups my cheek, giving my face a little shake. "Don't sound so defeated, girly. We could turn this around. Don't think we're already beat."

Hard to do, considering I feel like the both of us are work-ing toward an impossible goal. "Yeah, I know." The bell above the front door jingles, indicating someone's entered the café. "I should go check who's here." It's probably Gage, and my heart starts racing just thinking about seeing him.

I have got it so bad. And it is so wrong to feel this way.

"Don't keep your new man waiting," Gina teases and I stick my tongue out at her.

Someone clears their throat, drawing mine and Gina's at-tention. We both turn toward the front of the kitchen to find Gage standing in the doorway, looking downright sinful clad in jeans and a charcoal-gray sweater. He smiles at us, but I see the apprehension in his eyes.

He looks nervous. I think it's cute. Plus, his discomfort eases mine.

"Well, look who finally decided to show up," Gina declares in her booming voice as she moves away from me. She strides toward Gage, grabs him by his broad shoulders, and pulls him into an easy hug.

He looks startled, patting her back awkwardly. "Nice to see you again, Aunt Gina."

"Great to see you, too. You do casual very well." She pats his chest, her fingers lingering.

Oh, good lord. Talk about embarrassing. And are his cheeks turning pink?

"Look at him, Marina. Your Boy Toy is extra pretty to-night." Gina takes Gage by the hand and leads him to me.

"Boy Toy?" He raises a brow, stopping just in front of me. His full lips are curved into a secretive smile and a rush of memories floods me. How those lips feel on mine. How excel-lent he is with his hands. The smell of his skin, the way his soft hair curls around my fingers . . .

"I've upgraded your nickname. Thought Rat Boy was a little rude," Gina explains.

His expression goes solemn, though his lips twitch. "I appreciate that."

"Well, you two best be moving along. You've kept Marina here waiting long enough." She pushes the both of us, hurrying us out of the kitchen. I grab my purse from where I left it beneath the front counter, slinging it over my shoulder as I watch Gina bustle around the café, checking everything before locking up. "You two have fun tonight, all right?"

"Need any help?" I ask, keeping my voice low when I grab hold of her elbow before she can escape me again.

She flashes me a smile. "I've got this, sweetheart. You go have fun."

I release my hold on her, rolling my eyes as I turn to Gage. He's watching me; his gaze sweeps over me, slow and easy, and just like that arousal trickles through my blood, heating my skin. My aunt is forgotten, the bakery, everything else, and it's just me and him, standing in front of the door, the spot where just last night he had me pressed against the cold glass while he kissed me senseless.

"So I'm your Boy Toy?" he asks, his voice a husky murmur that sends chills down my spine.

"If the shoe fits," I tease, pleased when he opens the door for me like a gentleman should. He has manners. This is a plus.

"I have no problem with it," he teases back, his eyes twinkling. "I know you weren't complaining last night."

Glaring at him, I tilt my head to my thankfully still oblivious aunt. "Keep your voice down."

His expression switches to serious. "Sorry. Forgot myself."

I understand. I think we both forget ourselves when we're in each other's presence. Easy to do, considering the obvious chemistry sparkling between us.

This is going to be a long night.

Gage

She's so fucking gorgeous I can't get over it. All that long, tumbling blonde hair caught up in a high ponytail, showing off the pretty, irresistible curve of her neck. The neck I licked and nibbled last night, making her groan with pleasure, her hands clutching me tight . . .

Blowing out a harsh breath, I lead her outside toward where my car is parked at the curb. She stops short when she sees it, her wide-eyed gaze meeting mine. "*That's* your car?"

I nod, hitting the keyless remote in my hand so the doors unlock. "Yeah, that's my baby." I open the door to my newest purchase—a sleek, pearl-white Maserati Ghibli—and as I guide her into her seat, I can't help but like the way she looks settled inside my car.

I like the way she looks everywhere, as long as she's with me, if I'm being truthful.

What the ever-loving fuck?

Yeah. I've lost my mind. One night with a woman and I'm addicted. I think I want her even more because she's so damn indifferent.

"Your baby?" she asks me pointedly when I slide into the driver's seat, gripping the steering wheel. "This is a Ghibli."

Okay. I'm fucking impressed. Most women don't give a shit

about cars. Or they'll be able to recognize a brand but not the model. "You're right. I have a thing for cars. I like to collect them," I admit, starting the vehicle. It roars to life, the engine purring a low, sexy rumble that seems to vibrate throughout the entire interior.

I wonder if Marina would let me bang her in the back seat. That would make this a more than memorable date.

"I love Maserati. My dad has owned a few himself. He used to collect cars," she says, her voice wistful. "Not so much the last few years since he really doesn't have the time. Or the money."

Guilt assuages me at the money reference. But I can't help but be excited by the discovery that I have something in common with Scott Knight. "How many cars does he have?"

"Too many for me to count." She laughs and shakes her head, her hair rubbing against the soft Italian cream-colored leather. "He had an entire shop built to store them all. Most of them are vintage American classics mixed with a few Italian vehicles—homage to my mother's family."

"Nice." I pull out into traffic, shifting the car into gear as I slow down, and turn right. "I have a garage filled with the cars I've collected over the years. I started collecting when I was twenty-one."

"Really? How many do you have?"

I'm sort of blown away that we're having a normal conversation like normal people. No snarky remarks or rude comments. And that we actually have something in common—it's one of my favorite things to talk about, fast and expensive cars. "I have some in storage too. I think—yeah, I have close to one hundred cars in my collection so far."

"Wow. I know my dad had more than one hundred at one point, but I'm afraid he's sold quite a few of them." She nibbles on her lower lip, looking worried. "It makes him sad to lose them, but it needed to be done."

I can't imagine having to sell even one of my cars because times were tough. I'd do it if I had to but . . . I wouldn't want to. I feel for her father.

I also feel like an asshole. I want to buy property from her father for a steal, so I can turn it around and make a profit. Plus, I'm dating his daughter in the hopes I can get closer to him.

Though, really I like her. A lot. I'm not with her just so I can have an in with Scott Knight. I'm with Marina because I want to be.

"I'd love to see what remains of his collection some time." I would. Not just because I could get an in with him, but I'm genuinely interested. What if he has my dream car in his shop? Not that I have a particular car I'm yearning for, but hey, it could happen.

"Um, yeah." She fidgets in her seat, looking decidedly uncomfortable. "You know I still live at home, right?"

I'm shocked. I hadn't a clue. "You do? How old are you?"

She glares at me. Uh-oh. Here we go, right into "let's-see-how-out-of-hand-we-can-get-before-we-start-calling-each-other-names." "I'm twenty-three," she sniffs, all haughty Italian princess-like. "How old are you?"

"Twenty-eight."

"Really?" She sounds surprised. I glance at her to find she looks surprised too. "I thought you were older."

"How much older?" Shit, do I look old? I'm tempted to check myself out in the rearview mirror, but I resist the urge.

"I don't know." She shrugs, glances out the window. "Early thirties?"

"You like older men?" I tease.

She turns to glare at me again. "Not at all. I usually date men more *my* age." Her comment is pointed. Now she's really making me feel like a dirty, lecherous old man.

"I'm not even thirty," I mutter, shaking my head. Maybe we should quit talking. I never know what's going on in Marina's head. Our banter feels pretty comfortable at the moment, but we could slip into argument mode in a hot second. And I don't want us fighting before we get to the restaurant. Ivy will pick up on the tension rumbling between us and want to know what's going on. So would Archer probably, though he's pretty damn oblivious when it comes to that stuff.

Marina remains quiet, too; her hands curled in her lap, her head turned away, so she can stare out the window and watch the passing scenery. So I remain silent, sneaking the occasional glance at her hair, loving the multiple shades of blonde and brown mixed, knowing without a doubt that she's a natural blonde, now that I've seen her naked.

Thinking of her naked sends my thoughts into other directions. Dangerous, dirty, and unnecessary directions that I shouldn't be focusing on at the moment. Thinking of the two of us together leaves me feeling needy. Vulnerable.

Hungry. Starving, more like it. All for her.

Fuck.

"Can I ask you a question?" I gotta break the tension and talk about something else before I lose it and attack her.

She turns to look at me. "Go for it," she says warily.

"You're a blonde."

A smile teases the corner of her lips. "That's not a question."

"I thought Italians weren't normally blonde," I say lamely, feeling like a jackass. I'm trying to make conversation, and I feel like an idiot. This woman just makes me so damn . . . nervous. I can't explain it.

"I'm not one hundred percent Italian, you know. My dad is what he calls a mutt," she says, her voice light. She seems to like talking about her family, and I like it too. Any tidbit I can get on Scott Knight, I can turn around and use later.

But I also like learning more about her. I'm curious. I want to know. Usually I run the other direction when a woman wants to tell me her life story. So many of them do, going on and on about their past, their family, their friends. It all starts to sound like monotonous noise after a while.

Not with this woman. She offers these glimpses of her personal life so rarely, I cherish every tidbit I learn. Which is fucking crazy, truly. I shouldn't be that wrapped up in her, wanting to learn more, everything about her, wanting to kiss her . . .

"A mutt, huh?" I don't even know what to say to that for fear I'll mistakenly insult her father and piss her off.

She offers me a secretive smile, the sight of it sending a zing straight to my heart—and my cock. This woman twists me up into such complete knots, I don't know if I'll ever be able to unwind myself from them—or her. "My mother is Sicilian. There are a lot of blonde, blue- and green-eyed Sicilians out there. I happen to be one of them."

A beautiful one, too. She's so beautiful just looking at her hurts.

Not having her in front of me to look at hurts too.

Which means at the mere age of twenty-eight, I am completely ruined for any other woman. And I don't even care. I want to revel in the ruin.

My brain on overload, I drive the rest of the way to the restaurant in silence, taking the curves at high speed, enjoying the way the tires stick to the road, the squeal of rubber on asphalt making me smile. I downshift, the whine of the engine like music to my ears, and the faster I drive, the more I get into it.

"You're crazy," she whispers as I gain speed, going close to one hundred on a straightaway a few miles from the restaurant.

I roll down the windows, let the cool night air wash over my heated skin. Her hair blows everywhere, even restrained by the ponytail, and a long blonde strand hits me in the face, causing me to push it away. I chance a look at her, see that she's gripping the edge of her seat, her body on edge, her expression full of . . . excitement?

Really?

"You like it," I say, my tone practically a dare. "You're literally sitting on the edge of your seat."

"I do like it," she quietly admits, her wild eyes meeting mine. A shaky exhalation leaves her, and she nods toward me. "Go faster."

My foot presses on the gas pedal, picking up speed. She's watching me; I can feel her gaze on me, and I reach toward her, pushing all that sexy, wind-blown hair away from her face. Before I can drop my hand, she leans her cheek into my palm, then turns and presses a hot, wet kiss to my flesh, her tongue darting out for a quick lick.

I swear.

Ah, hell. I grow instantly hard, letting my hand fall from her cheek, but she wraps her fingers around my wrist, bringing my hand to her mouth and drawing my index finger deep inside her mouth, dragging her wet, lush lips along the length before she releases it, her eyes never leaving mine.

Easing my foot off the gas, I swallow hard. She's going to kill me. I tear my gaze from hers, keeping my attention on the road. It's dark, it feels like we're virtually alone, and I'm tempted. So tempted to pull over, kiss her until she's gasping my name, and then fuck her in the back seat just like I first envisioned.

I chance a glance at her, see the flushed cheeks, the parted lips. I recognize that look from last night. She's aroused.

Hell, yeah. So am I.

Downshifting, I pull over. I throw the car into park and lean over the center console at the exact time she moves toward me. We attack each other, lips searching, hands wandering, clinging, fighting to draw our bodies closer, but the awkward space makes it difficult.

"I want you," she whispers against my mouth before she sucks my lower lip between hers. "Please."

"Seriously?" I'm in absolute shock. She acted like having sex with me was the biggest mistake of her life. But here she is leaning into my hands as I curve them around her breasts, her breaths coming out in sharp pants as she rests her hands over mine, making me squeeze her breasts together.

Damn, she's hot.

"Seriously." Her voice tinged with amusement, she withdraws from my touch, moving closer to the passenger side door. Slowly she reaches for the hem of her shirt and tugs it up, then off, tossing it onto the back seat. Her bra is black, smooth satin and my mouth waters as she reaches behind her, unclasping it and tearing it off so it falls from her fingertips onto the floorboard.

I can't form words. She strips off each article of clothing until she's completely naked, coming at me like a woman possessed. I feel like a man possessed, obsessed with the feel of her soft skin beneath my palms, the taste of her. She climbs on top of me, pressing all that hot, wet deliciousness against my denim-covered cock, grinding against me like she's trying to get off.

Shit. Maybe she is trying to get off.

But no. She wants to involve me in the action too. Her nimble fingers undo my button fly and she's reaching inside my boxer briefs, sure fingers curling around the length of my cock. Knowing I'm about to blow, I lightly slap her hand away, reaching behind me to pull out my wallet and the condom nestled within.

I packed extra in the glove compartment earlier. I'm not an idiot.

"You make me crazy," she whispers, snatching it out of my fingers. She tears into it, rolling the condom onto my cock and then she's on top of me, slowly sinking until I'm completely imbedded inside her.

A car drives by, the bright white lights flashing across her, offering me a glimpse of her swaying breasts, her hips as they slowly move up and down. I grasp her there, steadying her, keeping her slow, afraid I'll ruin it by coming too fast.

Because holy shit, I'm ready to explode. I'm still fully clothed save for my open jeans and she's deliciously naked. All that fragrant, soft skin is wrapped around me, her breasts in my face, nipples teasing my lips. I draw one in deep, sucking, tonguing, teasing her until she's tossing her head back, riding me relentlessly. I shift away from her, wanting to watch. She's beautiful in her abandon, so lost as she races toward that delicious moment, and I want to mark this moment permanently in my brain.

"So good," she breathes, tipping her head back down so she can press her forehead to mine. I tip my chin up, brush her mouth with mine and she devours me. The kiss hot, wet.

Deep. I grip the end of her ponytail, tugging hard and she gasps.

Damn. She likes that too. If we didn't hate each other so much, I'd believe she was made just for me.

"Harder, Gage," she encourages, her hands gripping my shoulders. "Make me come."

Ah, fuck. I can't resist that. I increase my pace, thrusting hard, filling her again and again until she's crying out my name, her body quivering, sobs falling from her lips as she collapses against me.

I hold her close, tracing circles on her back with my fingertips, making her shiver. Her grip around my neck is like a vice, her face buried into my neck. I feel her warm lips press sweet kisses to my flesh, and I squeeze her closer, our racing hearts in complete and total sync.

"You haven't come yet," she whispers against my throat, her tongue licking.

My cock twitches. It's more than aware of that. "I know."

She lifts her head up, her arms loosely resting around my neck, her expression slumberous and full of satisfaction. "Let me make that up to you," she murmurs as she slowly starts to grind against me.

I wrap my hands around her waist, guiding her, my gaze locked where our bodies meet. She's moving on me slow and sure, little murmurs of pleasure escaping her, and I can't look away. I'm entranced by the way she moves, the words she says, the way she looks at me.

What am I doing? What is she doing to me? I feel lost . . . gloriously, deliciously lost in my need to have her.

Only her.

I'm closer to the edge, unable to hold back, when she reaches between us and touches my cock, then her clit. The sight of her slender fingers playing down there sends me right over the edge, making me gasp as my hips buck against her. She smiles her encouragement, murmuring my name, and I grab hold of her ponytail pulling her face to mine so I can drown in her kiss.

Fuck. I'm wrecked. All because of this woman.

Chapter 9

Marina

I enter the building with my head held high, pretending I have everything completely under control, while inside I'm a confused mass of jumbled nerves and rapidly growing insecurities. Smoothing my hair back from my face, I glance toward Gage as he stops just beside me, tall and commanding, earning plenty of appreciative glances from the various women sitting in the lobby and waiting to be seated.

He finds me watching him and flashes me a dazzling smile, making my heart race. I remember what he looked like only minutes ago, dazed and fascinated with me as I rose above him, naked and greedy and crazed with wanting him. Riding his thick cock straight into oblivion.

I don't know what came over me. Watching him drive that powerful, outrageously expensive car, his big hand shifting the gears, his thighs flexing as he pressed the pedals, sent me into a sexual tizzy. Just like that, I wanted him. Had to have him at that very moment or felt like I was going to die. I've never reacted like that to a man.

Ever.

"Do I look okay?" I whisper, leaning into him as I tuck yet another tendril behind my ear. I'd slicked on fresh lipstick while still in the car, pulling my clothes into place as best I could. He'd barely done anything, just tucked himself back into his jeans, tugged on his sweater, and he was good to go.

Men. They're disgustingly easy sometimes.

"Truth?" He smiles, and I sort of want to punch him for being so ridiculously good looking. I feel like a frazzled mess while he looks amazing. His hair is a little messy—from my eager fingers, I might add—but it's a good look for him.

Everything's a good look for him.

"Of course, tell me the truth," I mutter, irritated. Great, I must look a complete mess if he feels the need to tell me the "truth." I wonder if I have time to dash into the bathroom and put myself back together before we have to go sit down with Archer and his fiancé.

I really hope I like his fiancé. I'm more nervous meeting her than talking with Archer. Women hold such a strong influence on their men and their decisions. I know Archer's a respected businessman, but from what I understand, he's so far gone over this new and very steady woman in his life, I'm sure he listens to her opinion.

So what if she hates me? She could tell Archer how she feels and *bam*. My chance is over.

Gage grabs hold of my elbow and tugs me closer to him, his mouth right at my ear, hot breath fanning against my skin and making me shiver before he whispers, "You look . . . freshly fucked. And beautiful with it."

I pull away to meet his gaze, utterly speechless.

He grins. "It's a good look on you. One I suggest you wear as often as possible."

I smile and follow through with my earlier instinct, giving him a slug on the arm. He smirks, leans in once more and kisses my cheek, his lips lingering, warm and soft and so comforting I want to melt. "I can keep you in that look all night if you want."

"Stop." I shove him away from me, noticing the strange looks we're receiving from those waiting for a table. Great.

I so don't want to draw attention to the two of us together. What if someone recognizes us and it gets back to my dad that I'm out on a date with Gage? From what Gage told me, he's tried to get in contact with my father numerous times since our first encounter. And I know he's tried to talk to him prior to our meeting too.

I'm basically hanging out with the enemy. My dad would be furious, though I haven't talked to him about Gage. I'm too scared. It's bad enough I told my mom his name. It didn't dawn on me at the time since I was too busy looking for something to wear and not thinking with all cylinders firing. I'd been a little brain-warped after our night together, and now? After the incident in the car?

I'm toast. Done.

"Considering I know just how much you enjoyed getting that particular look, I wanted to make the offer," he says from over his shoulder as he moves away from me, approaching the hostess's counter and asking if our other party has already been seated. He flicks his head for me to follow and I do so like a good little girlfriend, letting him take my hand, loving the way he entwines my fingers with his as he leads me through the restaurant.

I can't believe I've fallen into this role so easily. I shouldn't want to. I shouldn't do it at all. I'm not his girlfriend and he's not my boyfriend. We're not even in a real relationship.

We're at one of the most expensive and revered restaurants in Napa Valley. Gage and Archer have exquisite taste, I'll give them that. The place is overflowing with beautiful people, all of them dressed to perfection. I can't see anything but a sea of suits and finely cut dresses. They all look like they just came out of work.

I look like I'm ready to hang out for the night and go clubbin'. Or worse, I have the freshly fucked look, according to Gage. Can everyone see we just had wild and crazy sex in his car?

God, I hope not.

My fingers tremble, and I feel him squeeze my hand. He comes to a stop, turning to look at me, his face etched with concern. "You okay?"

I shouldn't let it touch me that he's being so sweet. But it does. I want to melt at the concern I see reflected in his eyes. "A little nervous," I admit.

"Archer won't bite. You're going to be fine." He kisses me on the lips, right there in the middle of the freaking restaurant, and I want to both disappear and scream with glee that this man . . . this very fine man standing right here, is mine.

But he's not. Not really. We're . . . huh. I don't know what we're doing. He wants my family's property. He'd probably fall to my feet in gratitude if I introduced him to my father, which I so don't want to do. Helping him get that much closer to what he wants would be idiotic on my part. It would be the end of the bakery.

Besides, I want an opportunity to grow my business. Instead of pushing him away, I'm selfishly spending time with him. And we're gaining something from each other while we have wild passionate sex on the side. A totally unexpected bonus in this bargain we made.

It's so strange, so unlike anything I've ever done before. There is no definition for what I'm experiencing with Gage.

I just need to approach it day by day.

"What about Archer's fiancé?" I ignore the pointed stare the hostess is shooting us when she discovers we're not following behind her any longer. Just how big is this stupid restaurant?

"Yeah. Uh. She's great." He smiles and fidgets, releasing my hand so he can run his through his tousled dark hair. "I have a confession to make."

Dread fills my stomach. "What is it?"

"Sir? Miss? Your table is this way," the hostess calls, her voice full of hostility that we're not obeying her command.

We ignore her. "Tell me," I say when he still hasn't answered.

Shrugging, he reaches out, trails his index finger down my cheek. "She's my sister."

I frown. "Who? Do you mean Archer's fiancé?"

"Yeah." He winces. "My best friend is marrying my baby sister."

"Oh." I'm sort of offended that he didn't tell me from the first. Why keep it such a secret? I don't get it.

Sometimes, I really don't get him.

"Mister Emerson!" The hostess is practically shouting at us. "Please, follow me!"

We hurry after her, my mind awhirl after his confession. She leads us to the very back of the restaurant, where the private dining rooms are, and I blow out a slow, cleansing breath, trying to calm my agitated nerves.

I thought having sex with Gage in his car would take the edge off, but no, I couldn't have been more wrong. I feel edgier, more amped up than ever. He's not helping matters with how sweet he's being. You'd think I'd like his attitude and want more of it, after all the fighting and the arguing between us.

But I need the distance. I need to focus and think about what exactly I want to say to Archer. Now that I know he's with Gage's sister, that Archer is Gage's best friend, it puts a new spin on their relationship. Puts a new spin on the entire dynamic that's about to happen once we sit down with them. I knew he and Archer were good friends, but I guess I didn't realize they were *best* friends. They're practically family.

"Here you go." The hostess stops at an open door that leads to a small dining room, the interior done in cool greens and blues. Gage lets me walk in first, and I spot them sitting at the table. I smile nervously at Archer and his fiancé. Gage's freaking sister.

God help me, I hope I don't make a fool of myself in front of her. I want her to like me.

It doesn't matter if she likes you or not. You're not looking for a relationship with Gage. You're having dirty, awesome sex with him. Nothing more, nothing less.

I really wish I could believe that.

Plus, I need to focus on what I really want out of this dinner. A chance to gain exposure for the bakery and my aunt's desserts by having them featured at his hotel. That's what matters tonight.

Gage rests his hand at the small of my back, his simple touch making my heart hammer. I watch helplessly as Archer stands and approaches us, a warm smile on his handsome face as he stops in front of me. He's wearing a suit, just like everyone else in this restaurant save for me and Gage, and he's intimidating despite the friendly expression.

"Marina, it's wonderful to see you." Leaning in, he presses the requisite society kiss to my cheek. "You're looking ravishing tonight."

Oh. God. I want to die. He is so close to the truth it's embarrassing. Does he know Gage ravished me? Can he tell? Am I wearing a flashing sign on my forehead that screams *freshly fucked*?

Gage's low chuckle doesn't help matters either. If he doesn't watch it, he's going to end up with an elbow in the ribs.

"Thank you," I say, my voice shaky, and I clear my throat. "So glad you're able to have dinner tonight with us, Archer. I know it was last minute."

"Anything for Gage." He flashes him a quick, smug smile. "I may think he's a complete asshole, but considering he's going to be my brother-in-law in less than a year, I guess I need to start thinking of him as part of my family."

"Oh, stop being so rude." His fiancé approaches us as well, her expression open. Friendly. Curious. "I'm Ivy. Gage's sister. You must be Marina." She extends her hand toward me.

"Nice to meet you," I offer weakly, overwhelmed as she takes my hand and shakes it. I don't want to screw this up, and I'm going to if I don't watch it. I can barely keep my crap together as I stand before these two people.

I need to chill out.

Ivy's wearing a red wrap-style dress, looking effortless and elegant, and again I feel like an idiot in my jeans. I blame working at the bakery for my lack of dressy clothes. I have them, I just don't bother wearing them much anymore. I'm always in jeans.

Though Gage doesn't seem to mind me in jeans . . .

We all sit at the table, Archer and Ivy resuming the spots they occupied and Gage and I sitting across from them. The table is small, the setting intimate, and I keep my gaze on the place setting in front of me, trying to calm my racing heart.

Gage settles his hand on my back, reaching up to tickle

at the sensitive skin of my nape. I jerk my gaze toward him, giving him a look I hope he can interpret: one that says *stop touching me.*

He doesn't seem to get it. Clueless bastard. Instead he's smiling at me, as if he enjoys my slight discomfort, and I grimace at him, my breath catching in my throat when he laughs at me.

"Why are you so worked up?" he asks after the waiter sweeps out of the room with our drink orders. "You seem upset."

"I'm not upset." I glance toward Archer and Ivy, who are arguing over what to order for dinner. God, they're cute. "I feel woefully underdressed compared to everyone else in this stupid restaurant."

His smile turns wicked as he leans in closer, his voice lowering. "Baby, when we were in my car just a few minutes ago? Now *that* was woefully underdressed."

His words set my cheeks on fire, and he chuckles, shaking his head. "One minute you're the sexiest, most naked thing I've ever seen, and now you're blushing like a sweet school-girl."

"There's no such thing as 'most naked,' Gage," I say irritably, earning a bigger grin for my effort. "You're either naked or you're not."

"Well. You were *very* naked." He kisses my cheek. Again. It's like he can't stop touching me, not that I'm protesting. "And right now? You look amazing."

I feel my cheeks heat further, which is silly. Three simple words and my heart is hammering. He touches my elbow, my back, tucks my hair behind my ear, and I want him to touch me more. I think he sees it too. His knowing smile—which

I should find completely annoying—instead sends a shivery little thrill down my spine.

"You don't think I should be wearing a dress?" Why am I acting like a simpering, self-conscious girlfriend? I need to stop.

His gaze roves over me, taking me all in, and my skin heats as if he's physically touched me. "I think you look perfect," he says when his eyes finally meet mine, dark and serious and so intense I can hardly look away.

Oh. My. What is happening between us? I don't . . . don't know what comes over me when I'm with him. He's acting like he's truly interested in me and I . . . just don't think that's possible. Sexually, we're compatible. But two people can be in a sexual relationship that doesn't go beyond that point, right? Not that I've ever experienced anything like that, but I know people do it all the time.

So why is he looking at me like that? Saying such deliciously wonderful things to me? What in the world are we doing? This is supposed to be temporary between us.

Yet it already feels all too real. It shouldn't, though. Not at all.

Someone clears their throat, and I tear my gaze away from Gage to find Archer studying us, his expression full of amusement. Ivy's studying us as well, her delicate brow furrowed in confusion.

I can't blame her. I'm confused too.

"So Marina, I hear you've been spending time with Gage," Archer says, one brow lifting.

I want to squirm in my seat. Are Gage and I that obvious? Of course we are. We're hanging all over each other like we're together. He can't keep his hands off me. We just had sex in his car on the side of the road, for the love of God. The pheromones or whatever between us are probably off the charts.

And if they're best friends like Gage said, then surely Archer must know all about Gage's romantic past. Maybe I'm not Gage's normal type, and he's confused as well?

"Have you met Ivy before?" Archer asks me before he studies his fiancé with unabashed love in his eyes.

He knows the answer to this question. Is Archer trying to make this evening more awkward? What should I say?

Oh hey, Ivy. I know we haven't met and all but I've known your brother for a few days and we're having the wildest sex of my life. How do you do?

"This is the first time. I've only known Gage for a short time so . . ." I smile at her and she smiles warmly in return. "I had no idea Gage had a sister, so it's wonderful to meet you."

"I had no idea Gage was seeing someone, so the feeling's mutual." Her smile fades as her gaze turns assessing. "I don't believe I've heard my brother mention you before. How did you two meet exactly?"

"Um . . ." My voice trails off and I feel silly. I sought him out that night. *I wanted to meet the man who's trying to buy out my family.*

But I can't tell Ivy that. I'd sound like a cold, callous bitch.

"I'm so curious. Gage never lets me meet any of the women that he dates." Ivy's just about as determined as her brother. Scary.

And have there been a lot of women? There had to have been. He's charming, sexy, rich, and influential. What woman wouldn't find him a catch?

You, maybe?

"At that wine- and beer-tasting event I went to in Archer's place," Gage answers for me.

"That was only a few nights ago," Ivy says, frowning.

Gage shrugs. "Right. That's what I said. We met, and I asked her out. Now here we are." He sends Archer a pointed look, who just smirks at him in return, and I don't know what to think.

There's an undercurrent flowing between these three, unspoken messages, and I'm the one left out. I knew this would happen. I have no idea what's going on, and I don't like it. I wish we could go back to the car, where it's just the two of us. Wrapped up in our own little bubble, touching each other, kissing each other . . .

Getting lost in one another.

Chapter 10

Gage

|don't know if I want to go to your bakery," Ivy says with a laugh, making me glare at her. She waves her hand, dismissing me easily, considering she's been doing it since we were kids.

But damn, I don't want her to offend Marina. She's sensitive enough about her family business.

They're laughing, though. Having a good time together. Archer leans back in his chair with an arrogant expression on his face. Like he has me all figured out and knows that I'm already halfway whipped when it comes to this woman.

Not that I'd ever admit he's right.

"Trust me, I feel the same way sometimes! God, the things my aunt can create. Her breakfast muffins are to die for. If I didn't watch myself so carefully, I'd end up fat as can be." Marina laughs, the sound warming me deep inside, and I chance a look at her.

She's beautiful. Her eyes are sparkling and her smile is wide. My sister looks happy. This was exactly what I wanted to avoid and look at the two of them. Hitting it off and acting like they're old friends.

What a night it's been. We've actually been getting along,

making conversation that didn't involve us calling each other names or me saying something infinitely stupid.

I had one minor slipup. Well, a few, if I count the most recent blunder, me confessing that Ivy is my sister. I think that sort of blew Marina's mind.

We're getting along now. Everything's rockin'. I still can't believe the way she attacked me in my car. Talk about the hottest experience of my life. I've never done something that wild, never had a woman jump me after becoming aroused by my driving my freaking car.

I barely know her, and yet I feel like this woman sitting at my side was made for me.

Marina's had a couple of glasses of wine, and the alcohol has loosened her up. Maybe the sex earlier did too, I don't know. She's pretty damn easygoing, and I like it.

I like her.

The scent of her hair drives me crazy. It wafts toward me every time she turns her head, her ponytail swinging. I love the sound of her laughter. I haven't heard it very often, but I plan on changing that. I love her smile too. She's very expressive, all that cool blonde mystery from the first night I met her seemingly evaporated. In its place is an open, smiling woman. Full of laughter and easy conversation, sexy as hell wearing that thin, glittery black top that dips low in the front, offering me a generous view of her cleavage.

Breasts I had my hands all over not an hour ago. Her nipples were in my mouth. I can still hear her ragged moans when I sucked them deep. I remember her naked body, wrapped all around me as she rode me hard.

Yeah. Fuck. This woman . . . she's blowing my mind.

Ivy had been wary at first. I don't normally bring women

around her, and we threw her for a loop when she found out we'd only just met. She knows I haven't been serious about a woman in a long time. If ever.

"We should definitely do that," Marina says with an enthusiastic nod.

Her words bring me back down to earth. "Do what?" I ask her, glancing from my sister back to Marina.

She turns to look at me, those sparkling blue eyes trained on my face, making my blood burn. For her. "Oh, your sister suggested we go on a shopping trip together soon. I was just telling her how it's been forever since I went clothes shopping, and she offered to go with me into San Francisco for the day. Sounds like fun, don't you think?"

Reality butts its ugly head into my mind, and I frown. The two of them are almost getting too close when this . . . thing between Marina and I will go nowhere. Because that's what always happens. Yeah, I'm into this woman more than I've been with any woman, but I know my patterns. This won't last. It never does. "You're not constantly shopping, huh? I thought that's what all women do."

"Oh my God," Ivy mutters while Archer full-out groans.

Marina glares at me, her eyes narrow, her lips tight. "I cannot believe you just said that. Are you for real?"

There I go again, saying the worst thing ever and offending Marina. Thought I had it under control since we've been getting along so well tonight, but I guess not. I swear it's like my brain shuts down when I'm around her, and I blurt out the stupidest things with absolutely no thought. "I was kidding?" I offer weakly.

"Yeah right," she mumbles, her eyes hot with anger as they shoot daggers at me.

If looks could kill . . .

Hell, I can't tell if she's really mad or not.

Archer stands. "Hey Gage, come with me for a minute. I want to show you something."

"What do you want to show me?" Now I'm confused. Maybe I'm the one who's had too much wine. Or maybe I'm just drunk on Marina . . .

"Let's go outside," he says with a giant smile on his face, but it looks fake as hell.

I follow him outside wordlessly, the front of the restaurant still crowded with people waiting for a table. We end up around the side of the building, the cool night air washing over me as a breeze blows over us, relieving my overheated body and brain.

"What the hell is going on in there?" Archer asks.

Shrugging, I glance around, making sure no one is paying attention to us. "What are you talking about?"

"I'm confused. You seem way into Marina, and I thought you weren't interested in her. Marina and Ivy seem to like each other. Which is great, I'm glad to see the two of them getting along so well so quick, but I thought . . . I thought this dinner was all about Marina wanting to talk to me about some proposition she has," Archer says, running a hand through his hair.

"I think she's nervous. That's why she hasn't mentioned anything to you yet," I suggest. Hell, I'd told her not to say anything, and here's Archer asking why she's not. I'm just making up excuses, and it's not like we can call her out on it at the table. That would just be flat-out rude.

Since when do you care if you're rude to Marina or not?

It irritates that she hasn't even told me what she wants to

talk to Archer about. I'm just as much in the dark as he is. Doesn't she trust me enough with the information?

Of course not, asshole. Remember? She doesn't even know you.

"Well. She's hardly said one word to me, but that's fine. Maybe she doesn't want to talk about it in front of your sister, which I totally get." Archer pauses, studying me. "And then there's you."

"What about me?" I'm immediately defensive.

"If this is, and I quote, 'a business proposition,' and you're just using her, and I quote again, 'to get what you want,' then you're doing a damn good job of being the attentive, googly-eyed date."

"'Googly-eyed'? Nice description," I mutter. We're obvious. I didn't think it would matter in front of Archer and Ivy, but what the hell was I thinking? It didn't help that we just had sex before we stumbled into the restaurant. I still had a postcoital glow going on, for fuck's sake.

"It's true! Every time you look at her, you're like a lovesick puppy. I think you like her," Archer says.

"I do not," I answer way too quickly. Misery courses through me. Do I like her? I shouldn't like her.

You fucking like her, moron.

"I'm attracted to her," I finally say. "How could I not be? She's beautiful."

Archer shakes his head. "Then you better be up-front with her about this real estate deal you want to make with her dad."

"No way. She'll hate me for it." She called me a scum-sucking shark or whatever the first time we met, when she discovered who I am. She finds out I want to sweep in on the property the Molinas hold on St. Helena's Main Street—

including the very bakery she's running—she'll hate me for life.

Shit. She probably already suspects this. She has to. Marina's no dummy. She's smart and beautiful and—

"She'll hate you more if you keep the truth from her."

I absorb Archer's words, remaining quiet. Since when did he get so good at doling out advice? That's always been my thing. Now I'm the one making idiot moves, and he's the stable, secure one full of logic.

"You could always lease the property back to her," he suggests when I don't say anything. "Give her a deal and let her run the bakery that seems to mean so much to her."

"How do you know what it means to her?" I ask incredulously.

"Weren't you listening to what she said? She was talking about running the bakery, her aunt, and the amazing cakes she makes. I've tasted them, so has Ivy. She was totally engrossed in the conversation, offering Marina all sorts of marketing ideas to try." Archer shakes his head. "Are you oblivious or what?"

I look at Marina and all I can think about is the next time I can get her naked. I guess . . . I was tuning her out like a self-absorbed asshole.

"I'm going back in there and asking her what she wants to talk about. I'm not in the mood for a bunch of pussyfooting anymore. I'm too damn curious," Archer finally says, starting to head back to the front of the building.

I walk with him, the both of us striding side by side toward the restaurant entrance. "Come on. Let her segue into it on her own. I think she just needs to build up her courage."

"She's having fun with Ivy, and she's probably had a little

bit too much to drink. I think it's time for Marina to grow a pair and tell me what's up." Archer throws open the door, and I follow him in, wondering at his change of mood.

He's never been the most patient person. While I have no problem lying in wait, calculating my every move. Whether in business or personal matters, Archer gets too antsy.

"Give her time, damn it," I mutter, earning a hard glare from Archer.

"Why are you so protective of her, huh? You've only known her a few days. What gives?"

I care for her. It's the stupidest thing ever, but I do. I like her. A lot. The more I think about Archer's leasing sugges-tion, the more I believe it could be the solution to the prob-lem hovering over us. "I—"

"You like her," Archer says again, not sounding surprised. "A lot. I get it, man. Sometimes when it happens, it takes a while like it did for Ivy and me. Other times, it happens so fast you just know."

"I just know what?"

"You know you're in love with her."

I scoff. "I am not in love with her," I say emphatically. "I've known her a week."

"You have feelings for her, then." Archer grimaces. "Christ, listen to me. I've turned into Oprah."

"I blame Ivy," I say with a grin, though deep inside my stomach is knotted, my head spinning. Fine. I like Marina. A lot. I'm not in love with her. Not . . .

Yet?

I banish the thought.

"Be honest with her." Archer stabs his finger into my chest, making me wince. "If I can give you any advice, it's to tell her the truth. Be up-front. Let her know about the real estate deal. Tell her you want her help in getting to talk to her father."

"I sort of already did," I say, rubbing at my chest where he poked me. Damn, that hurt.

He's right, though. I don't have to take the bakery away from her. I don't want to. If it means that much to her, I'm sure we could work something out. I could lease the building back to her and her aunt and they could keep Autumn Harvest open. Keep the business in the family.

That's a freaking great idea.

"Great. Good. You're on the right path." Archer exhales loudly. "It's just . . . I like seeing the two of you together. Don't make fun of my ass, but you seem really happy with her. You're always so wrapped up in your work. It's nice to see you let loose and have fun."

I run my hand across the back of my neck, contemplating his words. "You're not saying this because of that stupid bet we made, are you?"

He rolls his eyes. "I already lost that fucker and you know it. Why would I want to sabotage your ass? I have no stake in it. This is between you and Matt."

"I haven't seen him in—forever." Matt's busy getting his new winery ready for its grand opening.

"Ivy's with him a lot lately since she's been working on the interiors. Ask her how he's doing." Archer smiles.

We head back to the private dining room. "What's up with the shit-eating grin?"

Archer shrugs. "Ivy thinks Matt's assistant has a major crush on him. He ignores her. I think it makes her want him more."

"Who the hell would have a crush on Matt DeLuca?" I ask indignantly. Only the majority of the female population in

California, let alone the entire United States. Back in the day, he'd been the star pitcher for the San Francisco Giants. Until a major knee injury put him into early retirement. Thank Christ for lucrative investments and endorsements. The guy sits on pile of gold bricks, he's so damn rich.

Huh. There's another reason why I'm not looking for a serious relationship. I don't want Matt to win this stupid bet. But is that good enough reason to not want to pursue something more with Marina? So I can beat Matt in a million-dollar bet?

Shit. Am I really considering if Marina is worth more than a million dollars?

You are . . .

Archer's out of the running with our bet. I'm close to being out without even realizing it. So that leaves Matt the winner?

Unless he finds himself attached as well in the next few weeks, months. Whatever. Then we'd have to call it a draw.

"You should have Ivy do some matchmaking," I suggest casually, knowing Archer will see right through me.

"Good idea." Archer nods as we stop at the open door of our dining room. "I'll talk to Ivy. She can work some magic and hook them up."

"And then I'm off the hook," I finish, making Archer grin.

We enter the private dining room chuckling, Ivy and Marina silent as we resume our seats. "You two okay?" Ivy asks pointedly.

I slip my arm around the back of Marina's chair, stroking her shoulder with the tips of my fingers. "We're great. How are you two?"

Marina turns to look at me, her expression full of confusion. "I thought you were arguing or something."

"I was just trying to set his ass straight," Archer pipes up. I send him a hard stare. Wish he would shut the fuck up. "So Marina, why don't we discuss whatever it is you wanted to talk about with me?"

She fidgets in her chair, glancing down for a moment and breathing deep, as if for courage, before she lifts her head, her gaze meeting Archer's. "You want to talk about it now?"

"Now is as good a time as any," he says with a shrug.

"Okay." She rests her hands on the table, her fingers plucking nervously at the pale blue tablecloth. "Like I was saying earlier, my aunt Gina makes amazing cakes."

"They are amazing," Archer agrees. "I can personally vouch for that."

She smiles. "Thank you. I'll let her know. Well, I wanted to see if you were interested in featuring her cakes at the restaurants within your hotels."

Archer studies her, doesn't say a word. He's thinking, I can practically see the wheels turning in his brain, but his silence is making Marina uncomfortable. "I like this idea," he finally says with a small nod.

"You do?" Marina sounds so hopeful I can practically feel the excitement vibrating off her.

"I do. We can call the cakes 'decadent desserts' or something along those lines. Our resorts have an almost . . . hedonistic quality to them." Archer smiles. "You and Gage should stay there sometime."

Very funny, motherfucker.

"Gina is a creative genius. Not only do her desserts and muffins taste amazing, but they're beautiful. Like little pieces of edible art."

"Hmm." Archer taps his finger against his pursed lips, then reaches inside his pocket and pulls out his cell phone, bringing up his calendar. "Can you meet with me on Monday? Come up with a written proposal, exactly what you want to provide, and I'll consult with my restaurant managers, see if they're on board."

Marina's mouth is hanging open. She looks totally shocked. "Are you serious?" she asks breathlessly.

"Absolutely. I was just telling Ivy how I wanted to stop by your bakery soon so I could get a cake. I have a not-so-secret sweet tooth and so does Ivy. Occasionally we indulge. And your aunt is amazing." Archer smiles. "I'd be honored if I could feature her at the restaurant. There will be some kinks to work out, but I know we can make it happen if you're both patient."

Marina pushes out of her chair and goes to Archer, throwing her arms around him and hugging him so tight, I'm afraid her cleavage is going to strangle him. I refuse to get jealous. She's so happy I can't begrudge her or her happiness. Ivy's laughter indicates she feels the same way.

"Thank you, thank you," Marina says, jumping away from him, the smile on her face saying it all. "We'll make this happen. I promise. You won't regret it."

"I know I won't," Archer says, smiling at her in return before he levels his gaze on me. "Hope everything works out for you and the bakery. If anything, your aunt could come and work for me if Autumn Harvest ends up getting shut down."

That fucking prick. I can't believe he would say that to her.

"Um, I'm hoping we can make it work, but I appreciate you offering a job to Gina. I know she would appreciate it too." Marina smiles, though some of the light has dimmed. "Thanks, Archer." The excitement has left her voice. She sounds disappointed and she glances down at the table.

Damn my friend for putting her on top of the world and then knocking her right off with a few choice words.

"Why would you say that to her?" Ivy slaps his arm, hard. "You give her good news only to bring her crashing down with bad stuff."

"Hey, I'd hire Marina too." Archer flashes her a smile, which Marina returns, but it doesn't quite light up her eyes.

Jerk. Thank God my sister spoke up. He's as bad as me, saying the wrong thing at the wrong time.

Hearing his offer makes me want to help her keep the bakery now more than ever. If I get my hands on those buildings, there is no doubt in my mind I will make that bakery hers. She can fight me all she wants, but I won't take no for an answer.

I want to do right by her. It's the least I can do.

Chapter 11

Gage

"I'm nervous." I tap my fingers against the steering wheel, nodding my head to the music playing on the radio.

Marina reaches over and grabs my hand, squeezing quickly before she releases it. "Don't be. He's going to love you. Maybe."

Ha. How honest of her. The "he" she's referring to is her father. The man I've been trying to see for months so I can make an offer hopefully he can't refuse. Scott Knight has avoided me. Yeah, I know he's been out of town a lot, but the least he could do is take my calls.

Now he has no choice. I'm going to dinner tonight with Marina at her house and meeting the parents. A big step for me, one I rarely make, but we've been seeing each other for over a month. Hopefully, Scott and I can discuss the real estate deal further. Maybe.

Funny how once I got involved with his daughter, that deal isn't as important to me anymore.

"I'm pretty sure your dad hates me," I say, because it's true. The guy must despise me. He's avoided me because he doesn't want to make the deal. Now he probably hates the fact I'm with his daughter. His only child. God, I'd hate me if I were him.

Could I sound any more ridiculous? I'm anxious as fuck and acting like an idiot.

She doesn't say a word in response to my dumb statement. Just sits in the passenger seat of my car with that blissed-out expression on her face. The one that says *I just got laid*, which she did since we had sex right before we left.

I frown. Hope her parents won't know that look. They might want to kill me for touching their baby girl.

"Stop frowning." She leans over the center console and gives me a soft kiss on the lips—while I'm driving. Thank God the road is pretty empty because I swerve a little when that sweet mouth brushes against mine. "You worry too much."

Ha. I don't worry enough. I've been letting myself forget everything and just enjoying my time with Marina. If we're not working, we're together. And lately, I'm not working much at all, which means . . .

"Turn here," she instructs as she points her finger, breaking my train of thought, and I hit the brakes to slow down, turning right onto a long, tree-lined driveway. It seems to go on for miles and my stomach cramps with nerves at the thought of coming face-to-face with Scott Knight. I haven't met a woman's family as her boyfriend since I don't know when. Ever?

This fact should make me feel like a twenty-eight-year-old loser, but damn it, I haven't found the right woman yet. As crazy as it sounds, in the little time we've known each other, I'm starting to think she's it. She's the one. Marina.

Shit. I know my friends love this. Archer doesn't fault me too hard because he's hopelessly in love with my sister. Matt, on the other hand, revels in my lovesick misery. He's also figuratively holding his hand out every chance he gets, demanding we hand over that one-million-dollar payout.

Jackass.

"How long is this damn driveway?" I mutter, earning a little laugh from Marina. Just as I ask, the thick trees disappear, revealing a circular driveway and a somewhat modest house with a spectacularly landscaped yard. I figured for sure Marina grew up in a sprawling mansion, the lone child who ran the house.

Guess I was wrong.

I park the Maserati in front of the four-car garage—the one sign of excess I see—surprised when Marina leans over and gives me another kiss. This one is longer, her lips lingering on mine, her hand curling around the back of my neck and holding me close. I exhale on a rough sound of pleasure and part her lips with my tongue, letting myself sink into her delicious, seductive mouth for a while. Forgetting all about my worry and the fact that I'm making out with Marina in front of her parents' home.

You're fucking making out with Marina in front of her parents' house, you asshole! What the hell? Are you sixteen and can't control yourself?

Well. That was like an ice-cold dose of reality.

Pulling out of the kiss, I smudge my thumb across her lush bottom lip, smiling at her as she glares up at me. I don't think she likes that I ended our kissing session. "We shouldn't be doing this," I whisper.

She pouts. "Why? I can't resist you. You know this."

Her simple admission makes me smile, but I don't let myself get too hung up on it. "We're at your house. Your parents are waiting inside to meet me, and I want to make the right impression. Not be the guy who's caught kissing and feeling up their daughter in his car."

"You weren't feeling me up," she points out.

I grin. "Yet."

Marina rolls her eyes. "Whatever. And don't worry about my dad. He'll take one look at your precious car and fall in love." Smiling, she leans in for another kiss, but I dodge her at the last minute, making her pout again. "Come on."

"Yeah, you got that right. Come on." I open the door and climb out, rounding the front so I can open her door. "Let's go meet your parents."

I take her hand and pull her out of the car, hoping like hell she doesn't notice my sweaty palm. She flashes me a sweet smile and leads me to the front door, her hips swishing seductively when she walks, her ass looking perfect in those jeans she's wearing.

Yeah. I'm a total goner for her. And she knows it too. I never, ever thought a woman would have me so totally by the balls, but this one does. I don't mind either. In fact, I like it, knowing she's mine. Knowing I'm hers.

Archer finds my capitulation into couplehood amusing. My sister thinks it's the cutest thing she's ever seen, and that's a direct quote. Matt laughs every time I talk to him, asking if I'm completely whipped yet. He knows how reluctant I was to let myself get caught by a woman.

Now I'm walking into the so-called trap and seriously thinking I never want out of it.

Marina doesn't bother ringing the doorbell, and we walk inside to find the living area empty. It's a wide, open space, full of comfortable furniture that has seen better days and lots of family photos on every available flat surface. On tables, bookshelves, hung on the walls, I'm surrounded by Molinas and Knights, all of them watching me, making me want to squirm where I stand.

Yeah. I think I've lost my damn mind. This is what a case of nerves does to a man.

"Dad!"

Marina lets go of my hand, and I watch as she hurries toward her father who's just entered the living room. She practically throws herself at him, giving him a big hug, which he returns. I know they're close. She complains that she hasn't seen him much lately since he's been out of town, working all the time.

He's scrambling. Trying to sell off property and cars and whatever else he can get rid of to gain some cash flow. I know this through friends and acquaintances in the business. They all talk. Knight's been going into San Francisco a lot lately to broker deals. Yet he's still holding on to that one property I want.

And I think if I work it just right, I can make it mine.

You are such a complete asshole. Marina's going to think you're using her to get to her dad.

That had been true, once upon a time. Not any longer. I care for this woman. Hell, I'm falling in love with her. Being in the middle of this situation, not quite knowing what to do . . .

It sucks.

"Good to see you, sweetheart." Her father gives Marina a kiss on the cheek, smiling down at her. "You look happy."

I stand there, at a loss over what I should do. Approach them? Clear my throat? Yell that his daughter looks happy because I put that smile on her face and the glow in her cheeks?

Yeah. Can't do that.

"I want you to meet Gage. Remember I told you about him?" She withdraws from her father's embrace and leads him over to where I stand. "Gage, this is my father, Scott."

"Nice to meet you." I offer my hand and he takes it, somewhat reluctantly. Or maybe I'm overreacting. The guy sets me on edge just looking at him.

He's tall, has a headful of salt-and-pepper hair, and his eyes are a pale, icy blue. Looking at me like he wants to hang me up by my balls too. "Gage. I believe you've been trying to get in contact with me."

"Let's not talk business today," Marina starts, but I interrupt her.

"I have been. I know you're a busy man, but when you get a chance, there's something I'd like to discuss with you."

"Call my office. We can set up a meeting," he offers breezily.

"I've been trying to do that for months," I tell him, needing him to know I'm not in the mood to play games.

Marina shoots me a horrified glare. "Gage," she whispers, trying to shut me up.

"Don't get mad at him. He's right." Scott's smile is easy. Too easy. "I have avoided his calls. I believe he's asking for something I'm not quite ready to give up yet."

Marina's mouth drops open. "How do you—"

"Just like you know," Scott says, smiling at her. "Everyone knows. This town is big, but it has a small-town feel, just like the gossip. And when a stranger comes into town, eager to buy up all the prime real estate he can, he gives everyone something to talk about."

I can't tell if this guy is merely tolerating me or hates my guts or . . . doesn't mind that I'm here and dating his daughter. His only child who I know he's very protective of.

Can't blame him, though. I'm feeling rather protective of her too. Something we definitely have in common.

"Ah, is this your young man?" Maribella Knight breezes into the room, a slight smile curling her lips. This is who Marina gets her looks from. Maribella is a beautiful woman, her features so similar to her daughter's, I pretty much know what Marina's going to look like when she's older.

"Yes. This is Gage." Marina smiles nervously. Just like her relationship with her father is so strong, the one she shares with her mother is a bit more fragile. "Gage, this is my mom, Maribella."

"Call me Mari." She extends her hand toward me, her gaze not as warm as her voice.

I take her hand and give it a shake, notice how limp it is in my grip. "A pleasure," I say truthfully.

"I'm sure." The smile she offers me is brittle, and her gaze narrows the slightest bit.

Yeah. I don't think Marina's mother likes me very much at all.

Marina

I knew my mother wouldn't like very Gage much. I don't think she'd like any man I brought home. She has these certain expectations I'm afraid no guy could ever meet.

So I pretend her cold disdain doesn't bother me. Throughout the afternoon and into dinner, she acts disinterested in him. But he does seem to get along with Dad. Now that shocks me. I figured my father would hate him on sight, considering Gage wants nothing more than to buy as much property from him as possible.

They have things in common, though. They're both savvy businessmen. My father's only downfall is that he owned too much, too fast. It's been hard for him to recover from the economic crash.

And they both love cars. In fact, their conversation revolves mostly around cars from the time we arrived. Gage even took Dad outside to check out his Maserati, which was love at first sight. At first I thought it was cute. After a while, I got bored.

Last, I'm hoping that they both care about me. Well, I know my dad loves me because, hello, he's my father. But Gage? He's never said the words to me, not that I think he would. He's never even admitted that he cares about me, but what can I expect? We haven't been together that long.

But Mom said something to me years ago, and I've never forgotten her words.

Sometimes, when you know, you just know.

That's how I feel about Gage. It scares the crap out of me and makes me want to punch him—because near violence is my usual mode of operation when it comes to Gage—but really, I'm excited. Nervous.

I'm falling in love.

Finally, I was able to drag him and my father apart, and we left long after dinner. Mom gave me a look that said she expected me to come right back. Dad told Gage to come by the office any time, or at the very least, call.

So strange. I thought my father would hate him. I thought I would hate Gage, but look at me. Maybe it's not such a bad thing, letting the bakery go. Gage could buy the strip of buildings, and my family would be in a better financial position. I know that's been my father's goal for a while. Maybe I'm the selfish one, wanting to hold on to a business that's nothing but a drain for my family.

"You're awfully quiet."

I glance up to find Gage flashing me a quick smile before he returns his attention to the road. It's near ten o'clock and he has the windows cracked, letting in the cool fall air. The roads are virtually abandoned, the night sky is like dark velvet dotted with brightly twinkling stars shining from above, and I haven't felt this content in a long time. If ever.

"I'm glad you and my father got along so well," I say.

"Truthfully? I'm surprised," he admits.

Laughing, I shake my head. "So am I. I thought he might hate you . . . or love you."

"I know." Gage chuckles. "He's a good guy, though. I like him."

"So are you. A good guy," I say softly, drinking Gage in, arousal heating my blood. It doesn't take much for me to want him. And seeing him behind the wheel of one of his powerful cars always makes me want to jump his bones.

When it comes to Gage, I'm incredibly weak. But I don't mind, because when I'm with him, I feel strong. Like I can do anything.

"Archer called yesterday." He sends me a quick look. "He said the two of you met a few days ago."

"We did." I nod. "He wanted to hammer out the details."

"That's amazing. I'm happy for you. Why didn't you tell me about it?" He sounds a little incredulous.

Leave it to Gage to get right to the point. Not that I can blame him. He deserves to know what's going on. "I was afraid I'd jinx it."

"Even to me?" He looks wounded. Silly man.

Leaning over the console, I press a kiss to his cheek, resting my hand on his muscular thigh so I can give it a squeeze. "Especially to you. You'll pump me up and get me so excited, I'll believe I can do no wrong. What if it didn't work out?"

"I would never let it not work out." His expression goes

tight and his lips thin. "I'd kick Archer's ass before that would happen."

"That's exactly why I didn't tell you," I say, laughing. "This is not about you kicking Archer's ass. This is about Archer and me coming to a business decision. I can't have you glowering in the background, out to tear anyone apart who dares defy me."

"Why not? I can't help it if I'm protective of you."

He is so sweet I almost want to cry. Or do him. I'd prefer the latter.

"I love how protective you are of me," I murmur, smoothing my hand up and down his thigh. God, I love his body. He's so hard . . . everywhere. "I've never had someone defend me before."

"Well, I'm all yours. Don't forget it." He flinches and yelps when I cup his burgeoning erection. "Damn it, Marina. I'm driving."

"Yes, you are. And I'm touching you. Don't mind me." I undo the button fly on his jeans and slip my hand within, encountering warm, thin cotton stretched across his hard, thick cock. My panties dampen just touching him, and I release a shuddering breath.

"Don't you dare do what I think you're doing," he admonishes, but his voice is weak. He's such a sucker for my touch.

Almost as much as I'm a sucker for his.

"I could give you a hand job while you drive." I scooch closer to him, my mouth at his ear, and I curl my fingers around his length. "Or a blow job. Remember when I did that last week?"

That had been fun. He'd been driving this powerful car, looking so sexy and in command I hadn't been able to resist.

Next thing I knew, I was sprawled across the front seat of the Maserati with my head in his lap and his erection in my mouth. He'd had to pull over so I could finish him off without him wrecking.

Hot. He makes me so hot it's ridiculous. I'm with him, and I feel like a giddy teenager just out for a good time. I think he feels the same way.

At least we're in this together.

"Baby, I love it when you put your mouth on me, but I'm trying to get us home in one piece so I can have my mouth all over *you.*" He stifles a groan when I deliberately stroke him. "Fuck, I swear you like seeing me in agony."

I do. I love torturing him. Only because I know he wants me so bad. It's a heady feeling, wielding this much power over Gage. And he has power over me as well, there's no denying it. I think we make a great team.

I can only hope my family feels the same. And eventually they can forgive him—specifically my mother—when he buys up our properties in downtown St. Helena and resells it. That's what his plan is. He doesn't even have to tell me. I already know.

And I finally think I'm okay with his plan. If I have to give up the bakery, then so be it. It chokes me up to think about it, but I need to act like a grown-up. Archer and I have discussed my possibly working with him very casually, and I know he means his offer. He's mentioned me taking on a management position within one of his restaurants. I don't know if I would actually pursue it, but hey, it's an option. One I appreciate Archer making for me.

"We'll be home soon, okay?" He settles his hand over mine, giving it a squeeze. I, in turn, give his cock another squeeze. His ragged moan sends a little thrill through me that urges me to keep going. "And then you can do whatever you want to me."

"Really? Whatever I want?" I raise my brows. There are so many things we haven't attempted yet that I'd love to try out. I'm so comfortable with him, I know whatever I suggest, he'd be game for it.

"Definitely whatever you want. But you need to get your hand off my dick. I feel like I'm gonna blow," he says through gritted teeth.

I burst out laughing. "I've barely touched you!"

"Yeah, but that's all it takes, Marina. Haven't you realized that by now?" He turns to look at me, the heated glow in his eyes so intense, it steals my breath.

And makes my heart expand. He's so far gone over me, I love it.

Especially since I feel the same exact way.

Chapter 12

Gage

I've waited for this moment for what feels like a lifetime. Hounded this man until I'm sure he was sick and tired of hearing and seeing my name. Now that the time has come, and I'm sitting across from him in my San Francisco office, and despite being on my turf, I'm so full of nerves I swear I'm going to be sick.

I am also a complete wuss. My biggest fear? That I'll somehow fuck it all up and lose everything.

Including Marina.

"My daughter likes you," Scott Knight says, his gaze razor sharp as it meets mine. I don't back down. Just keep my expression neutral and hope like hell he can't tell I'm sweating beneath my suit. "But just because she likes you doesn't mean I have to."

Jesus. Way to boost my confidence.

"I'm giving you the benefit of the doubt, though. Marina doesn't make bad choices. She's a smart girl. I like to think I had something to do with that." Scott turns his head toward the window, seemingly lost in thought. "So with that said, I think it's time we discuss you purchasing the property downtown."

Fucking finally. I practically sag in my chair. The relief

that's ready to consume me is strong, but I'd also have to be an idiot to believe all is well. This could be a trick.

I've been tricked before.

But no. Without hesitation, he launches into the specifics. Costs and current leases and documents and the details regarding the preliminary contract he had his lawyer draw up. Photos and the history of the buildings and that one single question: *I don't plan on tearing it all down so I can rebuild, do I?*

Hell no, I answer, knowing that I pleased him just by the look on his face.

I scan all the documents as he pushes them toward me, knowing I'm going to have my lawyer review them anyway, so I don't read them over too carefully beyond the asking price. Nod my head in all the right places and ask the appropriate questions when prompted. But all the while I'm wondering, why? Why now? Why me?

It's to the point that I can't hold back. I've gotta know.

"Why do you want to sell to me now?" I ask after he hands over a thick stack of papers. The contract his lawyer has drawn up. I'll be countering with a contract my lawyer will have put together, but there's no need to mention it at the moment. "After all this time, why me?"

Scott stares at me like I'm crazy. "Why not you? First, you barrage me with calls and messages for months. Practically to the point of harassment. My plan was to ignore you. I wasn't ready to sell yet."

Swallowing hard, I rest my forearms on the edge of my desk, remaining as neutral as possible.

"Then you start dating my daughter and I wonder." His all-seeing gaze lands on me again, and I can tell he's trying to figure me out. "Are you using her to get to me? Tell me the truth."

Damn. I can't confess that was my original intention. It's not anymore. If I'm being truthful with myself, I can admit I'm halfway in love with her. More than halfway. It's just hard to come to grips with that sort of thing and admit it, especially to her father.

I haven't even told Marina how I feel. Yet.

"Would that change your price if I told you I was?" I ask, pretending to be the shrewd, ruthless businessman I used to be.

We glare at each other from across my desk, neither of us moving until he finally shakes his head.

"You're a bullshitter. It's written all over your face," he says.

"What are you talking about?"

"I can see that you're in love with Marina." I open my mouth to protest, but he narrows his gaze, silencing me with a single look that reminds me eerily of Marina. "Don't bother denying it. I know the two of you have been spending most of your time together."

He hasn't really been around lately, so I'm surprised he's noticed.

"I keep tabs on everything where my daughter is concerned." Another pointed look delivered by the man who I'm thinking might be my—gulp—father-in-law someday. How I can even think that way blows my mind. "That she even gave you a chance despite knowing what you wanted shows me she somehow saw beneath your surface."

Agreed. She's perceptive, my Marina. Smart and strong and beautiful and sexy as hell.

"I want to give her the bakery," I blurt, clamping my lips shut as soon as the words leave me. I hadn't meant to admit that yet.

"I think that's a good idea." Scott doesn't even flinch at my admission. Like he knew I'd planned it all along.

Strange. But perceptive. Kind of like his daughter.

"I want to keep it in your family. Give her the bakery as a gift, though she'll probably freak out if I offer it as a gift," I say, muttering the last few words.

"My daughter is full of pride. Sometimes it's foolish, sometimes it's not." Scott smiles. "I'm sure she'll be very appreciative of your generous gift."

"And wary," I add with a shake of my head. "She'll probably think there are strings attached to it."

"Are there?"

"Not at all." She loves the bakery. It's a part of her and her aunt, and I hate to see them lose it. "It means too much to her, and I can't let it slip out of her fingers."

"That right there is exactly why I'm ready to sell you the property. Though I can't deny there are financial reasons as well." The grimace on Scott Knight's face is unmistakable. "We've suffered these last few years. The economy hit the family businesses so hard, it's been a struggle to recuperate. I held on to the bakery and the buildings that surround it specifically for Marina and my sister-in-law for as long as I could. I know they both love it. I couldn't stand the thought of taking it away from them."

He just earned points for that admission.

"And now that you've confirmed that you want them to keep the bakery, I know my decision to sell to you was the right one." I'm guessing I just earned points as well.

"I want to take care of her, that's all," I say, stunned that I'd even admit such a thing to her father. But it's true. I want to provide her with what she wants, what she needs. There's something about her that makes me want to give her everything.

"That's an admirable trait," he says carefully.

Damn. I didn't mean to turn the conversation in this direction, but I guess I can't help it. Marina has slowly seeped into my world, and I can't imagine her out of it. "I'd appreciate it if you didn't say anything about me giving the bakery to Marina just yet," I say, because damn it, I want to be the one to tell her. "I want it to be a surprise."

"Of course. I completely understand." The smile on his face is small but there. "She'll be thrilled."

Hell, let's hope so.

Marina

"I missed you today." I snuggled closer to Gage, feeling like the clingy, simpering girlfriend, but for once I don't care. I did miss him. I hate it when he goes to the city for business. I hate it worse when he's gone for a few days at a time, though that hasn't happened often. I love having him close.

Like right now, the both of us are naked in bed after an extremely sweaty bout of reunion sex. So we were apart for less than twenty-four hours; it's still considered reunion sex in my book.

Sighing, I turn my head and kiss his chest. Feeling his still-thundering heart beneath my lips. I've got it so bad for this man, it's ridiculous.

Ridiculously scary.

"I missed you too," he says, his deep voice gravelly. He's

trailing his fingers up and down my arm, his touch soothing. Arousing. Closing my eyes, I get lost in the moment. Being with Gage helps me forget all my troubles. My nagging
mother, my failing business, all of it slips away until I can
only focus on Gage and how good he makes me feel.

"How was San Francisco?" We hadn't bothered with the
preliminaries when I'd shown up on his doorstep not quite
an hour ago. He'd taken my hand, dragged me inside, and
proceeded to strip me of my clothing and kiss every bare
inch of my skin.

"It was . . . fine."

Hmm. I glance up at him to see his eyes are closed, his
brow furrowed. I wonder if he's keeping something from me.

"Who'd you meet with?"

"Investors. No one important," he answers quickly. Tipping his head, he kisses my forehead, his lips lingering, making my eyes shut again. "I don't want to talk about business."

He's definitely hiding something. But what? I don't get it.
Maybe he had a bad day and doesn't want to focus on it.
Maybe he's in secret negotiations with someone and doesn't
trust me enough to let me know what's going on.

Ouch. That hurts far more than I care to admit. I know
we haven't been seeing each other very long, but I've become
closer to Gage than any other human being on the planet. I
didn't think this was possible. When I first learned of him, I
hated him on sight, and I didn't even know him.

Now I'm falling for him. Scary.

"You should come with me sometime." When I don't say
anything he continues. "To San Francisco. We can stay a few
nights at the apartment I keep there."

"And what? Never leave the bed?" I tease.

He chuckles, then kisses my forehead again. "I could take you out."

"Maybe I don't want to go out." I tip my head back so I can see his handsome face. "Maybe I like keeping you all to myself."

Leaning in, he kisses me, soft and damp. "I like keeping you to myself, too."

"See? We don't need to go anywhere. We don't even have to leave this bed. We could stay here forever," I say.

He moves so fast I burst out laughing. He's over me, his hips pressed to mine, his growing erection nudging against my belly. Just like that he wants me.

And just like that, I want him too.

"Didn't we already do this?" I murmur before he kisses me deeply. Our tongues tangle, my brain empties, and I'm done with thinking. Talking.

All I can do is feel.

Feel his mouth on mine, already familiar yet delicious. The velvety glide of his tongue, the way his hands roam my body, the thrust of his cock against my belly reminding me he wants me. Again.

It's a heady, exhilarating sensation, knowing how much power I wield over Gage Emerson. He wants me always.

I feel the same way.

"You're probably tired," he whispers against my lips, one large hand cupping my breast, his thumb playing with my nipple.

I arch into his palm. "It's still early."

"And sore," he continues, rearing up so he's on his knees between my spread legs. He grips the base of his erection and brushes the head against my sex, making me gasp. "I sort of lost control with you earlier."

He'd pounded inside of me hard. My orgasm had been intense. But like the greedy woman I am, I want another one. Now.

"I liked it," I murmur, reaching out so I can touch him. I race my hands over his chest, down his stomach, until I'm touching his cock and making him groan. "Grab a condom, Gage."

He wastes no time, reaching for the stash he keeps in his bedside table and tearing one open. I watch in fascination as he rolls it on, loving how he moves, how he handles himself. He's a beautiful, sexy man and my heart literally fills with happiness knowing he's *my* man.

All mine.

"I wanna make this last," he whispers, sounding a little desperate as he grabs hold of my hips and flips us over so now I'm the one on top of him. "Give me a show, baby."

Smiling, I lower myself on him, until he's completely imbedded inside of me. He settles his hands on my waist, holding me there, his eyes glowing with some sort of unfamiliar emotion that makes my heart race.

He's looking at me like he can't get enough of me. And that's scary. Exciting.

Frightening.

Slowly, I start to move, trying to prolong it but already feeling anxious. He grips my ass, lifts up so he can take a nipple in his mouth and suck it, and I groan, tossing my head back as I slip my hands into his hair and hold him to me.

"You're beautiful," he whispers against my skin. "So goddamn beautiful I can't believe you're mine."

I feel the same way. The same exact way. I know my parents don't necessarily approve of us together. I know the way we met was sort of unusual. I didn't like him very much. I don't think he liked me either.

But the connection between us can't be denied. We're in so deep I don't think I ever want it to end. And I never think that way. I don't think Gage does either.

He leans back against the pillows, the satisfied smirk on his face downright arrogant as he watches me ride him. I increase my pace, gather my hair up in my hands and hold it there, sitting up straight so he can get that show he wants. Thrusting my chest out, I let go of my hair, shivering as the strands slide all over my breasts, tickling my hard, still-damp nipples. I shift forward, taking his cock deeper inside my body, and the agonized groan that leaves him makes me laugh.

"You're wicked," he murmurs, slipping a hand between our bodies so he can stroke my clit with his index finger.

It's my turn to gasp. "So are you."

"I want to watch you come." His touch firms, and I move faster, my entire body tingling with my impending orgasm. "Reach for it, baby."

Funny thing is I don't have to reach for it. He makes it so easy. His assured touch, the way he talks to me, looks at me: all of it sends me straight over the edge and into orgasmic bliss.

"Yeah, that's it," he says as I start to tremble, a little whimper escaping me. "Come for me, Marina."

I do. My entire body stills above his as my climax takes over. I moan his name, reaching out so I can grip his shoulders hard, and then he's coming as well, whispering my name against my hair as I collapse on top of him, the both of us shaking in each other's arms.

"Damn, woman," he mutters seconds, maybe minutes later,

his hands gripping my butt once more, holding me close. Like he never wants to let me go.

"I know," I whisper, pressing my lips against his neck, tasting his delicious salty skin. "I feel the same way."

God. It would be so easy to fall in love with this man.

In fact, I think I'm already close to being there.

Chapter 13

Marina

Alot can change in a few weeks; heck, even a month. I was single and lonely, working my butt off day in and day out with little reward beyond growing a relationship with my aunt, which I cherish, but still. I'd watched the business I love slowly start to fail and it was eating at my very soul. The disappointment from my family—my ever-traveling, too-busy father and overprotective mother—was growing harder and harder to bear.

I had no friends. Many of them had moved away. Or I had no time to spend with the few friends I had.

Life had kind of sucked. I latched on to the fact that Gage Emerson was trying to buy out my family and ruin our lives. I went to that stupid little event more in the hopes of talking to him rather than conducting business, which had been my original intent. Maybe sling an insult or three at him, too, and then walk out, satisfied that I'd let the guy trying to take away my family legacy know I was onto him.

Well. We got the insult-slinging part right, at least.

Everything is completely different now. I have a friend, one I spend a lot of time with. Ivy Emerson and I made good on that San Francisco shopping trip and went last week. She helped me try on a ton of clothes, things I would never have looked twice at. I ended up buying a few things, not wanting to go beyond my self-imposed budget. She helped with that.

She helps with a lot of things.

Archer and I finalized the deal and Aunt Gina's desserts are in his hotel restaurants. Gina's thrilled. Archer's taken her completely under his wing. I'll be lucky to keep her with me at the bakery, what with the way he coddles her. I think Archer wants to steal her away from me.

My dad is still traveling a lot for business. My mom is still overprotective. I can't change them, I just have to learn how to live with them.

And then there's Gage.

I still can't quite define what's happening between us, but we're definitely . . . involved. I can't get enough of him. It seems he can't get enough of me either.

My entire life has changed for the better. A lot of it I owe to Gage. The very man who I believed was my enemy. He's introduced me to my newest friend. He helped me put together a business deal with Archer, his best friend. And he's made me . . .

Fall completely in love with him.

Just thinking about it makes me want to both jump for joy and throw up.

Especially now, what with the headache I have going on. I don't know what caused it, but I had to leave the bakery to take a little break. I couldn't deal.

"So you're going out with him tonight. Again."

Great. Talk about now being able to deal.

I turn to find my mother standing in my doorway, her arms crossed in front of her chest, her expression sour. She's reluctantly gone along with me dating Gage. Only lately has she piped up and vocalized her opinions. I think she's afraid I'm falling for him.

Too late.

"I am." I mirror her position, feeling defensive. Since my dad has been out of town so much doing God knows what, she's become even more of a meddler. I know I live at home, but I'm freaking twenty-three years old. I'm hardly here anyway. I spend quite a few nights at the little house Gage keeps here in St. Helena. I stay there sometimes even when he goes back to his place in San Francisco to conduct business. Hopefully, someday soon I'll go with him.

But with my obligation to the bakery, I can hardly leave. Before Gage came into my life, I had no reason to leave.

Now I want to be wherever Gage is. Silly, but true.

"Do you know why he was in San Francisco last week?" She drops her arms at her sides and strides into my room, her expression full of fierce determination. "Do you? Did your new boyfriend tell you about the meeting he had with your father?"

"Wait. What?" I blink at her, not sure I heard her right. "Daddy and Gage met?" And Gage never told me? I knew they were getting along and had discussed setting up an appointment to talk further, but Gage didn't tell me they'd talked in San Francisco.

She nods, the satisfaction on her face painful to witness. It's almost like she wants to hurt me with this news. "It's happening, Marina. Gage Emerson is buying the entire strip of buildings the Molina Corp owns on Main Street. They'll belong to him within the next sixty days as long as all the paperwork is processed in a timely manner and they hit no snags."

Sixty days. I can't believe he didn't tell me. I don't understand why he kept this from me. What was his motive? Was he afraid I'd freak out? I'm more upset he kept it a secret. I'd finally come to grips with the possibility of losing the bakery. This revelation is throwing me for a loop.

"He'll most likely close down the bakery since it's the only business within the strip that's still owned by us. Unless the two of you can come up with some sort of lease agreement together? I'm sure he'd be willing to *work* with you," she says snidely.

"Why do you hate him so much?" I ask, my voice quiet. Inside I'm reeling, devastated by Gage's betrayal. When exactly was he going to tell me about this? Never? Right before he shut down my bakery? It makes no sense.

My mother trying to tear me down doesn't make any sense either.

"I don't hate him. I dislike what he's done to us."

"Mom." I go to her, grabbing her hands and giving them a squeeze. "We had to sell. You and Dad both worry about your retirement, about everyone in the family ending up with nothing when we've all counted on the properties to earn us income. This way you'll have ready cash flow and won't have to worry so much."

"He stole your future," she says bitterly, jerking out of my touch. "That man you're dating and spending the night with stole everything from you! Don't you get it? You're our only daughter, you have no real prospects beyond the very man who's ruining your life, and you act like you're making the right choice! What in the world is wrong with you?"

I blink at her, shocked by her outburst. Mom doesn't have outbursts. She's always calm and cool and so very, very wise.

I used to go to her all the time when I was younger for advice. She's great under pressure—the exception being when it comes to me and the choices I make.

"He's not stealing from me," I tell her. "Can't you see how this will help you guys? I'll be fine. I don't need the bakery." But I do. What will I do without it? Gina has a job lined up already. Archer is secretly trying to woo her. He's totally being a dirty rat, but can I fault him for it? No. And at least he tells me to my face.

Gage just keeps his secrets to himself and pretends everything's fine. So do I. But everything is definitely not fine. I don't know what I'm going to do with myself when I lose the bakery. There's no point in denying it now.

Autumn Harvest is done for.

"You needed to know," Mom says firmly, going to sit on the edge of my bed. "I can't stand that he's kept you in the dark. You need to come up with another plan."

"Like what?" I sit on the bed next to her, my mind too full trying to process everything.

"Break it off with him. Finish your time at the bakery until it closes. Then go to Italy and visit your cousins," she suggests hopefully. "You can have a nice three-month-long vacation there. Enjoy the sights. Meet new people."

Dread fills me. The trip to Italy is one all unmarried Italian girls make in the hope that they can find a husband. Either they end up staying there for the rest of their lives with their new husbands or they bring them home. I've seen a few cousins do this very thing. Only one came back, with a macho, irritating-as-hell Italian who refused to speak English and bossed her around all the time.

She eventually divorced him, not that anyone could blame

her. Though her mama acted like she thought her daughter was going straight to hell.

Sometimes, I really despise being a part of such a traditional family.

"I'm not going to Italy," I say vehemently. She needs to know that suggestion can't even make its way onto the table.

"Fine. Break up with him. Find something else to do. Go work with Gina at the hotel. You need to do something. Unless you have no problem living here with us for the rest of your life, unmarried and miserable."

"Are you living in the stone ages? What in the world is wrong with you?" I stand, glaring down at her. "You act like my being single and jobless is a kiss of death!"

She stares up at me pointedly, not saying a word.

She doesn't have to. I heard what I said. And it's slowly sinking in that yes, indeed, being single and jobless is the kiss of death.

For me.

Yet again, proving how life can change in an instant. I've gone from bad to fabulous to absolutely terrible.

All in the matter of approximately four weeks.

Gage

love Autumn Harvest." Ivy sighs, scrolling through the photos of the bakery I just uploaded on my laptop from my phone. "But we can definitely spruce it up for her. I'm almost finished with Matt's job and have something lined up right after it, but I can do this on the side. The bakery and café already have good bones, so it won't be too difficult. I can put something together quick."

"I don't want some slapped-together job, Ivy," I warn her, scrolling through the photos of the bakery that's so much a part of Marina, I can't imagine her not working there.

The bakery I now own. The building I'm going to give her as a gift.

Right before I ask her to marry me.

"I still can't believe you're doing this." Ivy smiles at me, slowly shaking her head. "I never thought I'd see you fall, Gage. You were such a jackass about Archer and me getting together. And now look at you."

"Hey, I was trying to protect you. I know how Archer is. Was," I correct when she sends me a pointed look.

"And I know how you were. A workaholic stick-in-the-mud who only found pleasure with the many cars you purchased."

Jesus. She makes me sound like a total loser. "Thanks a lot," I mutter.

She nudges me. "I only say that because I'm your sister, and I can be brutally honest." Pausing, Ivy contemplates me. "Can I tell you something else?"

"Can I handle it?" I ask warily.

"Oh yeah." She smiles, her eyes going soft, almost misty. She's so damn sentimental lately, I don't know what's wrong with her. "Marina is so good for you. And you're good for her. I love seeing the two of you together. I'm so excited. And thankful I like her."

"Yeah?" An ache forms in my chest, making me grab my sister and pull her in for a hug. "Thanks, Ive. It means a lot to have your approval."

"You're welcome." She pulls away from me, pressing her hand against the side of my head. Her eyes are swimming with tears. "I'm so glad I get along with Marina. She's going to make a great sister-in-law."

"Why are you crying?" I catch a tear with my thumb as it slides down her cheek, worry consuming me. My sister doesn't cry much. She doesn't have reason to cry. Archer keeps her too damn happy for her to ever be sad.

"Don't worry about me." She waves a hand, sniffing loudly. "I'm just pregnant."

"What the hell?" I stare at her, overcome with . . . all sorts of overwhelming emotions. Happiness. Shock. And plenty of murderous thoughts because holy hell, Archer impregnated my sister? I could kill him.

"Stop looking like you want to kill Archer." Reaching out, she grabs my hands, clasping them tightly in her own. "This is a good thing. We're going to have a baby." She sniffs, the tears streaming down her cheeks freely now. "I'm so ha-happy."

"You don't look or sound happy to me. Jesus, Ive, you're not even married yet! Mom's gonna have a cow."

Ivy burst out laughing, looking like a hysterical mess. Mascara-streaked tears line her face as she laughs. "You sound just like you did when we were kids."

"Well, it's true. She's going to flip. She's been working on your wedding for months." Years, probably, not that I'm going to say it. Our mom's been living for this moment and now Ivy's going to waddle down the aisle with a big ol' belly?

Yeah. That'll go over real well.

"We're bumping the wedding date up a few months. Mom already knows. So does Dad," she says.

"And Archer?"

Ivy rolls her eyes. "Of course, he knows. What, you think I'd leave the father of my baby as the last to know? I don't think so."

"No, you leave that honor to the uncle of your baby." I smooth her hair out of her eyes, feeling overprotective of my baby sister . . . who's going to have a baby. Holy hell, this is crazy.

"We haven't had a chance to talk, and you've been so busy." She grabs hold of my arm, giving it a squeeze. "Don't tell Marina. I want to tell her, but I couldn't tell her if you didn't know."

I hug her again because I can't resist, kissing her forehead. "I'm so happy for you, Ive. Even happy for that bastard you're going to marry. I hope you know what you're getting into."

"I do." She smiles as she withdraws from my embrace. "No regrets. I'm the luckiest girl in the world."

I hope someday I can make Marina half as happy as Archer makes my sister.

I LEFT ARCHER and Ivy's house to head back to St. Helena and the bakery. I've been planning this surprise for Marina for weeks, in the midst of taking over the properties her family sold to me. I kept that from her too, despite Archer's incessant nagging that I was making a huge mistake.

But it wasn't because I'm trying to hurt her or close down the bakery without her knowledge. This is my gift to her, ensuring the bakery stays within her family, where it belongs. I've already started the process and the paperwork's being drawn up. I plan on eventually handing over the deed for the bakery to her.

Now I gotta figure out how to make this surprise announcement to her without freaking her completely out. I can't make too big of a deal about it. I need to tell Gina too. Ivy's in on it because she can't wait to help redesign the interior, her services free of charge, a gift to both me and Marina.

Marina's going to love it. So is Gina. Archer, not so much, because he's trying to steal Gina away from Marina every chance he can get.

Such a greedy jackass, though I can relate.

I enter the bakery, the familiar, delicious scent of bread baking hitting my senses, making my stomach rumble despite not really being hungry. I wave to Eli at the counter and head into the kitchen where I find Gina shedding her apron and hanging it on a wall hook.

"Well, well, look who the cat dragged in." She tsks and shakes her head. "How you doing, Pretty Boy?"

Thank God I've been upgraded from Boy Toy. She still calls Archer Rat Boy, which he deserves. "I'm great. Where's Marina?"

"Not in. She went home earlier, said she didn't feel well."

I frown. She never let me know. "Is she all right?" I'm extra sensitive, I guess, because of my sister's major announcement, and I wonder: What would that be like, being with Marina? Getting her pregnant, watching her body shift and change, her belly full of my baby?

That strange ache seems to strangle my heart again, and I rub at my chest absently, wondering what the hell is wrong with me.

You're in love, you idiot. You'd do anything for that woman constantly in your thoughts.

"I'll call her," I say, watching as Gina gathers her purse from the closet she keeps it in and her sweater. "Mind if I go hang out in her office for a bit so I can call her in there?" I'm going to grab a few old brochures I know she keeps stashed in her bookshelf and give them to a marketing specialist I've worked with in the past. I plan on having some new materials created, along with a new logo.

Oh yeah, I have lots of plans. And all of them are going to blow Marina's mind. Make her love me that much more.

I wander into her office, searching her tiny bookshelf, plucking first one, then a few other old advertising pieces I can find. Two brochures, a couple of postcards, all of it's good to show the graphic designer.

Sitting behind her desk, I call her on my cell but get no answer. Send her a text asking if she's feeling okay, but again, no reply. Grabbing the brochures, I stack them neatly atop the desk, the edge of the cardstock nudging her mouse, and her monitor lights up, the security business site I know she uses at the bakery coming up on screen.

Squinting, I look at the black and white, slightly fuzzy image, noticing that it's a man, bent over . . . a woman? I see that the image is paused; this is actual footage taken within the bakery, and when I hit play, it all becomes too clear what I'm looking at.

That's me. And Marina. Having sex in the kitchen that first night we attacked each other.

I run a hand through my hair, glancing around like someone's going to walk up on me at any minute and discover what I'm looking at. I'm completely blown away. I can't believe Marina's kept this on her computer for . . . what? Her viewing pleasure? It happened over a month ago. We've had plenty of sex since then. Better sex, infinitely more satisfying sex. Every time we come together, it's better and better between us. We're lucky.

And now I'm . . . shocked, seeing us on her computer screen, me pounding inside of her, her head thrown back, her long legs wound tight around me as she clutches my shoulders with her hands. There's no sound, but I don't need to hear it to remember. She's panting hot, encouraging words, and I'm sliding so deep inside her I groan her name, ready to give in to the urge and let my orgasm take over.

Damn. It's sort of hot, seeing us together like this. Maybe I can understand why she kept it, but still. She should've let me see this. At the very least told me about it. I hit pause, catching her at a particularly good angle. The expression on her face tells me she's pretty damn close to orgasm.

I really like seeing that expression on her face, but live and in person. Not on a video I happen to discover hidden away on her computer. Why would she keep it? Was she hoping to somehow use it against me if I did her wrong? I've gone out with vindictive women before. Women out to get me before I got them, always on the defense when I never thought that way in the first place.

"What are you doing?"

I glance up to find Marina standing just inside her office, her eyes bloodshot, her expression tight. She looks terrible.

So, so sad.

Pushing away from her desk, I go to her, but she dodges me at the last minute. "What happened? Are you okay?" I ask, worry consuming me. She's acting odd. "Gina said you went home because you weren't feeling well."

"I'm fine. Really." She runs a hand over her head, messing up her hair rather than fixing it. She's looking at me like she doesn't quite know what to do with me. "I had a headache. So I went home. Had an interesting conversation with my mother too. Let me tell you, it didn't help with my headache whatsoever. I'd say after her news, it's even worse. I had to get out of there, so I came back here."

My heart skips over itself. Shit. "What did you two talk about?" I ask, afraid to hear her answer.

"Oh, you know. She's worried I'm going to die a bitter, single, *jobless* old woman." One delicate brow rises and I know exactly what she's referring to.

Double shit. This is not the way I wanted her to find out.

"Marina," I start, and she holds up her hand, silencing me.

"I don't want to hear your excuses," she says quietly, her expression flat, her eyes dim. "Tell me the truth. When were you going to let me know huh, Gage? *When?*"

She knows. I'd asked her father to keep it a secret so I could tell her she's not losing the bakery and I withheld the information too long. Now she's pissed. "It's not what you think—" I start, but she cuts me off.

"Then what am I supposed to think? I don't understand how you can keep something so incredibly important from me. Who are you? Why would you do this? The bakery closing changes everything, my entire life! I'll have nothing. No job, no nothing. All because of you." She rushes toward me, shoving at my chest so hard I take a step back, shocked at the force behind her push. "You're evil."

Wait. Her dad didn't tell her about the bakery. This is even worse. She thinks I'm trying to shut her down. "Marina—"

"Shut up. You're a liar. Withholding information is just as bad as lying. I can't believe you would do this to me. I thought you lo . . ." She clamps her lips shut, closing her eyes and slowly shaking her head.

"Let me explain myself. It's not what you think," I start, but she opens her eyes and glares at me.

"Don't bother trying to explain, Gage. You got what you wanted. I knew you wanted to buy those buildings from the start, so I don't know why I'm so surprised or hurt. I guess I got too caught up."

Damn it. She's not even listening to me. "What about *your* secret?" I toss out, my voice flat.

Her eyes widen, tears sparkling in them. Damn it, just the sight of them makes my chest ache. "What secret?"

I fold my arms across my chest, leaning against the edge of her desk. If she won't even listen to me, then I need to get the truth out of her regarding the security tape. It's weird that she never mentioned it. "I think you might know what I'm talking about."

Chapter 14

Marina

I have absolutely no idea what he's talking about. I'm not the secret-keeper in this relationship. He is.

And boy is his secret a doozy, one that's going to change my life forever.

He acts like it's no big deal.

"Stop playing games," I murmur, letting my anger fuel me. He's propped against my desk, his arms crossed in front of his chest, his biceps straining against his long-sleeved shirt, but I ignore the way my body responds to his. He always makes me feel this way. Hungry, desperate, needy. All for him.

I'm too mad. Angry sex with Gage is amazing—we've indulged a few times because we're sort of sick and twisted like that—but not like this. Not with this sort of horrible betrayal.

He's taken it too far.

"I saw what you keep on your computer." He waves his hand toward the monitor. "I had no idea we made a porn video, Marina. Wish you would've told me. Do you plan on selling it now that you know what a jerk I really am? Distributing it online so it can make the rounds? Maybe earn a few million hits on YouTube?"

Gasping, I round the desk, staring at the screen where

the video is paused. There we are in black and white. I can see my naked legs wrapped around him, his body hovering over mine, my arms around his neck. I minimize the screen, glancing up to find him studying me, his expression downright deadly.

"Why do you have that on your computer?" he asks, his voice scary quiet. "It makes no sense for you to keep it this long. Unless you did it on purpose so you could use it against me."

I'm in complete shock. Does he really think that low of me? What sort of women did he date in his past? "I . . . the morning after the encounter in the kitchen, kids smashed the pumpkins we had around the front door." I'm going to tell him the entire story, even if it kills me. "So I checked the videos from the night before and saw the kids but couldn't identify them."

"Okay," he says slowly, probably wondering why I'm telling him all this.

But there is a point to my story. "Then I clicked through, checking out all the cameras we have and I saw this. Us." Closing my eyes, I breathe deep, searching for strength. I can't believe I'm the one who has to explain myself when *he's* the one who kept the worst secret ever. I open my eyes and continue. "I—liked watching it. I was so confused after what happened between us. How could I hate someone and want him, all at the same time? You drove me crazy. Keeping this video was my way of . . . holding on to something that has sentimental value, you know?"

"A video of us fucking in your kitchen has sentimental value?" He laughs and shakes his head. "That's just great."

"I refuse to let you make me feel guilty. I had it up on my computer because I was going to delete it." I don't know why

I held on to it so long. Earlier I'd brought it back up, ready to delete when my mom called. I pushed away from my computer, talked to her a bit, felt the headache come on, and then left, forgetting all about it. "I realized it probably wasn't smart, having a video of us. What if it fell into the wrong hands?"

"No shit. Not one of your most brilliant moves, Marina." He snorts, shaking his head.

Ah, there's the old Gage. The one I want to slap across the face for saying such shitty, hurtful things. I stand, slapping my hands against the edge of the desk. "Don't try and make this all about what I've done to you. It's minor compared to what you've done and you know it. You're the one who bought out my dad and Molina Corp. Why didn't you tell me? How long were you going to wait? I deserved to know, Gage."

He glares at me, his green eyes cold. Hard. "You really think I would purposely keep this from you so I could *hurt* you, Marina? After everything we've gone through, everything we've experienced this last month? You don't know me at all, do you?"

I shrug, trying to blow it off. I have no idea what's real and what's not anymore. I don't care how gutted he sounds. As hard as it is for me to realize, I don't think I can trust him. "I don't know. It's only been a month. What could I expect from you?"

It's Gage's turn to rush me, coming round the desk so he's standing in front of me, his hands clasping my upper arms, shaking me as if he can knock some sense into me. "I'm in love with you, damn it. I wanted to show you how I felt by giving you the goddamn deed to this place. I was going to give it to you as a surprise and Ivy was going to redecorate the café.

I was putting together an advertising plan and everything. Anything you wanted for this place, I would've given you."

I gape at him, shock rendering me completely still. He was going to give me the deed? As a gift? And have his sister redecorate the café? I can't . . . oh my God. I'm such a jerk. "Why didn't you tell me though? You should've. My mom took great pleasure in being the first one to deliver the news."

I'm still so angry at him. I don't know if I'll ever feel the same way about him again. His words alone nearly destroyed me.

Now that I know he planned all of this? I don't know what to think. What to do.

How to react.

"Yeah, I know. I fucked up. Archer said I should tell you. So did Ivy. But I wanted it to be a surprise. It was a risky move, and look. I really ruined it now." He laughs, sounding borderline hysterical, and I want to go to him. Comfort him. Tell him everything's going to be okay.

But I can't. It still feels like a betrayal, just like me keeping the video of our first sexual encounter feels like a betrayal to him.

Now he talks about his plans in the past tense. Like I ruined my chances to be with him. Work with him.

Love him.

"You're mad at me, aren't you." It's not a question. He sounds so defeated, my heart is breaking for him. For me. My anger is slowly evaporating, turning more on my mother, which I know is pointless. She's my mom. I won't be angry with her forever.

Gage hangs his head, closing his eyes as he breathes deep. "I'm so sorry, Marina. I shouldn't have done it like this. I made a mistake. I know you can't trust me, but now I'm starting to wonder if I can't trust you either."

"Do you mean because of the video?" I ask him, my voice barely above a whisper. I can't believe it. He's that mad about the video?

"Yeah." He nods, opening his eyes to stare at me. "You should've told me."

"Right back at you," I automatically say.

We stand in front of each other, the both of us silent, as if we're waiting for the other to say something. Anything.

But neither of us do.

Finally he turns and leaves without another word. Just strides out of my office like I never existed and walks right out of my life.

Only after he's gone do I collapse into my chair, resting my head on my desk as I sob into the pile of overdue invoices that still haunt me.

Gage

"You're still going through with it." Archer sounds incredulous.

"I am," I mutter, watching the company I hired repaint the café walls. "She's given up on this place, but I won't."

Two weeks after our big blowup, she hung the closed sign in the door and shut down Autumn Harvest for good. I was stunned. Marina's no quitter. I have no idea what's come over her, and since she refuses to see me, I guess I'll never find out.

Luckily enough she still talks to Ivy, who keeps me fully informed. She says Marina's considering going back to school so she can get her master's degree. But this time, she'd like to travel elsewhere. Maybe go to an East Coast school. Start over with a fresh new life. I know what she's really referring to. She'd rather start over.

Without me.

I've taken over the business completely. Hell, I own it, so I can do whatever I want to it, right? I had new appliances installed, including a new oven, and I consulted Gina as to which I should purchase.

When I got off the phone with her, she called me Smart Boy—and in the same breath, a total dumbass. I'd reached both the pinnacle of approval and the absolute bottom of disappointment, all at once with Aunt Gina.

"It's going to look pretty damn amazing," Archer says, glancing around the room, which is still under a massive construction overhaul. "Ivy's been keeping me posted."

"How's she feeling?" We're both a pair of overprotective males watching out for her and I know she hates it. Yet she likes it too, all at the same time.

"Feeling a little better, not so queasy. The morning sickness is what's taking her down so hard. Plus she's so tired."

"I know. She tried to get me to let her come for this, but I told her no way. I didn't want her inhaling the fumes," I say.

"Good call." Archer exhales loudly before he turns to me. "Have you spoken to her?"

"Who? Ivy?"

"No, jackass. Marina. When was the last time you talked to her?"

"Not since we split." I shrug, acting like it's no big deal, but not having her as a part of my life feels like I'm missing a piece of me.

I fucking hate it.

"Seriously? And I thought *I* was stubborn." He shakes his head, looking ready to launch into a big ol' speech, and I brace myself. "Look, you need to go to her and tell her you're sorry. Ivy goes and sees her all the time and she says she's miserable."

"She never tells me that. Ivy acts like Marina's just fine."

"Yeah, well, I think she's trying to spare your feelings or worry or whatever. She's not fine. She's a wreck and plans on leaving to go to college across the country so she can escape her mother. She misses you. Not that you're supposed to know that." Archer points at me.

I keep my expression blank. "I have no idea what you're talking about."

"Good answer. I just . . . I can't stand to see the two of you suffer. I know she did wrong and you did wrong." I never told him exactly what happened, only that Marina kept something very important from me as well. The both of us weren't perfect in this situation. I probably overreacted, but I've been with some bat-shit-crazy women in the past who would've probably used a sex tape against me to get whatever they wanted.

Meaning I've dated some pretty awful women, women who weren't worthy of cleaning Marina's toilet, let alone be in the same league as her.

"You can't keep this up," Archer continues when I don't say anything. "It's killing you both. You're a wreck without her. Throwing yourself into your work, fixing up her bakery as some sort of homage to her? I mean, what the hell are you doing?"

"I want to do this. For her, whether she appreciates it or not."

"Right," Archer deadpans. "You're crazy."

Slowly I nod, knowing I sound crazy, but I'm not changing my mind. "This bakery belongs to Marina. It's hers, no questions. And if she doesn't want it, then I fully plan on giving it to Gina. This place needs to stay in the Molina and Knight family. It belongs with them."

A smile spreads across Archer's face. "You do have a heart, don't you?"

"Shut up." I shove at his shoulder. "Don't tell anyone. I don't want it getting out."

I miss her. My body, my mind, my heart, they all ache without Marina in my life. I refuse to go to her, though. Not until I have something to show her. Something that will prove my love to her and let her know without a doubt that I will do anything, and I mean *anything* for her.

Like revamp her business. From the kitchen to the front end of the store, to the new computer and ordering systems that are going to be installed within the next few days, everything's state of the art. Top-notch.

My girl deserves the absolute best.

"You're also a sap. You still plan on presenting the bakery to her, right?"

"As long as Ivy's still bringing Marina to the grand reopening, then yeah. I'm doing it." No one can say I didn't go for it with this, now can they?

"She is. Ivy told me. Marina's thrilled that Ivy's pregnant," Archer informs me.

"I bet," I murmur, not sure what to think. Why does he tell me stuff like this? Only makes me miss her more.

And damn, do I miss her. It's only been a few weeks but it feels like years. I miss her voice, her smile, the way she yells at me when I make her angry. The whispery little moans that escape her when I make her come. I miss her scent, the way she likes to cook my dinner, how she snuggles up against my back when we sleep together.

I miss everything about her. I want her back in my life.

Within the next two weeks, I'm hoping like crazy I can make it that happen.

Once and for all.

Chapter 15

Marina

Two weeks later

I don't want to go," I moan, hiding my head beneath the pillows. It's way too early for me to have to deal with this. Ever since Ivy's become pregnant, she's been on a tear. She turned into a total bossy little thing who has no problem pushing people into doing stuff they normally would never do.

"Tough shit." Ivy yanks the sheet off me, making me shriek. Damn, the air is cold. Almost as cold and unfeeling as she is. "We're going to this all-day spa and we're going to love it, even if it kills us."

That she's forcing me to go to a spa shows how ridiculous I am. I'm the biggest baby ever. Since I shut down the bakery and café, I've become a total recluse, barely getting out of my pajamas, let alone going to see anyone. I'd rather wallow in my misery.

"I don't want to be buffed and pampered," I whimper as I slide out of bed, shuffling toward my bathroom. Ivy's already dressed and looks adorable, her growing baby belly so cute everyone wants to touch it, which drives her nuts. She's not a big fan of complete strangers touching her and asking when the baby is due. I've even witnessed her pretending she has no clue what they're talking about.

That always freaks them out.

I force myself into the shower, perking up considerably once I stand beneath the hot spray of water for a solid ten minutes. I emerge from the bathroom a little over twenty minutes later to find the smell of coffee calling to me.

Dang. I should ask Ivy to move in with me.

We sip coffee and talk, Ivy telling me about Archer wanting to take her to Hawaii before the baby is born and how she really doesn't want to go. I tell her she's crazy, they need to savor all the alone time they can get before that baby comes and totally changes their lives.

Ivy agrees.

We're finally on the road in Ivy's car, ready to head to the spa resort when she turns toward St. Helena, a neutral expression on her face.

"Where are you going?" I ask her, my voice quiet, my thoughts a jumbled-up mess.

I miss Gage. My mom is thrilled we're finished and wants to talk about what a jerk he is, but I told her any discussion about Gage is off limits. Dad leaves me alone because he knows I'm heartbroken and Mom gave him the same talk I gave her.

No talk of Gage in the house. Ever.

But I want to talk about Gage. How happy he made me. How passionate we were together, both in bed and out of it. He made me think, he made me want to achieve something. Anything. He made me strong.

And now I feel weak and lonely without him.

"I needed to pick up something first," she says vaguely, waving her hand.

Huh. I don't like where this is going. I remain calm, though, and notice the colorful bunches of balloons hanging in front of . . . the bakery.

A giant crowd of people are waiting outside, and I see my familiar chalkboard easel, the words GRAND REOPENING written in bold script across the front of it.

No way. I had no clue the bakery was being reopened. Gage sure did move fast.

And doesn't that leave a bitter taste in my mouth.

Ivy drives by the bakery slowly, coming almost to a complete stop so I can see everything. God, she's obvious. "I wonder what's going on in there?" she asks innocently.

I don't know how she can keep a straight face. "Gee, I don't know, Ivy. Maybe we should go inside and see what's going on."

"That's perfect!" She claps her hands together and then parks the car. She's practically leading me by the hand toward the café, and my feet are dragging. I so don't want to go in there. I don't want to see the new owners, though I have my suspicions the only owner is Gage.

Still. I don't want to deal with this. Deal with him.

Not only is the outside of the café and bakery overflowing with people waiting in line to get in, but the inside of the café is packed too. Somehow, the determined pregnant lady gets us inside and I'm immediately shocked by all the changes.

The entire interior has been repainted, and Gage ordered all new tables and chairs, giving the location a cleaner, simpler feel. A new glass case has been installed, as well as new countertops, and I can't help but gape at everything, too stunned to study any of it for too long for fear it'll up and disappear.

"The kitchen is revamped too," Ivy says close to my ear so

I can hear her. The chattering crowd is absolutely deafening. "You should go check it out. There's all state-of-the-art appliances. Your aunt is in seventh heaven."

"Wait a minute. Gina is working here?"

"How do you think they're able to have the open house if they have no one here to bake all the goodies? Yes, she still works here. And she's loving every minute of it, despite Archer wanting to steal her away. Not that I can talk about it." She clamps her lips shut and does the universal sign for lock-them-up-and-throw-away-the-key. "Archer will kill me if he finds out I told you he's desperate to take Gina."

Yeah right. Like Archer would ever lay a hand on Ivy. "Take me to the kitchen," I tell her, needing her with me so I won't have to confront any of my fears—as in Gage—alone.

She escorts me back there, and the closer we get to that swinging door, the more heavily I lean on her. My heart is racing double time, my feet feeling like they have lead weights on top of them, and I stop just before we go through the door so I can look at her.

"There's no spa day planned, is there?"

"This is it." She throws her arms out, a silly smile on her face for a moment before it slowly starts to fade. "I hate nothing more than seeing my two favorite people in the entire world, besides the man I'm going to marry, so miserable without each other."

I hang my head, breathing deep. I hate that we're so miserable too.

"You two need to talk and listen to each other. He never meant to hurt you, Marina. I hope you've finally realized that."

Slowly I nod, not wanting her to see me. I feel weak and blink back the tears that are threatening to spill.

Ivy moves in closer so she can whisper in my ear. "Let him spoil you. He's so in love with you it's disgusting. He would do anything to make you happy." With a gentle shove, she pushes me through the swinging door, and I lose my footing, sending me nearly sprawling as I tumble inside the kitchen.

My gaze goes wide as I drink everything in. The layout is the same, but the appliances are all brand new. Big, gorgeous, stainless steel—and all top of the line.

That had to have cost a pretty penny.

"You like it?"

I whirl around with a gasp to find Gage standing before me, clad in an Autumn Harvest T-shirt, much like the one I used to wear, and a pair of jeans. He looks delicious, tired, happy, sad, and worried.

I can relate to him on every single thing except the delicious part. I'm not feeling very delicious.

"It's beautiful, Gage," I whisper, bracing myself when he approaches me.

"I did it for you." He reaches for my hands and holds them loosely in his. "I did it all for you. The revamp of everything, the grand reopening, all the new advertising materials, all for my girl. The local paper is going to do a write-up about you too. You'll be famous."

I'm only stuck on a few choice words he mentioned in that pretty speech. God, I missed him so much. Having him in front of me, so handsome but looking so unsure, makes my heart swell with overwhelming emotion for him. "Your girl?"

Slowly he nods, his fingers tightening around mine. "You're mine. Whether we're together or apart, I know it. I think you know it too." He takes a deep breath and exhales slowly. "I've been miserable without you in my life. I need you, Marina. I need you by my side, working with me, laughing with me.

Loving me." His eyes glow as he steps closer, and I hold my breath, waiting for him to say something more. "Tell me you still feel the same."

Gage

I wait with near unbearable anticipation to hear what she has to say. Ivy bringing her here to see the bakery and me is a good sign. If she hated me, she wouldn't have come in.

At the moment, I'm looking for any sort of positive sign—I'm that desperate.

"What you've done here is so beautiful." She smiles at me, her eyes shiny with unshed tears. "Thank you. I don't deserve this."

Ah, that's where she's wrong. She deserves all of this and more. So much more. "I know we've gone through our ups and downs. We've both made some dumb choices. But I don't ever, ever regret meeting you. Arguing with you. Having angry sex with you." My voice lowers. "Falling in love with you."

Her lips part, a shaky exhalation leaving her, and I pull her in, slipping my arms around her waist so I can crush her to me. I never want to let her go.

"Oh, Gage." She presses her face against my chest and begins to cry, leaving me feeling helpless by her tears.

"Don't cry," I whisper against her hair as I stroke it with my fingers. "I love you."

"I love you too," she sobs into my shirt.

I smile despite her tears. What she just said is a good thing. A very, very good thing. "I want you to marry me," I whisper close to her ear.

She withdraws from my embrace but I don't let her go too far. "What did you say?"

"I want you to marry me. We'll live here in St. Helena in the little house I'm having renovated and we'll keep the San Francisco house for all the cars. They all can't fit here. We'll only have a single-car garage," I say, earning a smile.

"Only if you promise to build a garage so we can keep a few of your cars here. I'd want to take them out for a test drive." She nibbles on her bottom lip, driving me wild just watching at her. "You know. Just for . . . fun."

Ah, damn this woman. She is just perfect for me in every way. "You've got it. Whatever you want," I vow.

"What about your real estate business?"

"I can do that from here." I have been for almost two months and everything's worked out fine. "We're not too far from the city so I can drive in when needed. It'll all work out. As long as we have each other, we can make it work."

She smiles up at me, her pretty eyes sparkling at me. "What about that proposal you mentioned."

I frown. "Proposal?"

Marina frowns back. "Yes, you know. The one where you mentioned marriage?"

"Ahh." I'm a complete bonehead. Reaching inside my front pocket, I pull out a small box and hand it to her. "Here you go."

She opens the box with shaking fingers, a small gasp escaping her when she sees the glittering two-carat diamond nestled inside. "It's too big," she immediately protests, glaring at me.

"It's perfect." Taking the box from her, I withdraw the ring and grab her left hand, sliding the solitaire onto her ring finger. It fits. "You're perfect." I kiss the tip of her nose.

"Hmm. I think you're the one who's perfect." Leaning up on tiptoe, she kisses me, turning it instantly deep and hot. She sways against me, I grab hold of her hips and let myself become acquainted with her delicious, persistent lips and tongue when I hear a voice clearing nearby.

Popping my eyes open, I find Gina starting at us, her expression irritable. "You two kids made up then?"

Marina turns within my embrace, her back to my front as I wrap my arms around her waist. She settles her arms over mine, our fingers interlaced, her head resting against my chest. I've never felt this content. "We have," she admits dreamily. "Gage asked me to marry him."

"And you said yes."

She nods her confirmation.

"What about your parents?"

I feel her stiffen and squeeze her closer, willing her to relax. She finally does. "I think I can convince them to come around. Dad is more agreeable then Mom," Marina says.

"Well, you have your work cut out for you then, don't you, Pretty Boy?"

I inwardly groan at her choice of nickname. "So we're back to Pretty Boy?"

"Well, you sure are pretty with that shit-eating grin on your face now that you've got your woman back in your arms." Gina smiles and tilts her head toward the café. "You two need to get out there. Everyone wants to talk to you."

"Really?" Marina asks incredulously.

"Really," I say, kissing her temple. "They all know I did this for you."

"How come I was kept in the dark?" She pouts.

"You did that by choice, by becoming a total recluse," I

tease, though it hurts me too. I hate that I made her feel so bad she could hardly drag herself out of bed.

She turns so she's facing me once more. We promise Gina we'll be out there in a few minutes just as she exits the kitchen.

"I am the luckiest woman in the world," Marina sighs against my lips before she starts kissing me again.

Damn it. She keeps this up, and we'll test out that new desk I had installed in the office. See if it's as sturdy as it appears. I set her away from me instead. "Later. Right now, we need to go greet our guests."

More mock pouting. Damn, her lips are luscious. Unable to resist, I drop a kiss on her forehead, her nose, lingering on those delicious lips. "Let's go out there and tell them our good news. You can show off your ring."

"Maybe I want to stay back here with you instead." A wicked gleam lights her eyes. "If there weren't so many people out there I'd suggest we reenact the first time we fooled around in the kitchen."

Damn. This woman blows my mind constantly. "You're out of control. Don't you still have the video? We can watch it later."

That wicked glow shines brighter. "I do still have it."

I drop a kiss on her nose. "Maybe we should make another one sometime." I can't even believe I made the suggestion, but that's how far gone I am for this woman. "Now come on, let's go talk to your customers."

"Gage." She stops me before I start out to the café front, a frown on her face. "So does our engagement mean you lost the bet?"

I frown, realization dawning as soon as I hear the words. "You know about the bet?"

Slowly she nods, nibbling on her lower lip. "Ivy told me a while ago, one night when we were hanging out. She said I had a right to know."

"And you're not mad?" I remember how Ivy had reacted. Not a pretty sight.

"Of course not. I wish you would've told me about it sooner." She loops her arms around my neck. "I would've helped you win."

Damn. More confirmation of just how perfect she is for me.

Gently pushing her away, I take her hand and we exit the kitchen, immediately greeted by the wild applause and celebratory shouts from our neighbors and customers. I even recognize a few friends in the crowd, though I hadn't noticed them before. The both of us step back, overwhelmed by the response, and she grins up at me, squeezing my hand.

My heart expands in my chest, filling up so much space, I'm almost afraid I can't breathe.

But that's okay. As long as I have Marina by my side, we can get through anything.

Together.

Can't get enough of the boys with the bet? Find out if the winner will take it all in the steamy final installment

SAVOR & INTOXICATED

Coming April 2024!

About the Author

Monica Murphy is a *New York Times* and *USA Today* bestselling author of over sixty novels and writes mostly contemporary, new adult and young adult romance. She is both traditionally and independently published and has been translated in over ten languages. She lives in central California near Yosemite National Park with her husband, children, one dog and four cats. When she's not writing, she's thinking about writing. Or reading. Or binge watching something.